Death Watch

Also by Jim Kelly

Death Wore White

Death Watch

JIM KELLY

Minotaur Books
New York

DEATH WATCH. Copyright © 2010 by Jim Kelly. All rights reserved. Printed in the United States of America. For information, address St. Martin's Press, 175 Fifth Avenue, New York, N.Y. 10010.

www.minotaurbooks.com

ISBN 978-0-312-64490-1

First published in Great Britain by Penguin Books

First U.S. Edition: June 2010

10 9 8 7 6 5 4 3 2 1

This book is dedicated to the memory of

Donald Webster Gillies

11 August 1920 – 13 December 2008

A proud *Son of the Rock*
And a great teller of stories

Prologue

Saturday, 5 September 1992

The moment Bryan Judd's twin sister died – that very instant – he was sitting on an abandoned sofa on the waste ground behind Erebus Street. He'd gone to the mini-market and bought a can of Special Brew which he was drinking slowly in the vertical summer heat, listening to his radio. The signal came and went, like an audible mirage, but he sang in the gaps, expertly finding the key, knowing all the words of 'Success Has Made a Failure of Our Home', mimicking the Elvis Costello cover, not this version by Sinéad O'Connor. The beer was warm, the tin damp, and the alcohol made him feel better about the night to come – about what it might hold for him. Ally had said she'd meet him outside the Lattice House. Her skin was always cool, even in this endless summer, and he'd found that to seek it, taut under his fingertips, had become an obsession. He smiled, tipped his head back, and drank, despite the taste of metal in his mouth.

And then his twin, Norma Jean, was there with him, a presence as physically real as the tin can in his hand. He never had any warning, there was never a sense in which she approached. She was just there. Inside him. They told people it wasn't a link between their minds, it was a link between their bodies, as if the intimacy they'd shared in

1

the womb continued now – nearly sixteen years later. But when she came to him there was always this sense of shock, or sudden arrival. The world he could see – the waste ground, the red-brick backs of the terraced houses, the distant crane on the docks – juddered, like a TV picture at home when his dad smacked the top of the set.

But this wasn't like the other times. This was a violent shock, a blow. The beat of his heart became slow and hard, thudding, as if he were running, or hiding; and in the background he could hear *her* heartbeat, a mirror image of his own. His blood rushed in his ears and he knew the emotion she was feeling was fear; then, with a jolt which seemed to tear at the muscles that held his heart in place, the fear escalated into terror. He tried to stand, wanting to go to her, but his knees buckled and he knelt, not feeling the shard of glass that cut into the soft tissue below his knee.

And then, despite the sun, a shocking coldness covered his face, and his neck; and all the noises of the day – the creaking dockside crane, the traffic on the inner ring road – became dull, and distant, as if heard under water. The coldness enclosed his head, his shoulders, inside his mouth, and down his throat. He tried to gulp air but there was something in his throat, something slippery and cold. He gagged, spewing vomit down his T-shirt. He tried to fill his lungs but there was nothing there, just this fluid cloak of suffocation over his head and shoulders.

He was drowning, on a summer's day, on a dusty piece of waste ground as dry as bones.

He tried to stand, but fell back on the sofa, blacking out.

He came to at the moment when that other distant heartbeat stopped, and for the first time in his life he felt alone. His world had changed, as if he'd been given tinted glasses to wear, and it made him want to cry out – the thought that this was how it would be for ever. Shakily, on his feet now, he listened to the sounds that had returned to him: a crane load of timber crumpling to the dockside, children playing on Erebus Street.

The lost heartbeat made him run to find her: across the waste ground, around the back of the Sacred Heart of Mary and down the street to his house, past the launderette where his mother worked, the windows clouded with condensation. As he passed he heard his baby brother crying from the pushchair by the open door.

The front door of their house, next to the launderette, opened as he got to it and his father came out, pulling it closed behind him, pushing a hand through a shock of white hair like a wallpaper brush, thick with paste.

'It's Norma,' said Bryan. 'Something's happened . . .'

His father brushed a hand over his lips and Bryan noticed the bib of sweat which stained his shirt.

'Jesus, Bry,' said his father, who was looking at the blood on his son's trouser leg, below the knee, and a cut on his cheek.

Bry pushed past, just stopping the door before the lock dropped, running halfway up the stairs.

'Norma!' He stood, listening to the familiar sounds of the house: a clock ticking, the cat flap flapping.

His father came to the foot of the stairs, looking at him through the banisters, as if they were bars on a cell. 'Your sister's gone out, son. She'll be back in her own time. Leave her be, Bry.'

The bedroom door to his sister's room was open, the bed inside made, but dented, as if she'd thrown herself on it. In the bathroom there was a trickle of water still running to the plughole, and a single bloody fingerprint on the edge of the bath.

He felt his father at his shoulder.

'I felt her, drowning . . .' said Bryan.

He could smell his father now. Cheap talc, and the cream he put in his hair. Bryan looked at his father and saw that he'd cut himself shaving.

'She walked out twenty minutes ago. She's fine.' Their eyes met. 'We argued, that's all – about the baby. That's all you felt, Bry – she's upset. Now leave it. Please.'

His father leant forward, pulled some toilet paper from the holder, and wiped the bloody print from the ceramic white edge of the bath.

I

Sunday, 5 September 2010
Eighteen years later to the day

When the lights went out Darren Wylde was at Junction 47. It was the last thing he saw – the big stencil-painted numbers – before the shadows rushed out of the corners. He stood still, the dark pressing in, making his skin crawl, as though he were hiding in a wardrobe full of fur coats. He looked at his luminous watch for comfort: 8.16 p.m. Down here, under the hospital, the lights often failed, but the back-up generator would be online in seconds. He started counting slowly and he'd got to forty-seven before the emergency lighting flickered on: which was spooky, because there it was – the big number on the wall: 47. Spooky. The weak emergency lighting didn't really help; stillborn, barely struggling free of the neon tubes, creepier than the dark.

It was a T-junction; and so he could see three ways. Left towards the incinerator. Right? He thought that might be the corridor to the hospital organ bank. And back, over his shoulder, was the zigzag route to the lift shafts which led up to the main wards, A&E, and out-patients. But down here no one moved within sight. He caught only the echo of one of the little electric tugs, hauling laundry, a specific sound against the background hum, which was persistent and steady, like wasps in a jar.

This was Level One: a catacomb; a maze, in which a map was useless. There were small signs at crossroads, and some of the T-junctions, but you needed to know your way. He'd done Theseus and the Minotaur at school, and he knew that the Greek word for the ball of twine that the prince used to find his way out was the origin of the modern word *clue*. A smile lit up his face, because he loved that, the way the past was part of his life today.

Every corridor on Level One was the same: the walls bare concrete, services in dusty pipes running overhead, humming like a ship's insides. That's what it was like, he thought, Jonah and the Whale, and he was down amongst the intestines, the lurid coloured pipes, like he'd been swallowed whole.

Turning left, he walked quickly towards the incinerator, trying to forget what he carried; trying to forget why he was down here at all, when he could have walked through the hospital, down the long bright corridor with the children's mural, the yellow bag swinging in his hand. But the theatre manager on surgery had spelt it out: Level One, and get it signed for. He felt the weight in the yellow plastic bag. His stomach gently flipped the full English he'd crammed down in the staff canteen for tea: runny eggs, sunny-side down, oozing out onto the greasy plate. Gulping, he tried to suck in some cool air; but it was fetid, unmoving, hot. Outside, above his head now, the hospital tarmac would be cooling in the dusk. Here, the heat went on, defying the sunset.

Darren hitched up his jeans with one hand and walked faster. It wasn't a bad job as summer jobs went. Usually, all he had to do was take the clinical waste to the chute at the end of the ward, punch the code into the metal tag, and fill the metal drawer before sending it on its way, down to Level One, where the tug drivers collected it and ran it out to the incinerator. Those bags were full of things he tried not to imagine: dressings – bloodied, stained – and tissue, perhaps, discarded by the surgeon. Organs, cancers, fluids in sealed plastic bottles.

But sometimes they sent him on foot. The yellow bag would be too big, an odd shape, and they didn't want any breakages in the chute system because then they'd have to have it deep-cleaned. Or the yellow bag would have that little sign on it: the three-cornered trefoil, the radiation symbol. Or the chemotherapy warning label. So those bags he'd have to take down to Level One himself. And at weekends, when they pushed through the private patients, there'd be hardly any tugs working, so they'd send him on foot then as well, because the last thing they wanted was a backlog, not in this heat.

He felt the heft of the yellow bag and tried to swing it, but the laugh he'd planned caught in his throat.

At last. Junction 57. A door, a radiation sign, a danger sign, and AUTHORIZED PERSONNEL ONLY.

He took the steps two at a time and burst through a pair of swing doors marked INCINERATOR ROOM.

It was like crossing the threshold into a kind of hell. The sudden brutal heat, the shearing scream of the furnace; but most of all the air – heavy with the fine white ash, and the heated fumes, making everything buckle like a mirage.

Darren tried to take a breath and gagged on the grit in

the air. The 'room' was the size of a school gym, the belly of Jonah's whale, the ceiling a mass of pipes, gantries, and extractors. The floor was concrete, the walls metal, windowless, held together by patterns of rivets. Half the floor space was taken up with the wagons the tugs dragged in from the hospital, each one full of yellow bags. Some came out of an industrial lift in one corner, but most came in through a tunnel which led in from the goods yard. The tugs could be tipped by a lever so that they spilt their waste onto a short conveyor belt which led across the room to the furnace itself, a dark metal mouth, a dim glow of fire just visible within, like a dragon's breath.

Above him, unseen, Darren knew there were several more floors of the incinerator building, smaller than this room, but rising up to house the various stages of the furnace, the cooling ducts, the filters, until at last, 200 feet over the hospital itself, the incinerator chimney trickled a cloud into what he imagined to be an otherwise cloudless evening sky.

The polluted air made his skin creep, as if he'd walked into a spider's web. Below him, *around* him, the furnace rumbled, as if he were part of the machine. And the heat was like a duvet, crowding out the last breath of cool air, sucking out his energy.

Emergency lights here too, running on the hospital generator, which had kept the furnace working – but, oddly, while the conveyor belt was running, it was empty of yellow bags, and unsupervised.

'Bry!' he shouted. The ash got into his mouth right away, and he had to lick his lips, tasting the carbon.

Someone, on his first day, had given him a mask to wear in the incinerator room, but he'd never bothered. A klaxon sounded, making his ears hurt.

Bryan Judd – Bry – had always been here on the late day shift, two until nine, watching the conveyor belt shuffle the piles of yellow bags towards the furnace doors, his pudgy fingers running over the dials on the control panel, sorting the bags, working alone. Darren didn't know why he liked him, especially as he always seemed annoyed that his solitude had been interrupted. Perhaps it was the music that created a bond, because Bry always had an iPod round his neck, like Darren. And, despite the age gap, they liked the same stuff: New Country, some Cash. And he knew what he liked because Bry was always singing, tunefully, hitting the notes dead on.

But there was no Bry.

One of the plant engineers appeared from behind one of the control panels wiping his hands with a cloth, a blue overall open to his waist, the hair on his chest grey, streaked with sweat. He shrugged. 'What's up?' he shouted, holding his mask out with one hand. Everyone shouted in the furnace room. 'The belt's empty – where's Bry?' he asked.

Darren knew the man; his name was Potts. Like all the engineers his damp, warm face was plastered with the white ash-like dust, a face devoid of eyebrows, wrinkles, or stubble. The face of a clown. Across his skin sweat had eroded a few channels, as if his skull was about to fall apart.

'I've got this,' said Darren, holding up the bag.

They heard footsteps on the open-lattice metal ladder,

descending from the floor above. Another one of the engineers, but this one had a tie, knotted neatly, and a clipboard in one hand. Bry had told him this one's name was Gerry Bourne, and he called him Mr Bourne to his face, 'The Git' when he wasn't there.

'Nothing's going in,' said Bourne. 'Better find Bry – he'll cop it otherwise.'

Potts shrugged. 'Probably having a fag outside – I'll get him.'

Both of them looked at Darren, and the yellow bag.

'It's a leg,' said Darren again, holding the bag out.

The two men exchanged glances.

'Left or right?' shouted Potts, readjusting the mask after wiping spit off his lips with the back of his hand.

'What?' said Darren, but he knew what he'd heard.

'Left or right?' said Bourne, tapping a ballpoint on the clipboard. He didn't have a mask, which marked him out as one of the bosses from the second floor. 'We need to know. You need a receipt, but we can't sign it in unless we know. So – left or right?'

'I don't know,' said Darren. He lifted the bag and read the written label attached to the metal tag. It was in code and meaningless. There was a signature, a squiggle in blue. Darren shrugged.

'Take it back,' said Bourne. Darren's shoulders sagged. He should be clocking off at nine.

'You could look,' said Potts, pouring tea from a flask into the plastic stopper cup. Darren didn't want to walk back, and he could feel they were judging him. He disguised a deep breath, then flipped the bag onto a metal worktop. The seal was plastic, poppable. He broke it open. The bloody stump was at the top, the bone cut clean to reveal the neat central core for the marrow. He forced himself to look beyond, down to the waxy toes. There was bile in his throat, but he was proud of himself for looking, so he didn't show anything in his face.

He resealed the bag with his fist; a savage blow.

'Right.'

Bourne was already laughing, Potts spat out his tea. They leant on each other, a little vignette of mirth. Darren thought, not for the first time, how cruel comedy could be.

'Priceless,' said Potts, leaving a smear under his eyes where tears had trickled out under the mask. 'Left or right!'

The main lights flickered back on, neon blazing, and – unbelievably – the noise levels jumped. A pain, quite sharp, went through one of Darren's eardrums. He grabbed the yellow bag, feeling tears well up in his eyes.

'Sorry, kid,' said Bourne, avoiding the youngster's eyes, pocketing the ballpoint. 'Here – come and have a look at this.'

Darren didn't move. He didn't trust Bourne. 'No,' Bourne laughed, loosening his tie. 'Really. I have to check the furnace now we're back on full power. Routine. Come on ...' He put an arm round Darren's bony shoulders. They walked to the wall and climbed a metal stairway to the next level. As they climbed Darren felt the temperature rise so that sweat sprang out on his skin and a cool thread of salty water ran across his left temple. Here, on the second floor, the space was subdivided into corridors lined with control panels, the ceiling an open metal lattice just above their heads. There was a steel wall in front of them, some rusted dials, a red panic button. And that smell of heated metal, the stench of the guts of the machine. Darren licked dry dust off the roof of his mouth. In the centre of the metal wall was a small hatch which Bourne flipped open to reveal a pair of eyepieces, like a set of binoculars, sunk into the wall.

'Ashes to ashes,' said Bourne, running a hand down his stiff back and licking his lips. 'Six hundred degrees. When we've done there's nothing left but a thimbleful of white dust. She can take anything . . .' He patted the metal wall affectionately. 'Radioactive waste, chemical waste, plastics, metals. Go on, have a look.'

Darren stepped up and sank his face into the plastic mould.

He was looking into the heart of the furnace. It wasn't fiery in there. It was like the sun; a searing yellow, with flares of aluminium white. And then, at the left-hand margin, a sudden intrusion of charred black, something extended, like a winter branch. Darren blinked, clearing his eyes. The vision edged across his field of view on the internal conveyor, and he saw it for what it was: a body, the head on the thin skeletal neck flexing, jerking, one of the arms thrashing with mechanical, inhuman spasms. A body in agony, combusting like newspaper tossed on an open fire.

Darren sprang back, angry, the tears welling again. 'Oh God,' he said. 'There's someone in there . . .' Vomit gushed through his hands as he tried to cover his mouth. Bourne stepped in, pressing his face into the mould, turning his head quickly, rapidly, left right, right left. He hit the panic button, hard, twice, and a siren screamed in the heart of the machine.

Darren's knees had buckled and he sank to the floor, then rolled over, lying on his back, looking up into the metal-mesh floor above. The noise level peaked and then died, like an aircraft engine after touchdown and throttle-back, so that what was left felt like silence. So he heard the footsteps, above them, on the metal floor. Not measured footsteps – he'd later tell the police officer who took his statement – not measured, but running, *escaping* footsteps. Briefly he saw those footsteps, through the wire, the base of a pair of fleeing shoes. But it was the sound that was wrong – the crack of iron on iron, of steel on steel. And the telling detail: the sparks – the little crackling electric sparks – as the shoes struck the mesh, creating a necklace of tiny lightning bolts.

2

Detective Inspector Peter Shaw was on the beach when his mobile rang – the ringtone a snatch from *A Sea Symphony* by Vaughan Williams. *His beach.* The death of an Indian summer's day, the sun already long set, the sand cool now, where it had once burnt the pale arches of his feet. He sat on the lifeguard's high chair, the RNLI flag flying over his head. Tracking his telescope from north to south along a falling wave he looked for the few late surfers prepared to stay out in the dusk, and found instead his wife, Lena, walking in the shallows with his daughter. Further out the swell spilt sets of waves in perfect sequence.

He'd been looking west, enjoying the last of the amber light. A broad face, wide open, matching the distant horizon, high cheekbones, almost Slavic, and short hair surfer-blond. His good eye was blue, as pale as falling tap water. The other blind, the pupil reduced to a pale circle like the moon edging its way into the sky above. He'd lost the sight in his right eye a year ago and he had only just begun to develop the skills which would allow him to judge distance. In the first months after the accident he'd tried to ignore his disability. Now he understood that it might give him skills he'd never had.

He twisted the top of a Thermos flask and let its lip sit on the edge of the cup before pouring out the cool juice within. In the early days after his accident he'd made a fool of himself more times that he could recall, pouring coffee onto his desktop rather than into his mug, his single eye unable to construct a 3D world. He twisted the top back on the Thermos and concentrated on a yacht which had dropped anchor out at sea. He tried to judge the distance using what artists called 'sfumato' or smoky perspective – the tendency for colours to dim to blue as they approach the horizon.

He watched as a family quit the beach, a straggled line from the mother, carrying beach bags, to a young child, reluctant to leave a ring of sandcastles. Soon, he thought, he'd be able to reclaim the beach for his own. The car park on the headland was nearly empty, a few barbecue fires flared along the waterline, but to the north the sands ran to a horizon as deserted as the Empty Quarter. He imagined a camel train threading its way into the night past Arab camp fires.

He shivered, zipping up a lightweight jacket, hugging himself.

He'd played with his father here as a child; between the lifeboat house and the old café. Detective Chief Inspector Jack Shaw, reduced to human scale by the tangled skein of a kite's string or a child's cricket bat. The beach had been their world, the only one they'd shared, the place they could both live life in the moment. Shaw remembered the day he'd traced the outline of an imaginary corpse on the sand, his first crime scene. Clues laid: a clamshell for the heart where the bullet had lodged, lolly sticks marking the shell cases, a cigarette butt between imaginary teeth. He'd been ten. His father had looked at the outline long and hard, and then he'd sat his son in the sand and told him for the first time about the rest of his life; that he could do anything he wanted, be anything he wanted. Anything but this – anything but the police force. There'd been no reasons, no duologue. Just a diktat. It seemed like a lifetime ago.

Somewhere on the beach he heard the time pips from a radio, and he counted nine. Then his mobile had rung. He'd held it at arm's length, as if that would help. But the text, from Tom Hadden's CSI unit, was one he couldn't ignore.

187 QVH

The code for suspicious death – 187 – and the scene of crime: the Queen Victoria hospital.

And now, twenty-three minutes later, he'd swapped his world for this world. He wore a T-shirt under a jacket, an RNLI motif on his chest, but that was the only link back to the beach. That and his suntan.

He stood in the incinerator room, watching the corpse emerge from the furnace doors, the conveyor belt set in reverse. Instead of a distant horizon, twenty miles away, he was surrounded by metal walls, greasy heat, and the stench of ash; ash that had had every ounce of life burnt out of it. His world, limitless on the beach, had been compacted, pressurized, to fit within this windowless box. The air had thickened, cooked, so that he felt sweat bristling on his face. A sparrow flew around, its wings clattering amongst the steel girders and pipes, prompting a snowfall of white dust.

The conveyor belt shook and the motion accentuated the vibration of the limbs. One hand was gone, the arm ending in a twist of charred tendons like a severed power cable. But the rest of the body was intact, the mass reduced by the extreme heat of the furnace, so that it seemed elegantly elongated, thought Shaw, like a reclining statue by Giacometti. Clothing, what was left of it, was burnt into the body, a leather belt still visible, on the chest a mass of molten plastic and metal which might have once been a mobile phone in a breast pocket. The shoes were gone except for the heavy soles. The head was twisted back on the apex of the spine, the jaws impossibly wide, the teeth black. A hole had been blown in the back of the skull where the brains had boiled and popped the cranial bones.

And the face, one of Peter Shaw's passions; but for now he avoided it, and especially the eyes, knowing he wouldn't find them.

Shaw had been breathing in through his mouth since entering the incinerator room. He sniffed the air: just ash, charcoal perhaps, and seared bone. Nothing of the body itself, as if the great incinerator chimney had sucked away its essence, setting the soul free on the night breeze.

The belt juddered to a halt. Smoke rose from the charred flesh. The only noise, just on the edge of hearing, was the metal cooling around them, creaking like a stiff joint, and the bird above amongst the piping, fussing.

'You said he was moving – when the witness saw him inside the furnace? What time was that?' asked Shaw, not taking his eyes off the corpse.

Detective Sergeant George Valentine was at his shoulder, a grey cotton handkerchief pressed to his mouth and nose. Shaw could hear his laboured breathing, air being dragged into shredded lungs.

Valentine might be an old-fashioned copper with thirty years' experience but he'd be the first to admit he'd never been happy in the presence of death. When he'd got the call he'd been in the Artichoke. Six pints, Sky Sports 1. He'd been planning a Chinese takeaway, crispy-fried duck. He didn't fancy it now.

'Eight thirty-one,' he said. 'The furnace is run by computer – so there's a record. It's Darren Wylde – the kid's name. He was being shown the works by the foreman . . .' Valentine flipped the pages of his notebook. Shaw noticed he had a fresh charity sticker on his raincoat lapel: Cancer Research UK, stuck over the corner of another one which read RSPB. There was always something stuck on the lapel, as though he couldn't pass a charity tin without emptying his pockets.

'Bourne. Gerry Bourne,' said Valentine. 'Foreman.' He didn't volunteer any other information because he didn't enjoy talking, so if he had to speak he kept it short and to the point, saving every breath. He'd smoked forty cigarettes a day all his adult life and he didn't need a doctor to tell him what was wrong with his lungs. He coughed with a sound like someone shifting coal out of a scuttle.

Shaw laid a gloved hand on the conveyor belt. 'How long would it take for something put on the belt here to get as far as the point where the kid saw the corpse?'

'Potts, the engineer on duty, says eight minutes.'

'So when this kid turned up here in the incinerator room it was just a few minutes after the victim had gone

18

on the belt ... And after he'd seen the body in the furnace you say he heard footsteps?'

'Right. Says he looked up and saw shoes, running.' Valentine pointed up at the metal-mesh ceiling. 'Second floor – so whoever was running was on the third.' He shifted feet, aware that his bladder was full. 'And sparks – which is odd. I checked – nobody on site wears metal boots. They're issued with rubber-soled shoes for grip, plus it's insulation. Place is a death trap.' He tried to focus on his notebook again, knowing that black humour was one of his many weaknesses. 'Wylde's twenty – student at Loughborough. English. This is a summer vac job.' He took an extra breath to finish the sentence. 'He's downstairs in the incident room, if you want a word.'

'Incident room?' said Shaw, impressed, reminding himself that George Valentine had probably run more murder inquiries than he'd had shouts on the lifeboat. Standard murder inquiry procedure required the incident room to be set up as close to the SOC as operationally possible. That way CID was on top of the crime, close to witnesses, and the forensic team.

'I'd better get on,' said Valentine. 'Get the statements organized. Unless ... ?'

Shaw shook his head. 'Hang about.'

There had been a note of insubordination in the DS's voice that Shaw couldn't fail to detect. And there was a note of something else – bitterness. Valentine had been up in front of a promotions panel on the previous Friday – his third attempt to regain the DI rank he'd lost a decade before. His third, failed attempt.

Shaw looked at his watch. It didn't just tell the time. It showed the tides at Hunstanton, the phases of the moon, sunrise and sunset. It was like carrying his other world around with him. He tried to suppress a wave of irritation with DS Valentine. The relationship between a DI and their DS was like a marriage; their problem was that it was a broken one, and the West Norfolk Constabulary didn't do quickie divorces.

'So,' he said. 'It's less than an hour since they found the body.'

'Right,' said Valentine, looking at his feet. 'Foot sloggers are checking the gates, car parks, the buses. We've looked at every inch upstairs. There's a door out to a ladder which drops down into the works yard. Running man got out there. It's all taped off.'

'ID on the victim?' said Shaw.

'Odds on he's a Bryan Judd,' said Valentine. 'Ran the conveyor belt on this shift for ten years. Last seen at 7.45 tonight by Potts – just before a brief power cut. The line went down at eight fifteen, back up at eight twenty-nine.' Another extra breath. 'There's a fault on the grid. Emergency generator kicked in – so the blackout lasted less than a minute.'

'Where was Judd last seen?'

'In his office, if you can call it that. Looks more like a kennel.' Valentine nodded at a small wooden cubicle, with smeared, dirty windows on three sides, like the deck housing on a small trawler. The only decoration they could see was a poster: country-and-western, a girl with flaxen hair and an acoustic guitar. The only thing she was wearing was the guitar.

Valentine's small, round head lolled forward on his neck, like a vulture's. He put a cigarette between his lips but left it unlit. 'They've tannoyed through to the main hospital, searched everywhere he should be. Fuck all.'

Valentine enjoyed swearing because he knew Shaw didn't.

'Absolutely fuck all.'

Smoke rose from the corpse like a barbecue. The CSI team had moved in and taped off the area, and were about to erect a small forensic tent over the body and the belt. Now that the machinery was switched off – including the extractors – white dust was settling everywhere like frost.

'Accident?' tried Shaw.

'Why climb on the belt?' countered Valentine. 'Nah. 'Fraid not.'

'Suicide?'

'Potts says last time he saw him, Judd was singing "The Wichita Lineman". Apparently he did that a lot – decent voice.'

'Right – so short of tap-dancing across the shop floor I guess we'll have to take that as an indication of robust mental health. Security?' asked Shaw.

Valentine stepped closer, tiring of the machine-gun delivery of questions he was supposed to know the answer to. 'Not great. To get in here from the hospital main building – the public areas – you need a tap-in PIN number. Changes daily – but it's not exactly the Enigma Code. Today it's 0509.'

'It's always the date?'

'Yeah. There are exterior doors but all the staff have

keys.' Valentine brushed the back of his hand across his five o'clock shadow. 'Or you can come up from Level One – that's the basement. I did. So did the kid. Admin. people say you've got to have one of these.' They both wore a visitor's pass looped round the neck.

Shaw shook his head. 'You got a white coat on they'll let you operate, let alone into the building. CCTV?'

'I've got Birley sitting through it now – but you know, there's five thousand people on site. It's a long shot. And what are we looking for? A bloke with iron shoes?'

DC Mark Birley was new on the squad. Ex-uniform, with an eye for detail, and something to prove. It was a good choice.

Shaw stepped under the scene-of-crime tape, then stayed down on his haunches so that he could get close to the skull, right inside the personal space. The thought struck him that our personal space begins to shrink at the moment of death – until it vanishes into the skin. He tried to sense that now, to feel the edge of the life that had fled – but there was nothing there, no line to cross. He got an inch closer, so that what had been the victim's face filled his field of vision. This close the loss of vision in his right eye didn't make any difference – in fact it could help, providing him with a crisp 2D picture.

Shaw had done a degree in art. That had kept his father happy. Anything but the police force would have kept him happy. But what his father didn't know was that the course his son had chosen at Southampton University included a year out at the FBI College in Quantico, Virginia, studying forensic art. It had been straight from there to the Metropolitan Police College at Hendon.

Shaw could read a face like an essay. His problem now was finding the face. The heat had seared the skin – leaving nothing of the ears, for example, but the concha, the funnel-like opening, and the tragus, the forward flap that protects the inner ear. The rest – the fleshy helix and fossa – were gone. All the skin of the face was missing, and the complex system of micro-muscles beneath had been reduced to gristle.

'A man ...' he said over his shoulder to Valentine. 'Plenty of hair. The forehead's exceptionally high, a ridge above the eyes – a bony ridge, but muscular too – the corrugator is pronounced.' That would be the crucial element of the dead man's 'lifelong look' – thought Shaw – the particular arrangement of features by which he'd always been recognized. Deep-set eyes, the brow dominant. Shaw would have called it a Celtic face.

Valentine hadn't said a word.

'Irish?' asked Shaw. 'Heavy build. Large head. Nothing of the nose left, or lips. Teeth charred, but we might get a dental match.'

Valentine stood at the tape. "Bout right. Foreman said the Judds were Irish – face like a front-row forward. Thirty-five, something like that.' He picked at a bit of tobacco on his lip.

'Justina on her way?'

'Ten minutes,' said Valentine. He'd be gone by then, he'd make sure of that. He'd kept his beer down so far, but watching the pathologist at work always brought on a sweeping nausea. It was something to do with the way she dealt with the corpse, like it wasn't a human being there at all, but some interesting fossil. 'I should get down to the incident room,' said Valentine, but Shaw didn't respond.

Tom Hadden, the head of the force's CSI unit, came over to the crime tape. He was ten years short of retirement, thin red hair now strawberry blond, with a scar just below his hairline where a skin cancer had been removed a year before. Freckles crowded round intelligent green eyes. Hadden had fled a broken marriage and a high-profile job at the Home Office for the West Norfolk Constabulary. A keen bird watcher and expert naturalist, he spent his spare time on the dunes and in the marshes, a solitary but never lonely figure, weighed down with binoculars.

'This is odd,' he said. He held up an evidence bag. 'Found these just by the conveyor belt where the victim worked. Don't quote me, but I'd say they were grains of rice.'

'Rice?' asked Shaw. 'So – he's a healthy eater, one of those salads you can get from M&S?'

'That would work nicely, if, and only if, it was cooked rice. Which it isn't.'

Shaw took the evidence bag. Three grains, almost translucent, twenty minutes short of al dente.

'There's blood on the conveyor belt, by the way – plenty of it,' said Hadden.

'That survived the heat?'

'No. There's two conveyor belts, Peter. This one,' he said, touching the belt in front of them with a hand inside a forensic glove. 'This one ... runs into the furnace, and then turns back under itself. Anything on it gets dropped onto an internal conveyor which moves the waste through the furnace system. It's more like one of those moving walkways from the airport. Steel.'

They looked at the victim in silence. 'Justina will talk you through chummy here,' said Hadden. 'But I'd caution against any amateur assessments at this stage.'

'Meaning?' asked Shaw.

'The hole in the skull. I don't think it's what it looks like. We can't get into the furnace yet to retrieve the blown bits of cranium, but one shard is here . . .'

It was on the belt, about six feet from the body, already in an evidence bag, its original location marked with a white circle and the letter 'D'.

Hadden tipped it slightly with a metal stylus, like a fragment of ancient pottery. 'You'll notice that there is a depression fracture on this piece of bone – just here.'

'Someone hit him?'

'Maybe. But we need the science to back that up, and at the moment, we don't have the science.'

Shaw brushed a finger along a gull's feather he'd put in his pocket from the beach. 'But blood suggests a struggle?'

'Or one of the waste bags burst a week ago. Don't assume it's his blood. I need to get the evidence back to the Ark.'

The Ark was West Norfolk's forensic lab, situated in an old Nonconformist chapel beside St James's – the force HQ in Lynn. It was Tom Hadden's kingdom, and the only place he was happy other than the saltmarshes on the coast. He plucked at his forensic gloves. 'You'll need to see outside too.'

He led the way to a door in one of the metal walls,

heavy duty, riveted, like one below stairs in a ship. They stepped through, Valentine reluctantly tagging along, and down a short corridor into a dark cavity beneath the giant piping which fed oxygen into the furnace. Hadden flicked on a torch which lit their feet as they edged through. A second metal door led outside.

'This door was unlocked when we got here, by the way,' said Hadden.

Outside was a small steel platform, an eyrie, at the base of the incinerator chimney. It housed one of the atmospheric testing units for the furnace. An encased stepladder led up, another down into the floodlit goods yard below. A line of yellow waste tugs waited, backing up now the furnace was cold.

Valentine pointed up. 'Is this how the running man got out?'

Hadden craned his neck. 'That's it – a small door, an emergency exit, about fifty feet above us. Again, unlocked.'

They were a hundred feet up with a view west over the town. Although the sun had gone there was still light in the west. A perfect night sky turned over their heads like a planetarium. The air was warm and sweet. There was a single chair on the little platform, office metal with the stuffing coming out of the seat, beside it a hubcap full of cigarette butts.

'Bourne, the foreman, says they knew Judd smoked out here – strictly against the rules, but it's a shitty job, so they bend them,' said Hadden.

'Yeah,' said Valentine. "Cos you wouldn't want to pollute the atmosphere,' he added, spitting over the side.

'We'll check the butts for saliva. But there's only one brand of cigarette – Silk Cut,' said Hadden.

'OK,' said Shaw. 'Let's arrest George.'

Valentine peered pointedly up at the distant apex of the incinerator chimney.

'One oddity,' said Hadden. He knelt by the hubcap. 'There was only one match. I've sent it down to the lab with a runner – single match, broken in the middle to form a V. We might get something off it. Potts, the engineer, says Judd used a lighter.' He stood, closed his eyes to think. 'And this doesn't help,' he added, producing another evidence bag from his overalls leg pocket. A torch in yellow and black plastic, hefty, as good as a cosh.

'Hospital issue?' asked Shaw.

'Nope. Not according to Potts. It was by the chair.'

Valentine took the torch in the bag and turned it 360 degrees. On one side there was a stick-on fluorescent label which bore the letters MVR in black marker pen. He held it up for Shaw. 'A company? Initials?' he asked. 'I'll check,' he added, beating Shaw to it.

Shaw took the evidence bag. 'It's dusty,' he said, noting that the matt black surface of the torch was scuffed.

'Yes – I'll let you know what kind of dust it is when I get it to the lab,' said Hadden. 'But visually I'd agree – dust, lots of it.'

'It's not white – the dust,' said Shaw, worrying at the detail that didn't fit.

But Hadden wouldn't be drawn. 'I'll get it analysed. No point in guessing.'

Shaw took one more look round, trying to imprint a

mental photograph of the scene on his memory banks. 'Any ideas – anyone?'

Valentine didn't like puzzles. He didn't think police work was a set of crossword clues. He leant back, his spine creaking. Up above them condensation still trickled out of the chimney, a thin line unmoved by any breeze, like a 747 contrail.

'It's nasty, clinical – it isn't amateur,' he said. 'If they hadn't shown the kid inside the furnace we'd have no idea the bloke was ash. So it's organized. Premeditated.' He shifted weight, trying to lessen the pressure on his bladder. 'But an inside job, 'cos you'd have to know the layout. So – a grudge. Sex is top of any list – we should check out wives, girlfriends. See who's knobbing who.'

That was just one of the things that irritated Shaw about George Valentine. He tried to solve crimes backwards. Dream up a motive and then see if any of the evidence could be made to fit. What was really annoying was that he was good at it.

'Let's do the legwork,' said Shaw. 'Check the staff here, check the victim's friends, background, then we'll evaluate the forensics when Tom's done, and see what Justina can find on the body.'

Check-It, that's what they called Shaw down at St James's. Check this, check that, check everything. As a nickname it was bestowed half in exasperation, half admiration. Valentine just found the meticulous approach annoying, like a hole in his shoe in wet weather.

Back inside beside the incinerator belt Dr Justina Kazimierz had arrived. The pathologist was kneeling on the conveyor, shining a torch into the shadows where

28

the victim's arm had come to rest shielding the face. Kazimierz was sturdy, a once-fine face overwhelmed by heavy middle-European features. She worked alone, and viewed interruptions as insubordination. Her only known pastime was dancing at the Polish Club with a diminutive husband who drank fruit juice but always bought her glasses of the very best Chopin vodka, the colour of lighter fuel.

She looked up as Shaw ducked under the SOC tape.

'Not now,' she said.

When he'd first met the pathologist he'd put her brisk rudeness down to the difficulties of learning a new language. That had been a decade ago.

'OK,' said Shaw, peeling off forensic gloves. 'But I'm not looking at an accident here – is that right?'

'It's not an accident,' she said, delicately taking a sample of singed hair from the side of the skull. 'Now go away.'

'One more thing,' he said, trying not to be intimidated. 'The kid who spotted the victim in the furnace said he was moving . . .' Shaw slipped the assumed gender into the question, knowing she couldn't let it pass.

'That's two things,' she said. There was a long pause and Shaw thought she'd leave it at that. Instead, she straightened her back. 'At temperatures like this the tendons contract violently. Sudden immolation could produce what looks like movement.' She sighed. 'And it is indeed a man, Shaw. And, at some point he's broken his arm in two places.' She indicated just above the wrist and about three inches higher, below the elbow. 'Now. *Go away.*'

She looked him in his good eye. Hers were green, like a field of cabbage. 'I need to work,' she added, without a trace of apology.

Hadden called them round to the other side of the belt. From there you could see there was something under the body. It looked like a melted strawberry ice cream with streaks of yellow custard.

'That went in with him,' said Hadden.

'One of the waste bags?' asked Shaw.

'Yes. The plastic label was burnt off – but there's a punched steel tag with some kind of notation. I can't read it – but let me get it back to the lab.'

'But no others on the belt . . . ?'

'No. A gap before and, not unsurprisingly, a gap after.'

'So – he was either holding it, the waste bag, or whoever killed him put it on the belt?'

Hadden sighed. 'Let me do the science. Then I'll have some answers.'

A uniformed PC gave Valentine a clocking-on card.

'Bryan Judd's,' said Valentine, reading. 'Address on Erebus Street – Bentinck Launderette.' His shoulders sagged. He'd broken enough bad news in his life to fill a newspaper. It had happened to *him* once: the hollow knock, the PC in uniform on the doorstep. An RTA, his wife in the passenger seat on the bypass, a hole in the windscreen where her head had punched through. DOA. Dead On Arrival.

'Let's do it,' said Shaw. He dreaded the knock too, the light footsteps down the hall, and then that look in their eyes as he stood there telling them their lives had changed for ever. It was like being the Angel of Death.

3

Late-night Sunday traffic was light so they swung across the deserted inner ring road to thread a path through the rotten heart of town, past the Guildhall, where a pair of drunks wrestled on the marble steps in the full glare of the floodlight designed to illuminate the magnificent chequered brick façade of the medieval building. Shaw checked the tide watch on his wrist against the blue and gold seventeenth-century version on one of the towers of St Margaret's – a perfect match. High tide had been and gone by an hour. And the time matched too: 10.17 p.m.

As Shaw drove, Valentine read Bryan Judd's file, retrieved from the HR department at the hospital after they'd dragged in the on-call manager. It was a bleak life in five hundred bleak words. Valentine offered a précis. 'Aged thirty-three. Born Lynn. Married. Left school for Tech College at sixteen. No GCSEs – that takes some fucking doing; even I got three. Apprenticeship as a mechanic. Been working on the incinerator for ten years. Before that general hospital porter.'

He found a set of passport-style pictures of Judd for his security pass and held it up for Shaw as they waited at lights, so that he could study the face, try to see through the skin to the bone structure beneath. There was little doubt he was looking at their victim. One notable feature not apparent from the bones and seared flesh was the serially broken nose, smudged flat, and to one side.

'Liked a fight,' he said.

They snaked through the old warehouse quarter, where dark archways led into cool courts of stone; then, suddenly, they were out into the Tuesday Market, a vast medieval square, ringed with Georgian gas lamps. Every Lynn pub crawl ended here, and a warm summer evening had drawn a big crowd; a heaving mass of drinkers. Someone let a firecracker off in the middle, the echo bouncing round off the stone façades, and a single scream was met with a chorus of laughter.

Shaw put his foot down, the sailboards on the roof rack of the Land Rover rattling in the breeze. Two minutes later they'd swung into Erebus Street – a cul-de-sac, ending in the old dock gates, clogged now with ivy and scraps of rubbish like prayer flags. The original iron rails for the dock freight trains ran down the middle of the street, rusted, the ruts clogged with grit. Shaw parked in the shadows.

This was a different world, and one in darkness.

'A power cut?' asked Shaw. 'That's odd. In one street?' And a coincidence, an echo of the brief electricity failure at the hospital. Shaw didn't trust coincidences; they got his mind working in circles, trying to construct links that didn't need to exist.

A full moon, hazy in the heat, hung over the street like a Chinese lantern. On one house a burglar alarm flashed blue. A woman stood by her front door in the moonlight, a candle set in its own grease on the window ledge, a cat snaking round her ankles. At the far end of the street a fire burnt in a brazier, while figures stood in a circle, the flames reflected in the frosted windows of the Crane, the pub by the dock gates. Cans were tipped back, the light catching stretched throats.

'Street party,' said Valentine.

In front of the dock gates was parked a white van, a motif on the side too shadowy to read, while beyond they could see a merchant ship at the quayside, as black as crêpe paper, a silhouette against the stars. Three storeys high, dwarfing the street. One of the giant quayside cranes bent over it like a praying mantis.

Shaw got out and stood in the heat, which seemed to radiate from the cheap red bricks. The air was still, all windows open; and it was an odd sensation – and you only ever got it in the city in a heatwave; a feeling that he wasn't outside at all, but in a huge room, a vast auditorium, a theatre perhaps, so that what looked outside was really inside, and that up beyond the illusion of the stars were the house lights.

They both stared at the shadowy house fronts, searching for the Bentinck Launderette. Several of the houses were boarded up, one's door had been kicked in, another's encased in a steel shutter. Erebus Street was the kind of address that came up every week at magistrates' court for all the wrong reasons. Its crimes were low, mean, and plentiful: domestic violence, street fights, muggings, benefit fraud, meter fraud, car theft, and a few RSPCA prosecutions for cruelty to dogs.

'P'rhaps they've nicked their own light bulbs,' said Valentine, stepping out into the street. He'd been to Erebus Street before. Another summer's evening. What? Ten years, twenty years ago? He flicked through the cases filed in his memory but it wouldn't come. There was something there – something unfinished.

The street party was high octane, the cheers ringing louder, the crowd swaying around the brazier. No one seemed to notice their arrival. Something went bang in the fire – probably an aerosol – and there was a scream. A child danced on the edge of the light, a boy in baggy joggers, maybe six or seven years old, with a mask Shaw recognized – one of the Cat People from *Dr Who*.

'Let's ruin the party,' said Shaw. 'It might be the best knees-up they've had since Mafeking, but I don't fancy telling some poor woman her husband's been incinerated against a backdrop of community singing. Have a word, George, tell 'em to keep it down. And *don't* tell them why we're here – they'll be selling tickets for the wake before we've got to the widow. I'll try and find the launderette.'

Shaw got out and walked into the middle of the street; six foot tall, his feet planted confidently apart as if he owned the place. He looked round, but you couldn't see far on Erebus Street. The docks one way, back to a T-junction the other. The two end corner properties at the junction were local landmarks: to the east the Church of the Sacred Heart of Mary, a black spireless cut-out of neo-Gothic; to the west the town abattoir – Bramalls' – four storeys of brick, with narrow fake arrow-slit windows and a crenellated top. A single tunnel entrance gave the cattle trucks access to an unseen yard. Over the arch there was the stone base of a sundial, its arm long lost, but still with the builder's motto in gold letters a foot high, catching the moonlight:

AS A SHADOW, SUCH IS LIFE

His mobile trilled and he checked it to find a picture message from Lena: his daughter Fran by a fire on the beach, her feet in jelly-mould shoes. He was going to text Lena back but heard Valentine's footsteps coming up the street. The DS wiped a hand across his mouth and Shaw wondered if he'd managed a swift short in the Crane. 'Power's been out since just after noon,' he said. 'Electric board are here – but they say they won't have mains back until midnight – earliest. The party's for three of the locals who got their redundo today – off the docks. Landlord says he can't stop selling booze. He's right. There'd be a riot. Beer's on electric pumps, so they're hitting the hard stuff, plus the high-alcohol lagers. But they're OK – pissed blind, but OK. I've told 'em to keep the volume down.'

He took his raincoat off and draped it over one narrow shoulder. 'St James's are gonna send a car past later. Just to check.' He spat in the dust and loosened his tie. 'I asked where Judd's wife might be ...' he held up a hand quickly. 'I didn't say why. Just a routine inquiry. They said if she's not in the launderette she'd be at the church on the corner. Bloke said she liked a quick prayer – they all seemed to think that was very funny. Wet themselves.'

'When you're that slaughtered, breathing's hilarious,' said Shaw.

They both looked up at the moon, low in the sky, magnified by the warm layer of polluted air over the town. It seemed to add to the heat.

'Launderette's back there,' said Valentine.

One of the houses had been converted to a shop at

ground level, the single window crammed with Day-Glo stickers in the shape of stars advertising cut-price deals: SERVICE WASH – £7 PER LOAD. SINGEL DUVETS £8. DOUBLE £10.00. KINGSIZE £11. The fascia read *Bentinc Launderett*, the last letters of the two words long gone. A neon sign over the door was off but they could still read what it said: 24-HOUR WASH. An upstairs bedroom window was open, a net curtain motionless.

Shaw rapped on the door, rang the bell, not expecting to hear a noise. But a buzzer sounded upstairs.

'Battery,' said Valentine. He'd brought the torch from the boot and flashed it inside the dark interior of the shop. Shaw realized he hadn't actually tried the door. It swung open easily. The smell that came out was warm, damp, and chemical.

'We're closed.' The voice came from behind them, out in the dark street; and then came a woman, dragging a laundry bag, a mop and pail.

She was tall, with lank blonde hair cut short at home. The kind of body which is just vertical, without curves, like a deckchair. If she was forty she hadn't been forty very long. No jewellery, no watch, no rings. Shaw thought she looked bleached, as if she'd been washed herself, too many times. And her hands were red, raw even, where the constant contact with powders and detergents had irritated her skin. But an odd detail. Shaw noticed she'd put lipstick on, ineptly, and most of it was gone, leaving an artificial edge of pink.

'Your shop?' asked Shaw.

'It's hot,' she said, ignoring the question, picking the T-shirt clear of her neck. A logo on the front read *Pat*

36

Green: The Wave-on-Wave Album, and the trailing lead of an MP3 player fell out of a pocket on her breast.

'The power's been down since lunch. I'm losing money here.' She put a hand on her hip in a practised gesture of rest. 'Anyway, who are you?'

The accent was local, with just a little of the Estuary English which had come to the town with the London overspill of the 1960s.

Sparks rose from the blaze up the street, crackling like fireworks.

'Mrs Judd?' said Shaw, standing straight, letting the formality in his voice act as an early warning of bad news. 'Josephine Judd?' He held up his warrant card and Valentine lit it with the torch. The DS tugged again at his tie, trying to loosen it in the heat, as she studied the picture of Shaw, tie-less as always, in a crisp white shirt. She touched the edge of the warrant card and Shaw knew she'd noticed the moon eye, but when she looked back at him she didn't stare.

'Yeah. It's Ally – second name. Never Josephine.' She waited for them to say something, but when they didn't she took her cue. 'It's Bry, isn't it?' She put the laundry bag down and put both hands on her hips. 'What's happened now?'

They heard footsteps slip on the flagged stones of the street. A man stood twenty feet away, reluctant to come closer.

'Ally? You OK? Someone said the police were nosing round – that right?'

'That's right, Andy,' she said. 'Just leave it.' She wasn't being kind, just dismissing him, as if he didn't count, like she was talking to a child. He walked over anyway, his steps unsteady, and in the warm air they could smell the alcohol. A shock of white hair like a wallpaper brush, a face lined unnaturally deep. A small man, but not a *naturally* small man; a bigger man diminished, shrunk down. He wore a white shirt, the sleeves rolled up, and the muscles swung as he moved, as if they'd almost wasted away. Behind him the dancing boy with the cat mask had detached himself from the party and was standing still, waiting to see what would happen next.

In a cupped hand the man hid a smoking cigarette butt.

'Andy is Bry's dad,' she said, as if he needed an excuse to stand in his own street. But she didn't take her eyes off Shaw.

'Bry? What's up with Bry?' said Andy Judd. The voice was Irish, but urban – Dublin or Cork.

'What's happened?' she asked Shaw, ignoring him again.

'Had Bryan ever broken his arm – here?' Shaw touched his left radius in two places.

The blood drained from her face as she nodded. 'Fell off his bike – that's years ago. So what?'

But Shaw could see she was working it out. He gave her a few more seconds.

'I'm afraid we're pretty sure Bryan's been involved in an incident at the hospital, Mrs Judd,' he said. 'I'm terribly sorry. He's gone missing, and a body's been found. It looks like very bad news. I'm afraid there's every chance it's him. I'd be prepared for the worst. We'll have to try and find a match with his dental records – but that could take time.' Shaw knew that *that* was the detail that always spoke for itself.

Ally's hands jumped, but otherwise she didn't react. Andy Judd almost fell over, quickly rearranging his feet to steady himself, a hand stuck in his hair, trying to comb through.

'Not Bry,' he said, shaking his head. 'No fucking way.'

'Shut up,' she said savagely, as if she'd been waiting years for a chance.

He looked at his feet, instantly diminished.

'I'm sorry,' said Shaw.

Her fingers jumped again and Valentine recognized the movement, so he offered her a cigarette. She fished one out of the packet of Silk Cut. Valentine leant forward and lit it for her. She looked pathetically grateful for the courtesy. In the harsh glare from the lighter Shaw could see she wasn't going to cry; not tonight, not for a long time, and perhaps maybe never.

Andy Judd knelt stiffly beside her on the pavement, but he didn't touch her.

'If it is your husband you should know it would have been very quick. He wouldn't have suffered,' said Shaw.

Valentine nodded, joining in the ritual round of misplaced comfort. It might have been quick, but it sure as hell hadn't been painless. He thought of the victim's charred spine, the wide-open jaws.

'Jesus,' said Andy Judd. 'Did ...' He looked at his daughter-in-law. 'Did he do for himself?' He wore a pair of soiled blue overalls and a bib of sweat had formed on his chest.

'No, we don't think it was suicide, or an accident,' said

Shaw. 'But we can't discuss the details just yet. As I've said – we don't have a formal identification, and that will take time. But for now I've just a couple of questions. At this stage we don't need to know much, but we do need to know quickly. Is that OK?' The question was for her.

She looked up then, the hand holding the cigarette vibrating slowly. 'Someone killed Bry?'

Andy Judd stood, touched his daughter-in-law's head briefly like a blessing, then turning unsteadily, walked away towards the fire. As he passed the boy in the cat mask he took his hand.

'Mr Judd,' said Valentine, taking a step after him.

Ally held up both hands. 'No, leave him. Please. I'll answer any questions – just leave him.'

They watched Andy Judd rejoin the group around the fire, a discordant chorus of 'The Fields of Athenry' petering out, the figures in the crowd gathering round, forming a tighter knot.

Smoking three more of Valentine's cigarettes Ally Judd told them the bare details of her husband's last day alive. Her voice had gone flat, bleached of emotion, and Shaw guessed she'd slipped into the early stages of shock. As soon as they'd got the basics they'd get someone from family liaison to stay with her, and a doctor.

Bryan Judd had got up at ten, she said, and went to pick up his magazine from the corner shop on Carlisle Street. *Country & Western News*. It was usually in on the Sunday, even though Monday was the right day. He'd come back with bacon sandwiches from the van by the new docks and they'd shared them in the shop. That day one of the driers had broken down so he fixed that, then

40

the power had gone. Bryan phoned the electricity company to complain, and they said they'd got a unit on the way. There wasn't anything he could do, so he'd taken his bike and cycled up to the hospital. His shift started at two and he always cycled – the bike would be in the shed by A&E. She'd made him sandwiches so he didn't go out for his tea break. It saved them money. Sometimes he picked up chips on the way home. Not tonight. She thought about that. Definitely not tonight.

She covered her mouth as if she'd suddenly remembered something shocking – but it was just the first time the fact that she was alone had really crystallized. She spread her knees, braced her hands on her thighs, and threw up on the pavement.

Valentine got on the radio for the doctor. Shaw put an arm around her. 'Can I get you a glass of water?'

She nodded. 'There's a sink at the back of the shop,' she said in a whisper. 'If the door's locked, knock. Neil – Bry's brother – he's upstairs.'

The launderette was fetid, damp. A line of silent driers on one side, machines opposite, wooden benches down the middle.

The door to the kitchen at the back was reinforced with iron bars. He shook the handle, playing his torch beam on the lock, but it wouldn't turn, so he knocked. Outside in the street he heard a cheer, and was thinking how out of place that was, when the floorboards over his head began to creak, then heavy footsteps marked a descent down uncarpeted stairs.

A key turned and the door opened, a young man blinking into the torchlight. 'Dad?' The voice was slurred, nasal, and very light, like a child's. Shaw guessed he was nineteen, twenty, in a black T-shirt, jeans. The light caught hearing aids in both ears – the transparent kind, fitted, and partly concealed by thick black hair.

Shaw held up the warrant card and spoke clearly. 'Lynn CID. Your sister-in-law needs your help – she's outside. She's had some bad news. A glass of water?' he asked, trying to look past him.

'What's happened?' he said. 'I've been asleep.' He rubbed his eyes. Shaw noted the stunted consonants, the flat toneless rhythm of the deaf.

'Neil?'

He didn't answer. The face held an echo of his father, but was much more delicate, a softer model, a more feminine version.

He stood to one side so that Shaw could see the kitchen in the torchlight. There was a metal sink, a pile of soap powder boxes, conditioner in catering bottles, a workbench and tools. Shaw ran the cold tap and filled a glass. They heard a bottle smash out in the street, then another, and a cheer. No. A jeer this time; angry and jagged. Neil Judd's head jerked and Shaw guessed he'd picked up the vibration, the shock wave, of the noise outside. He fled through the moonlit launderette in his bare feet.

Shaw followed with the glass of water. But Ally Judd had gone. Valentine was on his mobile. The street was transformed by light – a red, brutal gout of fire already roaring like a flame thrower as it burst through the upstairs bedroom window of a house up the street on the same side.

'Someone chucked something,' said Valentine, covering the mouthpiece.

The crowd in the street was melting into the darkness, retreating inside the Crane, or into the houses, leaving the street empty but strewn with debris – half-bricks, bottles, a few beer cans. Shaw ran out into the middle of the street to get a clear view. Andy Judd was stood in front of the blazing house with his daughter-in-law Ally. Then the downstairs window imploded and they all dived for the road, although Shaw had time to see a head within, glimpsed through the shattered glass, the mouth wide with a scream, quickly engulfed in smoke. But the scream remained, a constant, inhuman note, like a cat under the moon.

4

Andy Judd was throwing bricks through the shattered window, sobbing, his arms flailing at the flames; Ally was trying to catch at his hand and pull him back from the fire. Shaw ran to help her but the air pressure shifted, his ears popped, and he was knocked to the ground again as the front door imploded, releasing a tongue of fire like a Bunsen burner. By the time he was back on his feet he could see a light fitting melting in the front room, the hanging flex like a fuse, and beyond it the wallpaper peeling back in the heat. A shadow moved, an arm flapping at the corner of a burning curtain, the scream still sustained, cutting through the roar of the fire. The paint on the door was peeling because of the heat inside, the metal number 6 changing colour with the temperature.

Shaw got hold of Andy Judd's left arm and twisted it expertly behind his back, turning him on his heels, frog-marching him back off the pavement and out into the street, pushing him down onto the tarmac where the metal rails ran, set into the street. Overpowered, he went limp, like a marionette with its strings cut.

Then two things happened at once: they heard a police squad-car siren as it turned into Erebus Street, emergency lights flashing. Then, through the curtain of fire which filled the shattered doorway, a man stepped out, the coat he wore alight on his back and flames catching on one of his arms. He brought with him the inhuman scream, the single note unchanging. He strode into the road, stood for a second as if the act of moving his limbs was the source of the pain, and then fell forward, knees first, the skull striking the road with a crack like billiard balls colliding.

Shaw threw his jacket across him, then rolled him over, twice, three times, smothering the flames. The soprano scream died. Valentine knelt beside him too. 'Brigade's on the way – but there's upstairs,' said the DS.

They both looked back at the house to the first-floor window, but there was nobody there.

'I saw someone – a face,' said Valentine, his own bathed in sweat. 'Definite.'

Shaw turned the man at his feet over onto his back. He was young – maybe twenty-five – and although his eyes were open they were out of focus. 'Pete's trapped,' said the man, a line of blood trickling out from his hairline. 'My skin's cold.'

'It's burnt,' said Shaw. 'It'll hurt – soon. But help's on the way. Just be still. Pete – he's upstairs?'

But the man wasn't listening. 'I can't see clearly,' he said.

'It's OK,' said a voice, and Shaw turned to see that a young man was kneeling on the road beside him: late teens, early twenties, savagely thin, elbows jutting, with a head of black hair badly cut. He had clear skin, and a pair of thin, horizontal glasses, which made him look serious, professional. He was wearing a T-shirt with a motto: *Barnardo's – Believe in Children*.

'Please,' he said, edging forward, taking the man's hand.

'Aidan. Aidan, it's me – Liam. It's going to be OK. It's just shock – you'll be OK. I'll stay with you.' He looked up at Shaw quickly, as if there was a danger that if he broke eye contact with the injured man for long he wouldn't be able to re-establish the bond. 'It's a hostel,' he said, glancing at the burning house. 'Run from the church. I'm Liam Kennedy, the warden. This man is Aidan Holme; I know Aidan – I need to stay with him.'

Shaw stood, letting him get closer. Kennedy put an arm round Holme's shoulders and got his face closer.

'I'm going to die,' said Holme, the limbs beginning to shake to a slow beat. 'I told you . . .'

'No,' said Kennedy, trying to keep his voice light. 'No you're not. God's not ready yet, Aidan. Believe me. Trust in him.'

Shaw turned to Valentine. 'Watch the front,' he said. 'Get him into an ambulance. Both of them. Keep in touch . . .' He waved his mobile, then turned to look at the burning house. There was no way through the front door, still a rectangle of flame, the jamb and lintel burning like firelighters, but Shaw found an alley at the side of the house leading to the back yard, down a tunnel with an arched brick roof.

When he got through he could see the fire had a firm hold of the whole ground floor. The kitchen door was a single pane of glass, and beyond it the flames had already blackened a fridge and a microwave, and the thin chipboard worktops were curling in the heat. Cupboard doors were burning, revealing empty shelves. Smoke hung, trapped, a foot below the ceiling, as thick and grey as phlegm. A pair of French doors from the yard into the back room were wooden and alight, the glass cracked and blackening.

Shaw listened again, the sound of the fire like a giant gas ring burning, and then – at the edge of hearing – a fire engine's siren.

There wasn't time to wait. He put his foot through the French doors and ducked as the flames roared out, then stepped back, waiting for the blaze to take a second breath. The room was empty, with just the carpet to burn. A mural depicting a nude woman in savage orange and blue paint strokes covered the biggest wall.

Shaw ran through into the hallway, crouching, holding his breath behind his hand. In the front room there was a three-piece suite, a rug, and a TV set. Bubbles formed, then burst, in the plastic top of a coffee table. Disparate objects: a fitness cycle, a discarded game console on the bare boards of the floor, the metal foil packets from a takeaway curry in the fireplace. Shaw knelt, took in a breath from down near the floorboards, and felt the air burn his lungs.

The stairs, bare wood, ran up between two plaster-board walls. Smoke rose up, the stairwell acting as a chimney. He closed his eyes and took the steps three at a time. At the top he stopped, holding his breath, and for the first time he thought he'd made a mistake. It was supposed to be a calculated risk. But it felt like a posthumous medal. The fumes were blurring his vision and a sharp pain was pulsing in his head. He saw a vivid snapshot: Lena, standing in blue water, a still sea lapping at her thighs. Ten seconds; he'd give himself ten seconds.

He checked the back bedroom – empty – then the

front. A figure was curled up on the bare floorboards, white smoke leaking up through the gaps. He had scraggly hair held back in a pigtail with a black ribbon and wore an old suit, pinstripe, filthy. Shaw knelt, watching his lips move, hearing only the word: 'Jesu.' He opened his eyes, saw Shaw, then covered his face with trembling hands. But Shaw had seen his eyes nonetheless, and there are few emotions that can animate a face as effectively as terror, the white sclera of the eye visible around each pupil.

Shaw grabbed him by the shoulders but he tried to pull away, hands still over his face, his body twisting. 'I can't go out there,' he said, his voice oddly clear. Shaw knew then it wasn't the fire that terrified him. 'He's there.'

'You'll die if you stay here,' said Shaw. He could hear the staircase burning, blocking their escape, and the smoke coming through the floorboards was black now, toxic. 'Who are you afraid of?' he asked, while he tried to think what to do, tried to calculate how long was left before he had to leave him to die.

The man tried to say something but retched instead, choking with his head turned down to the floor. Shaw thought he'd heard three words:

'The Organ Grinder.'

The man's heavy boots pedalled on the bare floor as he tried to scoot back from the window.

'I heard the footsteps,' he said. 'They all hear the footsteps.'

'We're going out the back way,' said Shaw, deciding that this was some kind of twisted anxiety that he would have to address. 'He won't see you there.' He grabbed him by the ragged lapels of his coat, picking him up and pulling him over his shoulder in one fluid movement. At the top of the stairs Shaw pivoted, turning his back to the room, clasping his burden.

It was too late. The staircase was all flame. He thought then that Lena would never forgive him. He tried to blot out an image of his daughter, asleep, the duvet held to her chin by a fist.

He didn't understand what happened next. He heard a noise, a sizzling, like a giant frying pan. The air filled with smoke and steam. Then a jet of water hit him and threw him into the back bedroom. When he got to his knees there was an inch of water on the carpet, and he could hear it boiling, tumbling down the blackened, smoking stairs. He picked the man's body up a second time and stumbled to the staircase. Each wooden tread cracked as he moved their double weight quickly onwards, down-wards, to safety.

A fireman stood in the still-burning room below; full breathing gear, an oxygen tank on his back. The floor was a mirror of water, the sound of steam a hissing roar. Between them they carried the choking man out into the yard and laid him face down on the parched grass. He struggled when one of the paramedics tried to turn him over, covering the sides of his head with his hands.

Shaw got down so that he could speak into his ear.

'We're in the yard. Pete. Can you hear me? It's just us — the fire brigade, ambulance. You're OK.'

Pete's breath rattled, and when he coughed he arched his back, drawing up his knees under his chest. They rolled him onto a stretcher and gave him a blanket which he gripped, then pulled up to cover his head. They took him down the brick tunnel like that, and out into Erebus Street, as if he were a dead man.

5

An hour later Shaw stood at a bedroom window over the Bentinck Launderette looking down into Erebus Street, where hose water welled up out of blocked drains, creating pools to reflect the last flames of the fire at number 6, just out of sight, further up the street, towards the church and the abattoir. A single fire-brigade tender remained, and Shaw could just see two firefighters playing water into the burnt-out building. He knew that all that was left was a gap now, where the house had once stood, a rotten, blackened tooth, although the roof-line was left – slung like a hammock between chimney stacks. The power cut, confined to Erebus Street and the adjacent dock buildings, was ongoing, so most of the residents had been moved to the Kingdom Hall, a Jehovah's Witness meeting place a quarter of a mile into town.

Behind him on the single bed lay Neil Judd, Bryan Judd's younger brother. He'd demanded to speak to Shaw, insisting he had information crucial to the murder inquiry. Shaw had decided the remaining members of the Judd family should stay on Erebus Street that night – the emergency services had portable lighting, and he didn't want them mixing with the rest of the residents until he'd had statements taken. Shaw's wounds – some burns to his left hand, right leg, and a nail-gash on the right shin, had been treated out in the street. He was soaked, but had borrowed overalls from the fire crew.

The burnt-out house, as Liam Kennedy had told them, was owned by the church on the corner and run as a hostel. Both Aidan Holme and the man Shaw had rescued from the flames were at the Queen Victoria. Holme – accompanied by Kennedy – had been taken to intensive care, where he was fighting to overcome the shock of third-degree burns to his arms and neck. His friend was in better shape, but smoke inhalation would keep him in a hospital bed for forty-eight hours, maybe more. Andy Judd had been arrested at the scene. He'd spend the night in the cells at St James's after a thorough medical examination. The fire brigade's forensic unit had removed evidence from the house indicating that at least two home-made Molotov cocktails had been lobbed through the broken downstairs window, although the only thing Shaw had seen Andy Judd throw had been a half-brick. A team was taking statements at the Kingdom Hall – but Shaw knew the chances that any of them would incriminate Andy Judd for the arson attack were slight.

Ally Judd had been visited by the parish priest – Father Martin – then given a sedative and was asleep in her house, next door to the launderette, an officer from family liaison at the bedside. It was nearly midnight and Shaw had wanted to go home, grab some sleep, so that he'd be alert and prepared for the murder inquiry's first full day. Overnight Paul Twine, a keen, graduate-entry DC, would man the inquiry phone lines at the incident room Valentine had set up on Level One at the hospital, and keep a watching brief on the injured. Shaw had been about to swing the Land Rover out of Erebus Street and drive home when a uniformed PC had flagged him down with a message from DS Valentine: Neil Judd said he wouldn't sleep, couldn't sleep, because he had to talk to someone. He'd demanded to see Shaw.

So sleep would have to wait.

Shaw turned from the window and watched Neil Judd swig water from a bottle, sitting propped up on pillows on his bed. The bedsit was directly above the launderette, the kitchen shared with his father, a widower, who had a bedroom next to his son's. Neil's room was cluttered with teenage paraphernalia – neatly stacked magazines, CDs, DVDs. And the technology to go with it: an iPod and matching sound system, DVD player, a pair of cool dark Wharfedale speakers, a laptop.

All of which was in sharp contrast to the bare utility of the little shared kitchen, the rusted paraffin heaters in each of the rooms, the bare floorboards. The flat smelt of cheap talc, aftershave, and laundered clothes. Andy's room was like a cell: spotless, but without a single note of individuality except for a framed picture of Dublin's O'Connell Bridge. In Neil's room, by contrast, the walls were covered in film posters: *No Country For Old Men*, *In the Valley of Elah*, *Godfather II*. A Japanese cartoon, framed, blood dripping from a severed arm.

With the power still out Neil Judd had lit two night-lights on the windowsill and a candle on his bedside table. But the SOC team had set a halogen lantern in the corridor outside which splashed fake daylight into the room as well.

Shaw thought there was something wrong with the

room; it seemed to belong to someone younger, a fifteen-year-old perhaps. A fifteen-year-old you'd worry about. On the wall was a poster from *Taxi Driver* showing vigilante Robert De Niro stripped down, weapons taped to his body, a knife on a sliding rail on his upper arm, ready to slip down into his palm from within a jacket, a gun in a neat pouch at his groin. And then there were the magazines – arranged with disturbing neatness on two shelves. Shaw pulled one out: *Martial Arts Illustrated*.

'You wanted to tell us something,' he said, prompting. Shaw had noticed that, when someone spoke, Judd turned his head, bringing his ear closer to the sound. But there was nothing subservient about the tic, because a brief look of irritation went with it, as if it were Shaw's fault that his voice couldn't be clearly heard.

'I know why Dad did it – why he went for them – the dossers in the hostel.' Shaw observed that, when he wanted to, when he prepared the sentence, Neil Judd could almost completely disguise the dulling effect of his deafness on his diction.

Valentine stood with his back to the wardrobe, trying to do some mental arithmetic. He didn't know much about modern technology or wages on the quayside – Neil Judd said he'd just started as a stevedore, taking his dad's old job – but Valentine reckoned there was at least a few thousand quids' worth of gear in the room. And Neil Judd wasn't full time, he'd told them proudly, but on college day release.

Valentine knocked out a Silk Cut but Neil Judd got in before he lit it. 'Spare one?' he asked. They lit up together, from Valentine's lighter.

Judd worked a hand beneath his T-shirt, massaging his stomach, then grasped his bare right foot with the other hand, bending it back so that he could examine the sole. 'He hated them – the men in the hostel,' he said. 'Bry, he was a user, right? He'd always taken stuff – nothing hard, just dope. But they gave him this thing to drink. Green Dragon . . .'

He looked at Valentine, sensing the older man would know.

The DS nodded. 'Skunk and raw spirit.' He looked at Shaw. 'You get it – 'specially off the boats, in from Holland.'

Neil stretched himself on the bed, and Valentine thought how slight he was, how fragile the bones. Shaw wondered why Judd's face seemed to radiate an oddly smug expression, as if his evening was going to plan. The death of his brother seemed to be an emotional event confined to another world. When he exhaled his cigarette smoke he pushed it out in a long plume, up at the ceiling.

'Bry was trying to kick it – just ask Ally – and he'd done it, you know, for a year, maybe more. But they got him back on it and he couldn't get off.'

Shaw thought there was something cloying about Neil Judd, about the whole family, as though they were all victims, or looking to be victims. 'Where'd he get the money?' he asked. 'Job at the hospital can't pay enough for a habit like that.'

Judd swallowed hard. The question seemed to confuse him. He sat up on the bed, pulled his T-shirt up and over his head.

'It's hot,' he said, by way of explanation. But Shaw and Valentine knew why he'd done it. His body *was* slight, but beneath the T-shirt his muscles were clear, sharp with a textbook six-pack. He flexed a hand like a claw. 'He didn't pay. He gave them something back – stuff he got from the hospital.' He smiled. 'That's down to you lot . . . police use the incinerator to burn off drugs – street gear. The bloke in the hostel, Holme, he and Bry worked out a way of getting it out so it looked like it had gone up in smoke. But it hadn't. Bry got it, and gave it to him . . .' He stood and walked lightly on the balls of his feet to the open window.

Shaw looked quickly at Valentine, asking with his eyes if this could be true. His DS shrugged, unhappy that he'd worked out it was organized crime, but had missed the link with drugs. Now, looking back, it should have been obvious. Because drugs were the rotten heart of modern crime.

'Bry wanted to call the deal off,' said Judd. 'He'd told Holme – but there'd been a fight and Bry came back in a mess – his eye cut up. He was crying. Dad saw that. They weren't close, they hadn't been for years, but he saw that, and he knew Holme was making him do it, making him trash his life.'

'Hold on,' said Shaw. 'You're saying this Holme character, from the hostel, hit your brother.'

Neil Judd struck his solar plexus with a fist. 'Hit!' he shouted. 'Christ – Bry was terrified. Holme said he couldn't back out now, that they'd kill him.' Neil Judd nodded, kept nodding, leaving that idea to hang in the air.

'He said that?' asked Valentine, taking a note. 'Those words? When did he say this?'

Shaw went to the window as Judd went back to the bed, and, looking down, saw that a priest stood before the ruins of the burnt-out house. He watched him make a sign of the cross then punch a number into a mobile.

'A week ago, yeah – at the weekend,' said Judd, stretching out. 'A Sunday. Bry was on his way into work and he went over to try and tell them again – tell them he wouldn't do it. I think there was a big haul coming through – Bry got to know because he had to make room for the consignment, and be ready to make sure it all went in by batch. He said the place was always crawling with coppers, that it was risky – what they did. He said Holme had gone berserk, laid into him, and that it wasn't just Bry that would suffer if he pulled out now. Holme said they'd make Ally suffer too. He hit Bry, in the eye, a few times, so that it kind of ballooned up. The white bit was all bloody.'

As he said it he couldn't stop himself looking into Shaw's dead eye – the full-moon white pupil oddly piercing. He turned away on one shoulder so that he could pull up the pillow behind his head. Then he put an ashtray onto his knee, but Valentine didn't offer him another cigarette. Adrenaline was making the young man's foot shake from side to side, like a windscreen wiper, the underside of the foot black where he'd walked out into the street.

'We'll need a formal statement,' said Shaw. 'Tomorrow. We'll come here.'

'Right. No problem. It's only right – that fucker needs

to pay for what he's done.' The tone of his voice was flat, as if he was reading out his emotions rather than feeling them.

They left him to rest and made their way down the stairs and back through the launderette to the street. DC Jacky Lau was on the doorstep. Lau was in her thirties, short, stocky, and pugnacious. Her spare time was spent racing at the Norfolk Arena: hot rods, souped-up road cars. She wore a leather jacket now, despite the heat, and her Mégane, complete with aerofoils and spoilers, was parked at the kerb. She had a notebook in one hand and a bacon sandwich in the other, partly wrapped in foil. Valentine had told her she could clock off from the murder team an hour ago, but she'd insisted on checking out the two men from the hostel against the records at St James's.

'The men from the hostel, sir, I've got some details.'

She put the sandwich on top of the roof of the Mégane. Shaw heard footsteps in the street and looking towards the church saw the priest again, moving through the headstones set in the small graveyard.

'Holme, the badly injured one,' said Lau. 'Aidan Smith Holme – he's got a record as long as a needle-pocked arm. Thirty-two. He's up on a charge – supplying again. Third count. Guilty both times, but never jailed. Due in court end of the month. Bailed by a family member – an uncle, who must trust him; he's put up five thousand pounds. In another life he was a teacher at the tech. General science. Lost the job after the first offence. He was supplying the kids.'

'Plea this time?'

'Not guilty.'

If he can raise bail he can afford a decent lawyer as well, thought Shaw. But if he couldn't wriggle out he'd be inside for a decent stretch, two to five years on the third count.

Shaw pressed the heel of his palm into his good eye, massaging the skin, uneasy now that he hadn't known where the West Norfolk force destroyed street-haul drugs. He'd never worked on the drugs squad, and neither had George Valentine. It was a weakness – worse, a weakness they shared.

'And this "Pete"? – the one from upstairs?'

'According to the priest – a Father Martin – his name's Hendre, with an "e". It's a match for a name on our database too. Peter Hendre – if it's the same man – was an accountant. Struck off in 1990. He fleeced some old dears while sorting out their finances. One of the relatives spotted that the numbers didn't add up. Eight counts – down for three years. He's only just come back to the area; been away a year, here for just a few days. They gave him a spare room. Hostel's only for the dossers they trust, apparently. They have to be clean – no booze, no drugs, no sex. Martin says Hendre's got serious mental health issues: paranoia. But he doesn't touch stuff – any kind of stuff. He hadn't heard of anyone called . . .' She checked her notebook. 'The Organ Grinder?'

Shaw nodded.

'But he says the last time Hendre was here he claimed he was being followed by a man in a white coat with a butcher's cleaver. Mad as a hatter.'

Shaw walked out into the middle of the street. He was

past tired now, his mind invigorated by Neil Judd's statement. He took in a lungful of night air. Valentine looked at his watch, a Rolex he'd bought on the Tuesday Market for £1. It said 12.15. He hugged his raincoat to him. They had a suspect, a motive, and the inquiry was less than four hours old. If they tied up a few loose ends he might sneak in for the last ten minutes at the Artichoke. It had a late licence for Sundays till one. Then, maybe, a lock-in.

But Shaw had other ideas.

'Jackie,' he said. 'Get some sleep – then seven tomorrow at the hospital. George has set up an incident room close to the SOC. Be there.'

'Sir.' She crammed the last of the bacon into her mouth and fired up the Mégane, the engine rumble making a few loose windows vibrate.

Shaw watched the car turn the corner by the abattoir. 'We don't really need our beauty sleep – do we, George? How about some overtime?'

Valentine's shoulders slumped. 'Now?'

'Yeah – now. Ring the hospital – find me this Kennedy character. If he's the warden, does he live here, on the street? Find out. See if he's coming home, and if he is, tell him we want a word. He knows Holme, knows him well. I want to know what he knows, and I want to know now. Holme said something to him – here, in the street. When Holme said he was dying he also said, "I told you" – like he'd predicted it. I want to know what that meant.' He looked around, bouncing on his toes. 'If he's staying at the hospital we'll go to him.'

As Valentine made the call Shaw listened to the night. It was quiet now, in the witching hour after midnight, except for the trickling of water falling through the ruins of number 6 and pooling in the basement. As Valentine negotiated his way through the hospital switchboard to try and raise Kennedy, Shaw walked to the old dock gates, then turned, looking back towards the Gothic outline of the Sacred Heart.

Valentine stood by the car, cut off his mobile, and lit a cigarette. 'Kennedy's on his way back now in one of our squad cars – ten minutes. He lives at the church.'

'Great,' said Shaw.

And then, sharply, out of the night, came the sound of running footsteps. In the street, nothing moved. But the sound was as unmistakable as a chiming clock. Shaw could see the whole street and nothing in it was moving. Behind the houses on each side ran tarmacked paths. Is that where the sound came from? Not just footsteps. Metallic footsteps. Shaw imagined them conjuring up a line of sparks in the dark. And then they were gone.

6

Shaw and Valentine stood together in silence, examining the texture of the night for the sound they'd both heard. It was an odd facet of their relationship, one that neither would ever openly admit, that they did have this ability to know, unspoken, that they were thinking exactly the same thing.

'Get a couple of uniforms to check the back alleys,' said Shaw. 'Someone's about.' He checked the tide watch. 'Someone who shouldn't be about.' But Valentine went himself, walking stiffly but quickly to the nearest entry and disappearing down into the shadows, already on the mobile summoning assistance.

Then Shaw heard footsteps again, but this time they were scuffed and soft. Looking back at the dock gates he saw a man appear out of the shadows, opening a wire gate, and swinging a torch so that it danced at his feet. He had a badge on the chest pocket of a set of neat blue overalls which read NORTH NORFOLK POWER. Mid-fifties, with academic half-moon glasses, he looked out of place in the utility's overalls. A professor on a building site. He said his name was Andersen, head of supply, out on call.

'Police? Senior Fire Officer said I should talk to you – we're here to get the power back on? We sent out a unit earlier but they've just got me out too . . .' Shaw recalled the white van they'd seen parked by the dock gates when they'd first arrived in Erebus Street. 'I've got a problem, and frankly, I think it should be yours.'

'I'll get an officer to you asap. Ten minutes?'

Andersen shrugged. 'Sure. But I think you'll regret not taking a look yourself. Believe me.'

Shaw felt the tension buzzing in his bloodstream. He needed to get on, to focus; he didn't need a pointless distraction. But that, he knew, was an attitude which might lead to disaster. Because it was far too early to separate a pointless distraction from a vital lead, just hours into a murder inquiry. He forced himself to relax, letting his shoulders fall, his neck muscles unbunching, telling himself he was tired, stressed.

He followed Andersen to the wire fence, through the gate, and around some dusty shrubs until they could see the electricity sub-station. The building was bathed in the light from a small battery lantern hung from a branch. Shaw guessed the building was inter-war, a confection in concrete thinly disguised as a kind of Greek temple, with a row of half-columns, a decorated arch, and the rendering painted a delicate cream. There was even a frieze depicting naked Greek athletes: a discus thrower, a shot putter, and wrestlers. Genitalia had been added in spray paint to the original graceful classical lines, and a graffiti tag, 'TOG', in curled, bloated letters.

'Bit of a collector's item, this one,' said Andersen. 'Grade II listed; 1949. Renovated in the nineties. Build one these days you'd pick a brick-box out of a catalogue. They had some civic pride then.'

Shaw examined the engineer's face, noting the bags

under the eyes, the bloodshot sclera, the loose flesh. 'Long day?' he asked. 'Hope you're on overtime.'

Andersen laughed. 'You're kidding. This is all part of the job, Inspector. Our contract makes us solely responsible for restoring supply – till then I stay on site.' He yawned, revealing a pale pink throat.

There was a yard strewn with rubbish: beer bottles, cans, a CD player, and a buckled supermarket trolley. A dead cat lay amongst the litter, its lips drawn back from white teeth.

Andersen opened a reinforced metal door and switched on a torch.

'They cut the bolts on this,' he said, indicating a padlock hanging, the shackle sheared through.

Inside, there was a small area of bare concrete, while the rest of the building was crammed with what looked like a giant 1930s radio, or an antique computer: electrical switch gear, insulated wiring, printed circuit plates, brass, aluminium, steel and plastic. Despite the squalor of the yard the machinery was rustless. If electricity has an aroma they were overwhelmed by it now; the thin after-smell of warm plastic and heated metal.

'This is pretty much museum quality too,' said the engineer, swinging the torch beam over the scene. 'Upgraded, like I said, in the nineties. Past it now. We won't bother to repair it, put it like that. We'll rip it out. Which means the power'll be out for some time, so we're running in a temporary supply now by cable.' He looked at his watch. 'We should have the juice any moment now.'

The engineer knelt where someone had drawn a chalk line.

Before he said another word Shaw saw something which made his heart skip a beat: a single match on the concrete floor, spent, but snapped neatly in half and left to form a V – just like the one they'd found at the hospital, where Bryan Judd had sneaked away to smoke. But Bryan Judd had had a lighter.

Shaw squatted down. 'You smoke? Any of your crew?'

Andersen shook his head.

Shaw thought about the habit. You struck the match, you broke it with one hand, then flicked it clear. No ashtray – just on the ground. It was the kind of habit you'd pick up working outside, all day, every day.

Andersen played the torch on the concrete floor, revealing a stain like a spreading head wound. Shaw could smell evaporating fuel – probably paraffin. A bottle lay on its side unbroken – a milk bottle – a half-burnt rag in the neck. Scorch marks ran up into the electrics and a bunch of wires, like disembodied nerves, hung together in a melted mess. Shaw couldn't stop the flash of memory, seeing again the handless arm of the victim in the incinerator, the flesh fused by the heat.

They heard footsteps behind them, and Valentine appeared. He caught Shaw's eye. 'Nothing from the back alleys – they're checking out the rough ground but it's deserted out there.' He stepped forward, assessing the scene. 'Molotov cocktail?' he asked.

'Right,' said the engineer. 'Fire officer tells me there's evidence of others up at that house they burnt out. So there's a little production line somewhere – someone's a proper little Guy Fawkes.'

Shaw looked into the machinery. A set of black scorch marks had disfigured a circuit panel.

'I don't get it – looks like it didn't explode.'

'That's right, I think. They got two things wrong. The bottle didn't break – perhaps they chucked it in and then ran for it – and they've shut the door after them. These things are pretty much airtight. The fire's used up the oxygen and fizzled out.'

'But the power went?' said Valentine, shifting his feet because his back was aching, the tiredness making his head hang even lower on his neck.

'Yes. If that was what they wanted then they struck lucky. The flames from the rag have burnt those wires there ...' He pointed with an insulated screwdriver. 'The insulating plastic has melted away and left two of the cables touching – so yeah, bang it is. The short circuit has blown a load of fuses and cracked some of the insulated boards – so we can't even do a quick fix.'

'There were other power cuts,' said Shaw. 'We were up at the hospital and it went there too.'

'A few. When something like this shuts down it throws the grid. We have to juggle the power supplies. That puts extra load on areas not designed to take it and so we lost a couple of other units later in the day, when everyone put their kettles on. It's all up now – 'cept this.'

Shaw thought about that: the power cut at the hospital, the silent conveyor, the torch marked MVR. Pieces of the jigsaw that didn't seem to fit.

'The rag?' asked Shaw. What they could see of it was only burnt at one end. The rest had been white, defaced by a vivid red stain.

Shaw sniffed the warm air. He got closer, a few inches from the rag. He might be imagining it, but he thought he'd caught the thin hint of iron behind the reek of paraffin.

Valentine couldn't squat down if he wanted to, so he took a guess. 'Blood?' he asked.

'Maybe,' said Shaw. 'But a better question is why. Why cut the power, and why cut it in Erebus Street? And why cut it at noon?' He turned to Valentine. 'And is there a link to Bryan Judd and the hospital? Judd died between 7.45 and 8.31 tonight. The broken matches are the same – but that's hardly compelling. Take a thousand smokers, a few will do that – it's one of those black and white movie mannerisms: Bogart, Jimmy Cagney. That generation. But if there's no link, then it's a coincidence. And we don't like those, do we, George?'

Andersen wiped his hands on a J-cloth from his pocket and tugged his shirt collar away from his neck. 'Well – cutting the power is not going to have much effect on people's heating systems. It's got to be eighty degrees out there – more. But you lose power, you lose lots of things: TVs, radios, clocks – some clocks.'

'Doorbells, some doorbells,' echoed Valentine.

'Or lights,' said Shaw. 'You cut the power you get darkness. No street lights, no house lights. Just darkness. Then, if you don't want to be seen, you don't have to be seen.'

Valentine lit a Silk Cut, the sudden flare just managing to flicker in the hooded eyes. 'Yeah. That makes sense.' He couldn't keep a note of contempt out of his voice. He had a real weakness for insubordination. 'Then you light a

67

fire and dance round it.' He blew on the match, snapped it in the middle, then slipped it in his raincoat pocket.

They picked their way back out into Erebus Street where the unclouded moon still beat down. Valentine dabbed at the sweat on his forehead.

'Heat,' said Shaw. 'What you need – *really* need – in a heatwave is ice. Fridges, freezers. And air conditioning. You cut the power, everything cooks.'

'Then what?' said Valentine.

Shaw sniffed the night air. 'Something starts to rot.'

7

A minute later, at 12.46 a.m. precisely, the power came back on, flooding Erebus Street with light, sending the shadows dashing for cover. The street lamps flared Lucozade-orange, catching the drifting smoke and steam from the burnt-out house; while a neon cross, as stark as Christ's, now shone lime green from the roof of the church. Halfway up the street the launderette's 24-HOUR WASH sign throbbed like an insipid imitation. The oppressive heat still hung in the street, making the air thick, distorting the straight urban lines, like a mirage.

Shaw sat in the Land Rover, his knees up, head back, resting his eyes, waiting for the squad car to bring Liam Kennedy, the hostel warden, back to the church. Valentine waited too, on one of the trestle tables outside the Crane, smoking for pleasure, looking down at his shoes.

Shaw thought he was beyond sleep now. He was thinking about the milk bottle, full of fuel, and the bloody rag. He'd ask Valentine to ring the station and order swabs to be taken from all those they'd arrested in the street outside the hostel. They'd have taken fingerprints as routine, but swabs were a long shot, just in case they found any DNA on the bottle. He tried to keep his mind on the case but instead his thoughts went back to the beach, to his world, an antidote to places like Erebus Street, and the people who lived there.

The beach. Earlier that evening – which seemed now like a snapshot from someone else's life – he'd sat on the sand to watch the sunset, the world behind him, and nothing in front of him, the seascape alive with shades of shifting blue and falling white. And the blue above, the particular stretched-blue of a summer sky, made something rush through his bloodstream, just like the endorphins that made him run and swim. The kick from the ozone was tangible too, and came in waves like the sea, especially when the water had broken, sliding in over the flat sands in a sizzling pool.

If he sat on the beach alone, he always sat at the same spot, at the place where he'd come to rest as a child. This view, from this precise point, had been with him all his conscious life – in fact he often wondered if it was written in his DNA, an inheritance from an unknown ancestor. Or his father? He should have asked him before he died if *he'd* come here as a child. They'd certainly played here together. He'd often, in his turn, watched his daughter Francesca running in circles, then stopping, on the same spot, and looking out to sea. Shaw liked to think she had discovered in her head that precise set of images which he held in his. DNA as a map reference. It was a 360-degree panorama: the tufted dunes behind, with their hidden amphitheatres of sand, the beach running south towards the huts and the lifeboat station at Old Hunstanton, a barnacle cluster of wooden roofs, and the sea itself – not a single image, but two: to the west on a clear day the low hills of Lincolnshire across the Wash, while to the north the beach ran towards Holme, where the coast of England turned at last to face the Pole, a great sweep of sand, ribbed like a giant fingerprint, the line of high tide marked by pines, bent back, cowering from the wind.

When the Old Beach Café had come on the market its location had been perfect, combining his beach with Lena's dream – to live and work in the free air, out of the city. Two years ago it had been a derelict timber chalet, although Shaw recalled buying ice cream at a wooden counter there when he was a child. But it had closed before he was ten. He'd been on the crew of the little inshore lifeboat before he'd left for university, so he'd been able to keep a watching brief on the ruin of crumbling buildings. When he'd come back from the Met he'd joined the crew of the rescue hovercraft, installed to cover the sands and marshes of the north Norfolk coast, so he'd checked it out again, secretly, for Lena.

She'd been looking at properties along the coast, at Cromer, Sheringham, and beyond. He'd let her search, then suggested she take a look at the Old Beach Café, just when he thought the price would be at rock bottom, at the point when the roof beams looked like they wouldn't make another winter. She'd been looking for the right place. It took her thirty seconds to realize she'd found it. For the asking price of £80,000 they acquired the old cottage behind the café (no roof, no services) and the boathouse beside it (wet rot, no roof). Lena had worked hard, but most of all she'd kept going, surmounting each crisis, amending the business plan with the bank as they got to know their customers – the weekend/summer-cottage London crowd who were turning north Norfolk into 'Chelsea-on-sea', *and* the kiss-me-quick hordes who descended on Hunstanton in the high season from the East Midlands. Families, raw with sunburn by the time they headed back for their cars, or clustered on blankets, the women in shell-suits or saris, giggling at the men.

Two ends of the market, with nothing in between. The boathouse was now called Surf – selling beach gear from £300 wetsuits to plastic windmills at £1.50. The Old Beach Café was just that. The cottage was home. A night-light would be burning now in his daughter's room. He imagined her in the narrow bunk bed, a pale arm hanging down from the duvet through the gap in the wooden slats. And Lena? She had an ability to wake when he came home, then slip away again at will, as if sleep could be dismissed, then summoned, without taking offence. But he could touch her now, because he'd found that he could do that in his mind – feel the salt drying on her skin, the dampness at the nape of the neck, the slight inward curve of her back. Only her face, animated and fluid, was less easily conjured, like the shape of a cloud.

The first time he'd seen that face the black skin had been splashed with blood. She'd been sitting on the bottom step of a staircase in a house on Railton Road in Brixton, holding a young boy to her chest, with both arms around his neck. Shaw had never forgotten his name: Benjamin Winston Azore. He was fifteen years old and would get no older. Lena, a field lawyer for the Campaign for Racial Equality, had been working in the neighbourhood for a year. She'd been in the house seeing Benjamin's mother about a complaint she'd made against the Met when someone had knocked on the front door. Benjamin had answered it. He'd had several suppliers in a short and brutal life, but this one was new, and he'd run out of cash. Benjamin didn't have any cash. He'd been shot twice – once in the shoulder, once through the heart. Shaw, straight out of the Met training college at Hendon, had answered a 999 call from a neighbour. When he came through the door Lena was holding Benjamin, the boy's mother was on the landing above, gently pressing both her pale palms against the wall, keening gently.

Shaw was going to speak but Lena asked him a question. 'Are his eyes open?'

He'd nodded, aware that his own pulse rate had soared, and a muscle had started to tic below his left eye.

'In the front room, over the fireplace, there's a family picture . . .'

Shaw had noticed the slight cast in her left eye, and the easy way she'd withdrawn one arm from the boy's neck. He took those thoughts into the front room. It was cold, despite the June day outside, the grate holding a folded white paper flower and a dusty Palm Sunday cross. Standing there, trying to focus on what he'd been asked to do, he thought he might be in shock, because he'd never seen death up close, not the moment of it, despite all the hours in the morgue sketching faces.

The picture showed a boy on a beach, bedraggled palm trees in the background, a parent in either hand. He took it back to Lena.

He stood on the doorstep waiting for the ambulance, straining to hear the siren. Behind him he knew, without looking, that she'd got him to look at the picture, so that that would be the image he took with him.

8

Shaw's memories had slipped into a dream-like sleep, so that when a double tap sounded on the roof of the Land Rover he'd jumped, his heart racing. He opened his eyes to see a face at the open passenger-side window, a face he recognized but couldn't name. He wore a fire helmet – white, with a black comb insignia and a black band. Shaw glanced at his epaulette and saw the two impellers which signified that he was the watch manager – senior officer at the scene.

'Peter,' he said. 'George and I think you should see this.' The voice gave Shaw the name – Jack Hinde, an experienced officer, who'd been friends with his father. Hinde was popular in the CID room at St James's, and had been for twenty years, because he was a superb expert witness in arson cases. He was looking at retirement now, but Shaw guessed he'd pick up a consultancy from one of the insurance companies, and spend the last decade of his life being paid for what he knew, not what he did.

Hinde led the way to the threshold of number 6, the burnt-out house, where Valentine stood looking down into the gutted basement. Water still splashed amongst the blackened beams. The fire brigade would be here until first light, making sure the fire didn't flare up again. The blaze had been an inferno at its height, and it was still possible its embers were alive, deep inside the charred wood and bricks.

Valentine pinched a dog-end between finger and thumb before slipping it into his pocket, then followed them into the ruined house. Shaw looked up through the smoking rafters to the room where he'd rescued Pete Hendre. The floorboards on the ground floor were burnt through in the living room, revealing the flood beneath. The smell was one of the saddest Shaw knew – a home, all the lives in it, reduced to charcoal and soaked bedding. A metal stepladder had been fixed to a floor joist down into the basement. Hinde led the way, Shaw followed, while Valentine watched from above.

'You see, Peter,' said Hinde, stepping off into a foot of water. 'That's experience for you. George is keeping a professional distance – right, George?'

Valentine was backlit by a floodlight, so they couldn't see his face.

The basement was a single room, less than half the area of the ground floor. Shaw stood with one foot on the bottom rung of the ladder, the other on a stone step which just cleared the water.

The room was empty but for a workbench, in heavy wood, which had survived the blaze. On it were various pieces of laboratory equipment. Most of the glass was smashed except for a spherical jar, a rack of test tubes, and what looked like a filter. 'Big boy's chemistry set,' said Hinde.

'Drugs – it's a factory, right?'

Hinde shook his head. 'Don't think so, Peter. Fire Investigations Unit took some stuff away, but they know their drugs – they reckon no. It was mostly household goods: salt, some garden chemicals, hardware too – creosote, that kind of thing. If you're firing up crack, or anything like that, you need the right gear – and this ain't it. This is for something else. And it's not kids – there's the remains of a set of electrical scales. It's not rocket science but it's not cheap either. And there's no literature – someone had it in here.' He tapped a gloved finger against the helmet.

'Right – thanks for the heads up.' Shaw looked round the basement walls. Up against one was the shadow of a set of shelves, not horizontal but criss-cross, creating a pattern of lozenge shapes, like a garden trellis. Within each of the spaces was the ghostly outline of the bottom of a wine bottle.

'Château Dosser,' said Hinde, laughing. 'But not a single bottle. And before you ask – this isn't a wine-making kit, or a still.'

Shaw filed the image away in his mental library.

'Find much?' asked Valentine, intrigued, when Shaw was back in the street.

'A chemistry set, but no sign of drugs, and what looks like the remains of a wine cellar – long abandoned. So no – nothing that makes sense, anyway.'

They'd arrived at the church and Shaw cricked his neck looking up at the lime-green cross. 'Where's this Kennedy, then?' he asked, checking his watch, surprised it was still just 12.58 a.m.

Valentine shrugged. 'Squad car rang – Kennedy's pretty tired, so they stopped for a tea at one of the all-night places on the Tuesday Market. Should be any minute.'

The church was adjoined by a Victorian presbytery, which had its own front door; the building was like a folly, in a playful style – a gingerbread house in a forest of gravestones: lancet windows, a small tower carrying a bell, and a porch in wood with carved saints as doormen. Ivy had once engulfed it, but had been cleared away, to leave the marks on the brickwork like veins seen through thin skin.

There was a light in the downstairs window, but as they watched it went out. Then a bedroom light came on, for a few seconds only, before it too went out.

A police squad car took the T-junction turn at 60 m.p.h. and slid into the kerb. Liam Kennedy got out, picking the sweaty T-shirt away from his narrow chest. He stood looking at the church, fidgeting, switching his weight from foot to foot.

Shaw nodded. 'You OK? We need to talk – briefly.'

'I need to check inside,' said Kennedy. 'We could talk then. I've got a room here, in the basement.' He broadcast a smile, which Shaw judged he thought was charming.

The main doors of the Sacred Heart of Mary, under a high-pointed neo-Gothic arch, were locked, but along the side of the building ran a path to a single door over which hung a light bulb in a metal frame, like a miniature iron maiden.

Kennedy laid a finger to his lips and pushed the door open. The nave was unlit, a little moonlight struggling through the sickly blues and reds of the Victorian stained glass. Shaw stood, waiting for the subtle jigsaw of greys and blacks to form itself into an image. The smell was pungent: human sweat, lavatory cleaner, and something meaty in a school-dinner way – shepherd's pie, liver and bacon, mince.

Kennedy stepped close. 'The hostel – number 6 – is home to only four men at any one time. It's designed to provide a bridge – a real home, for a month, maybe three – for those who've got themselves a job. Here at the church we look after the less fortunate. A dozen, twenty a night. We do our best.' He held out his hands to indicate that, while that was not enough, it didn't mean God wasn't pleased with him.

Shaw tried to keep his reactions to Kennedy as neutral as he could, but he recognized it would be a struggle. In his short career he'd found more evil than good in organized religion, more exploitation than salvation. And he couldn't suppress the question: what were this young man's motives for working here, amongst the broken? Perhaps, he thought, he was broken too.

The front sets of pews in the church had been removed, stacked to one side, and in their place mattresses laid out in two neat rows. On each lay a man; most of them just covered in a sheet, wrapped by constant movement into mummies. One lay on the cool wooden floor, only his hand left on the mattress. The outer door closed behind Shaw with a thud on an automatic spring, and one of the figures stirred, crying out '*Slainte!*' – an Irish toast.

They followed Kennedy behind the altar into a small room. A table with green baize had a rip in it, and the unshaded light bulb made the bare, unpapered walls look stark. A row of pegs was empty except for a surplice and a Tesco bag. In one corner stood a large metal filing cabinet, scratched, dented, with a calendar taped to one side, the Sundays marked with felt-pen initials in red.

Kennedy opened a narrow door with a key, flicked a switch, and turned his body slightly to one side with practised ease so that he could drop down a flight of stairs.

'It's a bit hot,' he said, greeting them at the bottom. Behind him was a lagged boiler, oil-fired, ticking in the silence. 'We can't shut it down because it provides hot water – for here, and the house. In winter, it's snug – in summer, I try and keep the skylights open.'

At ceiling level there was a line of frosted-glass windows in one wall, heavily barred and letter-box narrow. The boiler room was neat and swept, as was a corridor which led away down the length of the church above, lit by three more bare light bulbs. Off it was a door into a bedsit, with a kitchen and toilet to one side. The narrow horizontal window here was open too, held up by a wooden stay, revealing the leaves of a fig tree in the graveyard above.

'It's not the crypt of St Paul's, is it?' said Shaw.

'It's home,' said Kennedy. In one corner stood an easel, half a dozen twisted oil-paint tubes in the wooden gutter. A light sketch in pencil covered a piece of cartridge paper, the lines too thin to reveal the subject. There was a desk and a computer – a slim white laptop. Kennedy touched it like an icon. 'I'm setting up a website for the church. I can do that – design and so on. I've done it before.'

He tucked his fingers into the front pockets of his jeans. 'How can I help?' he asked, the accent leafy-suburb London. 'Ask anything – I won't sleep, not now. Those poor men,' he added, his eyes pressed quickly closed.

79

'How are they?' asked Shaw.

'Aidan has some very serious burns; he's still unconscious. I think there are concerns the shock may be too much – although he's still young, and strong.' Kennedy looked away, his voice catching. 'Pete's got minor burns, and the smoke's really got his lungs, but he'll be fine. He's under sedation.'

'Four beds, you said. Where are the other two men?' asked Valentine, noticing a crucifix set above the door. The last time he'd been in a church had been for a funeral, and the memory, suppressed for so long, was making him anxious. He didn't recall the service itself, or anything anyone had said about his wife, but he could catch the precise smell, a kind of polished dampness. It was there again now, like a spirit.

'Well – Pete was only stopping a few nights – he's one of our old boys.' Kennedy laughed, but didn't get any response. 'He was here last year, in the summer, but he's up on the coast now at St John's, Hunstanton. And doing very well. He had to come back to Lynn – probate on a will, I think; I don't know the details. So there are actually three places vacant – Aidan's the only permanent resident at the moment. But we can't push people who aren't ready. The hostel is supposed to be a haven, you see, a safe place. So there's a process: criteria,' he added, proud of the word.

'A process you're in charge of?' asked Shaw.

'It's my job,' said Kennedy. 'I'm the hostel warden,' he said, puffing up. He stood up a bit straighter, too, knowing he'd just taken responsibility for something that might have gone badly wrong. One of the boiler pipes gave a curious liquid thud.

'You're very young for the job . . .' said Shaw, smiling.

'Father Martin trusts me. That helps a lot,' said Kennedy.

'So it was your decision to give one of these rooms to Aidan Holme – a serial offender with a record in peddling drugs?'

Kennedy nodded, as if considering an obtuse point in an academic debate. 'Yes. Yes, I did. Well – I recommended. Father Martin has the authority. But Aidan's past was not a secret. He's on a registered scheme for addicts. He takes medication to help him with that – and I collect prescriptions for all the men. He's stuck to the course – which is not easy. Father Martin gets regular reports on his progress from his social worker and they have been excellent. I believe he's clean. I have faith in him.'

Kennedy's confidence was, Shaw guessed, as brittle as the trendy glasses on his face. He tried to remind himself that this was a young man, that life hadn't yet taught him to see the people around him as a blend of good and evil, lies and truths.

'But supplying? He's been charged with supplying,' said Shaw.

'He denies it. I've asked him about it and he's adamant that he is an innocent man. I'm sorry – that was my judgement.'

They heard a brief blare of a car alarm through the narrow graveyard window.

'OK,' said Shaw. Kennedy might be a fool, he thought, but at least he was a decent one. 'So when the Judd family tell us Aidan had drawn Bryan Judd into taking drugs, and in fact into stealing drugs from the hospital to peddle on the street, they're lying, are they?'

'No. I think that's what Bryan Judd probably told them. I'm not surprised they believed him. Is that why they attacked the hostel?'

Shaw wasn't answering questions, he was asking them, and he thought Kennedy's answer had been smoothly glib. 'When you were with him in the street – earlier. What did Aidan mean when he said he was dying, and that he'd told you that would happen?'

'Aidan's not stupid, he's highly intelligent. He felt – feels – he's wasted his life. Here – in the church – we've talked about that many times. He said his greatest fear was that now – now he'd decided to sort his life out – God would take his life from him. I had to try and make him believe that wouldn't happen. Father Martin too. We told him that there is always time to repent, and that, if he did, there was no reason why there couldn't be rewards in this life, as well as the next.'

Shaw couldn't fault the logic, even if it was based on what he saw as superstition. 'Is it the first time there's been trouble at the hostel?' he asked, switching tack.

'There have been incidents in the past – in the street, at the Crane. People want their church, you know, but they don't seem to want what it stands for.' He said it as if reading the words, and Shaw wondered if he was mimicking Father Martin. Perhaps the priest was a father figure in more than one sense of the word.

'But I knew something would happen. Something terrible. I knew there'd be a fire. *Flames.*' Kennedy closed his eyes.

'How?' said Shaw, aware he'd been inveigled into the question.

'I hear voices,' said Kennedy, opening his eyes.

'Anyone we know?' asked Valentine.

Kennedy's smile froze. 'I'm sorry if you don't believe. I hear voices all the time and they said there'd be a fire. I told Father Martin we should have hydrants fitted – and smoke alarms. I *am* responsible.'

'So you keep reminding us,' said Shaw.

Kennedy licked his lips and Shaw noticed, for the first time, a stud in his bottom lip in the shape of a cross. 'Mary told me,' he said, glancing over Shaw's shoulder. They turned to see a painting, mass produced in a cheap frame, of Christ's mother revealing the heart in her chest, rays emanating, a chain of thorns producing drops of blood.

'Does anyone else hear the voices?' asked Shaw, trying to keep the tone unchallenging. Something in Kennedy's voice told him that for this man the voices were real enough.

'There's a network. We all hear – but not the same voices.' He looked from Valentine to Shaw. 'We're not mad. The doctors encourage us to listen to the voices, not deny them.'

'Doctors?' asked Shaw. Kennedy's face looked like it was about to crumple and Shaw instantly regretted the question. He held up a hand to stop the answer. 'Sorry.' He turned to go and noticed again the easel, and now, up close, he could see what the drawing was – fruit, in a bowl, set on a table covered with a cloth. 'Yours?' he asked.

'A study,' said Kennedy, laughing again. 'The work itself is in the church – would you like to see?'

Valentine ground his teeth. What he wanted was to go home, what he needed was a drink. He willed Shaw to say 'No'.

'Yes,' said Shaw.

Kennedy took them back up into the vestry, then into the nave, to the end, by the closed main doors. To one side a temporary kitchen had been set up; a stainless-steel unit, gas stove, sink, counter, and a fridge-freezer. The smell of shepherd's pie was stronger here, and stewed greens.

'The council provides food – we're trying to raise the funds for a proper kitchen. But the men appreciate it – a hot meal.' Kennedy had lowered his voice in deference to the sleeping men, and lowered his head too, as though in prayer.

'The men in the hostel at number 6,' said Shaw. 'I saw the kitchen – it didn't look like they cooked their own meals. The cupboards were empty.'

'No. They eat here. We are a community. God provides.'

Shaw recalled the empty silver takeaway curry trays; perhaps God didn't provide enough.

Kennedy flicked a switch. A spotlight illuminated the high whitewashed wall above and around the neo-Gothic doors. Valentine took a pew, suddenly aware that he might be overwhelmed by sleep. He closed his eyes and felt dizzy, so he snapped them open, looking up at the lit wall.

Shaw stood back. The whole surface had been prepared for a wall painting – but only one corner, at the bottom right, had progressed. It was in classical style, a velvet drape on the corner of a table, upon which were several objects: a skull and a bunch of grapes in a silver bowl. The grapes were ripe, beyond ripe, blushed with a thin layer of white mould. And some animal bones on a gold plate, picked clean of the flesh. To one side was a second bowl – just pencil lines, the subject of the study in Kennedy's room.

'You did this?' asked Shaw. The work was amateurish but studied, like painting-by-numbers. It was a work of dedication, not inspiration.

The fingers of Kennedy's right hand pulled at the left. He nodded, not taking his eyes off the images.

'Memento mori,' said Shaw. 'Remembrances of death.'

Kennedy nodded. 'Yes. Mortality.'

'And the rest?'

'*The Miracle at Cana*. Father Martin's favourite reading. It's a great honour to be asked.'

Shaw couldn't be sure but he thought he recognized the composition, the Italian colours. 'It's a Patigno? A copy?'

Kennedy blushed, as if copying a masterpiece was a sin. 'Yes, of course. That's clever of you. I did design at college – A Level. Mostly websites, actually. So this is a challenge. I've got a large print of the original in the back – if you'd like to see ...'

Shaw held up both hands. Valentine stood, walked

over to the fridge-freezer and lifted the lid. Ice and frost lay over plastic boxes, bags of frozen vegetables, packs of beef burgers. He touched the snow, and felt it was soft. 'You gonna use this stuff?'

'Don't think so,' said Kennedy. 'It's a waste, but we can't really risk it.' He looked to the clock over the door. 'It was down twelve hours. Too long. The freezer's old – and not very efficient even when it's working, and it's –'

Shaw cut him short. 'We need to speak to the men, these men, all of them. Some of them must have known Holme? Or Hendre even? Where were they during the fire?'

Kennedy looked shocked, which Shaw thought masked some anger as well. 'I told them to stay inside – but most were asleep because the lights were out. I can't wake them, not now.' He looked at a wristwatch, a Swatch. 'It's past one in the morning.'

'No, it can wait till first thing. But can you keep them all here for us?'

Kennedy looked back at the sleeping men as if for the first time. 'Sure. Well, until breakfast. That's nine o'clock. Then most of them walk – in the summer – down to the river, or the parks. That's their right.'

Shaw turned to go but noticed an electronic organ set to one side, and looking up he saw the original Victorian pipes. On the pew end was a pile of hymn books. He picked one up, leafing through, thinking about the 'Organ Grinder'. 'You still hold services here?'

'Yes. Oh yes. It's part of a team ministry – based at St Anne's. So we get a Sunday service once a month, and

86

other special services. Funerals, of course – and the odd wedding. We had one yesterday.'

'Someone plays the organ?' asked Shaw.

Kennedy shrugged. 'Father Martin sometimes, for the men. A few parishioners too, but not often.' He kicked at the floor with his trainer, and they could hear the gritty sound of something covering the tiles.

'I'd like their names, please,' said Shaw. 'The parishioners . . .'

Kennedy looked down, irritated. 'Since we banned confetti we have to deal with this . . .' He crunched something with his heel.

Shaw knelt quickly and picked up something, juggling it into the centre of his palm, holding it out for them to see.

It was a single grain of rice. Uncooked.

9

'Rice?' asked the man behind the counter of the all-night mobile kiosk. He wore a Chinese shirt, dragons and little willow-pattern bridges, but the accent was London overspill and he had *Red Devils* tattooed on one hand.

'Chips,' said Valentine. 'Curry sauce.' He didn't recognize the man; normally it was a woman with cutaway gloves.

He took the tray and a plastic fork and left without saying anything, leaving the right money in loose change on the counter: 90p. It had been that price for a year now.

The quayside was deserted, it was 2 a.m, the light from the all-night takeaway spilling out to the railings over the water. Valentine touched the iron, a little ceremony of luck, then walked, picking at the food, until he got to South Lynn, the network of streets he'd lived in all his life. He put the tray of half-eaten chips into a bin, crunching it down so that the seagulls wouldn't tear it back out.

His terraced house stood dark and still; but the street light outside his bedroom was on, buzzing like it always did. Briefly, he wondered if the power had been out here, then dismissed the thought. There was nothing in the fridge anyway.

In his imagination he could see into the rooms, through the bricks, as if it were a doll's house standing open. He knew what would be on every table, on every shelf, every wall. It spooked him now if he found something where it shouldn't be, because it meant one of two things – either he was losing his memory, or there was someone else in the house.

His keys were heavy in his pocket, and only a few minutes earlier he'd been dreaming of his bed, but now he couldn't face it, because sleeping was about letting go, and he wasn't very good at that. He walked on instead, past the corner shop and its security grille, to the graveyard of All Saints'. Someone had put an empty can of Special Brew on top of his wife's gravestone. He sat on a bench and lobbed grit at it. He unpeeled the charity sticker from his lapel and stuck it on the stone. There were twenty, thirty, others in various states of rotting away, all over the granite surface.

Julie Anne Valentine
1955–1993

Asleep

The beer can clattered down on the tarmac path.

He walked; zigzagging through the terraced streets behind the London Road, trying to shake off the illusion that he was being followed, an illusion which haunted him now when he was alone, at night, in the silent streets. Near the old city gate there was a pub called the Honest Lawyer, the sign a headless clerk; closed down now, the windows stopped-up with breeze blocks. Beside it stood a funeral parlour. Granite stones in the window, lilies in green glass vases, the paintwork gloss black. Beside the shop was a chapel of rest, the single window dark.

On the other side of the shop from the chapel was a house, two-up two-down, with a front door in matching gloss black. And beside that a set of garages: four roll-up doors. Valentine knew what was inside each: a sleek black car with glass panel sides for the coffin, a Daimler estate, and a glass-casket funeral coach; he'd often seen the plumed black horses pulling it towards the cemetery at Gayton Road.

The fourth roll-up garage door was never open in the week except in the evenings. Inside was a souped-up Citroën, stripped down for stock-car racing, up on blocks, with a bonnet logo that read TEAM MOSSE.

In front of the house, parked at the kerb, was a battered BMW, rust on one of the wheel arches.

There was a chestnut tree opposite the house on a triangle of open ground and the branches came right down to the ground, creating a perfect canopy. By the trunk of the tree was a bench, a hidden gazebo. And that's where he always sat. It was a bit like his other addictions now, watching this man – like the booze, the fags, and the gambling. He did it without thinking, and wouldn't have admitted that it wasn't fun any more. He'd started after Christmas because January was always his worst month. His generation – born in the fifties – didn't do depression, but if he'd known a little he'd have spotted the symptoms. He felt cold when it was mild, tired when he woke up, and alcohol deepened the feeling that he'd forgotten how to get through a day, like suddenly losing the ability to tie your own shoelaces.

So he'd made himself do this because he felt there was a chance that if he got to know everything you could know about this man, who lived and worked with the dead, it might unlock the mystery of the day when he'd seen his own life change for ever, the day his career had stalled, the day he'd lost track of the person he'd always wanted to be.

July 26th 1997.

He'd set out that night for the Westmead Estate, an up-and-coming DI, with a career ahead of him. His partner had been DCI Jack Shaw – Peter Shaw's father. The body of a nine-year-old boy, later identified as Jonathan Tessier, had been found dead at three minutes past midnight in the car park beneath Vancouver House – a twenty-one-storey council block in the heart of the estate – a sprawling warren of deprivation, the kind of place that official statistics said didn't exist.

The body was still dressed in the sports kit the boy had put on that morning to play football on the grass triangle by the flats. He'd been strangled, with a ligature of some sort, the condition of the body pointing to a time of death between six o'clock and eleven o'clock that night. A witness who'd found the body had seen a car leaving the scene – a Volkswagen Polo. The driver had failed to negotiate the narrow ramp to ground level and clipped one of the concrete pillars, spilling broken glass from a headlamp on the ground. Valentine and Shaw had stayed at the scene – overseeing the forensics team, organizing a door-to-door of the flats above, setting up an incident room in the community centre in the row of shops across the waste ground.

And then they'd got the break every murder inquiry needs: a Polo found abandoned at two that morning on waste ground two miles from the flats with a broken offside headlamp. Forensic tests would later provide an exact match between the shattered glass in the underground car park and the damaged Polo. The driver was listed as Robert James Mosse, a resident – like Tessier – of Vancouver House. He'd already reported the car as stolen. Jack Shaw and George Valentine interviewed Mosse in his flat at just after 3 a.m. He was a 21-year-old student taking law at Sheffield University, at home during the summer vacation. He'd been to the cinema with his mother, but they'd seen different films, and he'd come home alone.

Shaw and Valentine confronted Mosse, showing him evidence found at the scene – a leather, fur-lined glove, in a sealed evidence bag. They searched the flat but could not find a matching glove. Later DNA analysis of the skin residue inside the glove produced a close match for Mosse. And there was a motive, of sorts. Mosse's car had been vandalized on several occasions in the previous month – each time separately reported to back up insurance claims. Had Mosse caught Tessier damaging the car? Had an attempt to administer summary justice turned violent, then lethal?

The case was thrown out of court just after lunch on the first day. Shaw and Valentine had made an elementary procedural error in taking the glove to Mosse's flat. The defence argued that the glove had been contaminated in the process. Mosse's original statement, and that of his 62-year-old mother, was that the glove had *not* been in a sealed evidence bag. Even if it had been bagged, Shaw and Valentine had broken the rules. But if they hadn't bagged the evidence it raised another possibility, one that the judge was forced to highlight when dismissing the case. Had they taken the glove to the flat in a deliberate attempt to frame the suspect? Because without the glove there was no other physical evidence to link Mosse to the scene of the crime.

Jack Shaw's career ended in early retirement a few months later. George Valentine was busted down a rank to DS and sent out into the wilderness that was the north Norfolk coast; ten years of petty crime, traffic offences, and community policing. For George Valentine it felt like the start of a long slow death. But he'd kept his nose clean, and he'd worked hard, and he'd finally been given one chance to get his rank back. He'd been recalled to the CID at St James's.

Since becoming partners a year earlier he and Peter Shaw had tried to reopen the case into Robert Mosse – now a solicitor practising in Lynn. What they needed to do was build a fresh case against him – one that did not rely on the contaminated glove. They'd managed to link Mosse to a gang of teenage thugs who'd imposed some rough justice on the Westmead Estate. Mosse – away at university – was already living a different life. But it was clear that at one time he'd been part of this violent and unstable clique, and that they'd been a force to reckon with on the estate. On at least one occasion they'd meted out a violent lesson to a child in the very same underground car park where Tessier's body had been found. And Shaw and Valentine had found forensic evidence linking the murder victim to this gang – microscopic traces of paint found on Tessier's clothes suggested the boy had been close to an industrial spraying machine in the hours before his death. Three members of the gang worked for an agricultural engineering firm which used that precise make of paint – which included a rare chemical sealant used to protect farming gear.

They'd put all the new evidence they'd collected before Detective Chief Superintendent Max Warren, asking for the case to be reopened. At the very least, reviewed. They'd got a flat refusal. It was a notorious case, which had badly dented the reputation of the West Norfolk force. Warren said he needed more than circumstantial evidence to reopen old wounds. Worse, Warren warned Peter Shaw that any further attempts to interview witnesses or approach the one-time suspect would result in disciplinary action. Shaw had, in turn, warned Valentine off. The case was closed.

They'd never discussed it again. Valentine knew, although it had barely been said, that Jack Shaw's son still harboured a lingering doubt that his father might have planted the evidence that night. Valentine could see he'd been tortured by not knowing the truth: and now, perhaps, he'd accepted he never would – which meant that in part he not only distrusted his father's honesty, but Valentine's too, a judgement which lay at the heart of the animosity between them.

Valentine had not accepted the order to drop the case. He'd tracked down the remaining members of the original gang of four other than Mosse. One had emigrated to New Zealand, one was in a secure psychiatric unit on the edge of Lynn, having spent most of his life in prison serving sentences for various petty crimes.

Which left him with Alex Cosyns. He'd been watching his house, here, opposite the chestnut tree, for twelve weeks, picking up threads, and using police records and the odd spare moment in CID to piece together a biographical jigsaw. What had he learnt? His age – thirty-seven – born St George's Day in Lynn Royal Infirmary. Brought up on the notorious Westmead Estate, sixteenth floor of Vancouver House. Valentine had found a cutting from the *Lynn News* for 1980 – a picture of Cosyns's father, with his young son, and a litter of prizewinning dogs. Labradors. Dogs had been their shared passion. Then came a school record unblemished by achievement, followed by a course in mechanics at the tech college. Awarded the Griffiths Medal for best student 1989. Worked at Askit's Agricultural Engineers, Castle Rising until 1998. Then Kwik-Fit. Now a driver-mechanic for Gotobed's Funeral Services. Married, the father of one daughter, and divorced – all three life-defining events crammed into the same year, 1999. Affected dark glasses and driving gloves. When he wasn't working he was caring for the stock car or driving the third-hand BMW down to a semi in Manea, near Ely, to see his daughter. That was twice a month, always a Saturday. They went shopping in Peterborough, the cinema, a pub meal, then home.

And that was the first clue: those shopping trips round the Queensgate Centre were just a little too generous for a man who drove a hearse for a living and still paid child support. And then Valentine had checked out the stock car. There'd been a new engine six weeks ago, and a set of wire wheels, and a new roll-bar to weld. Team Mosse had a track record at the Norfolk Arena, Belle Vue, Stretham and Mildenhall. From the start the team had been run and bankrolled by Robert Mosse. Back in 2000 there'd been three cars in the team. Now there was just Cosyns's. And a trailer for the car, but Valentine didn't know where they kept that. As hobbies went, it was just about as expensive as you could get on dry land.

And that was the life he'd pieced together. All that, and the dog.

Valentine checked his watch. It was fifteen minutes past two. He wouldn't be seeing either of them tonight. The usual pattern was a late-night walk at around midnight. The lights would wink out, then the door would open. The dog was a Jack Russell and had seen better days, grey fur around the narrow snout, too much fat round the middle. Cosyns would tug it along the path towards the park, stooping down, ruffling its fur, talking. Like the extra cash, thought Valentine, the dog didn't fit. People *do* end up looking like their pets – a process of nature and nurture. They choose them, and then they mimic them. But the stumpy Jack Russell, despite its age, was hyperactive, fretful, skittering. Its owner, on the other hand, was tall, with unhurried movements, the lead always held firmly in the hand – and the hand always unseen in a leather driving glove. Mismatched partners, thought Valentine.

While Cosyns walked, Valentine would check out the front door just in case he'd left it off the latch. Then he'd look in the last of the four garages. Inside there'd be the

Citroën, a new paint job between each race. Although there was never any sign of the paint – so that must be done somewhere else too.

Next time he'd spring the front door lock, check out the inside of the house. This time he'd just wait, think, and see if he felt more like sleep. He fished in his pocket for his hip flask and drank.

He pictured Erebus Street, the dock gates, and the Crane. He knew that Shaw and he had come, silently, to the same conclusion; that Bryan Judd's killer had not only come from Erebus Street, but that the heart of the mystery was there too. Because too much had happened in one night: the blackout, the murder, the sabotage, the attack on the hostel. Then there were the potential forensic links with the murder scene – the rice, the broken match. But what was cause, and what was consequence? Surely, within one of those houses, a motive must have been born, strong enough, and dark enough, to set in motion such a violent series of events.

And then there was that curious knowledge that he'd been to Erebus Street before. He snatched at the memory, but it slid past, like a fish just seen under reflective water. All it left was a phrase in his mind, almost slipping off the hook: *missing person*. Now he knew he wouldn't sleep – not in his bed, anyway. So he stood abruptly and set out towards The Walks, across the silent park, picking up the long sinuous path which skirted the medieval Red Tower, and led back to police headquarters at St James's.

10

Ally Judd stood at her bedroom window looking at the harsh neon sign that read 24-HOUR WASH, buzzing on, buzzing off, buzzing on, flooding the double bed with green light. Through the party wall she heard the washing machines return to life in mid-cycle, the driers turning like whispers. She hadn't thought of that – that with the power back on they'd restart.

On the bed she'd laid out some photos. She'd slept for an hour after she'd taken the sedatives, then started awake, crying out, so that the WPC on the step had come up to check she was all right.

Alone again, she'd laid out Bry's life in pictures.

Her throat was dry and she still hadn't cried. It was the guilt, she knew, that held her back. The knowledge that now she wouldn't have to tell him that she had to leave, that she'd loved him once, but that the love had been ground out of her, drained, by her life on Erebus Street, and the bad blood which seemed now to be in the very nature of the Judd family.

She sat on the edge of the duvet and picked up the first picture: a snapshot of Bry and his twin, Norma Jean, her teeth encased in a brace. They'd be eight or nine, Ally guessed, and already the mirror-like resemblance was being torn apart by the difference in sex: Bry's brow getting stronger, his face broadening, while Norma Jean's was lengthening, and the mouth bowing with full lips. She flipped the picture over to see the date: August 1984.

Then, the picture she'd taken on her first day out with Bry, on the front at Wells, taken by a stranger from Scotland – Pennycuick, she remembered, because they'd laughed at the name and got her to spell it out. Ally looked bitterly at her seventeen-year-old body in its shorts and bikini top – lithe, the waist impossibly slim. She'd had curves then, not this drab figure like an ironing board stood on end. Bry didn't like the sun, so he was shading his eyes, an arm draped round her neck. The year they met – 1991. The year before everything changed, the year before they'd lost Norma Jean. After that, Bry hadn't smiled much, but she'd still been drawn to him – a vulnerable, damaged man she thought she could fix.

The wedding day next; what was left of his family, all of her family – worse luck. But at least Bry's smile was real enough amongst the sullen smirks. She'd been three months pregnant with the baby they'd lost. Andy in the background. She thought the cruelty of it was almost unbearable; Andy, alone after Marie had died, hiding in a family photo.

Next, holidays. The Grand Ole Opry, Nashville, just bliss: the music, the heat, and the thought of all those miles between them and Erebus Street. They stood together, astonished at how much fun life could be.

Back home it was always family. She bit her lip. A picture of Neil next, a laughing six-year-old, thrown over his brother Bry's shoulder, her grinning behind. And then, finally, Christmas this year: her and Bry on the beach at Old Hunstanton. Bry, trying to be happy, but disorientated by the drugs and alcohol, winching up a smile, just to make her happy. There was a new café on the beach, and they'd opened Christmas morning for teas and coffees. Snow on the sand, and the sea as green as Bry's eyes, and Neil's shadow running away from the camera. The three of them, with Andy back home in the Crane, keeping an eye on the turkey from the public bar.

And a new picture. A secret picture.

It had lain on the bedside table slipped inside the psalter he'd given her. A snapshot, him in swimming shorts, on a beach. She covered her mouth with her hand. She had a right to be happy, just like anyone else. She propped the picture on the bedside table beside the night-light they'd lit together. And they'd said a prayer for Bry's soul. They hadn't even thought about the future. That would have been a sin too.

She broke the line of thought. Next door she could still hear the washing machines. Neil and Andy shared the flat above the launderette. But Andy was at the police station, and would be all night. Neil slept heavily, and noise wouldn't wake him anyway, unless he picked up the vibrations. She'd leave it until the morning. Then she thought about sleeping, in this bed, their bed, and decided she could deal with the machines now.

The female PC had retreated from the front step to the squad car parked at the T-junction, blocking traffic, the thin squawk of the radio just audible. Looking up, Ally saw a clear night sky, the moon, going to earth now, over behind the abattoir. She put the key in the lock of the launderette and turned the Chubb – but the door wouldn't open. She turned it back and it did. She'd left it open.

Inside she turned her back to the door and looked down the centre of the launderette.

'God,' she said, thinking she might cry now. One of the washers had malfunctioned and there was a pool of water in front of it; a detergent slick. She grabbed a plastic laundry basket, knelt down in the water and pulled open the porthole, dragging out the contents.

Inside was a pair of heavy-duty overalls. They were covered in red stains. Pressing the material to her nose she caught the unmistakable scent of blood: ferrous, acrid. She fumbled for the name tag inside the collar.

'Oh God,' she said. 'No.'

11

As the seagull flies, Peter Shaw lay twenty-two miles to the north, on the cool sand of Old Hunstanton, watching the moon set. Despite the hour, nearly 3 a.m, along the high-tide mark small fires still burnt, the remnants of the surfing crowd staying up to see in the new day and enjoying what might be the last night of the Indian summer. Wavelets curled over to fall on the beach, creating the night's only sound – a rhythmic whisper. Fran had made a seat in the sand in front of the café. He sat in it now, his skin drying after a swim, wrapped in a beach towel.

Lena swam fifty yards offshore, the rise and fall of her arms hypnotic. When he'd got back she was up, in a chair on the stoop, unable to sleep through the heat. He watched her coming out of the sea: black skin, white bikini, slim and compact, treading heel-to-toe as if following a line in the sand. She grabbed a towel from the café and sat down, their bodies touching at the hip and shoulder. She dug her toes into the sand. 'We made some money today,' she said. She had brown eyes, only ever half open, but with a cast in the right. 'Fifteen hundred pounds in the shop – a thousand in the café.'

Shaw whistled, insinuating a hand around her waist. On his lap he had a reference book – *1001 Paintings from the Louvre*. He'd had it open at Patigno's *Miracle at Cana*. One of the many ways in which he was less than the perfect detective was this obsession with apparently incidental detail. But, he consoled himself, this was his time, and if he wanted to waste it, he could. He certainly wasn't going to sleep. He'd wanted the swim to cleanse him of the day, but it had simply prepared him for the next. He held the book open on his lap, the hypnotic scent of the quality paper almost as enticing as the smell of the sea.

Liam Kennedy's copy on the walls of the Sacred Heart of Mary had been faithful to the original – at least in the corner he'd finished – in every detail except one. A tiny omission amongst the memento mori.

Lena kissed him on the neck as he closed the book, but then he slipped a cutting out that he'd hidden between the pages of the index.

'I found this,' he said, knowing he'd just ruined the moment.

It was from the *Lynn News* of 1997. July 22nd.

An accident on the outskirts of town. A Mini had hit a Ford Mondeo at a lonely T-junction. The driver of the Ford – a 45-year-old woman – survived but the two passengers, both over seventy, died at the scene. CCTV footage showed clearly – the report said – that the Mini had jumped the red light. They'd got out of the car to inspect the wrecked Ford – three young men in peaked baseball caps, their car side-on to the CCTV. According to the police the footage showed the driver was alive – her forehead slumped over the wheel turning side to side, and one of the passengers in the back of the car, a hand at a rear window, pawing at the glass. Then the Mini drove away. It was nearly thirty-five minutes before another driver arrived at the scene and alerted the emergency services – thirty-five minutes in which both the passengers died.

It was just the kind of crime Lena said damaged the way you looked at the world. Just the kind of crime she didn't want to know anything about, not any more. She folded the cutting, handing it back. 'Nice people. Perhaps they've paid the price for it – we'll never know. I don't want to know.'

But Peter Shaw did want to know. This was what he found almost impossible to tolerate: an open-ended question, the puzzle with no solution. Lena knew it was one of the things that made him a policeman.

'The date,' he said.

She nodded. 'I know. It's a few days before the day we don't seem to be able to ever forget.'

She looked out at sea, annoyed – angry – that an almost perfect day had ended like this.

They both knew the details of his father's last case: the murder of nine-year-old Jonathan Tessier on the night of 26 July 1997 – three days after this fatal car crash. The case that had left his father to retire under the shadow of that dreadful epithet 'bent copper'. The case that had seen George Valentine busted down to DS, and banished to the coast.

Shaw held the cutting lightly. Lena watched the sea, hugging herself.

'Tom Hadden's done a re-examination of the forensics on Tessier. Remember there were tiny spots of paint on the kid's football shirt? We linked those to the factory where some of Mosse's mates worked. But there was *another* flake of paint on the football shirt that child died wearing – and this flake was different. It was bevelled, as if from an impact. Grey-blue. It was never considered in the original inquiry. I got Timber Woods in archive to run through all the car crime in the month running up to the murder. The car involved in this fatal crash,' he waved the cutting, 'was silver – but there were flakes of paint from the other car, the Mini, embedded in the offside door and boot. Grey-blue. Not just any grey-blue – *seascape* blue. It's a commercial make used widely in the 1980s.'

He flicked the cutting. Lena looked out to sea. 'Widely,' she said, expertly picking at the hole in the logic.

But she'd walked into a trap. 'Tom's done a mass spectroscope analysis and the paint is one produced for this specific model of Mini by British Leyland at Long-bridge in 1991. That's about eight thousand cars in the batch – most went for export. That's a very small number, Lena. Think about it – eight thousand in the world. What are the chances that fleck of paint *didn't* come from that Mini?'

He gave up waiting for his wife to react, and watched the waves breaking instead. 'So – a gang of youths in a fatal car smash do a runner from the scene. We know Mosse was involved in such a gang. Less than a week later we find Tessier's body under the Westmead – and there's a flake of paint from the Mini on his clothing.'

Lena looked her husband in the eyes. She was always saddened at how much of their lives seemed to get sucked into this other world.

'This is it,' he said, raising both hands in frustration. 'They know there's a camera at the junction. They prob-ably guessed you couldn't do an ID on the registration number from the footage – and they're right. But they've got a hot car – a two-tone Mini with a crushed offside wing. So the kids take the Mini back to the Westmead, my guess is to one of the lock-up garages – there's dozens. They respray the car. Tessier is playing football, he runs off to get a ball – he loses interest – perhaps he can't find it. He strolls on – around by the community centre, then into the lock-ups. He stumbles on them – somehow, I don't know how. But he pays for it with his life.'

She laughed without a trace of humour. 'And you think that makes sense?' Shaw had been at New Scotland Yard when he'd met Lena in Brixton. She probably knew more about crime on the streets than he did. 'Why kill a nine-year-old kid because he's seen you respraying a car? They knew where he lived. A threat would have done – sweetened with a five-pound note. Why would the sight of a Mini being resprayed have registered with the kid? You'll have to do better than that, Peter. Max'll have you for breakfast.'

Shaw snagged an ankle round hers.

'Have you told George?' she asked.

'No. I can't. I don't know why.'

She threw her head back. 'He's a boozer – not far short of an alcoholic – and a nicotine addict with an aversion to exercise and a weak bladder who lives alone. You're married, with a daughter, have an addiction to exercise, an aversion to cigarettes and no apparent need for a bladder at all. I've seen you drink a pint of Guinness, but never two. And you don't get on? That's a big surprise, is it?' She rubbed the salt on her cheek, suddenly desperate to be in the shower. 'And, while we're on the subject, there is your father. George knew him better than you did. Let's be brutal – he knew him better than you ever will.'

'I don't trust him,' said Shaw, trying not to recognize how cruel she'd been to point that out. He was haunted by this simple conundrum: were Jack Shaw and George Valentine just old-fashioned coppers who'd bent the rules, or were they old-fashioned bent coppers? He was convinced now that Robert Mosse was involved in the murder of Jonathan Tessier – but he was aware that his guilt didn't necessarily mean his father and George Valentine hadn't twisted, or planted, the discredited evidence.

Lena stood, brushing sand from her skin. 'You don't trust him because you still think there's a chance he and Jack planted that glove. Which would imply that George's enthusiasm for reopening the case is simply a cover for his earlier dishonesty. Which means you don't trust – didn't trust – Jack, either. Who do you trust?'

Shaw narrowed his eyes, watching a light at sea. 'I just want proof.'

Lena stretched her fingers out, making her hands into two bird's feet. Shaw could see that she was struggling to keep her temper. 'All right. What about doing something practical – getting this over with? And if you can't do that, Peter – let's see if we can live without it.'

She stood, took a step forward, looking out to sea. 'Other than Robert Mosse, who is presumably fairly easy to find, where are the other three kids you and George have identified as members of this gang?'

'They're not kids.'

107

'They were.'

Shaw worked his hand into the muscles at the back of his neck. He'd been down this route, trying to track them down in the odd spare moment George Valentine wasn't around. All he'd found were three dead ends.

'One emigrated – two years after the murder. New Zealand. Another turned out a small-time crook – East Midlands somewhere. But he's in a psychiatric unit now. The ringleader – well, the oldest – took up driving, car mechanics. He crops up in 1999 – drink-driving. Got off with a suspended sentence when the court was told he needs to drive as part of his job. Divorced, one child. Since the drink-driving he's led a blameless life and appears a model citizen.' He stood, kicked some sand. Out of his pocket he took his RNLI pager, checked the signal and the battery – a little ritual before sleep.

'And he's got a steady job. Even if it's a peculiar job,' he added. 'A touch of the macabre – he drives a hearse.'

I 2

Monday, 6 September

The SDM crew had that Monday-morning feeling, so that when the foreman, Joe Beadle, lifted the manhole cover, the stench of the air they'd all soon be breathing made them choke. It was always bad like this in hot, dry weather. The storm-drain system, which took rainwater off the streets and out to sea, was almost empty, so anything down there that shouldn't be down there had time to rot between the tides. And the rats moved in and out of the sewerage system, rivers of them, following some phantom piper.

The crew's job was storm-drain maintenance – SDM. They swept out the channels, checked the brickwork vaulting for cracks and settling, then cleared the gratings which stopped anything too big being brought into the system from the sea. There were twenty miles of storm sewers under Lynn, a lot of it medieval. So they had jobs for life, the three of them, and they never complained to anyone but each other, because the money was good and they spent half their time drinking tea, or at the greasy spoon by the dock gates. And they set their own hours, because they had to work between the tides, which was why they were here now, at just after six.

Trance, the kid they'd taken on a year earlier from

Direct Labour, zipped up his overalls. It hadn't taken them long to see where he'd got the nickname; he lived in a world of his own, behind glassy eyes, his lips often rippling with an internal conversation.

But he was young – just seventeen – and they needed a gofer, and someone to send down the narrow vaults. Trance took one last look along the narrow street they were in, full of closed shops, and lowered himself athletically into the hole, searching with his boots for the metal rungs of the ladder. Then he jumped, and they heard a splash, but there was no bass note, nothing to indicate depth. Beadle clapped once. 'Well done, kid.' He turned to Freeman, who was black, but the life underground had robbed his skin of its sunny lustre so that he looked grey, like a dead fish. 'You next.'

Beadle, last down, pulled the cover closed and they were in the dark until the torches came on – and then they were in *their* world, and despite the stink, they felt better. Trance whistled, picking up rubbish with a grip on a stick, popping it in a black bin liner. They walked at a steady pace, Freeman searching the curved brick arch of the tunnel for signs of cracking, ticking boxes on a clipboard that hung from a lanyard on his belt. Beadle checked a map in a cellophane wallet. The tunnel they were in was Victorian and ran for nearly 400 yards parallel with the quay. Overhead they could feel the early rush-hour traffic, a visceral rumble which made their guts vibrate. A thin trickle of water ran at the centre of the channel, but the rest was dry, the bricks stained and bleached by the daily inundation of salty seawater.

Beadle checked his watch: 6.04 a.m. They had two

hours to get to the grating at the head of the Purfleet and back before the seawater came in, sluicing the drain. Then, they had a tunnel to check under the park, and then they could knock off, get a fry-up, be home by early afternoon.

Trance's torch beam shone directly ahead, not strong enough to reach the distant sharp turn. The rats, uncannily, were always on the edge of the light, a faint shimmering movement, retreating as the men advanced. But the noise was there if you listened for it, a feral, high-pitched chorus, just on the borderline of the inaudible. Trance used the pick-up stick to bag a few dead rats, a supermarket bag, and the shreds of a shell-suit. They trudged on, all of them smoking now, the turning in the tunnel coming into view, a graceful 90-degree angle in arched brick. They regrouped and Beadle poured coffee – black – because the milk always went off in the summer and anyway the acrid, unadulterated caffeine helped take away the taste of salt on their lips.

Now they were at the elbow-turn they could see the tidal grid, a perfect half moon exactly the same shape as the tunnel, beyond it the pale glow of daylight in the channel of the Purfleet. But it wasn't a perfect grid, it never was, because the tide brought flotsam in, which stuck in the metal grating, so that the little squares of light were often fogged. One day they'd found the rotting carcass of a dog on the grid, and there'd been mattresses, and fishing buoys, and the flesh of a basking shark. Jessop – the supervisor back at the depot – had worked on the SDM crew in the seventies, and he said once a coaster had gone down on the sands in the Wash and the cargo had clogged the grids all along the Cut – women's knickers, bras, sexy stuff. But they'd never been that lucky.

They trudged forward and the rats funnelled away into the channels which fed the main sewer, giving up the ground to the crabs which scuttled out of the mud of the Purfleet. For the crew this was the worst bit, and the main reason they wore the heavy boots, so that when the shells cracked with every step it didn't feel so immediate, so like a killing. But even then they avoided the larger specimens: green-shelled shore crabs a foot across which made an odd hollow tumping sound when they scuttled, the carapace rocking on the brick floor. Trance began to sing, something tuneless and angry. Beadle smoked manically, chalking up a code on the wall to prove they'd been down.

Trance waded through the clicking, snapping crabs until they were twenty feet from the grid. But it was Freeman who made them look. 'Well,' he said, loosening the bandanna he always wore around his neck. 'It was bound to happen one day.'

Almost exactly at the centre of the semi-circle of the grid was a human body, spread-eagled like a sky-jumper, left hanging by the tide.

'Fuck,' said Beadle, fumbling for his mobile. He looked round, then unfolded a map. They all shuffled forward to get a better look. It was a man, in jogging pants and a T-shirt that looked too big. The face had been pressed up to the grid and by chance the mouth filled one of the open squares so that they could see teeth, and a dark gullet, but the lips were colourless. He was hanging there because he had something round his wrist, like a charity bracelet, white, strong, and caught on one of the grid's metal edges. And one of his legs had gone through the grid, and broken below the knee, so that a bone showed, but again the flesh was colourless even where the muscle and flesh were exposed.

'Weird,' said Trance, a smile widening as he imagined himself telling his mates that night at the Globe.

But they couldn't really see any detail because the body was up against the light, a silhouette, the light beyond blinding now that the sun had risen, and was bouncing off the water. Outside, on the distant quayside, they could hear the sounds of everyday life: a car alarm, seagulls, a buzz of muzak.

'Why's it moving?' said Beadle, stepping back, catching his heel and falling. It was a nightmare, to be down there in the crabs, thrashing, feeling their shells and legs, unable to get a hand down to the brick floor. He felt a fool but he screamed, and went on screaming, until Freeman and Trance helped him up, hauling him by the arm, laughing.

Then they all looked again. And it *was* moving, because the crabs had latched onto the skin as the water level fell, and now they were stranded up there, although every second or two a few would fall. It was like when they'd been kids, and you dangled rotten bacon over the dockside and waited for the crabs to latch on, but when you pulled it clear of the water you always lost some, dropping off, plopping into the water.

So many crabs had clung on that the edges of the man were moving against the light, like he was an animated sketch, shivering in the light.

Then the wristband broke, the body swung to the left, then out, then down, into the mud. A few crabs were left on the mesh, like an outline at a murder scene, a surreal confirmation that they'd seen what they'd really seen.

Freeman kicked one of the crabs up in the air so that it hit the wall with a crack. But Trance waded forward because he'd seen the wristband drop. He picked it up – and saw that it bore three stencilled letters . . .

MVR.

13

Sergeant Ernest 'Timber' Woods had let George Valentine bring a bacon sandwich into the records room. They'd worked together in the seventies with Jack Shaw. But Timber was never in their league: he couldn't catch a cold without uniformed assistance. He'd embraced early retirement and a nice little job to pay for his domino nights at the Institute – he was working the early shift that day: six till noon. West Norfolk had still to secure government funding to transfer all the force records to computer. Anything before 1995 was still on paper. So they needed Woods and the dusty box files which filled the old gunpowder magazines under St James's – a Grade II listed relic of the barracks which had stood on the spot before the city walls had been demolished to make way for police headquarters.

Valentine had got two hours' sleep at his desk, his feet up, then he'd gone out to the bus station to get his breakfast. He'd brought Woods a tea and a round of toast and dripping wrapped in silver paper.

'Missing person, you say?' asked Woods, pulling himself up from behind the steel desk they'd given him. He was built like an armchair and walked like a fisherman, with a roll of the shoulders.

'Not my case, Timber, but I think Jack was involved. And Erebus Street – I know that address.' Valentine followed, the aisles of shelves opening up on the left and right. The room itself was as long as a Tube carriage, with a barrel roof in fine brick, spotlit, the side aisles leading off for a distance of about thirty feet. It was as quiet as libraries used to be, before banks of PCs introduced a patter of keystrokes.

'It's got to be the early nineties,' said Valentine. 'It's before I teamed up with Jack – I know that. That was '94. I'd have been a DI – so that's after '91.'

Woods came to a halt. 'Right – there's one of these for each year; missing persons in alphabetical order.' He tapped a printed sheet inside a metal frame holder. 'Here's 1990 – then go that way,' he added, pointing down the room. 'I'll eat my toast,' he said, hobbling away.

Valentine didn't know if he'd recognize the name. But he liked long shots, especially when he was this tired. It was like gambling, a kind of listless excitement. There was nothing on 1990 – from Brent to Wynch. Or 1991. He was at the bottom of the list for 1992 when he knew his concentration had gone. He pressed two fingers on either side of his nose, and read them again. And there it was: JUDD, N. J.

'Well, well,' he said, the adrenaline flooding his blood-stream. 'Family secrets.'

He found the box file using the code provided. There was a table and chair at the end of the aisle. He set his packet of Silk Cut to one side, the lighter beside it, and opened the file in the box to the first page, a typed sheet with a single line . . .

Investigating officer: DCI Jack Shaw.

It took him an hour to read the file: thirty-two pages, including a Home Office forensics report. When he'd finished he gave it back to Timber Woods without comment – simply asking for a copy of the notes and enlargements of all the pictures – then got the lift to the canteen, which opened at seven. He ordered the full English, and a mug of tea, and methodically ate, reordering what he'd read into a coherent timeline. Then, out on the fire escape platform, he lit the long-delayed Silk Cut and rehearsed the whole story of Norma Jean Judd as the nicotine cut in, making his heart race and his vision suddenly sharpen. In his mind he formed a précis of the story ready to give Shaw.

Norma Jean Judd was fifteen years old when she disappeared; fifteen years nine months. Her home address was number 14 Erebus Street – the house occupied by her twin brother until his violent death. Norma Jean was last seen alive on a summer's afternoon in 1992. She was at Lynn Community College but on a day-release scheme in hairdressing – NVQ Level 2. She'd been at Fringe Benefits, the hairdressers on the London Road, from 10 o'clock that morning until 3.45 that afternoon. Colleagues said she'd always been tidy, dutiful, and polite. That day, however, she'd been unusually quiet – a trait which had been deepening for several weeks. She'd explained that she was worried about her exams. She'd walked home. A neighbour saw her in Erebus Street at 4.30, talking to a neighbour, a man called Jan Orzsak. The witness said their voices had been raised and that Norma Jean appeared upset by the encounter. She ran home to number 14. She was never seen again by anyone

outside her family. To get home she'd run past the launderette where her mother — Marie — worked. Her father,
Andy, was outside the Crane, drinking at one of the tables
set on the pavement, having completed a shift working on
the dockside. The gates had then offered direct access
to the quayside. He saw she was upset, and followed her
into the house.

It was not a happy house. The problem was Norma
Jean: attractive, precocious, and independent, and four
months pregnant. The father was Ben Ruddle, of number
31 Erebus Street. He was nineteen at the time, in a young
offenders' centre up the coast at Boston, awaiting trial for
burglary. Andy Judd wanted her to keep the baby. Marie,
her mother, wanted her to have a termination. A brief
note from Norma Jean's doctor was included in the file;
it confirmed that another GP had been asked to review
the case notes on the grounds that a request had been
made by the patient — on 1 September — for the doctors
to consider a termination under the 1967 Abortion
Act, on the grounds of the damage it would cause to the
mental health of the mother.

In his statement to police Andy Judd said he'd gone
home, found Norma Jean crying on her bed, and had
comforted her. Norma Jean said — according to her father
— that she was upset and confused about what to
do about the child. Andy said he'd run himself a bath
because he and his wife were planning a night out at
St Luke's — the Catholic club in nearby Roseberry Street.
While he was in the bathroom he heard Norma Jean
going down the stairs — he said he presumed she was
making herself a cup of tea. But when he came down he

found her gone, the back door still open into the yard they shared with the launderette.

Marie Judd, in her statement made that evening to DCI Jack Shaw, corroborated her husband's version of events. She'd said she'd seen Norma Jean crossing the yard at about 5 o'clock – it had to be before that because one of her friends had come into the launderette to listen to the local weather forecast on the radio. They both wanted to hear it because they'd planned a trip to the beach at Heacham the next day – a Sunday.

Andy Judd went back to the Crane. The landlord said he was certain he was back by 5.30 p.m. It was the mother who raised the alarm when she went home to get ready to go out at 7.30 p.m. There was no sign of her daughter. She rang friends, and – after dragging her husband out of the pub – they checked neighbours as well. At 9.30 p.m. they called the police.

The prime suspect was Jan Orzsak. Aged forty-eight. An engineer. Polish. A bachelor whose mother had died two years previously. When she was much younger, he'd made friends with Norma Jean and a few of the other children in the street. They went to his house to see his tropical fish. Orzsak said he'd asked Norma Jean to feed the fish while he'd been out of the country on an assignment for the company he worked for – in Africa, installing a power plant in a village near Lagos. When he got back the fish were dead. She'd lost the key he'd given her. He admitted they'd argued in the street. Orzsak said he'd simply expressed his disappointment. CID had him in that first night while an extensive house-to-house search was conducted. He was released without charge the next morning. While a back alley did link Norma Jean's yard to Orzsak's house, there was no forensic evidence she'd been in his house that evening.

Nothing was ever heard of her again.

Jack Shaw had next hauled the father – Andy – into St James's. Marie Judd, re-interviewed, admitted that there had been family arguments about the baby. The issue was deeply divisive. Marie Judd was from a sprawling Irish Catholic family. She'd watched her own mother worn down by bearing eleven children: three boys and eight girls. Her death at fifty-eight had been a release from grinding poverty. It was a fate Marie was determined her daughter would not share. Her father, a teetotal wages clerk at one of Dublin's linen mills, had seen in the size of his family the only evidence that his life had been a success. Andy, as devout a worshipper at the Sacred Heart as his wife, could walk away from the consequences of childbirth; he considered all forms of abortion to be infanticide.

The CID team asked themselves the obvious question: had Andy, on that last evening, discovered that his daughter had finally decided to take her mother's advice? Had an argument turned to violence?

It wouldn't have been the first time. Andy Judd had a violent criminal record; often linked to alcohol abuse. In 1984 he'd been convicted on a charge of ABH – he'd coshed a workmate from the docks with an empty beer bottle after an argument over a card game in one of the North End pubs. In 1993 he'd been before the magistrates court on three counts of breaching the peace – all in the Crane. Each time excessive alcohol consumption had reduced his ability to inflict serious injuries on those he'd attacked. He'd been fined, and placed on community service orders. More than one neighbour was prepared to go on the record to say that the sounds of a fight had been heard in the Judds' house two days before Norma Jean had gone missing: a scream, glass breaking.

But despite an extensive forensic sweep of the house no evidence could be found of a violent struggle, let alone murder. If he had killed his daughter, where had he put the body in the few minutes during which he'd an opportunity to cover his tracks? And there was Marie Judd's eyewitness account of seeing Norma Jean alive *leaving* the house. She insisted her husband was not capable of hurting their daughter and had never struck her, despite the bitter family row over the unborn child. Jack Shaw had believed Marie Judd's statement, although the suspicion would always linger that she might have been persuaded to lie to protect her husband.

If they couldn't find a killer perhaps there was another possibility: had Norma Jean simply left home? She'd talked to at least one school friend about running away. But extensive checks on buses, trains, and the major roads out of Lynn drew a blank. The Garda visited relatives in Dublin to make sure she had not fled across the Irish Sea. The file on Norma Jean Judd remained open for almost two years. There was a single sighting of the teenager in 1993 after an extensive poster campaign in eastern England. She was 'seen' buying *Hello!* in Peterborough by a woman who ran a newsagent's. *Hello!* was Norma Jean's favourite magazine. The woman said she was 'nearly certain' it was the girl in the poster. Lynn police set up a mobile unit outside the cathedral for two weeks, and a leaflet campaign was mounted in the city, but no other sighting – however tenuous – was ever reported. Belated checks on the witness uncovered the fact that her own daughter had gone missing in 1981. She had received a single card, postmarked Canterbury, asking her not to worry. She had been receiving intermittent treatment ever since for depression.

Valentine finished his cigarette and threw it from the metal fire escape outside the canteen, watching it corkscrew down five floors to the St James's car park. What did Norma Jean's story tell him about the dead man – her twin brother Bryan? What did it tell him about the Judds? Only, perhaps, that they were a family who lived with a secret and a question: if Norma Jean was dead, did her killer live amongst them? Or just a few doors away?

He asked himself how many families could withstand that kind of distrust, that intensity of internal tension, before blowing itself apart. And he knew the answer was none.

14

Shaw had slept fitfully until six, then, relishing the cool air, he'd left Lena in bed, running to the Land Rover along the high-tide mark. The team would be in place at the murder incident room at the Queen Vic at seven. He had an hour. He'd considered a swim, but a single image made him hesitate – the lights going out at the presbytery beside the Sacred Heart of Mary the night before. He'd found the interview with Liam Kennedy unsettling; he sensed he'd been told less than the whole truth, worse – that Kennedy was an unreliable witness, someone *unable* to see the difference between reality and the world in his own head. He wanted to get to the parish priest before he'd had an opportunity to discuss with the hostel warden what had happened in Erebus Street. Shaw closed his blind eye, massaging the lid. He wanted two views of Aidan Holme, not one, merged.

In the dawn light Erebus Street was desolate, the blackened ruins of number 6 no longer smouldering, the debris cleared from the road, the light outside the launderette, thrown out of sequence by the power cut, flashing now despite the low sun slanting in as it rose above the slaughterhouse on the corner. Shaw picked his way through the headstones in the small walled graveyard to the front door of the presbytery, which was painted locomotive green, and stood open.

Shaw called down the hall. A light spilt from a door-way showing piles of newspapers, magazines, and food supplies – tins of Fanta, baked beans, tomato soup, and toilet rolls.

He could hear a voice, just one half of a conversation.

'Yes. Of course. I've got the policies out now. Yes – I'll make the calls. I understand . . .'

Shaw called again.

'A second,' said the voice. A head appeared round the door. 'Come in, please – I won't be a moment.' The voice was high, with an accent, a sibilance which suggested Spain, Portugal, or South America.

The front room held a desk on which was an oil lantern, the flame out, but the room still haunted by the scent of paraffin. The lantern was brass, with an inlaid design and coloured glass panels. The light came from an electric desk lamp which Shaw had guessed had been on since well before dawn. Two walls of books, a Victorian standard lamp and a sideboard which hadn't seen polish in the reign of Pope Benedict. A priest stood at the desk making a note on a foolscap pad with a fountain pen, the scratch of the nib purposeful, businesslike.

'Thank you. Every prayer is needed,' he said, then cut the mobile, slipping it into a wallet on a leather belt. Shaw could see that mentally the priest continued to play the conversation on the phone through his head.

'I am Father Thiago,' he said, trying to focus. 'TEE-AR-GO.' He emphasized the syllables so that Shaw would get it right first time.

His skin was dark, the hair lustrous, receding from a high academic forehead. Shaw noticed a gold signet ring and, despite the simplicity of his clothes – a white linen shirt and collar with black trousers – there was a gold buckle on each of his black leather shoes. He was slim, perhaps forty years of age, with graceful self-conscious movements. He ran a hand back over his hair as if he were stroking a cat.

'Thiago Martin,' he added.

Shaw showed the priest his warrant card.

'The fire,' said Father Martin, a hand covering his eyes. 'That was the bishop. There's so much to do. Insurance – I'm just checking our policies. I'm afraid our affairs are not in the best of order.'

'Any news of the two men from the hostel?' Shaw asked.

Martin shook his head. 'And Bryan Judd – killed, murdered? Can that be true? The radio hasn't given a name.'

'Yes. Nothing's cast in stone, Father,' said Shaw. 'But we found a body, and Bryan is missing. Still missing.' He broke off, walked to one of the bookcases and teased out a spine. 'The men in the hostel, Father – Holme and Hendre. It's Holme I'm particularly interested in. Specifically his relationship with Bryan Judd. You know Holme?'

Father Martin sat, holding both hands to his face to cover a yawn. 'Aidan? Of course – he's been with us some time, although the hostel is really Liam's kingdom. Liam Kennedy – the warden. I have a parish to run, there's no time to duplicate our responsibilities. Liam's a young man, but very able.'

Shaw was always shocked at how businesslike religion could be. He could have been interviewing the MD of a small waste-disposal company, or a double-glazing firm. 'Yes. We've spoken – last night. But what do *you* know, Father?'

'About Aidan? What can I tell you? An intelligent man who regretted his past. A teacher once, I think. Science. I spoke to him at Christmas, about how beautiful science was – that it was one of the proofs of God's presence. All that order out of chaos.'

He looked down at his hands. Out in the street they heard a beam crash from the roof of the burnt-out house and splash into the basement. The priest looked to the window, distracted.

'He took drugs, sold drugs, did you know that?' asked Shaw, irritated by the priest's miniature sermon.

'Yes. But Aidan had professed a desire, a determination really, to reform himself, and his life. We encouraged that. And we believed in it.'

Before Shaw could ask another question the priest pressed on. 'It was, and is, Liam's responsibility to choose those men offered the privilege of a room in the hostel. Most sleep in the church – we run a shelter there. I'm very busy running the parish, as I've said. I've always been happy to cede that duty to Liam.'

Shaw noted how expertly he'd suggested that he might not be so happy to do so in the future.

'But you must remember that almost all the men who come to us for help have a criminal record.'

'So Holme's intelligent – anything else?' asked Shaw. 'He feared death, didn't he? Why was that?'

Martin searched for the right words. 'It's not an uncommon emotion, is it, Inspector? The fear that just when we've grasped what we want in life, it will be taken away. Aidan had seen his salvation. He was troubled – no, terrified – by the idea that it would be taken from him. And it wasn't all . . .' He searched again for a word. 'Psychological. The drugs he'd taken had pronounced physical effects. Anxiety, certainly.'

'I see. And Bryan Judd?'

'I don't know him well. The mother died – some years ago, before I came here. She'd been a stalwart apparently; my predecessor had felt the loss greatly. Marie, I think. It is a broken family. The father is broken most. But he has faith. Andrew. But a deeply troubled man.' He nodded to himself, pleased that he'd retrieved both their names from his memory.

'But Bryan . . . ?' asked Shaw.

'We know Alison – his wife.' He stopped, and Shaw sensed he'd talked himself into an awkward cul-de-sac. And the use of the royal 'we' was beginning to grate.

'Why do you know her?' he asked.

The priest licked his lips. 'Alison does the laundry for us, and for the hostel, and the church. Also, a little house-keeping. She sings as well, when we can muster a choir.' He shrugged, still distracted, perhaps, by his conversation with the bishop. Shaw recalled the first time they'd seen Ally Judd, appearing out of the darkness with a mop and pail. He wondered how efficient that was – house cleaning in a power cut.

'But Bryan?' he asked, aware it was the third time he'd asked the question.

'No. I'm sorry – just a face. He certainly didn't attend Mass.'

'It's possible Aidan Holme had something to do with Bryan Judd's death,' said Shaw.

Stillness must be a great virtue in a priest, thought Shaw. He looked Shaw directly in the face. 'How?'

'Too early to say,' said Shaw, deciding it was *his* turn to be elliptical.

Martin went to the desk and screwed the cup off the top of a small metal Thermos flask. He filled it with black coffee. The aroma in the fusty room was deeply exotic. He walked to the bay window and looked out to the street.

'I am disappointed in the people here, many we know, many worship here. To do that … to burn down the hostel. They say it was Andrew Judd …' He laughed, as if the irony was an impossible one.

Shaw studied the walls. There was a framed degree certificate from the Universidade Federal do Paraná. And a framed poster in a language he didn't recognize: a vibrant colourful Christ, armed with a pistol, standing on a barricade in a city street, red flags flying in the mob behind him.

'A mob,' said Shaw, touching the frame.

'A crusade,' said Martin, looking at the picture. He gestured through the door. '*That* was a mob.'

Shaw checked his watch, wanting to press on. Father Martin's shoulders relaxed at the prospect of being left alone.

'You're a long way from home, Father,' said Shaw, walking into the hall.

'I go where I'm needed. I am not needed in my own country,' said Martin, following.

Shaw stopped, and let the silence stretch.

'Brazil,' Martin said at last.

'Brazil must have its poor parishes,' said Shaw.

'It does. But I believe that Christ wants us to fight for the poor, Inspector. Fight. I believe Christ wants us to drag down the rich, and that money is a sin. Once this theology was popular. A revolutionary theology. Not now. So I go where I am wanted.'

'And your degree? Theology then, or politics?'

Martin took a deep breath. 'Medicine.'

'Don't the poor need a doctor?'

'Christ wanted me to do this,' he said, and Shaw thought what a smug answer that was.

Shaw had one last question. 'What about Neil Judd, the youngest? I don't see him as a church-goer.'

'No. Christmas – with his father. They *are* close. Ally says he holds the family together, despite them. That is sometimes the role of the youngest. I don't know why.'

Shaw nodded happily, wondering if the priest had noticed his error; replacing the stiff and formal 'Alison' with the familiar 'Ally'.

15

Shaw stood back to let one of the hospital tugs go past, the electric motor straining, the driver rhythmically hitting the horn with the heel of his palm. Eight trucks, all crammed with yellow bags destined for the incinerator. He held his breath, making sure he didn't pick up a trace of the smell, then watched it diminish for fifty yards, trundling into the heart of Level One, until it turned a distant sharp left, and was gone.

He stood looking at the face of his mobile phone. He'd just had a short conversation with Valentine, who'd filled him in with a fifty-word summary of what he'd discovered about the disappearance of Norma Jean Judd. Was it relevant? Maybe. But they needed more information, so he'd asked Valentine to track down DCI Jack Shaw's DS on the case – Wilf Jackson. Retired now, he lived in a bungalow at Snettisham on the coast. But he had a mind like a gazetteer, and he'd remember the case like it was yesterday. Shaw had a specific question: where was Bryan Judd the evening his sister went missing in 1992? And Neil – the youngest? Valentine was to get out to the coast, flesh out the story, then get back for the full briefing at 10.30.

The murder incident room was at Junction 24. Shaw pushed open a pair of double doors marked BIO-MECHATRONICS: STORAGE.

He relished this moment at the start of any murder inquiry; the sudden plunge into a room full of focused energy. DC Twine, the graduate-entry high-flier, had done a thorough job overnight, setting up a standard serious incident suite. Six computers were already online along one wall, each showing the force badge in shimmering colour. The rest of the room was given over to three nests of desks, a tea/coffee station, a fax machine, two photocopiers, and a line of three switchboard stations on the opposite wall to the computers. There were already half a dozen detectives in the room, most of them focused on delivering the first caffeine hit of the day.

The original contents of the room – a series of metal shelves holding artificial limbs – had been pushed back against one wall. Shaw could see rows of arms, lower legs, claw-like hands and feet; in plastic boxes swaddled prosthetics with pink fake skin, tangles of cable and pulleys, balls and sockets in sickly-white and perspex. And a rack of sticks and crutches, some in metal, but many in worn wood. On the wall was a glass cabinet, with shelves like a Royal Mail sorting office. In each, held in cotton wool, was a glass eye. The sight made him look away. He'd avoided having a glass eye himself, but it was always a possibility, as over time his doctor had warned him that healthy single eyes often deteriorated in sympathy if their injured partners were left in place.

Shaw took off his jacket and rolled up the sleeves of his crisp white shirt, nodding at the watching eyes. 'Are they all looking at me, or what?' he asked.

Twine handed him a short report summarizing developments since they'd last talked by mobile just after six. While most of the CID team came to work in cheap suits Twine wore a well-cut open-necked shirt, jeans, and soft leather boots.

'DS Valentine asked for a shakedown on Potts and Bourne – they're the incinerator workers who were there when the victim was found,' said Twine, holding a sheaf of statements. 'Potts was the last to see Judd alive at 7.45 – but he wasn't alone. There was a third man on early duty – Kelley. He saw him too. By the way, all of them had noticed he'd picked up a black eye recently, but none of them can recall when he got it.'

Twine's summary had brought silence to the room, but his voice didn't alter. 'We know Judd was dead at 8.31 when the furnace was stopped by Bourne. Between 7.45 and the arrival of Darren Wylde, Potts and Bourne were with Kelley in the control room. They were brewing up some tea on a gas burner after the power went out. Bourne got on the line to the electricity company to see what had gone wrong, and Potts was on a mobile to the generator room – checking that they could go on taking up the demand. Then Potts went down to see what the situation was on the incinerator belt. So – unless they're all in it together – they're all in the clear.'

Shaw sat on the edge of a desk and reread the statements, looking for a loophole. There wasn't one. Valentine had been right to insist on a fast-track check because the odds on a killer being the person who found the corpse were surprisingly high. A fact almost constantly overlooked in those first anxious hours of a murder inquiry.

The core of the CID team had been on site since five

thirty. There were eight DCs in the room now, four more out on door-to-door interviews. Civilian admin to run the phone bank would be in by nine. DC Mark Birley had been there all night with Twine, who'd volunteered, viewing CCTV footage. He had a bank of six screens, all miniature, and one widescreen to which he could switch any one of the smaller images. Jagged pictures came and went, a jigsaw of sunlight and shadow.

'Anything?' Shaw asked.

Birley swung round, his six foot two inch frame and fifteen stone of rugby-playing muscle crammed into a plastic bucket seat. His wrists seemed to bulge where they emerged from his suit. He'd spent a decade in uniform and his outfit was still hanger-new. There was a plaster over one eye.

'Match?' asked Shaw.

'Argument with the fly-half's boot. I lost, but you should see him. He could do with one of those sticks.' Birley nodded at the rack. 'And no – nothing yet.' Birley had been on Shaw's team before in a major inquiry and he'd learnt one good rule early: if you've got nothing to say, keep it short.

Twine handed Shaw a coffee and a printout of personnel. 'That's everyone, with mobiles.' The young DC had been a good choice for 'point' – a key role, the lynch-pin between Shaw and the team, channelling information, pulling everything together, then sifting out what needed to be shared, keeping the information moving. It was like being a human mini-roundabout.

'Right, what we need to find out, Paul, is this ... Is it really possible – feasible – that Bryan Judd was able to steal large quantities of drugs from the hospital which were earmarked for incineration by law-enforcement agencies? If it *is* possible, then we have a motive which would put Aidan Holme in the frame for Judd's murder. We're told they fought. We're told threats were made. But all that depends on Judd being able to supply . . .'

Twine tapped a fountain pen on his teeth, then flicked the screen into life on his PC. 'I figured we'd want to have a walk-through of the incinerator system – the waste bags. From top to bottom. We can go ahead with that then see where the drugs consignment fits in. I've got the man in charge of human waste ready now, for a quick tour. Dr Gavin Peploe – Level 10, Mary Seacole Ward.'

'Well done,' said Shaw. That's what he wanted in his team, the kind of straightforward logic that made a murder inquiry hum. He put a £20 note on the desktop. 'In the meantime get someone up to Costa Coffee on the main concourse and get everyone a decent coffee – that was truly awful.' He lobbed his empty cup fifteen feet into a bin.

'One other thing,' said Twine. He clicked the screen. 'Duty book . . .' The front desk at St James's kept an online record of all crime. It was standard inquiry procedure to cross-check with the last forty-eight hours. 'Familiar litany,' said Twine. 'Two house burglaries in Gayton – next door to each other, that's cheeky. A mugging in Greyfriars Gardens, an affray outside the Matilda, some vandalism in the town centre during one of the power cuts – six shop windows gone in the Arndale. Local paper wants to know if that's looting, which is a good question.

And a body in the docks – so far no ID, no obvious cause of death.'

'Keep an eye on the floater,' said Shaw. 'Whose case?'

'Creake,' said Twine. DI William Creake was a slogger, with a reputation for wearing cases down by sheer bloody footwork. Inspired detection was not his strong suit. 'I'll get the basics off him, then make sure he gets an update from us too,' added Twine.

'Get me a copy, Paul. And I'd like a summary on the Arndale – anything to do with the power cuts we should see too. OK – press office? What are we telling the great unwashed of the British media about Bryan Judd?'

'Bare details for release.' Twine hit a key and a sheet of A4 slipped out of the printer. 'We've stuck to suspicious death at the Queen Vic, no name yet, or address. The fire brigade released the basics on the blaze in Erebus Street and listed it as suspicious. If anyone finds a link we'll stonewall for now.'

'Fine,' said Shaw, not bothering to read the release through. That had been one of his father's maxims – trust people in a big inquiry, because if you try to do everything yourself, you'll fail. 'Going forward, Paul, I want to keep back the initials on the torch – MVR. The torch isn't Judd's, so there's a good chance it's the killer's. If we get any nutters claiming they did it I want something to catch 'em out with. That'll be it. And I don't want the killer knowing for sure he's left it at the scene.' He saw a millimetre jump in Twine's left eyebrow. 'Or she, for that matter.' Twine smiled. 'And something for the door-to-door on Erebus Street, Paul. See if there's any gossip about the Judds' marriage. Something's not right there –

see if they can get a sniff. George picked up a couple of snide remarks last night. Seems like she's close to the parish priest – but don't give that out yet. Let's see if they pick it up on the street.'

'Housework' done, Shaw took the lift to the tenth floor of the main hospital block. The view over the town was already lost in heat and smog, a toxic layer of pollution like a blanket, deep enough to obscure everything but Lynn's own skyscraper – the Campbell's soup tower, down by the river. A tug was bucking the tide coming down the Cut from the sea, a wake behind like a slug's trail. Out at sea a summer storm cloud like a giant chef's hat drifted east. It would be a fine day on the beach, thought Shaw, squinting to see a distant line of surf.

Mary Seacole Ward was for infectious diseases, so he took care to squirt plenty of gel on his hands before entering. Dr Peploe met him by the nurses' station. He was a paediatric surgeon, and the Lynn Primary Care Trust's spokesman on the disposal of human tissue, a post required under the Infectious Diseases Act. A neat Glaswegian with a widow's peak, Dr Peploe possessed one of those asymmetrical faces that the Celts seem to breed: one eye slightly more open than the other, the mouth off the horizontal. Handsome enough, with taut healthy skin stretched over a muscular face. And there was nothing Hebridean about his tan, which was an Italian brown. Stern, but playful – an image enhanced by the small cuddly toy sticking out of one pocket.

He laughed at himself, stuffing the teddy bear's head out of sight.

'Sorry – Human Tissue isn't my day job. It pays to

keep the wee customers happy, however little they are.'
He smiled, and Shaw noticed the scar left by a harelip.

'We think someone, somehow, infiltrated the waste
system to steal street-haul drugs before they were incinerated,' said Shaw. 'Consignments from law enforcement,
customs, the lot. Is that possible?'

Peploe thought about it, and there was a long intake
of breath. 'Right. You want the Cook's Tour or just a
run-through?'

'For now, just the basics please,' said Shaw.

Peploe picked up an empty yellow waste bag from the
room behind the nurses' station. Each bag, sealed, had a
metal tag. This one read *NHS: W 10.*

'This bit's pretty obvious,' he said. 'Every ward gets its
own supply.'

On the bag itself was a plastic label on which had been
printed a further code: *1268. Non-R. Non-C. I.*

Peploe took him through it: the label was filled out by
a nurse, 1268 was a patient number. Non-R – no radioactive material. Non-C – no chemotherapy residue. I –
infectious.

Twice a day the bags were taken by a ward orderly to
the metal chute in the cleaners' room. A drawer, opened
then shut, tipped the bag down a gravity-driven pipe
system. They listened to it rattle away.

'Let's go get it,' said Peploe, light on his toes. As they
walked down the corridor he slid a hand in his pocket
and pulled out something small, plastic and colourful;
then he tapped it quickly, twice, in the palm of his other
hand and quickly swallowed whatever he'd dispensed.
Self-medication, thought Shaw, or a sweet tooth.

In the lift Peploe continued a virtual tour. 'Clearly the system is different in the operating theatres – they're all running today otherwise I'd have taken you in. But the principle's the same, it's just the volume that's different. Any body part or other waste takes this route.'

'The young man who found the body said he was sent down to Level One with a waste bag,' said Shaw.

Dr Peploe nodded, as if that fitted the system he had just described, which it didn't.

'Anything that might stick in the system, or break, goes by hand delivery – but never through the public areas of the hospital.'

The lift dropped to Level One and he followed Peploe through the maze of corridors to the tug depot, beneath the hospital's main concourse. A metal chute descended into the depot room, cut off in mid-air, so that they could glimpse up into the darkness. They heard a sigh, then a rattle, and a yellow bag fell out of the darkness and into an angled bin below, which deadened the impact, then allowed it to slide down an aluminium ramp into a waiting tug.

'That simple,' said Peploe. He walked to the tug truck, looked amongst the yellow bags, and retrieved the one he'd put down the chute on Mary Seacole Ward. 'Tugs take it all to the furnace. Then we monitor what goes up the chimney in terms of chemical composition. We can – broadly speaking – match input and output. It's a good system.'

'Tell me they didn't just put the drugs down the chutes?' said Shaw.

Peploe grinned. 'I know this is the NHS, but we're not that stupid. No – that system doesn't cross this system until we get to the incinerator room.'

They walked through Level One to Junction 57. Shaw was braced for the cacophony when he brushed through the doors, but it was like a hammer blow, the bass note making one of the bones in his ear vibrate. And the air was laden with the white, lifeless dust.

But they weren't stopping.

'We can't talk here,' shouted Peploe. 'Follow me.' He took them beyond the incinerator belt, where a man worked with ear protectors and a plastic mask, and to a door marked simply CONTROL.

Shaw was about to step through when someone shouted his name. He turned to see Tom Hadden standing by the belt, waving him over. He used his hands to tell Peploe to carry on – he'd catch up. Hadden pushed what was left of his strawberry-blond hair back off the pale forehead, took a breath, and shouted. 'I had someone brush all the metal surfaces in here for prints. Nothing, but we found this instead.'

Beside the belt and next to Bryan Judd's small office was a control panel in beaten metal. A few dials, an LED display which, Shaw guessed, showed the temperature at various levels of the furnace, and a set of brass switches sticking out, each with a small bulb of metal at the end, like a chapel peg. One of them was darker than the rest, smeared.

'It's blood,' said Hadden, into Shaw's ear. 'And brain and bone. The switch has been impacted by some kind of collision.' Hadden opened his palm out and mimicked hitting the switch. 'I think this is what punctured Judd's skull.'

Shaw went to speak but the dust caught in his throat, so that he had to turn away, coughing violently. 'So – what – not a fall?' he asked eventually, holding the back of his hand to his lips.

'No, no. A fight perhaps.' Shaw moved closer. 'Judd was medium height,' said Hadden. 'My guess is his assailant got him by the neck and threw him back against this wall – the switch would be just right for here ...' He touched the base of his skull at the back of the neck. 'There's a lot of force – see, the whole thing's dented.'

Shaw stood to one side so that the light played across the metal. A dent, around the switch, and again below where Judd's hips would have crashed into the metal panel.

'One other thing,' said Hadden. He gave Shaw a piece of card marked *NHS: W 22*.

'That's what was on the metal tag with the bag that went in with the victim.'

Shaw took it. 'Tom,' he patted him on the back. 'Thanks.'

He went after Peploe, climbing an enclosed spiral staircase until he stepped into a room with a glass wall looking out onto two large gas turbines. Peploe explained that these were used to drive the air through the furnace and up the 200-foot chimney. The surgeon pointed up and Shaw craned his neck; the ceiling was glass too, giving them a view up through the mesh floors of the furnace.

Shaw's mobile trilled. It was Valentine. 'I've just touched base with Twine – picked up some bad news. Hendre – from upstairs at number 6? He did a runner overnight.'

'What?' Shaw's voice buzzed with frustration. 'He had someone on him?'

'Yeah. But he went for a pee. They told him chummy was out sparko – couldn't lift a finger. When he got back he'd gone, plus the dusty suit. Last seen legging it over the car park.'

'Get a description out through Paul – let's find him before he goes to ground.' A tiny detail, but Shaw hadn't missed it. Valentine could have given him the name of the DC who had bungled the job, but he'd kept it to himself. There'd be a quiet word later, a warning, nothing bureaucratic, no paperwork, just a note added to the Valentine memory banks.

'I'll be at the briefing,' said Valentine, cutting the line before Shaw had a chance to check on his progress with ex-DS Wilf Jackson out on the coast.

There were two engineers in the room monitoring a bank of dials and LED displays. But Peploe affably took charge. He tore off a foot of printout. 'So, you want to know how the drugs fit in . . .'

He tapped the printout. 'When a consignment's due we put aside an hour in the schedule. That's what they pay for – and they pay by the minute. The drugs arrive with a certificate from the Home Office lab which lists the contents of the batch. The drugs are in sealed metal containers – old fashioned, but effective and simple. The seals are wax. They're signed over to us downstairs.

There's normally a senior officer with the police, or whichever agency we're dealing with, present for the handover. He or she comes up here while our head of security stays downstairs and personally – *personally* – puts each container on the belt.'

He tapped the printout again. 'This shows the chemical composition of what's going out of the top of the chimney ... This is state-of-the-art technology. Every drug has a chemical signature. As it burns we can match it up with the printout. These are very sensitive machines. If any of these emissions breach EU guidelines, for example, the furnace shuts down. It's that strict, there's no margin for error. Half a mile away the cars on the ring road are churning out carbon monoxide like there's no tomorrow – a self-fulfilling prophecy if ever there was one. But here – a few milligrams of toxic gas slips through the filters and we're out of business.'

'And it is a business,' said Shaw.

'Of course. Every penny we make goes back into the NHS. But this kit costs millions, so, like any business, we have to sweat the assets. We run it twenty-four hours a day. Shutting down's too expensive, so we need to make sure we can generate income full-time. We have several contracts – vets, private hospitals, doctors' surgeries, pet cremation – and then the whole range of law-enforcement seizures – police, customs and excise, British transport police, the lot. And not just West Norfolk, of course, but several other forces without access to this kind of facility. But it doesn't matter how busy we are, Inspector – what goes up in smoke is what goes on the belt. Believe me. You can watch it yourself ...'

He led the way to a porthole door, like an airlock. One of the engineers spun a lock and it popped open. They stepped through into a circular room, then looked up. The sky was a hundred feet above them, blue, with white clouds, but shimmering as if caught in a permanent mirage.

'The gases come in about thirty feet above our heads,' said Peploe. 'What's left behind is lifeless ash.' They could see the pipes, the gases churning out, colourless but distorting, like a fairground mirror.

'You mentioned the head of security,' said Shaw. 'Name?'

'Nat Haines.' Shaw knew him – a retired DI from Norwich he'd once worked with on a migrant workers case – an illegal gangmaster running a prostitution business from a chicken farm.

'When was the next consignment due?' asked Shaw.

'Tomorrow – five p.m. That's not Norfolk, actually – it's Cambridgeshire. There's a manifest.'

'How much notice do you normally get?'

'Ten days,' said Peploe. 'Usually longer. This isn't a cheap form of disposal, but bulk cuts the price. So most forces stockpile seizures for a month, maybe six weeks, then we burn a job lot.'

'Would Judd have known the consignment was coming?'

Peploe nodded. 'Yes. Bryan Judd's job is to coordinate the waste disposal, so he'd be told in order that he could make sure there was a gap, and also ensure that anything that needed to go up went up before the security van arrived. So, if there was something radioactive from the cancer ward, for example, he'd make sure that was dealt with. We can't have that kind of waste just sitting around.'

A seagull crossed the circle of sky above. 'Bryan Judd was a registered drug addict – was that sensible?' asked Shaw. He'd disguised the question by keeping his voice light. Peploe climbed back out through the door and Shaw wondered if he was buying himself time.

'I'm sorry – your question again?' asked Peploe.

Shaw repeated it, though he was certain he didn't need to.

'Well, at the time, it seemed to be sensible. The trust has responsibilities as an employer,' said Peploe. His pager buzzed and he read the message.

'You need to go?' asked Shaw.

'No. No – it's fine. I need to get up to the theatre. But this is important.' He gathered his thoughts, looking down at his shoes. 'We give opportunities to those with criminal records. Judd was one of those. Given the fact that drug disposal is so closely monitored, none of us saw any potential danger in letting him work the conveyor. It's not a pleasant job down there. He did it well.'

'I've got a note of the annotation on the metal tag on the bag we found with the victim. Can you trace it back for us? Our forensic lab is testing the waste itself, but we're pretty sure it's a human organ. But this would help.'

He showed him the note marked *NHS: W 22.*

'That can't be right,' said Peploe, putting both hands in the neat white pockets of his house coat.

'Why?'

144

'That's the children's ward. We don't carry out surgical procedures on the ward – never.'

'But there *was* body waste in that bag,' said Shaw. 'The CSI lab's checking it out, but we're pretty sure it's human.'

Peploe nodded. 'Well. Then we've got ourselves a problem, Inspector. A very serious problem.'

16

Shaw took the ten-thirty briefing in the murder incident room at Junction 24. It was as much for him as for the team, a chance to lay some of the jigsaw pieces out flat, to step back, and see if they saw the same picture he did. The mood was electric, because they all knew these were the crucial few hours – the first day that could make or break the whole investigation. Voices buzzed with adrenaline and a wave of laughter ran through the team like mains electricity.

The clock flipped its digital numbers to 10.30. There was still no sign of Valentine but Shaw binned a paper cup of Costa Coffee espresso and stood. Behind him was a perspex display board, bare but for an enlarged print of Bryan Judd's face: their victim. Dark Celtic features, heavy swollen flesh, the curly hair unkempt, the skin blotched.

'OK – listen up, please.' The room was silent anyway. They all knew Shaw's reputation, a high-flier, going places. None of them would object to catching hold of his coat-tails. Getting on to the squad was the first step. Now they had to perform. Get noticed. Stand out from the crowd – without showboating, because they all knew that was fatal.

Shaw tried hard to ignore the rows of disembodied arms, legs and hands lining the wall at the back of the room – and the sets of eyes, each in their own pigeon hole. He decided then that he'd get one of the civilian staff to drape some sheets over the stuff while they were using the room. He noticed that his voice had an echo, bouncing round the concrete walls, as if they were in a crypt.

'We have a scenario, and it works. That doesn't mean it's the right scenario. And it is most certainly not the *complete* scenario. But let's run it, for what it's worth.

'Our victim ...' He slapped his hand on the portrait. 'Character: the silent type, morose even, nervous too, but a dry sense of humour – like he was secretly laughing at the world. According to his colleagues – and the young-ster who spotted his body inside the furnace – music was his life: New Country, Johnny Cash. He'd wear an iPod, even though it was against the rules, and he'd sing with it. Wife made him lunch, so he didn't go to the canteen, but he'd go down to the staff bar once a week with the rest of them for a beer. Recently, according to the foreman, he stopped that too.'

'According to his younger brother he's a drug addict, a user. And not any old stuff – Green Dragon, skunk dunked in pure alcohol. He gets his stuff from this man ...' He put a mug-shot of Aidan Holme up on the board, extracted from the files held in the locked cabinet in the room behind the altar at the Sacred Heart. 'He lives in the hostel on Erebus Street. One-time addict, now clean, but a serious supplier. Due up in court next month on his third charge – pleading not guilty. He's escaped going to jail twice before, maybe it's third time unlucky.

'Our victim – Judd – pays for his stuff by helping

147

Holme steal large quantities of hard drugs seized by various agencies and destined to be incinerated here at the hospital. That's what he told his family, anyway. The problem is we don't know how – and having just had a tour of the disposal system, we may never know how. On the other hand, perhaps he lied to his family.'

DC Fiona Campbell, standing at the back, put up both hands.

Over six foot, flat shoes, shoulders rounded to make herself look shorter. A career copper from a family of coppers – her father was a chief super at Norwich. She'd come out of school with enough qualifications to do anything she wanted in life – and this was it. Not just a bright girl, she had street cred too, earned the hard way. The scar from an eight-inch knife wound ran from below her ear down the side of her neck. A chief constable's commendation had been her only reward for trying to save the life of a violent man who didn't want to live.

'I don't get it,' she said. 'He helps this Holme character get a haul worth thousands in return for a bottle of the green stuff worth – what – a couple of hundred?'

'Good point. But it does work if the only role our victim plays is simply to look the other way. And there's no evidence Judd was ever on crack, tabs, poppers, heroin – anything like that. Green Dragon is highly addictive, but it's nothing like the usual cannabis derivatives we pick up off the streets. It's a middle-class drug, and we all know we don't even get close to that trade. I think this was a deal Judd just fell into. For minding his own business – maybe little else – he gets a supply of what he likes. Then, one day, he decides that life would be better without it and he tells Holme the deal's off. Someone kills Judd. Is it Holme? Maybe.'

Shaw took a deep breath, aware that adrenaline was making his heartbeat pick up. 'Evidence? Neil Judd's statement provides us with the basis for motive. At the moment we don't know anything about opportunity because we don't know where Holme was at the relevant times – that's a priority. Forensics are pretty thin. Holme's house is all ash and smoke damage, so don't hold your breath. We have the rice at the scene of crime, which might be a link to the church where Holme ate. But it's pretty flimsy evidence.'

Two hands, DC Campbell again.

'Sorry,' she said, amid laughter. 'I still don't get it. If Holme's not using drugs himself, but he's got this supply line through Judd, why's he eating at a church kitchen? Why's he living in the hostel? Why does the arse hang out of his trousers?'

Laughter again. 'My guess is that this is early days,' said Shaw. 'Neil Judd says his brother had been working the scam for a year, maybe less. The hostel's a brilliant cover. *And* we know Holme got caught trying to supply. We've requested the notes from the drug squad but I had a word – when they picked him up he had nearly a hundred and fifty grand's worth of stuff in a rucksack. He was trying to do a one-off sale in the docks. That was six weeks ago, so maybe that's all of it so far. Which would explain why he was pretty keen on getting his hands on the *next* consignment. Maybe it was his pension. Maybe he thought he was going down and this was going to keep his spirits up while he ticked off the days on the calendar in his cell. Who knows?'

DC Campbell folded her arms. She'd got her answer, but she wasn't happy.

'Now,' said Shaw. 'The things that don't fit. We've got human tissue waste on the incinerator next to Judd's body which is not traceable to any operation or procedure on the ward marked on the metal tag which survived the furnace. What's that about? An admin mistake? Unlikely. We need to drill down on this . . . Judd died with this yellow bag of human tissue under his body. Is it what he died for?

'Then we've got the arson on Erebus Street in the power sub-station. Unlike the arson at the hostel, this *pre-dates* the murder. Is there a link with Judd's death? It's a coincidence, certainly, especially as the power failure disrupted the grid and eventually put out the hospital power too – although that's a random outcome according to the power engineers, so you couldn't have planned it. There's no cause and effect – there can't be. And remember, coincidences happen, so let's not get hung up constructing a link where there isn't one. Although . . . there *is* the broken match found at the spot where Judd smoked at the hospital – and a similar one found at the electricity sub-station. A possible link, but nothing more than that.'

Shaw took a marker pen and wrote CONCEN-TRATE in red on the board. 'It's that simple. First twenty-four hours keep focused. Don't disregard anything. Be thorough, don't cut corners, and don't keep anything to yourself. If I find anyone's tried to steal the show I will introduce them to the one-way traffic system in town and they can spend the rest of their careers making sure it keeps moving.'

They all laughed, happy to be a team, thankful that so far no one had earned Shaw's disapproval.

'There's something early from CSI,' said Twine. 'Tom said to say they'd got a fix on the blood-soaked rag used in the Molotov cocktail at the power sub-station. Pig blood. But there's an abattoir on the corner. So maybe a link with the workforce?'

The store door banged open and Valentine came in, carrying a copy of the *Daily Telegraph* in one hand, a bacon sandwich in the other.

'Sorry,' he said, walking forward. The rest of the team watched the chemistry, knowing there'd be sparks. Everyone knew the story of George Valentine's career: he'd come back from the coast to reclaim the rank they'd taken off him thirteen years ago. And they knew he'd been Jack Shaw's partner in that last disastrous case. The question was whether he could really shake off the cynicism, the bitterness, and principally the booze, for long enough to impress the brass.

'It was worth it,' he said to Shaw, flapping his note-book.

'OK. Tell 'em,' said Shaw, noting his DS had picked up a fresh charity lapel sticker: Wood Green Animal Shelter.

Valentine gave them the story of Norma Jean Judd – the one he'd rehearsed on the fire escape that morning. It was a faultless performance, delivered without a trace of either nerves or self-doubt. What they didn't know was why he'd rehearsed it – not just to impress, but so that he could time those extra breaths, keeping his lungs full, so he didn't wheeze. All he had to add was what he'd learnt from Wilf Jackson. He'd found the former DS in an over-heated greenhouse in a sandy garden, happy to sit on a camp stool to talk, wiping sweat from his face, crumbling lumps of dry clay between his fingers.

'Wilf Jackson remembers the case well,' said Valentine. 'He said one disturbing facet of the inquiry was our victim Bryan Judd, Norma's twin. Always "Bry", by the way – never anything else,' he hauled in some extra air. 'They had all the family in to check out Andy's story. Wilf said Bryan was lying – holding something back. He said he'd been drinking on the rough lots behind the houses that day and that when he'd gone home he'd met his dad coming out the house. He'd checked upstairs to see if Norma Jean was there because he wanted to speak to her – he didn't remember why. Wilf said they didn't believe that – and he still doesn't.'

Valentine fished a packet of Silk Cut out of his pocket and put a cigarette between his teeth. 'Bryan said her room was empty. Bathroom too. He says he went back out 'cos he had a date that evening. Odd thing was there was a neighbour – the woman who helped Marie Judd run the launderette – and she said she'd gone home about 6.30 and she'd heard Bryan out on the waste ground calling Norma Jean's name. So – question: why was Bryan looking for his sister at least an hour before anyone thought she was missing? When they asked him he came up with some crap about wanting to find her, that they were close, and he thought she needed him. Wilf said they put a surveillance unit on the family for ten days –

nobody put a foot wrong. Were they all in it? Maybe. Andy could have killed her, Marie gives him an alibi, and Bryan goes out making it look like they were worried. Maybe – but they couldn't get a lead. The family stuck together.

'So they went back to Orzsak. Anniversary came round in '93 so they leaked a story to the *News* that CID had new evidence. Close to an arrest – total crap, of course, but we've all done it. Still got nothing. Six months after that they wound the case up – cold case, as cold as they get. She could even still be alive, in theory. But there's been nothing since that day except one dodgy sighting. No, she's dead. Got to be.'

Valentine took a seat, trying to make it look like it wasn't a relief to do so. 'One coincidence worth mentioning: Orzsak lived at number 6 – the house that's now the hostel that was firebombed last night.'

There was silence in the room. 'Thanks, George. Pictures?'

Valentine got out the copies Timber Woods had made of the originals in the file.

First, Norma Jean Judd. Dark Irish looks. 'Look familiar?' Valentine said, pinning it next to their victim's face, scanning the room, for once the deep-set grey eyes catching the light. Shaw examined the faces of the twins. The bone structure was similar, the colouring identical, and there was something about the withdrawn intensity of the dark eyes which marked them out as twins even now.

Second, Jan Orzsak. A child's face sunk in a full moon of white flesh. A double-chin obscured his neck, the cheeks pendulous, the eyes sunk like raisins in a cake. And something Shaw didn't like the look of: a shadow of bruising across one eye, the white around the iris bloodied. From the code letters and the background you could see it was a police snap. The date and time of the picture were printed in one corner.

Third, Ben Ruddle, the father of Norma Jean's child. The resemblance to his girlfriend was uncanny; the same Celtic colouring, the street-urchin's face with the delicate bone structure. The difference was in the eyes: Ruddle's were small and lifeless. There was something cynical about the look into the camera, something knowing.

'George,' said Shaw, standing. 'Great work.' He let that sink in; the squad needed to know that despite their personal issues George Valentine had been given this last chance to save his career because he'd once been a first-rate copper.

'We need to keep all that in here,' said Shaw, tapping the side of his skull. 'At the very least it gives us an insight into the Judd family. But maybe there's something else too. It looks like Bryan knew something about his twin sister's disappearance – something he didn't want to share with us. Did he think his father was the killer? Did he *know* he was the killer? There's a secret here – could it explain why Bryan Judd is dead? We need to keep that possibility in our minds going forward. So, a couple of loose ends to check. Are we sure Andy Judd was in Erebus Street all day? Let's check that. And I want to know where Ruddle, the boyfriend, ended up.'

Valentine took a note.

'And the address, sir?' asked Birley. 'Coincidence?'

There was a break in the tension in the room, a round of group coughing, because nobody liked that word: *coincidence*.

DC Jacky Lau tried to speak over the sudden hubbub. Lau's voice held a vibrant tension, like her small, compact body.

'Just a thought, sir. If she was still alive – Norma Jean – she'd be thirty-three, and the child would be eighteen.'

She'd got her silence. None of them had thought of that – a child, a young man, a young woman. Shaw looked at the picture of Norma Jean, rearranging the lines, trying to see the possibility of other faces from the same gene pool. Then he looked at Ruddle, trying to blend the pools into a common stream.

'But given she's probably dead – and the child with her. Where's Orzsak?' asked Birley, switching tack.

Valentine shrugged. 'He'd be sixty-six – we'll trace the pension if he's still alive.'

'Sir?' It was DC Fiona Campbell. 'I've got the electoral roll for the house-to-house this morning – a D. J. Orzsak lives on Erebus Street – number 47, next to the dock gates, opposite the pub.' Someone whistled and chatter broke out. 'So the prime suspect still lives at the scene of the crime.'

Shaw was looking at the pictures on the board and he'd just noticed the stencilled date on the mugshot of Orzsak.

'Hold on …' He put a finger on the date. Valentine stiffened, aware that he'd missed something he shouldn't have missed. 'That's a coincidence we can't ignore. The day this picture was taken – presumably the day the girl went missing. Fifth of September 1992. Yesterday, the day her brother died, was the anniversary. Eighteen years to the day.'

17

The front door of number 47 Erebus Street was an old-fashioned ceramic blue. The downstairs window was barred, the letterbox covered with a metal plate. Across the blue wood a sharp object had been used to write one short word in tall capitals: PEDO. And a green estate car parked right in front of the door had a lazy scratched line down the offside.

Shaw checked his tide watch: it was 11.41 a.m. and low water at Brancaster. Standing on Orzsak's front step, he saw just how close the house was to the electricity sub-station which had been vandalized the night before. Number 47 was the last house of the terrace, a high fence, clogged with blackthorn, shielding its backyard from the Grade II listed building. A power company van was still parked in the street, and from behind the thorns came the sound of a pneumatic drill cracking concrete as the engineers replaced the unit's electrics.

Valentine knocked once. He went to knock again but the door opened to the sound of an electric lock buzzing, then a chain being pulled. Jan Orzsak stood in his pyjamas and a pair of wrecked slippers, one of them squashed flat, as though he'd channelled all the weight down one leg. His mouth was open, his tongue too big to hide behind the small lips. For a face as odd as Orzsak's the most striking feature was its agelessness: it was almost identical to the one in the file from nearly twenty years earlier.

'Mr Orzsak?' Valentine showed his warrant card. Close up to the front step he could smell dog, the stench engrained in the door itself.

'Did this happen last night?' asked Shaw, touching the paintwork, nodding at the car.

'Yes.' It was the first word he'd said and the syllables were indistinct. The tongue again, fighting to find space to articulate the words.

'Could we come in, sir?' asked Shaw. 'We're investigating the death of Bryan Judd. You may have heard?' Orzsak didn't meet his eyes but nodded, the flesh round his neck swinging. 'Just a few questions . . .'

Orzsak turned away without another word and walked down the hallway into the through-lounge. One side wall of what had been the back room was obscured by a series of fish tanks built into a wooden frame. Each tank had been smashed, the glass scattered in the thick-pile carpet. The air was cool, but damp, and for the first time in weeks Shaw shivered.

Orzsak walked to the nearest tank, lifted the lid, which was fitted with what looked like a small electric heater, and set it on the table beneath. He turned to face them with the corpse of a fish on his hand: a gorgeous fish – black velvet scales, with a rainbow splash of tangerine orange and lemon yellow. It was a diamond shape, as thin as a sheet of paper; a resplendent corpse.

Orzsak went to the second tank. Same story. In the last tank the glass had not been smashed completely from the frame so that one fish had survived – an inch long in see-through silver, with a go-faster stripe in pink, gliding in shallow water amongst the shards of glass.

Shaw and Valentine exchanged a look. 'When exactly did this happen, Mr Orzsak?' asked Valentine.

'My neighbour – Elspeth – she said she heard them at one; her husband was watching the football.' He touched one of his cheeks and a sudden gout of tears spilt out of his eyes. Shaw felt a rush of sympathy, prompted by a vision of what this man's life was like on the inside.

Orzsak turned and went into the kitchen. They found him sitting with a quart mug of tea in front of him on a plain wooden table. Valentine recognized the kitchen of a lonely man. Shaw noted that the rear window was barred too, and that an electric Maglock had been fitted to the rear door, just like the one on the front. A plate lay on the draining board covered in burnt crumbs. Rubbish collected in a black bag slumped in the corner like a corpse. There was a wine rack, not a flimsy dozen-bottle one, but a solid homemade piece of furniture. Shaw estimated it had held up to a hundred bottles. Now, per-haps twenty. There was an echo of an image in his mind – the faint shadow of the criss-cross marks on the wall in the flooded basement of the men's hostel.

'What's happened here?' asked Shaw. 'Have you reported this?'

'A Sunday,' said Orzsak. 'They know that on a Sunday I am out all day. Mass at St Casimir. Then the Polish Club. I get back at ten – sometimes later. I found all this. They cut the power – so the locks pop. It's an old system – cheap. They are better now.'

'You think someone cut the power to do this – to you?'

'I live for the fish,' said Orzsak. It was a statement without a trace of irony. He opened his fist, which had been closed, and they saw that he still held the tropical fish. 'And they helped themselves to wine.' A sneer disfigured his face. 'But they don't know the good bottles from the rest . . .' he added, looking at the wine rack. He slurped tea. 'Last year they tried to break in, so I got the locks, and the bars. I didn't want to be here to see if it was enough. One of them said in the street I should be castrated.' He shook his head. 'With a bread knife.'

'Who did this?' asked Shaw, still incredulous. 'And why didn't you report it?'

Orzsak laughed silently, the folds of fat around his neck shaking. 'The same as always. Each year – on that day. The dogshit through the letterbox. The rotting rubbish over the fence into the yard. The broken window. The telephone calls when no one is there.' He studied his mug and Shaw noticed that it bore a picture of Pope Benedict.

'On that day?' asked Shaw. 'The day Norma Jean disappeared?'

This time when he laughed the tiny mouth opened to reveal milk teeth.

'Yes. Eighteen years ago.'

'Why didn't you come to us?' asked Valentine.

The change in Orzsak was frighteningly quick. He was almost across the table, the chair legs screeching on the lino, his face congested with blood.

'Never.' He hit the table, the mug of tea slopping over. 'I am never going back to that place.' He shook a finger at Valentine. 'Men like you,' he said, looking at Valentine.

'Yes. Maybe you. Four of them – and then just one of them.' Holding up his right hand he separated the fingers so that they could see that at least two of them had once been broken, then badly set. 'They beat me,' he said, subsiding into the chair. The anger drained away, like air from a punctured child's paddling pool. He drank his tea, looking everywhere but at them. Shaw thought of the blush of the bruise on the side of Orzsak's head in his police mugshot.

'You were interviewed – about Norma's disappearance,' said Shaw.

Orzsak looked away.

'Who does this?' asked Shaw. 'Is it the Judds – Andy, the boys?'

But Orzsak was smarter than that. 'I didn't kill the boy.' He laughed. 'He knew – as do I – who killed Norma Jean.' Blood flushed into his face. 'Andy Judd *knows* who killed Norma Jean.' His eyes bulged. 'When we were friends, Norma and I, we talked.' He laid one hand on top of the other, showing how close they had been. 'How he beat her. Beat the boy. I knew both the children. Their father killed Norma Jean. They fought – I know this. I've said this to his face.'

Orzsak tapped a pudgy finger on the table. 'Bryan knew too. And one day, I think, he would have told me *why* he knew.'

'What makes you say that?' asked Shaw.

'He had no part in his father's feud with me. Never. He stood apart. I think that each year it was harder for him to keep his silence. But now . . .' He cut his hand through the air like a cleaver. 'Silence for ever.'

161

The kitchen window was open by an inch and through it they heard the dull rumble of an HGV on the quayside.

Orzsak looked at Valentine, his large head on one side. 'Once – eighteen years ago – you, people like you, took me to a police station and beat me. They said I killed this girl. I told them the truth then, I tell you the truth now. I did not.'

Shaw set his jaw. 'We need a statement, Mr Orzsak,' he said. 'And we need to talk to people who can verify where you were last night.'

But Orzsak wasn't listening. 'Because I tell the truth the people here want to push me out. As others drove us out ... the Russians, the Nazis, always ... pushing us on.' He hit the table and his mug slopped again on the Formica top. 'But this is my home.'

'But it wasn't always,' said Valentine, smiling. 'You used to live at number 6.'

Orzsak looked down at his hands and Shaw could see he was calculating something before he spoke. 'Mother's house. When she died I didn't like those memories, and the house was noisy. So I moved when I could. But not away. I will not run away.'

Orzsak licked his lips and Shaw sensed he'd been going to say something else, but had checked himself. He pulled a face, and sipped tea to dispel the bitterness.

Valentine was standing by the kitchen window. He looked out on the yard, strewn with rubbish, and the high fence of the electricity sub-station, a fig tree, leaves sticky and shiny in the sunshine. He dotted his pencil on his notebook. 'Names, sir. Times. Specifically between seven and nine yesterday.'

Orzsak held a hand to his face and Shaw saw that the tiny fingers vibrated. 'I walk – after tea, and before the dance. The town, then the quayside.'

'Alone?' asked Shaw.

'Alone.' He drank from the mug.

'See anyone you knew?' pressed Valentine.

He didn't seem to understand the question. Shaw guessed that Jan Orzsak didn't collect casual acquaintances.

'Mr Orzsak – we're going to have to talk again,' said Shaw. 'And I'm going to ask our forensic crime unit to check the house; not least to see if we can find any fingerprints belonging to the people who did this – to the fish. And the car. Do you have any objections to us checking that out too?'

Orzsak stood, one hand on the table for support. He shook his head, then led the way to the front door.

'But one question now,' said Shaw. 'Do you ever pray at the church across the street?'

They could see him struggling with the question, trying to work out what the answer should be. Finally, he nodded. 'Not often. Because of Andy Judd. He is there, sometimes, praying, like a Christian.' He shook his head.

Shaw couldn't stop himself coming to Judd's defence. 'He wanted Norma Jean to keep her baby. So on that, presumably, you'd have both agreed?'

Orzsak's jaw worked, eating food that wasn't there, struggling with that contradiction.

'And the priest ...' He left some unknown accusation unsaid. 'I do not have time for him. But yes, sometimes

I go – a prayer – maybe, in the morning, for the dead.' He meshed his fingers. 'And sometimes I play the organ – when I can. Music is one of God's gifts.'

18

Valentine lit up on the kerb. The sun was high now and their shadows crowded round their feet. The street reeked of the town – hot pavements, carbon dioxide, and something rotting in the drains. He spat in the dust. Was he braced for the inevitable question, thought Shaw, or did he think Orzsak's casual accusations of police brutality would be left hanging in the air between them?

Shaw looked into the distance, up towards the T-junction and the abattoir. 'So, George – they roughed him up. First night of what looked like a child-murder inquiry, tempers fray, lot of pressure from upstairs, right – to get a conviction, get the press off your back. What's a couple of broken fingers against the slim chance Norma Jean was still alive somewhere? Maybe you *were* there . . .'

Valentine's eyes were in shadow. His bladder was hurting, and he wanted – more than anything – to walk to the Crane and use the loo. Then buy himself a pint.

'Wasn't my case. I wasn't in the room. I think I did some of the house-to-house next day – maybe.' But he wasn't going to let it lie there. Why should he? He looked Shaw in his good eye. 'But if I had been in the room,' he said, stepping closer, so that Shaw could see the ash which had blown into his thinning hair, 'I'd have twisted his little fingers till they snapped just as happily as they did.'

'And Dad? It was his case. Think he was in the room?'

'Yes. Course he was fucking in the room. For all they knew, Norma Jean was lying out there somewhere . . .' He pointed to the docks, then round to the waste ground where Bryan Judd had plaintively called her name that night in 1992. 'Lying there. Dead, dying, they didn't know – did they? So you tell me if it's worth it – sir.'

Shaw went and got in the car, leaving Valentine to finish the cigarette. When the DS joined him he took a deep breath and tried to imagine they hadn't just had the exchange they'd had. Valentine wanted the conversation to continue, because he hadn't got to the heart of it, to the fact that Jack Shaw had a nose for scum; for the kind of man who'd take a fifteen-year-old girl from her family, kill her – probably worse – and then spend the rest of his life watching that family rip itself apart in the aftermath of the one moment in their lives they couldn't forget – the moment they knew she'd gone.

'Jack –' he said, but Shaw raised a hand.

'Leave it.' They sat in silence for thirty seconds. 'Let's think this through. Let's remember which murder inquiry we're supposed to be on. If Orzsak killed Bryan Judd last night, what are we saying happened?'

'My guess is he comes home at about seven,' said Valentine. 'He knows it's Norma Jean's day. The day she went. All that stuff about being out all day doesn't wash. He'd be back to check.' He flipped the seatbelt to give himself room to struggle out of the raincoat. 'The timings fit nicely – Judd and his mates fire up the electric sub-station at noon, wait an hour to make sure the power's staying out, then ransack the house. By the time Orzsak

166

gets home the fish are long dead. He's distraught.' He looked at the front door of number 47. ''Cos it is a nightmare, and he's living it. He wants it to stop. It must stop.'

'But why Bryan? It's Andy he'd go for . . .'

Valentine shook his head, took an extra breath. 'Andy's outside the Crane. Beered up. Surrounded by his mates. They'd tear him apart. And anyway he's not going to *listen*, is he? No, Bryan's the one he thinks he can get through to. So he goes up to the hospital to try. He said it himself, Bryan thought his father had killed Norma Jean.'

He turned in the seat to look at Shaw's face but caught only the moon eye – unseeing. They heard a cow bellow from the back yard of the abattoir, setting off the rest. A kind of keening.

'He's had eighteen years of it,' said Valentine. 'Being treated like a piece of shit. Kids shouting at him. People spitting. Crossing the street to keep away.' There was an edge in Valentine's voice and Shaw wondered if it was how he sometimes felt – an outcast.

'But this time he's had enough. He pleads with Bryan to tell the truth at last – but Bryan's loyal. It is eighteen years since she went missing. If he was going to tell us, tell anyone, he'd have done it by now. So Orzsak doesn't get what he wants – and that's when the fight starts. He's a big bloke, I wouldn't like to get on the wrong end of a fist – Christ, if he punched his weight he'd kill you.'

He tried a laugh, then pressed on. 'Orzsak kills him – maybe accidentally in the heat of the fight – then stuffs the body on the moving belt. Back in town he goes down the Polish Club for a shot of the hard stuff.'

Valentine wound the window down. 'That works.' He

was pleased with himself, even more so because he knew being pleased with himself made Shaw seethe.

'Any evidence you'd like to offer for that scenario – or do we just take your word for it, George? What about Andy? Are we sure – really sure – he was here on the street all day? Perhaps Bryan *was* going to talk to us at last; perhaps Andy went up the hospital to try and talk him out of it.'

'Nah,' said Valentine, looking away. 'If it's not Holme and the drugs, it's Orzsak and Norma Jean. It ain't Judd – the feud's too old, the blood's cooled.' It was an odd image for Valentine to use, and they waited in silence for him to take up the thread. 'Andy could have belted Bryan any time he wanted – why go up the Queen Vic when the street's rocking?' He pinched his nose, trying to stop a sneeze. 'No – the action's all here for him. On the street. By the time we got here he was out of his tiny warped little mind, content that he'd made sure his little vendetta rolled on another year.'

'Maybe,' said Shaw.

Across the street they could see Fiona Campbell on the doorstep of the Bentinck Launderette with two PCs.

'Ring Twine,' said Shaw. 'Get him started on checking Orzsak's alibi. Let's talk to the family.'

19

The Judds' house had the same layout as Jan Orzsak's, so it was an odd sensation, stepping over the threshold, as if they'd come back to the same house years later, newly decorated, the stench replaced by the acrid smell of washing powder, even here, next door to the machines. DC Campbell handed Shaw a file: a printout of Andy Judd's statement in custody at St James's, given the night before. DC Twine had texted earlier to say the CPS was still considering charges, but that at this point the chances of any resulting conviction were slim and Judd had been released on police bail in the early hours. No witness at the scene had agreed to give a statement. Shaw had seen Judd lob the brick into the blazing house – but nothing else.

Ally Judd pushed her way out through the kitchen door and into the hall carrying a tray with a teapot, a bottle of milk, and a packet of sugar. She nodded at Shaw and Valentine and led the way into the living room. She'd aged ten years overnight, but of the many expressions tussling for control of her face grief wasn't one of them. If Shaw had to put a name to it he'd have chosen fear. Again, he noticed the washed-out look, the almost colourless light grey eyes. Beyond the party wall they could hear the driers turning in the launderette.

The front room had been knocked through to the

French windows looking out on the yard, a Moorish sixties arch between. In the back section an acoustic guitar stood on a stand. In the front, over the fireplace, was a framed print of the cover of Johnny Cash's *At Fulsom Prison*, signed.

The three Judds sat apart: the wife, brother and father of the victim. Andy Judd had been given the alpha male's chair, padded leather, set square to a widescreen TV. He didn't look comfortable with the honour. Beside him, Shaw noticed, on the floor, was an empty milk bottle, the sides still slightly glazed with the full-fat liquid. Ally was on the sofa. Neil sat on the carpet barefoot, legs folded easily into a yoga posture. Here, in daylight, next to his father, Shaw could see how vividly Neil must be his mother's son, the features finer than the heavy Celtic clichés of his father. The sleeves of his sweatshirt were rolled up to reveal over-developed biceps.

Andy Judd looked down at his hands, which were large, awkward, and clasped either side of his mug of tea. 'I saw you,' he said, before Shaw could speak. 'Over at the pedo's house.' The colour of his skin, seen in daylight, was extraordinary – like rancid butter. Liver disease, thought Shaw.

'We're investigating the murder of your son, Mr Judd, and both the vandalism which brought the power supply down, and that at number 47 – Mr Orzsak's home. Three incidents which may be connected.' Shaw paused, looking at each of them, but coming back to the father. 'Mr Orzsak can account for his movements last night. We're checking that out. I'd like to concentrate for a second on *your* movements.'

'What does that mean?'

Ally Judd poured tea and Neil gave his father a fresh mug, adding sugar and milk. 'Dad's not been well,' he said. 'He's got problems – he needs medication.' And that, thought Shaw, was Neil Judd's role. The family peace-maker. He sat back on the carpet, cross-legged, like a dog at his father's feet, a hand adjusting one of the hearing aids.

'The power cut yesterday at noon was caused by an incendiary device – a Molotov cocktail, if you will – at the power station,' said Shaw. 'A successful device, I guess, if the aim was to cut the power, which released the electric locks on Mr Orzsak's house and enabled someone to gain entry at about one. I think that someone was you,' added Shaw. 'But we'll wait for the forensics to come through. Do you have a car, by the way?'

'Like I could afford to run a car . . .' He slopped the tea in the mug. 'I've got a bike – why?'

'Because I want to know where you were, Mr Judd, at the time your son died. That was between 7.45 and 8.31 last night. How long does it take to get to the Queen Vic – fifteen minutes?'

Judd didn't answer.

'Did you kill your son, Mr Judd?' asked Shaw. Valentine's muscles tightened. He had to give it to Shaw – he had balls.

Neil Judd looked at his father, then at his hands. Ally covered her mouth with one hand, then turned the move-ment into a flick back of her lifeless hair. Andy Judd got up stiffly and walked to a 1950s glass cabinet. He took out a tumbler and a bottle of Johnnie Walker and poured himself a three-inch slug, which he drank with his back to them.

'No,' he said.

Then he put the cap back on the bottle. As he sat down again he fished a packet of cigarettes out of his pocket, lit one with one hand, snapped the match carelessly between thumb and palm, and flicked it into the grate.

Valentine knelt, using his Silk Cut packet to jiggle the spent match out of the ash. He held it up to the light for Shaw to see.

'Mr Judd – we found a match, just like that, where Bryan smoked up at the hospital.'

'Bry did that with matches too,' said Neil. 'It's a family thing – he got it off Dad. Dad got it off Humphrey Bogart.' They laughed, for a split second a family again.

'Your brother had a lighter,' said Valentine.

Neil Judd shrugged, and Shaw thought how easily the young man's brittle confidence could be broken.

'I was out there . . . in the street, all night, all day,' said Andy Judd, the smoke dribbling out of both nostrils. 'Half a dozen of the old regulars in the Crane break their matches. Jesus. Is this a joke?'

He went back to the bottle for a second glass. 'You think I killed Bry? Is that what he told you – the pervert? Neil's told you who killed him – it was that fucker in the hostel.'

'And your daughter, Mr Judd. Norma Jean. Who killed her?' asked Shaw. Valentine glanced at the door, thinking that if this went on they might need uniformed assistance. Judd, he thought, was close to breaking point.

The effect of the missing girl's name on the family was instant, each immobile, as if a video tape had been freeze-framed.

'We've talked to the original officers who led that inquiry, Mr Judd, and they agree that your son Bryan was withholding evidence in the period after her disappearance. That he knew something about what had happened to her. Perhaps, they thought, he knew who killed her.'

Shaw tried a mock shrug. 'Why would he protect Jan Orzsak? Or was it you he was protecting? Was he always going to protect you – or did he threaten to talk in the end? It was the anniversary of Norma's death – that must be a difficult time for you, for the family. The power went – the drinking started – the night came. I'm asking you again, did you kill your son?'

Even Valentine had to admit Shaw had framed the accusation beautifully. Andy Judd seemed to rock back on his heels.

'Jan Orzsak killed my daughter.' He'd said it between clenched teeth. 'If anyone feared the truth coming out it was him. He lives in my street.' He walked over to Shaw and stood just within his personal space, but when he spoke it was in a whisper. 'The only thing I've ever wanted is to bury her.' He choked on the word *bury*, whisky coming back up his throat, making him gag. 'I just want him to tell us where she is.'

'Shall I tell you what really worries me, Mr Judd?' asked Shaw. 'It's the fact that no one in this family seems to think it remotely possible that Norma Jean ran away. That she's still alive. Perhaps she had the child after all – like you wanted her too. Why is that so unthinkable?'

Neil rubbed the tattoo on his forearm. 'Bry said she was dead – so we knew, we've always known. Bry . . .'

Andy silenced his younger son with a look of contempt, for daring, Shaw thought, to talk about Norma Jean when he could have had almost no memory of her. Instead, he went back to his chair and took up the story. 'Bry and Norma Jean had a kind of link,' he said, putting his hand on his chest. 'Every moment she was alive he could feel her there. But that day she went. He always said she was dead – and that's good enough for me. It's been good enough for all of us.' He looked around at his family. 'That's not to say we don't see her – all of us. Like a ghost in the street, in a queue at the post office, getting off the bus, in the crowds at the Arndale. We see her – but it's never her. It's never going to *be* her.'

Andy Judd gripped the padded arms of the chair. 'Jesus, do you think this is *just* about Norma Jean?' He threw himself to his feet again and picked up a picture which was on the mantelpiece below Johnny Cash and next to a fifties austerity clock and a box of Swan matches. Judd weighed the picture in his hand, as if judging its worth. It was a family snapshot, all on the sofa, the lights of a Christmas tree behind. The twins, Bryan and Norma Jean, young teenagers clutching each other, cheek-to-cheek, Andy Judd with jet-black hair, an arm round a woman with a low-cut blouse emphasizing a show-stopping bust.

Andy Judd thrust the picture into Shaw's hands.

'That's what that pervert did to us.' He spat when he spoke, a thin line of saliva on his chin. 'This is us – 1991. Marie died in '99 – she was forty-five. Breast cancer – but

174

she didn't fight it, didn't want to fight it. Norma Jean, gone. Now Bryan, gone . . . '

'Who took the picture?' asked Shaw, trying to buy himself some time. Judd's aggression had thrown him, and the note of self-pity was almost unbearable.

'My oldest. Sean. He was at sea when Norma went missing. Trawlers out of the Bentinck. When he got back he found this . . .' He spread his hands, including them all. 'He didn't stick around and I don't fucking blame him.'

Andy grabbed the picture back and staggered slightly, slumping back into the armchair. 'He'd always looked out for Norma, did Sean – more than Bry. Like a guardian angel. She was dead because he'd left her – that's what he said. And now she was gone there was no point in staying. He said he wouldn't be back, and he hasn't been back. It broke what was left of Marie's heart. She never forgave him – burnt every picture we had of him.' He looked at Shaw. 'If he'd stayed he'd have done what I should have done. He'd have killed Jan Orzsak.'

'We should kill the fucker,' said Neil.

His father laughed at him, and Shaw wondered just how much satisfaction he got out of humiliating his youngest son. 'Yeah, right,' he said.

'Where are you, Neil? You're not in the picture,' said Shaw.

Neil looked at his father. 'He's in his cot.' Andy laughed, pulling at his shock of white hair. 'This is nothing to do with him.'

Neil didn't know where to look. Instead his skull twitched to one side, like a boxer's.

'And where's Sean now?' asked Valentine.

'He doesn't write to me – ask them,' said Andy, self-pitying again, finished with the conversation even if Shaw wasn't.

'I get cards,' said Neil. 'So did Bry. He joined the navy – shore crew, as a chef at Portsmouth. He won't come back, like Dad said. He's done with us.' He sensed a re-action to what he'd said, adjusting one of his hearing aids, and Shaw wondered if he knew how loud his voice could be. There was a silence and he rushed to fill it. 'Dad didn't kill Norma,' he said. 'Mum always told me she'd told the truth – she'd seen Norma Jean, crossing the yard.' He glanced to the French windows, beyond which they could see the brick back wall. 'But Bryan used to feel things . . .' He searched for the right words. 'He could *feel* what Norma Jean was feeling. He blamed Dad when she went – we don't know why. He never told me what he'd felt. And after she went he couldn't feel . . . anything.'

Ally smiled at Neil. 'That's why we all know she's dead,' she said. 'If she'd been alive, Bry would have known. Andy's right. She's not.'

Shaw tried one last time. 'Mr Judd. Did you see Bryan yesterday – at the hospital?'

'I've said no. I won't say it again. I've told you who killed Bry – it was Holme. He got him hooked on that green slime he used to drink – then he made him steal. When Bry said he wanted out – Holme killed him. You've got your killer – he's in a bed at the Queen Vic. Don't let him get away with it.'

Shaw stood. 'We need to get on. I'd like you all to stay in Lynn, please. Mr Judd, you will be formally interviewed a second time about the events last night after we've completed the forensics. If you plan any journeys, please inform St James's. We will need to talk to you all again.'

Andy Judd spat in the grate.

At the door Shaw turned. 'Two other things – any of you heard of a character known as the Organ Grinder?'

Neil shook his head. 'You don't see them any more, do you? Not here – it's like rag-and-bone men. They've gone.'

Andy Judd had his eyes closed, back in the armchair, breathing heavily.

'And you should all know that on the incinerator belt with Bryan's body we found some human tissue – in a waste bag. We can't find any record of its contents. It might have been put there by his killer. Do any of you know why that might be?'

The members of the Judd family swapped glances, a cat's cradle of looks, then Andy Judd stood and went to the window, looking out into the street. 'Human waste,' he said. 'The low life in the hostel. That's what *they* were.'

20

The Ark stood just off the inner ring road, a broad avenue of swirling carbon monoxide and dusty plane trees which bypassed the medieval town centre. A former Nonconformist chapel, it had been converted into the West Norfolk Constabulary's forensic laboratory in the nineties. Like most of the town's Victorian red-brick buildings it seemed to suck up the heat on a summer's day, its simple architectural lines buckling slightly in an exhaust-induced mirage. Shaw parked the Land Rover at St James's and they walked across for their appointment with the pathologist, Dr Justina Kazimierz.

Inside the Ark the light was sea-green, filtered in through the original Victorian glass. The rectangular box-like nave – the origin, with its simple pitched roof, of the building's nickname – was divided by a metal partition six feet high. Beyond was the pathologist's lab: a small morgue, six dissecting tables, and the only piece of the original statuary to remain in the building – a stone angel, set on the wall, its hands covering its face. On this side of the partition was Tom Hadden's kingdom – six 'hot-desk' PC stations, two lab tables bristling with racks of test-tubes, and an array of forensic kit. Along one wall, running through the partition, was a heavily lagged horizontal chute – a closed shooting gallery for the analysis of bullets. In one of three fume cupboards they could see a green gas billowing.

Hadden sat at a desk, a laptop open, the screen saver a flock of marsh birds over a Norfolk beach.

'Toy shop's open, then,' said Shaw.

'Justina's ready,' Hadden said, closing his eyes, as he always did when he was thinking. 'Then I've got something for you. You'll like it – not all of it – but some.'

Dr Kazimierz pushed her way through a pair of bar-room doors, topped up a mug of coffee, and retreated without a word.

They followed her through. The blackened corpse of Bryan Judd lay on the central autopsy table. To one side a white sheet covered another corpse – two limbs partially visible: a foot, the veins marbled blue, and an arm and hand, fallen to one side and outwards, as if the victim were signalling a left turn.

Dr Kazimierz saw Shaw's interest. 'That's the floater. One of Rigby's.' Dr Lance Rigby was a former Manchester pathologist who had retired to the north Norfolk coast to be close to his boat. He picked up routine cases, private work, and consultancy. Dr Kazimierz had expressed the view to Shaw at the St James's CID Christmas party that she knew several high-street butchers who were better qualified pathologists.

Something had caught Shaw's eye. He knelt by the hand. The skin around the wrist was rucked, red, and showed the distinct imprint of a band of some sort. 'Watch?' he asked.

'Maybe,' said Kazimierz, refusing to quit her position

behind Bryan Judd's head. 'Rigby thinks it's a suicide from up the coast – clothes and valuables left on the beach. Hence – presumably – no watch.'

Shaw looked again. It didn't look as if a watch strap had made the mark.

He put the detail aside and joined them. A mortuary assistant fussed, setting out instruments on an aluminium side-table. Valentine found himself a spot to one side where he could see Judd's corpse, but where he could also see the clock which had been fixed on the chapel wall. He concentrated on the second hand, the juddering, metro-nomic movement. If he felt sick he'd look at this, thinking about the clockwork within, imagining the interleaving cogs, clean, crisp, and inhuman.

'So – externals first,' said the pathologist. She tapped the teeth with a metal tweezer. 'Perfect match, by the way, for Judd's dental records – so there's no doubt, if there ever was any.'

She'd reconstructed the broken skull – as neat as a child's jigsaw in 3D, held together with a plastic glue, clearly showing the small puncture-hole depression at the rear towards the apex of the spine.

'This is an impact point,' she said. 'Don't ask me what – I can't tell. Tom says you've got a ball-head switch? Well, I couldn't rule that out. But that's as far as I'll go.

'One surprise is this . . .' She had a large magnifying lens on a tripod which she positioned over the chest. The blackened skin was taut, but just below the collarbone on the left side was a small hole. She worked the tweezers into the wound. 'I need to cut through the tissue here to see how deep this is, but even from here I'd say three to six inches.'

'Knife?'

'Yes. Maybe. But it's not a traditional kitchen knife, or a switchblade. The point is very narrow, almost like an épée – the heavier of the fencing weapons. So something very sharp, and narrow. It's not fatal – that's the skull wound, then the furnace. But it's traumatic. His blood pressure would have collapsed pretty quickly if it severed any major arteries.

'Now for inside.' She began work, opening up the abdomen to gain access to the principal organs. While the exterior of the corpse had been sucked dry of any moisture the chest cavity had survived largely intact. The sound of trickling body fluids was set against the swish of cars on the ring road outside.

'I've tested the blood,' said Kazimierz. 'We're talking high levels of alcohol – twice the limit for driving, plus cannabis.'

'Really?' said Shaw. 'Ingested when?'

She spilt the contents of the stomach into a metal bowl. 'Here's the culprit,' she said, drawing off a sample by pipette from the pool of vivid green liquid. She removed a length of intestine and, effecting a precise longitudinal incision, examined the contents.

'Well – it's mostly still in the stomach. Let's say eighty per cent – with the rest in the small intestine. There's nothing in the colon ...' She held a length of large intestine up to the light and Valentine watched the second hand of the clock judder.

'So – two hours maximum.'

Shaw and Valentine exchanged glances. Had Aidan Holme brought a bottle of Green Dragon to the hospital to help persuade Judd that his drug-supplying days were not over after all? The next major consignment for incineration was due within twenty-four hours. Holme would have been desperate to intercept it before it went up in flames.

'We're saying he was dead by the time he went in?' asked Valentine, switching tack, trying to see what had happened beyond the technical jargon. He risked a glance at the blackened canines.

'Yes. Or past saving. The lungs ...' She used her gloved hands to spread out the tissue on a metal drainage board. 'The lungs have some toxic contents, I would say — but we need to test for that. There's a tiny bit of inhalation from inside the furnace. Ash — as hot as any ash in any fire. He'd have taken half a breath, maybe less. The heat has scorched the tissue.'

Shaw imagined being half-conscious for that excruciating second as the body jerked along the incinerator belt, then in through the opening to the furnace. Darkness, then heat, with a soundtrack out of hell.

'Hell,' said Valentine, seeing the same image.

Dr Kazimierz removed the major organs and trepanned the skull, setting what was left of the brain in a glass dish. In another thirty-five minutes she was done. Valentine led the dash back to the coffee machine. As they turned away Shaw caught the movement in the pathologist's right hand. A sign of the cross.

She followed them back to her desk on the far side of the partition and speed-read a page of handwritten notes.

'Nothing else. The clothes were largely burnt into the skin. Coins in one pocket, a lighter, a penknife. Mobile in the shirt pocket. What's left of a cardboard packet – cigarettes, but we can't get a brand for you until they've done their stuff . . .'

She nodded once at Shaw, then at Tom Hadden. 'That's it.' She turned away without another word.

Hadden sipped a cup of espresso from the Italian coffee-maker on the desktop. 'No joy on the snapped match, I'm afraid. Dry as bone. I thought we'd get some saliva if he held it in his teeth, but no go.'

On Hadden's desk lay an evidence bag holding the torch they'd found beside the hubcap ashtray. 'Bad news first. I've checked MVR online and it's not a company. We're talking to the manufacturers of the torch – they're Finnish.'

That was a detail Shaw liked, so he filed it away.

'But it's the dust on the torch itself that's interesting . . .' He touched a key on his laptop and the screen filled with a microscope shot. A mass of fibre, unspeakable horror-movie bugs, chips of material.

'It's smeared in this stuff. This is it at ten thousand. All dust is different – like a fingerprint. This sample is very low on human tissue – skin and the like. It's very high on two things . . .'

He brought up another shot. 'This is some kind of fibre – man made, like a polythene. I don't know, maybe wrapping or packaging of some sort. And this . . .'

The third shot. Splinters of something red.

'It's wood dust – sawdust. But really, really, fine. But it's the wood that's odd – Muirapiranga. Bloodwood. A South

American hardwood – valuable stuff. Looks like teak. I've checked online and it's used widely for expensive flooring. Imported, obviously. You want to see a bloodwood tree in its natural environment, you could try the banks of the Amazon. If you want it on your kitchen floor it's five pounds a square foot.'

'Right,' said Shaw. Another detail that didn't fit. Or did it? He thought of Father Thiago Martin, an exile from Brazil. He'd get Twine to organize a background check on the priest.

'Other results . . .' Hadden flipped a file. 'The blood on the conveyor is Judd's – and his alone. The rice you found at the Sacred Heart of Mary is a match for the grains at the scene. But it's a standard import long-grain variety from the US – Tesco stocks it. Cash 'n' carry warehouses too. So it helps, but I wouldn't dream of taking it into court. And we're still struggling with the waste in the bag under the body. Another twenty-four hours – maybe less. Oh, and I've sent the milk bottle away – the one from the electricity sub-station. There's a trace of saliva round the neck.'

Shaw thought of Andy Judd in his alpha male's armchair, the pint of milk empty by his foot.

Hadden smiled, as rare a sight as one of his beloved Ospreys. 'Where we did strike lucky, however, was with this.' Hadden scrolled through his image file on the laptop until he reached a picture of the metal seat they'd found on the balcony by the hubcap. 'This was covered with Judd's prints – and those of his colleagues who cover the other two shifts. But there was a print that didn't match – and it was on *top* of Judd's . . . It was very difficult to lift – we had to use a new methodology which I won't bore you with, although you will become familiar with it, Peter, because you'll have to defend the bill when it goes upstairs. Eight thousand pounds.'

Valentine whistled, delighted that wasn't going to be his job.

'Anyway, once we'd got it, I ran it through the database Twine's set up of all prints taken in the case so far. Suspects, witnesses, victim. I got a direct match.' He let them sweat for a full second. 'It's Aidan Holme's.'

Valentine clapped once, and started searching for a Silk Cut. At last, a solid piece of forensics which put one of their prime suspects on the spot. Shaw let his naturally contrarian nature kick in, because that single print proved only that Aidan Holme had been there. It didn't prove he was a killer. But then he told himself that a break was a break and he should be thankful for that.

'Let's hope Holme lives,' he said.

2 1

On Erebus Street three pairs of uniformed PCs were working the doorsteps and a team of builders were shoring up the ruins of number 6. DC Jackie Lau was on the kerb to meet them as Shaw parked the Land Rover in the shadow of the Sacred Heart.

'Sir. Sorry – but I'm absolutely sure you need to see this.' She led the way inside the church, out of the sun, the nave already a cool haven amongst the red bricks of the North End. Valentine hung back, trying to get a decent signal on his mobile so that he could check Aidan Holme's condition at the Queen Victoria.

Inside, DC Lau checked a note. 'According to the warden – Kennedy – there were fourteen homeless men here last night,' she told Shaw. 'There's thirteen here now. All the statements we've taken match – except one. Most of them ate a big meal at 7.30, then went to bed because there were no lights. The fracas in the street woke some of them up, and a few went out to have a look. Then they all went back to bed. But one of them has a different story. He woke up some time *before* the attack on the hostel. He says he saw a man being abducted.'

She let Shaw take that in. 'The witness is well short of 100 per cent reliable, sir – but I think he's telling the truth. Either that, or I can't see why he'd lie.'

'Let's see him,' said Shaw.

Valentine joined them. He studied a text message on his phone. 'Holme's still bad,' he said, sniffing the air, laden with the smell of huddled people.

In front of the altar the team had set up a pair of tables and two uniformed officers were taking statements. The homeless men were sitting in the pews, drinking tea from paper cups or reading bits of newspapers. Lau took them into the vestry they'd seen the night before. A man sat at the table on which stood an empty mug and a single biscuit on a large plate. The door to the boiler room, and Kennedy's bedsit, was open. 'This is John William,' she said. 'He's from London, hitched up in a lorry to Cambridge some time ago. He says his surname's gone. But he might remember it later.'

Shaw shook the old man's hand, noticing as he often did that age seemed to add weight to the limbs, as if they were seeking a place to rest.

'It was his first night here at the church,' said Lau. 'He's very tired because he says he walked here from Cambridge – he thinks it's taken him a month, sleeping rough.'

John William nodded, helping himself to the last biscuit.

'Can you tell us again, John William?' asked Lau, putting a hand on his shoulder. Shaw looked into his green eyes, the colour of lichen, floating in watery sockets, like lily-pads. It was the only colour left on him: his skin and thin hair were like parchment and his shirt, which had been washed to destruction, was handkerchief-grey.

'I slept,' he said. 'I was tired, like she says. And the

food was good.' He opened his hands and Shaw saw the pale band where a ring had once encircled his wedding finger. 'Liver and bacon. But I had to pee in the night, I always do. 'Bout ten.' His mind disengaged from his story for a second, then clicked back into gear. 'When I came back in I saw a match flare – someone smoking. That's against the rules. He didn't see me – and there was noise outside, so he didn't hear. I thought, something's up.' He searched their faces, checking that this was what they wanted to hear. 'So I got close – in the shadows.'

He grinned, showing wrecked teeth.

'What did you see, John William?' said Shaw patiently.

'There was a man, standing beside one of us – one I'd seen at the meal, everyone called him Blanket because he had this old grey thing, like a horse blanket, but he wore it, like a poncho.' He shook his head, still scandalized by the impropriety. 'He had long hair, so you could hardly see his face. That's against the rules too – so I don't know what's going on.'

It was Valentine's turn to act as prompt. 'And did they talk, these two?'

'Yes. He was sat hunched, Blanket, smoking too. And then this stranger, the outsider, he said . . .'

John William looked into the middle distance, trying to get the words just right. 'He said, "That's the deal – take it or leave it. Like you'll get better."'

'Then?' asked Shaw.

'This Blanket smoked the fag, and then when he was done he looked away and said, "I'll leave it." – No. "I'll leave it – so should you . . ." Yeah, that was it. And he started to get back in his bedroll, but then I saw the other man lift something out of his jacket – a spanner? I don't know. Anyway, he hit him. Not hard, but enough ...' He touched the back of his head. 'Then he got him under the arm and he took him out, through the side door, into the dark.'

'And what did you do?'

'I was scared,' he said. 'Really scared. I went back to the loo and hid. I thought he might come back – and Liam, the warden, he's always ...' He leant forward, lowering his voice. 'He's on stuff ...' he said, making small 'mad' circles with one finger at his temple. 'He's always asleep, so I just went back to bed – but this morning, at breakfast, I told him then.'

He looked at Shaw, the lily-pads floating. 'I should have done something last night – I'm sorry now I didn't.'

Shaw stood. 'Show me, show me where you saw the torchlight.'

John William shuffled out into the nave, holding his trousers up with one hand even though he had a belt. He took them up the aisle and then to one side, where a small altar held an alabaster Virgin. On the floor was one of the church's standard bedrolls.

'Here,' he said.

Shaw could see his hands were shaking, and his body above the waist swung rhythmically from side to side.

'Thank you, John William. Is there anything else you can tell us about what you saw – anything unusual, perhaps, about the outsider?' he asked. 'Height? Age?'

The tramp shook his head. 'I didn't see him – just a shape in the shadows. He had the torch in his hand so all the light kind of went away from him.'

'Clothes?' prompted Valentine.

'There was a noise,' said John William, ignoring the question, suddenly animated by the realization he might, after all, be of some use. 'His shoes – I noticed that because he did everything else so quietly. But when he dragged Blanket out I could hear them, on the wooden floor, like a tap-dancer's.'

'Metallic?' asked Shaw, almost in a whisper.

'That's it. Yes – drive me mad, shoes like that, like you were being followed everywhere by yourself.'

Shaw and Valentine stood back, both trying to see if it was possible, trying to see if the man who had killed Bryan Judd at the hospital had time to get back to Erebus Street and abduct the homeless Blanket. And if it was possible, which it *was*, then why?

Lau led John William away, an arm under his elbow, keeping him on his feet, taking him down to sit with the other men. Then she came back, rattling a silver bracelet on her wrist, getting down on one knee by the bedroll. There was a Tesco bag under the bench, and she slipped on a driving glove and lifted it out. But she'd left something behind, so light it almost fluttered out when she moved the bag – a £50 note on the parquet floor.

Shaw was down on his knees too, and Valentine stood back so he could see as well.

'OK, let's get Tom here,' said Shaw. 'Bag that for a start. I take it Blanket isn't this character's real name?'

'It might as well be, sir,' said Lau. 'We just don't know. To qualify for the doss they have to fill in a form. But Kennedy – the warden – is clearly no stickler for the rules. Blanket's was pretty much, well, blank. He put thirty-six for age, Middlesbrough for place of birth, and as his former residence before here, Newcastle.'

She looked inside the Tesco bag. There was a carpeted step in front of the small side-altar and on it she arranged the five objects in the bag.

A picture in a wooden frame without glass. A child, pale with black hair, on a man's knee. Blanket had clearly been touching the face of the man, because it was gone now, smudged into a pale, featureless oval.

Lau nodded. 'I reckon he's ten, eleven years old – the kid. There's a date on the back: April, 1984. So it could be our missing man.' Next, a folding fisherman's knife made by a French company – Opinel – the handle well worn. Then a National Express bus timetable; a packet of Nice biscuits, and a copy of *Moby Dick*. Inside was a library sticker, the due date a week away.

The blanket-coat still hung from its impromptu hook. It was filthy, heavy with engrained dirt. Shaw took it down, twisted it, so that they could all see that there was a mark on the back; in chalk, a single vertical rectangle, narrowly drawn, with a wispy elliptical circle just over the top, like a fat dot on a wide letter 'i'.

'That's odd too,' said Shaw. 'Someone's drawn that.'

'It's a candle,' said Valentine.

Liam Kennedy walked up the aisle from the altar carrying a tray with mugs. He had on a fresh T-shirt, this one with a VSO logo.

He took orders, then handed out teas, adding sugar and milk to taste. Then he stood, mug in one hand, the other tucked into the front pocket of his jeans. Shaw thought that now, in the daylight, after a night's sleep, he looked younger, fresher. A teenager. He'd handed Shaw a tea – white with sugar. Shaw always took it black without. He sensed that Kennedy was one of those infuriating people who enjoy bouts of complete self-confidence without any justification.

'You're not exactly running a tight ship here, Mr Kennedy. No proper documentation for this man who's gone missing. And his violent abduction unreported – largely because the men here seem to think they can't wake you up at night. You *were* here?'

Kennedy's good humour froze on his face, but he seemed to fight back the inclination to meet Shaw's accusations with anything other than humility.

'I'm sorry. Yes. The paperwork's never been my strong point, and Blanket was a difficult case. He wouldn't tell us his name, so if I followed the rules I'd have to deny him a bed, or food, which seemed unfair.'

Kennedy saw John William still sitting on the pew, waiting to give his statement, his head buried in his hands. Kennedy said he'd be a moment, and went to sit beside him, an arm along the shoulder. They heard sobbing and looked away. Shaw thought how often flawed people led flawless lives.

When Kennedy returned Shaw got back to the question, but he couldn't keep a note of conciliation out of his voice. 'This happened about ten – John William seems to think you were asleep then – but that's not right, is it?'

Kennedy looked at his trainers. 'Not at all – although I would be most days. I take medication.' The admission seemed to diminish him, and he looked younger still. 'I was outside – by the abattoir actually, watching the street.

You could tell, couldn't you? That something might kick off. So I took a coffee outside, and just watched. There's a low wall by the corner of the street – I often sit there, before bed. I'm usually asleep by nine – bit later; but yes, I stayed up. When I saw the flames at the hostel I went to see if I could help, and I popped into the presbytery because I knew Father Martin was in and he needed to know. He phoned the fire brigade. When the ambulance came I went up to the Queen Vic with Aidan. Then I came back and talked to you downstairs.'

'How did you know Father Martin was in?' asked Valentine.

'I'd seen a light earlier, and I'd noticed, because of the power cut. Father Martin has this old lantern, oil fired. I think it's a family heirloom. The light's multicoloured.'

Valentine scuffed his slip-ons across the parquet flooring. 'Where was the light?'

Kennedy swallowed hard. 'Bedroom.' He stirred his tea, adding sugars from little paper packages that he'd collected in a dish.

'We need to find this man – the one called Blanket – Mr Kennedy,' said Shaw. 'Can you tell us anything more about him, anything that wasn't on his form?'

Kennedy sat, composed himself, as if he were a prisoner in the dock. 'Most of these men are short on words, Inspector. I doubt I heard him string three together. He wouldn't give us a name, as I said, which is why he got the label he did. Alcohol he didn't touch, that was clear. His mind was good and he read a lot of the time – we get a travelling library. Good stuff, too. I always try to notice so that there's something to talk about –

Buchan, Innes, Greene. It's odd: if they do read, these men, then it's often the best.' He laughed, shrugging his shoulders.

'And he'd been here how long?' asked Valentine.

'Two weeks – I can check the record. But about that.'

'Description?'

Kennedy laughed. 'Well, that's a sore point. Once the men have been here a few days we insist they get their hair cut – it's a health issue. Most of them have been on the streets for years so there are various skin complaints, lice, that kind of thing. But Blanket said he wasn't having that – that he'd leave if we made him. We just agreed to differ. I hoped he'd come round. And he was pretty clean – he used the showers at the town baths. But the hair stayed, and the beard. He looked like Ben Gunn.'

Another hidden face, thought Shaw.

'But Middlesbrough – so an accent?' said Valentine.

'Not really. Ask the men – they'll say the same. One or two are from up north and they said no way was he from Teesside, or Tyneside, for that matter. And there was something else. It was weird.' He pressed his narrow knees together. 'The first day he arrived it was mid-morning and we lock the church between ten and four – usually, anyway. But he rang, and I came out. I said he could come back at four, but he could fill in the form now – it saves time, and people get upset when all they want is to grab a bed and some food and they have to fill in a questionnaire. I watched him walk off. He went down the gravel path round the back of the church, there's a bench there – wrought iron, Victorian. Anyway, the point is you can't see it from the street. But he went *straight* there. Sat in the shadows, filled in his form, then stretched out for a sleep. He knew, you see. But he said he'd never been here before. He said that a lot.'

22

Shaw was standing by the Land Rover, a polystyrene cup of coffee balanced on the roof, when his mobile buzzed; he looked at the incoming ID – it was Tom Hadden, calling on the landline from the Ark. He picked up the call, watching Valentine in the distance briefing the door-to-door teams on what they'd discovered at the Sacred Heart.

'Peter. Look, I've got some tests back on the waste bag found under Judd's body.'

Shaw didn't speak, trying to refocus his mind on the scene in the Queen Victoria's incinerator room, the blackened corpse shivering as it trundled out of the furnace.

'It's a human kidney, Peter – or at least what's left of one.'

Shaw's hand moved involuntarily to his back.

'But the real conundrum is that, as far as Justina and I can be sure, this kidney is in no way diseased. It should be working away keeping someone alive. But it isn't. It's been discarded – and I don't think that makes much sense.'

'Unless . . .'

'Well. Let's take it step by step, backwards. Someone has deliberately falsified the documentation on the waste bag to slip this organ into the incinerator. Either that or they opened a bag on the belt and switched the contents.

This organ has been surgically removed, and the only possible reason that would happen – if it is a healthy organ – is that it was being readied for transplant. A transplant that didn't happen.'

The words echoed in Shaw's head. *Organ transplant.* He felt they'd crossed a Rubicon; but the image was in colour, the river red.

'Bryan Judd died with this thing under his body,' said Shaw. 'He was either holding it, and didn't let go, or it was deliberately put with the body.' It was a statement, not a question, and Hadden greeted it in silence.

Even in the noonday sun Shaw shivered, the hairs on his neck bristling, because his mind had only just made the big leap. He thought about the stifling smoke in the upstairs bedroom at number 6 Erebus Street, the fumes pouring through the gaps in the bare floorboards, the figure of Pete Hendre, curled in a foetal ball under the window ledge, and his whispered plea to make sure his face stayed hidden; hidden for ever, from the Organ Grinder.

He thanked Hadden, briefed him on what they'd found in the church, and asked if he could get a team on the scene as soon as resources allowed.

Twenty minutes later he was in a lift rising to the eighth floor of the main block of the Queen Victoria. He stepped out when a bell pinged, escaping the piped-in Bach and a trolley on which lay a man heading for theatre, his face mirroring the helpless fear he must have been feeling within. Shaw thought just how trusting you had to be to lie on a stretcher, to let strangers decide where to take you, and then to let them put you to sleep – the definition, surely, of 'defenceless'. And that awful double-edged euphemism: 'put to sleep'.

Mrs Jofranka Phillips, head of surgical services, had an office in the executive suite. The whole floor was air-conditioned, and the sudden chill made Shaw feel uneasy. The door was open, the office an uncluttered glass box empty but for a desk, a filing cabinet, and a full-sized skeleton hanging from an aluminium stand. Phillips stood five foot two in – Shaw noticed – her stockinged feet. She shook his hand and he thought that surgeons always had hands like that – the fingers preternaturally long, slender. And that stillness, an ability to remain calm at the very moment when ordinary people would begin to shake, as they made the first incision.

Shaw took a seat, noticing the skeleton had hands like that too.

'Thanks for seeing me so quickly,' he said. 'My CSI team have passed on the details . . . ?'

She nodded. 'I thought we should talk,' she said. She looked him squarely in the face and saw the dead eye for the first time, her familiarity with trauma reducing her reaction to the merest flicker of her eyelids.

'I'm sorry.' Shaw raised a hand. 'I realize you have responsibilities in the hospital but we're dealing with a murder scene here – and now with the discovery of a human organ without the relevant documentation. I've talked to my superior at St James's – Superintendent Warren – and to the chairman of the primary care trust . . .'

He flipped through his notes but she didn't have the patience for that.

'Sir John Falcon,' she said.

'Right. Him. And we're all agreed that these two issues are now inextricably entwined.'

Phillips looked shocked, and she couldn't stop a hand rising to cover her mouth.

'So I'm going to investigate all of these issues in the round, as it were – with your help. I can rely on your assistance?'

He'd been brutal, but it was the only way. There was no point pretending anyone was in charge of this inquiry except him. What he hadn't said was that Sir John Falcon had made it clear that any inquiry within the hospital would have to involve clinical experts brought in from other hospitals. Phillips would be answering questions, not asking them – although he'd added an encomium to the effect that she was one of the finest surgeons in the NHS and that they were very lucky to have her on the staff. Don't be fooled by the 'Mrs', he'd added – it didn't mean she was married, it meant she was a surgeon. 'So don't call her doctor,' he'd warned, laughing, 'because that *is* an insult.'

'Of course,' said Phillips. She touched the phone on her desk and Shaw guessed she'd thought about arguing the toss with Falcon, but decided it was a lost cause. 'I'll do anything I can.' Her accent was heavy – Cypriot, perhaps. Luxuriant black hair was swept back off her face, a contrast to the white clinical coat and pale-olive skin. Her jewellery was black too, a jet stone bracelet, and a black pendant necklace. Black and white, light and darkness – Shaw sensed this was a person who dealt in certainties, or sought them out. But the eyes, an extraordinary luminous grey, made sure that light was the dominant force, and it was in her eyes that Shaw could see a fine intelligence.

'What have you done already?' he asked.

'I've notified the Human Tissue Authority, Lynn Primary Care Trust, and the Department of Health. A team from HTA will undertake an audit of our tissue and organ bank within the next forty-eight hours. In the meantime I've had it closed. The locks are sealed. No one is to enter without my written approval. The press office have prepared a release, but it won't go out until I say so.'

Any note of resentment at Shaw's hijacking of the inquiry had disappeared from her voice. He sensed a woman whose self-confidence was robust, and anything but fragile.

'Good. That's prompt. Thank you. I'm sorry – two points. I need to sign that approval as well – for entry to the organ banks. Can you make that change? And the press office needs to sit on the news until I say so. I don't want this aspect of the inquiry made public.'

She nodded.

'Now, please,' said Shaw. She flicked through a plastic internal telephone directory and made the calls.

When she'd finished she held the directory in her hand, shaking her head. Then she sat with it on her lap. 'I'm sorry,' she said, running a hand into her black hair until it stuck, the fingers lost in the thick plush locks. 'This is really stupid of me. Stupid of all of us. One of your officers was asking if any of us recognized the initials – MVR.' She put an unvarnished fingernail on one of the telephone entries, stood, and showed Shaw. Motor

Vehicle Repair: MVR. 'There's a garage over beyond A&E. I'm sorry, we should have thought.'

'It's OK,' said Shaw. But it wasn't, and sorry was the most overrated word in the language. They could have had a forensic team in the garage while Judd's body was still smouldering; now the chances of finding relevant evidence were slim. He stood, walked to the glass wall of the office, and rang Valentine on his mobile, telling him to get over to MVR with back-up. Then he took his seat again.

'The kidney that we've found on the incinerator belt,' he said. 'To what degree can we be sure a crime has been committed here? What's the best-case scenario, and the worst?'

Without knocking, Dr Gavin Peploe joined them. He let a smile begin on one side of his lopsided face and slide to the other, shaking Shaw's hand. A crumpled figure, in a £500 suit, he folded himself easily into a chair, the crossed legs and folded arms revealing not a trace of anxiety.

'Gavin, thanks,' Mrs Phillips said, adroitly reinforcing her authority by making it clear she'd summoned him. 'DI Shaw's first question is a good one, if he doesn't mind me saying so. Could this be nothing – a one-off?'

Peploe's small feet did a little shuffle. 'I've been thinking about that,' he said. 'At this moment we don't have any other evidence of illegal traffic, unauthorized procedures, or organ or tissue retention against anyone's wishes. Our records are complete for the disposal of tissue and organs from both live patients and cadaveric supplies.'

Shaw licked his lips, unsettled by the appalling double euphemism.

'So. Here's a scenario. What if the kidney *is* diseased – I think the pathologist is still doing tests – it could be something very difficult to detect in an organ which has been partly incinerated. Glomerulosclerosis, for example. What if an earlier bureaucratic error left such a kidney in the system which could not – retrospectively – be matched to documentation? All the NHS theatres run at near full capacity – everyone makes mistakes. We've completed nearly two hundred kidney transplants within the trust this year. Organ and tissue disposal is a priority, but it's only human nature if people spend a bit more time on caring for the living patient. So – an error. Someone panicked, forged the tag, or switched a bag, and tried to slip it onto the incinerator belt.'

'And what are the chances that actually happened?' asked Shaw.

'Nil,' said Peploe, smiling, his teeth very white against the expensive tan. 'One in a billion. Organ tracking is the surgeon's responsibility, then the theatre manager's. Senior professionals in both cases. If there'd been an earlier error they could just have reported it. It's a misdemeanour. Why risk a career by trying to cover it up? It doesn't make sense unless it's a panic reaction. The one thing experienced theatre staff don't do, Inspector, is panic.'

'Worst case?'

Phillips stood and walked to her filing cabinet, leaving Peploe to answer. Shaw noticed for the first time there was a picture on the top in a gilded baroque wooden frame. A formal portrait of a man, seated, a photographic salon backdrop showing trees and a hillside, a church tower just visible. It looked like Mitteleuropa, before the war. The picture of a man seeking to confirm his respectability. A man who wanted to belong.

'The world,' said Peploe, spreading his hands, 'is divided into the rich and poor. The poor supply human organs, and the rich receive.' He tossed a thick file onto the floor beside Shaw. 'In 2002 the *Washington Post* reported from a small village in Moldova that fourteen of the forty men had sold body parts. We're talking liver parts, kidneys, lung, pancreas, colon, corneas, skin, bones, and tissue such as Achilles tendons – even marrow.

'This is a worldwide trade. The poor selling to the rich. A Turkish peasant can get two thousand seven hundred dollars for a kidney he doesn't need. Someone who does need one will pay a hundred and fifty thousand. Note the profit margin. In 2000 eBay auctioned a kidney and reached one hundred thousand dollars before the FBI stepped in. There is also plenty of evidence that children were sold for body-part harvesting out of eastern Europe and Russia – largely through orphanages set up to feed a burgeoning black market.

'There are *darker* corners of this market,' he added, laughing again. 'An entire human body is worth about a quarter of a million dollars. It did not take the market long to realize that if people wouldn't donate parts, or sell them, then systematic murder would provide one source of supply. Tissue brokers, who supply the major bio-med companies, may not be as punctilious as they should be when checking the provenance of body parts.'

Shaw took a deep breath.

'And one other sophistication . . .' added Peploe. 'The Chinese government uses prisoners on death row as a source for harvesting tissue and organs. Prisoners may undergo several operations before they are deemed of no more use. Until that point they are effectively kept alive to provide fresh body parts. They're *farmed*, with regular harvests. Then they are executed. This happens. There is fragmentary – anecdotal – evidence it happens elsewhere, too.'

Somewhere, a hundred feet below, they heard a car alarm sound.

'I need to read about this,' said Shaw, picking up the file.

'That's all I could download this morning,' said Peploe. 'UN report, some background stuff from the HTA, and a few case studies from Organ Watch – a pressure group. If you want any more, let me know. It's my specialist subject – at least, it's going to be.'

'If we're talking illegal operations, could they be taking place here? At the Queen Vic?' asked Shaw.

'It's unthinkable,' said Phillips, leaning against the filing cabinet.

Her voice had been sharp, too sharp, and she knew it. She took a deep breath. 'It is not possible for an illegal organ transplant to be completed in an NHS hospital without being detected.' She gave Shaw a list. 'This is a roll call of all surgeons working within the trust. There are twenty-eight names here. Any one of them *could* perform this operation. But, as I say, I find it impossible to believe it happened here.'

'If not here, then where?' Shaw said bluntly. 'How easy is it to complete a successful kidney transplant in a backstreet operating theatre?'

Peploe steepled his fingers. 'Well, a lot easier than it was. New drugs mean you don't need a blood match, or a tissue match for that matter. And the chances of organ rejection are significantly lower. Plus, you've got keyhole surgery for the removal now, so the donor can be up and about in hours. By the way – so you know – when you give someone a new kidney you don't take out the old one. So if this is a transplant, we're not *missing* the diseased organ. The new organ goes in here . . .' He indicated a spot in his groin. 'Joined to the urethra.'

'Well, we have to begin somewhere,' said Shaw, holding up the paper Phillips had given him. 'We'll start by interviewing everyone on this list.'

Shaw stood. 'For the record, I am going to have to ask both of you this question. Do either of you have anything to do with illegal organ removal in this hospital, or with the death of Bryan Judd?'

There ensued what might have been a stunned silence. 'I'm sorry, but I need an answer,' said Shaw.

'Nothing.' They said it together, in perfect unison.

23

The Red House had been the CID's out-of-office office for nearly thirty years. Its principal original attraction had been the rarity of its public telephone in the corridor leading to the loos – a vital link with the outside world before the advent of the mobile phone. Now it had no attractions at all. There were four drab rooms, a tiny bar in a lobby by the door. Its local trade – mainly stall-holders from the town's two markets – crowded into the front bar. The CID took the larger of the back two, a room dominated by a lithograph of the Guildhall and an old photo of the city walls before they had been demolished to make way for St James's police HQ.

Shaw always got a thrill walking over the threshold, having spent many childhood evenings sitting outside on the kerb, waiting for his father, bought off with crisps and squash. Its interior had been part of his father's secret world. Now it was his world.

'Mark,' said Shaw, nodding at the door. DC Mark Birley wedged a stool against it.

They were crammed into the room. Pints and alcopops bristled on the table tops. No one was on fruit juice, and everyone would drive home; one of the police force's abiding ironies. Everyone had a single-sheet briefing note from Twine – all the major developments summarized.

Valentine stood, leaning his back against the nicotine-yellow wallpaper, nursing his second pint.

Shaw sat on the wide window ledge, his back to the stained-glass picture of the pier at Hunstanton. He took one sip of Guinness, annoyed to find a shamrock doodled in the white head.

'Anything we should know that's not in the note?' he asked.

DC Campbell waved a lime-green bottle of alcopop.

'MVR – Motor Vehicle Repair. The garage appears completely legit, they don't issue torches. Staff of thirteen. We're talking to everyone who was on duty yesterday, nothing yet.'

'OK. But we don't have an alternative, Fiona, so let's dig deeper. What about the vehicles themselves? All accounted for? Any out over the weekend – that happens. Nice little sideline. Bit of pocket money. They rent out the hospital vans for forty-eight hours and no one's the wiser – as long as someone's fiddling the mileage. Really dig – OK?'

'We'll check it,' said Campbell.

Check-It. A few of them grinned into their drinks.

Twine stretched his legs under a round iron table, leather boots screeching on the wooden floor. 'Door-to-door picked up plenty of gossip on the Judds' marriage. Tongues wag – mainly because Ally Judd seems to spend most of her spare time dusting Thiago Martin's bedroom furniture.' That got a laugh.

'I've got a file getting fatter on the priest – he's right about not being welcome in his own country. There's a police record. He's been telling fibs about his medical

207

degree as well. He was struck off in 1994 – a decision which, incidentally, means he can't practise in the UK.'

'Why was he struck off?' asked Shaw.

'He tried to prove that a contaminated water supply in one of the shanty towns was causing lead poisoning in children. He ran a study based on blood and urine samples. The parents worked for the company that supplied the water. He didn't get their permission. When he tried to publish there was a legal action. Big money talks – he got struck off. The church wasn't too pleased either. His own parish, in one of the up-market suburbs, hadn't seen him for eight months.

'We're checking his movements yesterday. He helped someone move house early evening, out of council care, but he was back by seven. He says he's doing an MA with the Open University and was upstairs studying. He says he was alone. Ally Judd says she went to the presbytery to sweep and wash the floors while the light lasted early evening. She says she left her gear there, thinking the power cut would end and she could go back and carry on. When it didn't she went and got her stuff. Says she called up the stairs to the priest both times – once at 7.30, then about 10.30. Which is convenient as it provides a neat alibi.'

He leant forward, elbows on the table. 'And just to say we got hold of Norma Jean's medical records. Her baby was due in early 1993. So we tracked down abandoned babies for the Eastern Counties – nothing even close. And certainly no record of a regular registered birth in hospital. There's also a blank on bank accounts, driving licence, and passport – she didn't have one in 1992. She's gone,' he finished, his palms open.

A thunderstorm had been brewing for an hour and now it broke, rattling the windows, chugging in the downpipes. The room got darker, the wall lights warmer, and they could smell the sea.

'And one loose end,' added Twine. 'Bill Creake says the floater who fetched up on the storm grid down in the docks looks like a suicide from Cleethorpes. Wife says he went for a walk four days ago along the beach, didn't come back. Left his dog tied to a post in the dunes, his shoes and socks neat and tidy. Age is about right – mid-fifties. He'd just been diagnosed with Alzheimer's. They're getting the dental records down.'

Shaw thought about the body in the mortuary at the Ark – the single arm protruding from the shroud, the marks at the wrist. 'OK – thanks.'

Then he stopped himself going on, annoyed that he hadn't tracked down that detail. 'Just one thing – ask Bill to ask the wife if he wore a watch. Perhaps he left that on the sands too? Only there's a mark on his wrist – odd. Maybe one of those copper bands to guard against rheumatism. Just let me know.'

Twine made a note, the Mont Blanc's nib scratching on notepaper.

The chatter in the room had begun to rise so Shaw pitched his voice just a little louder. 'Right. George and I have just interviewed Aidan Holme at the hospital,' said Shaw. 'He was brimful of pain-killers, but he *was* compos mentis. He understood that we'd found his fingerprints at the murder scene. I think he's told us the truth – so here it is . . .'

The room in intensive care had been like one of Jan Orzsak's fish tanks. Tubes bubbled, air tanks hissed, and the light was a sickly low-spectrum blue. Holme looked like he'd been smuggled out of the Valley of the Kings: bandages around his chest, throat, and one half of the skull – the right. The left half was red with the heat in the room, the visible eye encrusted with sleep.

Holme's voice was a whisper, but clear enough, if Shaw sat with his head bowed down to his lips, like a priest. Valentine had sat opposite, trying to take a note, and hadn't asked a question.

'I'm going to die,' said Holme, before Shaw could speak. They'd been briefed in the corridor outside by the consultant who said the patient's vital signs were poor. The burns had put a burden on his heart which had not responded to medication. He had a lung infection, septicaemia, and internal bleeding inside his skull where he'd struck his head on the road. He was too ill to survive an operation to relieve the pressure on the brain.

'You're in good hands here, the best,' said Shaw, resisting the urge to take his hand. On the side table by the bed were two cards, stiff and slightly formal, both asking the recipient to 'Get Well Soon'. There was a bowl of fruit and a bottle of Lucozade, unopened.

Shaw outlined what they knew. Holme listened with his eyes closed, each swallow making his Adam's apple creak.

When Shaw had finished he realized that Holme had been saving his strength, because when he opened his eye it was clearer, brighter.

'It wasn't difficult – at the furnace,' he said. 'That's my subject, right? Chemistry. I used to teach it. I'd make a package for each drug to swap for the canister. I'd know what was on the belt because Bry got to see a note telling the engineers what would be in the consignment. Take crack. The chemical signature is hydrogen, carbon, oxygen and nitrogen. But the key would be traces of sodium from the bicarbonate of soda used to make the rock.' He smiled, and winced with the pain of moving the flesh on his face. His throat started to spasm and it was only after a few seconds that Shaw realized he was laughing.

'You put it together in the basement of the house ...' said Shaw, recalling the chemistry lab equipment. He got his lips close to his ear. 'But how did you do the swap?'

'I got inside. Inside the machine. There's a maintenance door, you can slide in by the belt, so you're right there, just before the inner doors of the furnace. It's hot – too hot to touch anything. But it only takes a few seconds. When the stuff came through I'd take a stash; not all – just one canister, maybe two. That's the trick – don't be greedy. Then I'd put the package I'd made up on the belt. Straight swap. Once the last batch was on the belt the coppers were off anyway – so I'd only be inside for two, three minutes, max. Bry would knock and I'd slip out. I never told him how easy it was – best that way.' He tried to wink, the encrusted eye jerking open.

'How'd you get into the hospital?'

'Up the ladder, where Bry smoked. Foolproof – you just walk in off the street into the goods yard and wait until they take a break. You don't have to wait long. They brew up in a hut by the gate. You can't see the ladder from the yard.'

He closed his eyes.

'But then Bry wanted out? Like the family says?'

The eye came open, angry. 'Shit. No.' He shook his head despite the pain. 'That's Bry's story because they all *wanted* him to stop. But Bry – he was happy. Happy as he'd ever be. No. *I* wanted to stop. We'd fought over it; I'd been telling him for months. But this big shipment was coming in and he wanted to do it. And he wanted some serious money back – a full share: fifty-fifty. I went up there that last day to tell *him* I wouldn't do it.

'I had a life once. I wanted it back. I stopped using about eighteen months ago. So I was looking for a new start – a bit of cash to get me out, and up. So I tried a couple of deals, and got caught. I was going down, what-ever the lawyers say. I know enough people who've been down. If you supply it's OK. But you use too – no one can resist that. I thought, if I go in it'll kill me.'

He laughed silently, overcome by the irony.

'The lawyer'll tell you – we're looking at a deal that'll get us an open prison. One last chance. So I told Bryan we'd stop. I gave him a bottle of the Green Dragon – I told him if he wanted the stuff there's a bloke on the docks can get it. But, like, it costs too – top end, two-fifty quid, more. It's money he hasn't got. But that was going to be his problem, not mine.'

'What time did you see him?'

'Three – maybe half past. I met him up on that ledge where he smoked. I told him again, that it was over. He wasn't happy but, like, what's he going to do about it?

He said he'd find someone else. I told him, that's dangerous, but if he wanted to, it was his life. But I was out of it. I left him about four – alive as you or I. Well, maybe just you.' The effort of speaking had overcome him, and the laugh made him choke. Then he'd closed his eyes and slept.

Shaw sipped his Guinness. The Red House was silent.

'So, there was a drugs trade. But Bryan Judd didn't die trying to get out of it. He wanted in, not out.'

'We believe this stuff?' It was DC Lau, a bottle pressed to her lips. 'What if they argued anyway? Judd might have gone for him, they struggle, and whack!' She knocked the bottle on the table top.

'What was there to argue about?' asked Shaw. 'Holme *was* going down – and they needed his expertise to do the switch. And we've checked his story with the brief and it all matches up. They'd agreed a change of plea, to guilty. There was too much hard evidence – CPS has the case, I've looked at the file. No, Holme was up for a plea bargain and there was a good chance he'd get it. There was nothing Bryan Judd could do about it.'

Chatter filled the room.

'Let's put drugs to one side,' said Shaw, and the room fell silent. 'I'm not saying forget it – I'm saying to one side, for now.'

Birley went to the bar to get refills, while Shaw nursed the Guinness, reading some of the reports from door-to-door. And three notes. The first was a progress report on tracking down Pete Hendre, the hostel resident Shaw had saved from the burning upper floor of number 6 Erebus Street, who'd slipped out of the Queen Vic despite police surveillance. CID at Hunstanton had checked out the church where he worked as a volunteer – no sign, and nothing at his flat, a one-room bedsit in sheltered housing in the town. But Shaw recalled that Kennedy had said Hendre was in town to see a solicitor about a will. Maybe it was an appointment he couldn't afford to miss. He scrawled a note to remind himself to get a message out to the local branch of the Law Society, see if they could track down the lawyers.

The second note was from Newcastle CID. He flicked over a few pages. They'd traced Ben Ruddle, the teenager who'd got Norma Jean Judd pregnant in 1992. He'd been released from Deerbolt, County Durham, in 1994, having been found guilty on the burglary charge. There was no record of him returning home. He was back inside in 2000, for burglary again. The case came up at Castle Barnard, County Durham – thirty-one other offences of a similar nature taken into account. Out eighteen months ago from Acklington, again County Durham. Probation service had a record of him working in a market garden, outside Middlesbrough. He went missing six months ago, after picking up his wages. Teesside Social Services had a record of him turning up in a homeless shelter: six nights. He was interviewed – then, next day, off the radar.

'Middlesbrough,' said Shaw, handing the note to Valentine to read.

The third note was from Twine. The Military Corrective Training Centre at Colchester, the military's last remaining 'glasshouse', had contacted St James's. They needed help tracking down Petty Officer Andrew Sean Judd, who had absconded from custody while serving an eighteen-month sentence imposed by a military court at Portsmouth. He'd stolen canteen supplies and sold them on to corner shops in the city. Judd had been missing for three weeks. His home address was still listed as 14 Erebus Street.

Valentine read that note, too.

'Let's dig a bit more on both of those,' said Shaw. 'This final Ruddle interview – with the social – see if we can get a transcript. And pictures. Colchester will have a mug of Sean Judd, and Acklington'll have Ruddle. Let's get both.'

'What you thinking?' asked Valentine.

'I'm thinking I'd like to see the faces.'

Shaw stood, fished a handful of drawing pins from his pocket, and pinned a foolscap piece of white paper onto the jaundiced wallpaper. Someone whistled and a couple clapped. It could have been a drawing of anyone, but there was no doubt that in its own way it was a work of art. Shaw's skills as a forensic artist were known to them all – he gave regular lectures at Hendon, the Met's training centre, and was one of only half a dozen officers with the qualification in the country. He wrote articles for *Jane's Police Review*. But seen in the flesh, as it were, the result was startling. This wasn't a police ID with pencils. It was a living person, a classic example of the kind of animated graphic which was making forensic art part of mainstream police work around the world, replacing the disjointed jigsaw of the traditional photofit.

It *was* a striking face. The principal feature was the gap at the bridge of the nose, especially wide, pushing the eyes apart. One of the front teeth was chipped. The bone structure was heavy, the hair thick and black; but the jaw was an oddity, unusually fine, weak even, and dimpled. It wasn't a face you'd forget.

Shaw was proud of this because it was the first time in a live investigation he'd used the techniques of age-progression to produce an image. And it was the first piece of work he'd done since losing his right eye a year earlier. He'd been told by the occupational therapists that his ability to sketch – and to take photographs – would actually improve with monocular vision. In effect he didn't have to close one eye, the classic artist's pose. What he saw now, with one eye, was a 2D flat image – exactly the image he could transfer to the sketch pad. He hadn't believed them, but now he could see the proof.

Shaw cut the chatter by tapping his Guinness glass with Twine's Mont Blanc.

'OK. I'll come back to our friend here. But first – the big picture. We've all read the briefing note, so I won't waste your time. The last few hours of the inquiry have opened up two possible ways forward. First, Jan Orzsak and Andy Judd. They're tangled up together in the case of Norma Jean. Did one of them go up to the hospital last night – the anniversary of her disappearance? We need to re-examine the Orzsak alibi minute by minute; that's a priority for tomorrow. The father's still an outside possibility – let's dig some more. George will put together a team. And when we can, let's gently see if we can get Ally Judd and the priest to talk – what if Bryan Judd knew about their affair? Come to that, is it an affair, or is it just gossip?

'Which leaves our major line of inquiry: illegal organ disposal. A human kidney was found under Judd's body on the hospital incinerator. Question: is this a one-off illegal transplant in which Judd plays the key role of incinerating the incriminating tissue, or just a glimpse of a wide-ranging illegal system of organ trafficking and transplant run from within the hospital? If it is, and we have to be prepared for that, we're looking for two groups of people.

'One – clients. The rich, the unscrupulous. So far we've haven't had a whiff. So let's think about that. Two – donors, either willing, or unwilling. Pete Hendre, the man we got out of the top floor at number 6 when the place was on fire, said he didn't want to come out because there was someone in the street he was afraid of: the Organ Grinder. Just that. I said afraid, but terrified is closer. Hendre's done a runner – we need to find him. And we've got a missing person, violently abducted. The man with no name except Blanket. Someone came and found him under cover of darkness. Someone offered him a "deal" – which he declined to take. And there's a chance that that someone was Bryan Judd's killer. Obvious question: was Blanket, *is* Blanket, an unwilling donor? If he is we need to find him, fast.'

Shaw put a finger on the sketch. 'I think this is what he looks like. We don't know his name. He's a tramp who says he's spent most of his life in Middlesbrough but has no accent to match and, according to Liam Kennedy, an unnerving amount of local knowledge. He was never seen without his blanket coat. Last night he was dragged, unconscious, out of the Sacred Heart of Mary by an unidentified man. The coat – which was left behind – was marked on the back with a rough sketch of a candle. I repeat, we need to find him. Let's call in a few favours, try all our contacts, really rattle the cage. Separate question: who is he? We don't know. But two long shots: Sean Judd – the victim's oldest brother – is on the run from the Colchester military prison. Did he come back to Erebus Street? If he did, he'd know the Red Caps would be watching the house – or getting us to – so was that why he hid in the hostel? Or is it perhaps Ben Ruddle – the father of Norma Jean's baby? Did he have unfinished business on Erebus Street? After all, if Norma Jean was murdered then the killer robbed him of two things – a wife-to-be, perhaps, and a child.'

They all studied Blanket's face. Campbell, her six foot two inches perched on a tiny stool, asked the question they all wanted answered.

'This image – where did it come from?'

'Blanket's possessions included a snapshot of a small boy in 1984. The picture – like most from that far back – is actually very high quality. I blew it up, then aged it thirty years. It's not rocket science – but then it doesn't have to fly.'

Everyone laughed except George Valentine.

'How do you do it?' asked Birley.

'The FBI leads the world in this. In the eighties they started using it to track down missing kids. Usually there are two methods combined. On one hand you study the family and see if you can pick out genetic patterns. On the other there are general principles of craniofacial development – it's obvious stuff, just look at your own kids if you've got any. Their faces grow down, and forward. Stuff like that. But the good news for us is that most faces retain an essential lifelong look – for anyone taking notes that's gnomatic growth. We've all done it – looked at family pictures and instantly recognized Grandad seventy years ago. The trick is spotting what elements of the face will remain static.'

He sipped his Guinness. 'Lecture over. The health warnings are clear, though – we've got no DNA input here, no parentage to feed into the mix, and I've used my instincts not a computer program to run the progression forward. That might be a plus, maybe not.'

'Does it look like Sean Judd?' asked Twine. 'I mean, does it look like the family?'

They all looked then, trying to see Bryan Judd's face.

'Maybe,' said Shaw. 'But maybe not. We're getting pictures of Sean Judd and Ruddle. We might strike lucky. Until then, keep an open mind. I ran it past Kennedy and he says it's a close likeness – but then he didn't really see that much past the curtain of hair so let's not get too excited. Anyway, there is no doubt it's the best picture we've got. You'll all have a copy tomorrow. And I'll get one to the *Lynn News*, *Look East* and *Anglia Tonight*.'

They drank in silence.

'Paul's going to go on summarizing all the evidence,' continued Shaw. 'Statements, anything we think's relevant, all boiled down into a single online file. A thousand words, no more, every day. I want you all to read it when it's posted. We'll update as we go along. It's links we're looking for, so I want everyone up to speed. The organ transplant information remains confidential. Talk to nobody. If I see it in the press I'll find out who leaked it. That's not an idle promise.'

He stood, then drained his pint. 'My round.'

He bought everyone a drink except himself. The some-times cloying bonhomie, the esprit de corps of the CID, was never his natural environment. He could imagine his father staying late, chewing over the fat, eking out ideas. But that wasn't his style. After being knocked out of a darts match at nine thirty he bought a few more drinks then slipped out to the loo in the yard, and from there through a gate in the fence, straight out into the street. The windows of the pub were open so that the sounds flooded out into the flagged street. He walked away from the noise of other people.

24

He'd booked the video suite at St James's for nine forty-five. A windowless room behind the front desk, stinking of Flash and stale coffee. Closing the door he sat down, knowing that if Lena knew this was what he was doing, she'd effortlessly unleash that high-pressure anger he knew she kept just beneath the cool surface of her skin. Because this wasn't what she'd meant when she said he needed to make or break the Tessier case; the chances of him finding anything on the video that was new after thirteen years was close to zero. No, this was an obsession, and he was feeding it. He felt furtive, guilty, and strangely excited. Outside, the desk sergeant was trying to book in a pair of drunks picked up on the quayside, their voices overloud, cloyingly cooperative. Around him he could hear the sounds of St James's: a phone ringing unanswered, cars being shuffled in the vehicle pool, the cleaners running floor-polishers upstairs in CID.

Slipping in the video cassette he'd picked up from records he concentrated on the black, flickering screen, until he saw a white caption roll up.

I.O. DI Ronald Blake.
Tape owned by BC KL&WN.
Case. GV 5632 HH.

Then a picture, the usual grainy CCTV footage, black and white, made worse by the late-night lighting and a steady drizzle.

A T-junction Shaw knew well, where the road from Castle Rising crossed a long straight stretch of the B-road which ran out towards one of the bird reserves and a few lonely farmhouses. A deadly spot, even now, because of the thick woods which obscured the view left and right as you approached the junction. There'd been crashes before, despite warning signs, not least because the arrow-straight mile of open road was a magnet for joyriders. The junction was lit by a set of high lights on which was set the CCTV camera. The ticking digital clock showed the time on screen: 12.31 a.m. No date. But he knew that: 21 July 1997.

Shaw found himself trying not to blink in case he missed it. A fox trotted happily across the picture from the woods towards the village. Then the first car, on the dual carriageway, swishing past at a steady 60 m.p.h., wipers going.

A rat dashed along the verge.

Then it happened, so quickly it made him jump. A car crossing the picture on the dual carriageway at 60 m.p.h. – perhaps a little faster. And out of nowhere a second car, from the village, cutting across, swerving at 80, 85 m.p.h. It caught the first car side-on, shunting it to the far carriageway, where it turned over once and then bounced on its suspension. Then an unnatural stillness. The street lights caught the smashed glass on the tarmac. The second car, the one that had caused the accident, had left the picture.

He replayed it to that point in slow motion. Since the tape had first been viewed in 1997 new technology allowed the images to be viewed in separate frames, enhanced, magnified. But Shaw saw nothing new, except perhaps the smudge of debris and splinters at the point of impact, like a breath on a cold day. He froze the film several times and zoomed in on the licence plate of the second car but a combination of the speed and the poor film quality made it impossible to read.

Then he let it run on – still in slow motion. The second car, its bonnet buckled, trundled back into the picture, at the edge of vision, up on the verge in the shadows under some trees. Nothing moved for forty-five seconds – then three youths got out, two from the rear seats, one from the driver's. In the shadows where the car was Shaw could just see the windscreen and the wipers still wiping. The three wore baseball caps, T-shirts, jeans, and each had something wrapped round his lower face – a sweat-shirt, a football scarf ... That's what they'd done in that dead forty-five seconds – because they knew there were cameras, so they'd masked their faces. The three walked to the other car and peered in through the shattered side windows. One of them vomited at his feet, the other two started fighting, pushing, almost hugging. Then they all stood still, watching a spreading black stain which had formed beneath the passenger-side's buckled doors.

One walked towards the CCTV mounted by the T-junction and looked up between the peak of his cap and the scarf round his neck and lower face. Cool, appraising. He looked back at the Mini parked under the trees, perhaps satisfying himself the camera couldn't read the plates. But they couldn't be sure the camera hadn't caught the licence number on the way past, thought Shaw. Another one of the three went to the far side of the wrecked car and pulled open a door, leaning in, appearing again holding something in the crook of his arm. Something fragile, something wrapped. Then they all went back to the car. When they drove off they backed out of the picture, to avoid getting close to the camera again. The victim's car stood alone, and Shaw watched it until he saw a small movement in the rear side window – a hand, splayed once, then dropping out of sight.

The written report which went with the CCTV had formed the basis of the press article Shaw had read to Lena and laid out the details found at the scene: the two dead OAPs in the rear seats. The driver, neck broken, but still alive. The tyre marks. And the evidence of the CCTV itself – a narrative description of the film Shaw had just watched. No IDs possible for the three men, or the car, although the paint job on the vehicle was distinctive – a central white band over the doors and roof – leaving the boot and bonnet in another colour. From the hue it looked grey-blue.

The film was eight minutes long, and Shaw watched it six times. At first he concentrated on the fragile bundle, not mentioned in the report. Too small for a child. It was a guess, and only a guess, but it may have been that the original CID team had withheld the fact one of the youths had taken something from the car – a detail they could use to weed out crank confessions. But what was in the bundle?

He watched the film again. There *was* something

wrong. But what was it? Something that didn't fit. Something that jarred.

'Who's in the passenger seat?' he asked himself. 'Why would two teenagers go out on a joyride and sit in the back? Is there someone in the front seat – or is there something on the front seat?'

He found the image again of the windscreen when the car came to rest under the trees. He drew a cursor round the darkened area on the passenger side and blew the image up: ×10, ×20, ×50. But the film's original poor quality made the images chaotic, an illogical patchwork of black and grey.

Shaw printed out half a dozen stills from the footage.

He looked at one frame of the three men standing on the road. Could one of these young men be Robert Mosse, the 21-year-old Shaw's father and George Valentine had arrested for the murder of Jonathan Tessier? He'd been a member of a gang of juvenile thugs in his teenage years before leaving for university. A gang of *four*. In the weeks leading up to Tessier's murder he'd been at home, back amongst his roots. Had he gone out for a joyride, a few drinks with old friends, and then a late-night high-speed romp, just like old times? Or – another possibility – had he gone for the joyride but been smart enough to stay in the car after the crash? Was he there, amongst the grey and black shadows, in the passenger seat?

He looked at a still image of the Mini, the wind-screen speckled with raindrops except where it had been cleaned by the wipers. There was still something wrong. Something *else* wrong.

He popped out the cassette, put it in the machine above, and made three copies. He took his copies, and the stills, and deposited the original back at the duty desk. When he got in the Land Rover he pinned that same image on the dashboard. He looked at it for ten minutes, then gave up, turned the ignition key and swung out into a deserted St James's.

25

Tuesday, 7 September

Two hours after dawn, and low tide in Morston Creek; no view except the mudbanks, oystercatchers planting webbed feet in the sticky ooze. The boat nosed its way through the maze of creeks out into Blakeney Channel. The sky was stretched-blue, dotted with clouds which would later billow into chimneys of heated, moist air. But the morning was cool still, the smell of the tidal waters salty and fresh.

Shaw sucked the sea air in like a drug. He'd had a call from DC Twine in the murder room at 5.30: a body had been spotted by a fishing smack on a sandbank in the Wash. Tom Hadden had gone out on the Harbour Conservancy launch with his night-duty CSI officer. He'd texted Twine to say there was a link with the Judd murder – no details. Shaw didn't need to go to sea himself – but he was awake, and he had his father's mantra: if you *can* see it for yourself, see it for yourself. And if he was losing sleep, he didn't see why DS Valentine shouldn't too.

The tourist boat *Albatross* broke into open water, following a channel marked by buoys past the small craft moored in the shallows. Hadden had called out anyone on the CSI payroll who wasn't tied up on the Judd inquiry. Half a dozen of them sat morosely in the boat cradling their kit, smoking, drinking tea from flasks. Valentine stood at the back talking to the man at the tiller, an eye on the sooty net-curtain of rain which fell from a lone storm cloud, edging inland.

Twine had the bare details from the crew who'd spotted the body. The *Kittyhawk* had landed three men at sunrise on Warham's Hole, a stretch of sand the size of a football pitch. Basking seals had scattered as soon as they'd come ashore, to retrieve a string of crab pots which had broken loose during the night. When the seals were gone something was left: one of those industrial bags, incredibly strong, used on building sites to carry rubble, or sand, or hard core. It held assorted rubbish – tin cans, oil drums, and what the *Kittyhawk*'s captain reported as 'human remains'.

Valentine sat, pulling his raincoat up to his ears. 'Here it comes,' he said, looking up at the sky. The rain began to fall in drops the size of paperweights, leisurely, then in a frenzy, turning swiftly to hailstones which stung the flesh. Visibility dropped to twenty feet, the air white with plummeting ice, the hailstones lying in the boat and in the folds of Shaw's all-weather jacket. They chugged on, the summer boat trip suddenly transformed into a snapshot from some Antarctic expedition. Valentine felt ice-cold water beginning to insinuate itself down his neck. He thought about the coke fire in the Artichoke; the intensity of the heat on the palms of his downturned hands.

The blue sky appeared overhead even before the hailstones had stopped falling. Then the sun broke through, and Shaw saw that they were there – fifty yards off the island of sand. About forty grey seals lounged amongst the melting hailstones. Two or three pairs half-heartedly cuffed each other or rolled in tumbles. Around the *Albatross* heads appeared in the sea, disappeared, like fairground targets.

'There,' said Valentine, pointing at two figures on the far lip of the sand working beside a grey bag, long and narrow like a deflated balloon. The spot had been marked by the *Kittyhawk* with an orange distress buoy.

In two feet of water Shaw stepped overboard. The seals, mildly inquisitive of the floating boat, panicked as the humans stepped ashore, shuffling towards the sea, trapped, it seemed, in sleeping bags. Within a minute they'd deserted Warham's Hole.

The CSI team jumped ship and unloaded a mobile SOC tent and lights. Shaw led the way about eighty yards across the ribbed sand – hard, crystalline, surprisingly solid. Beside the asbestos-grey bag Hadden had laid out its contents in military rows: about thirty tin cans, some metal tubs which had once held machine oil, and three black bin liners – one of them torn – to reveal more rubbish, mostly discarded food wrapping. Shaw could see a cardboard pizza box and a plastic curry tray. All that was left in the bag, which had been stretched open, was a corpse on its side, one hand thrown backwards, the fingers of the hand stiff and swollen, the arm extended like a waiter's offering a salver of champagne glasses.

Hadden was examining a piece of nylon rope which had been threaded through the four handles of the bag. Shaw could see where the rope was still kinked by the memory of the knot.

'Weights?' asked Valentine.

Hadden nodded. They were all thinking the same thing. The sack, weighted down with the rope attached to an anchor or lead weight.

'If the knot hadn't slipped we'd have never seen chummy again,' said Shaw. 'He'd have been fish food within the week. How long's he been in, Tom?'

'Rigor's still apparent,' said Hadden. 'So – given the water's not that warm – forty-eight hours? Maximum of forty-eight – maybe less, Peter.'

Shaw still couldn't see the face. But he could see the victim was male, white, middle aged, wearing jogging pants and a sweatshirt, the head shaved. The skin showed all the signs of immersion, puckered and swollen, but was otherwise intact, free of feeding marks. There was a washed-out bloodstain on the sweatshirt chest. Hadden used gloved hands to lift the material, revealing a gunshot wound.

'Justina needs to tell you about this,' he said. 'But if you want an amateur's opinion, I'd say this killed him. It's very close to the heart.'

'Calibre?' asked Shaw.

'Nine millimetres – a handgun. Difficult to tell range, Peter. He's been in the water too long for any residue to be left on the skin. But it's not point-blank. I can't say any more.'

Shaw leant in. He couldn't smell anything except an intense aroma of the sea, like oysters on a bed of ice. He noted acne on the body's exposed neck. 'It's not Blanket,' he said. 'Height and weight are wrong.'

And one detail he didn't see first time – only three

fingers and a thumb on the right hand, an old scar where the index finger should have been.

'This is why I called . . .' said Hadden, handing Shaw an evidence bag. Inside was a plastic charity wristband. Valentine had seen Shaw wearing one in the spring – red and blue, with RNLI printed on the ring. Shaw turned it to catch the early slanting sun and saw that three letters were stencilled in the white plastic.

MVR.

Shaw thought about that – about what kind of organization would have charity bands made, and issue torches with the letters on as well. Silently he decided that he needed to make a personal visit to the hospital vehicle pool.

'The band's luminous, by the way,' said Hadden. 'If that helps.'

Shaw handed Valentine the bag. 'Can we see the face – you've not turned him over?'

Hadden called up one of his team, who took a set of pictures. Then Hadden took hold of the dead man's shoulder, Shaw his thigh, and they rolled him over, the dead arm flailing.

The face was almost perfect – untouched. The lips were blue, a light stubble on the chin, the nose slender and almost feminine. There were only two things missing.

The eyes.

26

Valentine watched a thin line of tourists in blue and red cagoules walking out over the tidal mud on duckboards, queuing to climb aboard one of the seal trip boats moored on Morston Creek. Valentine had brought 'solids' from the National Trust shop – a game pie, a coffee, and a packet of Hula Hoops.

Shaw was on the mobile, tracking down DI William Creake.

'Bill?' he said, cupping the phone, turning his back on the sea breeze.

'Yeah – fine, good. She's well. Look. I need your help. You know this stiff down on the docks – the one they found on the storm grid? Right. I know. Have you got the records down from Cleethorpes yet – the missing person?'

Shaw looked at Valentine and couldn't help a weary glance up to the sky. 'No? Yeah – it takes time. But you're sure of that – the widow says he never wore a watch? Right. I was in the Ark for the autopsy on our man from the hospital and I couldn't help noticing your one had marks on his wrist. So, if it's not a watch . . .'

Shaw's shoulder sagged. He listened for a minute, then cut the line.

He walked towards Valentine's Mazda talking over his shoulder. 'Creake's just read the original witness statements. Something he'd missed – one of the workmen who found the floater said he was caught on the grid by a plastic band on his wrist, snagged on the mesh. It's with the victim's personal effects at St James's – Bill's checking it out. But I think we know what letters are stencilled on it, don't we?'

Shaw was angry, but not as angry as George Valentine. He'd spent ten years of his life on the north Norfolk coast – busted down to DS – running a case load dominated by petty theft at weekend cottages and the odd half-hearted armed robbery at an amusement arcade. Meanwhile police officers as incompetent as Bill Creake had been made up to DI.

'Ring Justina for me, George. Tell her I want another examination of the floater – tell her to make up any excuse she wants to get it off Rigby. It doesn't usually take much.'

Valentine made the call. He threw the mobile onto the dashboard. 'Why wristbands?' he asked.

'I don't know, but I can have a guess. They're ID bands; last thing you want to do in a transplant operation is mix up donor and recipient. Maybe it's that simple – white for donors, red for recipients. Like I said, I don't know. But if Bill Creake had done his job I could have started trying to find out yesterday – which would have been a big plus.'

Valentine thought how often it was that the simple details brought a crime to life. He still couldn't get the image of the victim they'd just found out of his mind. 'There's a market for human eyes?' he asked, avoiding Shaw's.

'Yes. There's a market for everything. There's a market for the bones.'

'And MVR?' asked Valentine.

'I still think it's the motor pool – especially now. This isn't some backstreet one-off op, George. This is trade. This has to be a donor. Bill Creake's floater too. Then there's Blanket – where's he gone? This isn't just about Bryan Judd's murder any more – although as he isn't a donor, he may be the key to this. We need to get this info to people who can help us. As soon as we get to the incident room get on it, George – Interpol, the Yard, Customs, the lot. And we need to shake down the hospital – surgeons, nursing staff, everyone.'

Valentine drove, lighting a Silk Cut from the Mazda's dashboard lighter, keeping his eyes on the road. He had that trick of being able to keep his eyes open even when the smoke got in them. When they parked outside A&E, they slapped a 'Police' sign on the windscreen. Twine was in the incident room, with Birley still running through CCTV footage.

'Where's Jofranka Phillips?' asked Shaw, taking a coffee from a tray.

'Organ bank, sir, with the inquiry team. She'll be there all day.'

'Right.' He told Twine what they'd found on Warham's Hole, and the link with Bill Creake's floater in the storm grid. 'MVR. There has to be a link,' he said. 'So let's shut the garage down – seal it. Get a description of the body out on the sands to all the papers. Hadden says there's a missing finger – the scar's an old one, so that helps. Don't mention organ removal. We'll hold off for another twenty-four hours on that – then make a splash. We need to get the team trawling through the hospital staff, Paul. Let's start at the top. Do we have anything on Phillips and Peploe? Background, HR files . . . anything?'

Twine nodded, expertly sifting through documents on the computer, then printing out two sheets of A4. Shaw read Peploe first – a life in 350 words. Standard education for the son of a Perth doctor. A good school, then Edinburgh University, then a post at a New York clinic specializing in restorative cosmetic surgery for young children. He was forty-five, married, with two grown-up children. In 1989 he had taken part in the Whitbread Round the World Race as part of a team based in Southampton, sponsored by Goldman Sachs.

Jofranka Phillips's life story had been defined by her father – Kalo Kircher. A surgeon at a private hospital in Neustadt, western Germany, in the 1930s, he was a pioneer in early operations to remove cataracts. At the outbreak of the Second World War he had been rounded up and transported to a Jewish holding centre at Mannheim, and then sent to the death camp at Chelmno in Poland. He was not a Jew. He was a member of the Roma, the once-footloose people who had dispersed across Europe; the true cultural forebears of the gypsies. He was a Roman Catholic. Like many Roma, he'd simply taken on one of the religions of his adopted country.

For the Nazis the Roma were as eligible for extermin-ation as the Jews. Kalo's medical qualifications enabled him to escape the mobile gas vans of Chelmno. Instead, he was forced to assist staff under the command of Dr Eduard Wirths. A series of barbaric experiments were undertaken at Chelmno in an attempt to prove the Nazis' racial theories. In 1945, when the camp was liberated, Kircher was found hanging from a roof beam in the block reserved for those prisoners who had worked for the Nazis. He wasn't dead. A medical team with the Soviet Army saved his life.

Kalo returned to Neustadt, then part of West Germany, and helped reorganize surgical services in the city. In 1958 an application was made by the State of Israel for Kircher's extradition to stand trial for war crimes committed at Chelmno. Kircher was found hanging in his holding cell where he had been awaiting interview. The noose had been fashioned from the stethoscope in the medical bag he'd been carrying when picked up outside his surgery. This time he was successful. His daughter was born posthumously in early 1959. She moved with her mother – a GP – and her three elder brothers to London in 1962. A private school, a degree in medicine at Bristol, and a series of positions at major hospitals followed. Phillips was divorced, with no children. The brothers had all taken medical degrees and practised in the US – two in California, one in Maine. All the brothers supported a charity which provided free medical care for the poor in Israel.

Shaw folded the two sheets of paper inside his jacket. It was one of the oddities of police work; that you got to meet people, then strip down their lives without them knowing. He'd never got over the sense of intrusion. He swigged back the last of the double espresso.

DC Birley had been waiting for Shaw to finish reading. 'Sir,' he said, nodding towards the bank of CCTV screens. 'I've got something.' He pulled up seats for all of them, then began running a cassette on the main screen. 'Got to this an hour ago,' he said. 'Paul's got some software which cleans up the image – this is the original . . .'

The main screen flickered, then showed a sunlit car park.

'The camera's over the entrance to the Bluebell – that's the maternity hospital. I left it till last – big mistake.' The Bluebell shared the site with the main hospital, a single covered walkway linking the two main buildings.

A man and a woman came into view from beneath the camera position and shared a cigarette. Then a large figure in what looked like a set of workman's overalls walked surprisingly quickly into shot, then into the hospital. Movement was jerky, the figure seeming to disappear, then reappear, with each small laboured step.

'This is the best image after we'd run it through the clever stuff,' said Birley.

The image cleared, then reappeared, sharper, the grey edged out by black and white. It was Jan Orzsak, glancing up at the sky as he stepped into the shadows of the Bluebell maternity wing.

'Time and date?' asked Valentine.

'That's the really good news. Seven thirty on the target day – Sunday evening.'

They'd already checked out Jan Orzsak's alibi and they'd been able to track his movements throughout Sunday except for the two hours before he'd arrived at the Polish Club at nine. Now they knew why.

'Let's get him in,' said Shaw. He leant back in his seat, looking up at the neon strip above. 'No, forget that. We'll go to him.' He checked his watch. 'One hour. George and I will be there.' He shook his head. Every time he set aside the story of Norma Jean Judd he regretted it. Her disappearance eighteen years earlier seemed to run through the case like letters through seaside rock. Letters in code. But the link between the two sides of the case – the trade in organs and the disappearance of Bryan Judd's sister – eluded him still. And he had to fight now, to keep the broader view in mind. This wasn't a single murder inquiry any more. It was a multiple murder inquiry.

'Orzsak plays the organ at the church,' said Valentine, their thoughts marching side by side. 'Maybe he's the man – the man on the street, the collector, bringing in the donors.' Valentine thought about the crushed slippers, the weight on the shoes. 'Maybe he needs special shoes – he's bad on his feet. You get those built-up ones, they'd make a noise.'

'I'm going to check the organ bank audit,' said Shaw. 'Then we'll see Orzsak. Meantime, get over to MVR, George. Inch by inch – it's got to be the place we're looking for. Paul, when we've got the resources get started on the staff checks. And I want everything you can find on Orzsak: employment records, family, the Polish Club – check it all. Then get anything relevant to George, fast as you can.' He stood. 'Because we know one thing about Jan Orzsak,' he said, laying a hand on top of the CCTV monitor. 'He's a liar.'

27

The organ bank was at the far western perimeter of Level One. Shaw walked alone, telling himself that the gentle echo of footsteps behind him was just that – an echo. And that the soft footfall contained no hint of a metallic click. He started listing the turnings in his head, following the little red direction arrows for A5, the code for the bank. Left, left, right, left, right. The full lighting petered out, to be replaced by the occasional neon tube on half power. Lines of tugs and trucks were stored in the wide corridors. He passed a single maintenance man working on a water-pipe junction, the irregular percussion of a hammer on metal. And then, bizarrely out of place, a line of tug trucks decorated with Disney-style characters, a float for some long-forgotten parade, a platform on the back for a carnival queen.

Eventually there was just one corridor, a hundred yards long, with a single light-bulb at the far end where a uniformed PC sat on a chair in front of an unmarked door. The sight was bizarre, surreal, like a snapshot from some Cold War movie. For the first time Shaw *had* to look over his shoulder. Nothing – and the echo stopped too, instantly. The PC stood and opened the door. Another corridor, twenty feet, with four doors. Shaw suddenly realized he had no idea what to expect to find in an organ bank. It was a semantic cliché without a corresponding visual image. The corridor was dusty, empty, and narrow, the doors alphabetically labelled. It reminded Shaw of a Czech fairy tale he'd seen on TV as a child where the hero was given a choice between doors – three to hell, and one to heaven. Here, he thought, the odds weren't as good.

He pushed open door 'A' and stepped into a floodlit room, about the size of a railway carriage, with one long wall lined with what looked like standard supermarket freezers except the tops were opaque, not glass. But the electrics were sophisticated – each white box attached to a panel of blinking lights. LCD screens showed flickering temperatures in blue light.

One of the freezer boxes was open, like a white coffin, cold air spilling over. The contents had been laid out on a plastic sheet on the top of the next freezer. Phillips was watching two orderlies repack the open box; she was dressed in white, spotless trousers, white forensic gloves, the black hair under a white cap, although a strand hung down by her cheek in a coal-black corkscrew. The frozen plastic bags of tissue provided the only colour in the room – the lifeless blood-red of a supermarket meat counter.

Phillips smiled, her face flooded with what looked like genuine relief, and those extraordinary eyes, which were a living contradiction of electric grey. The chill in the room made her look paler, an even starker contrast to the black hair, the jet bangles. She shook Shaw's hand. 'So far, so good,' she said. 'The audit team's in B now. But this one's been cleared. They've matched all the stored material with operations listed in the six NHS theatres. They've taken one out of every ten specimens away for analysis –

to make sure what's in the bags matches the coded labels. But as I say, so far, so good. We couldn't hope for more.'

Shaw told her what they'd found on Warham's Hole.

She brushed the back of her hand against her cheek, and Shaw noticed again the long flexible fingers.

'Tell me about cornea transplants,' he said.

She lifted the edge of the freezer. 'No,' said Shaw quickly, holding up both hands. 'Just *tell* me.'

'OK. Well, it's pretty much like most transplants, except the donor's always dead. No surgeon would remove a healthy one from a living patient. Like kidneys, there's two, but the comparison breaks down pretty quickly – we need two eyes to see stereoscopically.'

She stopped in her tracks, suddenly aware this was a topic on which Shaw was probably well up to speed. She forced herself to look him in the eyes. 'Op's been around for a century. I guess the only material difference is that you can gift your eyes and they can be removed up to twenty-four hours after death – that's much longer than usual. There are no blood vessels in a cornea, you see, for obvious reasons. You wouldn't get a very good view out.'

'But they're valuable?'

'Oh yes. Very. Especially those of younger donors – obviously most are from donors over sixty-five. There's a special technique for keeping them once removed – I think there's a centre for storage in Manchester. But you'll have to ask Gavin. He's done some work up there. I think a friend of his runs the unit.'

It was the way she said 'friend' that invited Shaw to ask the question. 'What kind of friend?'

She smiled, as you would over the exploits of some

mischievous but gifted child. 'One of his lady friends. That's Gavin – our very own playboy. He's a charming man.'

Shaw thought about the quick CV he'd just read. 'And the wife?'

'Divorce, I think – but then that's none of my business,' said Phillips. She buttoned her white coat one notch higher against the cold. 'One thing, speaking of Gavin. The audit team will give you chapter and verse, but we do have a private operating theatre here at the hospital. Theatre Seven. They have a facility for storage here in bank D. They haven't checked that out yet, obviously, but on the paperwork side there are, in theory, spaces in their theatre schedule.'

'What's that in English?' asked Shaw.

'The NHS system runs pretty much at capacity – and when the theatre's not in use in normal hours it's usually being cleaned up or the maintenance crews are in. The private side's different – intermittent. So there are gaps in which an operation might take place illegally, if unrecorded. It's only a theoretical possibility, but one you should know about.'

The orderlies had repacked the bank. The lid closed with a pop.

'This isn't what I expected,' said Shaw, looking round.

'You mean it's a bit like Iceland?' Phillips laughed, the professional coolness thawing.

Shaw recalled DC Twine's brief biographical note on Phillips's father, Kalo Kircher, the concentration-camp doctor. He tried to imagine what kind of legacy that had left for his daughter.

'It's clinical,' said Shaw, laughing too. 'Gives me the creeps,' he said, laying a hand on the cool lid of the nearest freezer. 'I always feel guilty in hospitals – it's the not being ill that does it.'

'Yes. That disappears when you have a role. A job to do. Otherwise you feel like a spectator, don't you?'

Shaw nodded. 'It ran in your family, didn't it? Medicine.'

'Yes.' The chin came up. She was shrewd enough to know that Shaw had already done his research. 'My father was a fine doctor.'

Shaw let the silence stretch.

'He had little choice but to do what he was told to do, Inspector Shaw. They'd have killed him instantly if he'd refused.'

'Just following orders?' Shaw raised an eyebrow, knowing how inflammatory the question was.

She slipped her hands in the white coat pockets and looked at her shoes, not rising to the bait. 'He did what he could – many small kindnesses. There would have been witnesses at the trial to speak for him. It wasn't that he couldn't live with the victims, it was that he couldn't live with himself. We're outsiders too – the Roma. Just like the Jews.'

'But at home here,' said Shaw.

'Yes. At home here.' She led the way out, then locked the door behind them. 'I have the key back,' she said, adding it to a bunch hanging from a white belt. 'Let's hope the others follow.' She turned, knocked on the door marked B. 'Goodbye,' she said, and slipped inside.

Shaw tried to retrace his steps towards the central lifts,

but like many journeys attempted in reverse he found himself lost very quickly. He got to a junction marked 41, stopped, and looked three ways. There were no coded signs. Then he heard the distinct sound of footsteps, out of sight but strangely rhythmic, the shoes clipping down hard, unnaturally hard, on the concrete floor.

To one side there was a door marked DRY RISER, set back, so that there was a threshold. Shaw stood within, in the shadow, listening. Opposite him was another inset door, a sign that read HEARING VOICES NETWORK.

The footsteps became louder, crisper, until Shaw sensed the walker was almost upon him. He stepped out into the corridor. The figure, in silhouette, was ten feet away. Shaw held up his warrant card. 'Sorry. Police. Can I ask why you're down here?'

There was a neon light on half power and the figure kept walking until it was directly underneath.

'DI Shaw?' It was Gavin Peploe. He laughed, spreading his hands wide. 'You've caught me in civvies.' Shaw noted a cycling top, Lycra shorts, and a small pack over one shoulder. 'This is how I keep fit.' He patted a flat stomach. He checked his watch. 'I've got an hour, then back to work.'

Shaw pointed at the doorway opposite. 'What's that?'

Peploe considered the sign, one foot jiggling with impatience. 'Hearing Voices Network? New one on me, I'm afraid. But this section is used by the psychiatric wards for storage – maybe ask there?'

Shaw turned so that they could walk together. 'Where does this lead? I'm lost.'

'Senior staff car park – the bike's on the back of the BMW.'

Shaw looked at Peploe's feet. 'They make a racket.'

'These? Sure – cycling shoes, they're rigid. It saves your feet, believe me.' He lifted one leg and tapped the bottom of the shoe. 'Nothing gives with these.'

They turned a corner and ahead saw sunlight spilling through two exterior doors. 'I'd better go back,' said Shaw. 'I need the lifts.'

Peploe raised a hand in farewell.

'Theatre Seven,' said Shaw. 'Spare slots for private ops; I'm told you're the man we should see.'

Peploe looked at his watch again, and for the first time the charm didn't quite shine through. 'Well. The HTA team is still in the banks, right? So if they find anything suspicious in D, we can talk. As to the theatre, sure, there are gaps. It's mothballed at times. Did Mrs Phillips bring this up?'

Shaw didn't answer.

'I take exception to the idea that just because there is a private health facility here – and it's within the NHS – then it's bound to be involved in some scurrilous trade. If we have some evidence for that, perhaps we can talk. I –'

'We'll talk anyway,' said Shaw, cutting him short, checking the tide watch. 'Three o'clock, your office. No – could we meet at Theatre Seven? I'd like to see the set-up.'

Peploe shrugged, then nodded. 'I can make the time,' he said.

'And where were you Sunday evening, Dr Peploe?'

Peploe couldn't stop a sneer disfiguring his top lip where the ghost of the harelip was just visible.

'I was on my yacht. A mile off the coast. Entertaining.'

'Your wife able to back that up?' asked Shaw, wondering what version of the truth he'd get.

'If she can, she's psychic. I haven't seen her in five years. We're divorced. But I can give you a name, if it helps. I'll leave it with my secretary. In fact, coincidentally, it *was* my secretary. Now, I'd like to get some exercise before going back into the theatre. That's Theatre Four, by the way – the NHS – so that's all right, I presume.'

He turned on his heels, and Shaw listened to his shoes clacking.

Walking the other way he tried to concentrate on finding his way back to the lifts, but an image intruded: a grey industrial sack being quietly slipped over the polished teak gunwale of a white yacht.

28

Two children were playing football outside the Bentinck Launderette in Erebus Street despite the fact that the state school summer holidays had finished two weeks earlier. One of them could have been the child they'd seen dancing round the fire that first night in the Cat People mask. If it was, Shaw had been right about his age: seven, less. He had a snub nose and a brutal haircut designed to combat nits. The boys had scrawled a chalk goalmouth on the wall, the heads of an imaginary crowd added in for effect.

A voice shouted. 'Joey!' The boy with the snub nose ran to a door at the side of the Crane. Holding it open was a young woman with long, pale legs. She couldn't stop herself looking their way. Then she clipped the boy round the head and dragged him indoors. Opposite the pub stood Jan Orzsak's house; the curtains drawn, the scrawled insult on the door gone under a fresh coat of paint. But a splash on the woodwork below looked like fresh dog's pee. Orzsak's estate car, which had yielded no evidence, was back, parked at the kerb, behind the electricity van and a builder's flatback pick-up and skip.

From beyond the razor wire and hawthorn they could hear a pneumatic drill munching concrete. On the back of the truck was a new power unit for the sub-station, much smaller than the original Shaw and Valentine had glimpsed that Sunday night by torchlight, covered in polythene, the metallic connections gleaming in the sun. Power to the houses was still coming in by cable, gaffer-taped along the gutters, from which a smaller cable ran to each house, looped through letter boxes or open windows.

'New gear,' said Valentine, looking across the street to the Crane. The front doors were wedged open and they could see a cleaner wiping tables. A man in a white shirt holding a coffee cup played a one-armed bandit.

The hot street, the atmosphere of aimless boredom, seemed to suck the energy out of Valentine. That and the sight of Peter Shaw, bouncing on his toes, knocking smartly on Orzsak's front door.

They heard the crushed slippers shuffling down the hallway. Orzsak had a napkin at his throat, and his mouth worked, chewing. He let them in without a word and went ahead into the front room. The shattered glass had been cleared up, but the tanks still stood, cleaned out, dry. For the first time Shaw noticed a portrait, in oils, on the chimney breast, showing a man in formal Polish national costume. There was a small table in front of the barred bay window on which was a plate of cheese and rye bread, which Orzsak pushed aside as he sat. And a bottle, beside an elegant balloon glass a fifth full of red wine.

Shaw walked to the portrait. 'This your father?'

Orzsak's eyes were suddenly alive. 'Yes. He was a vintner, import and export, based in Gdańsk.'

'Wealthy, then?'

'He died in the war,' said Orzsak, shrugging. 'Then the Russians came. I was a baby. We had a little, which did

248

not last very long. My mother worked hard. We came here. I worked hard. Everything I have we earned.'

'And you still like a glass of wine?' asked Valentine. He looked at the bottle. 'Not cheap, right? Dipping into the savings? Or do you still earn money, Mr Orzsak?'

But Shaw remembered something else. 'Of course — the basement, at number 6. A wine cellar — the marks are still on the wall. But no cellar here?'

Shaw looked around; there was no little door in the hallway. He recalled that there'd been none in the Judds' house either, or at the launderette. He'd check with door to door — was it the only basement in the street?

Orzsak ignored him, sipping the wine, circulating the blood-red liquid.

'Did your people find Judd's fingerprints in my house?' he asked, although Shaw sensed he didn't want an answer, that the question was a diversion.

'Why did you lie to us about where you were on Sunday evening when Bryan Judd was murdered?' he asked.

Orzsak seemed to deflate, his chin sinking further onto his chest.

'I didn't,' he said, but it was barely a whisper.

Valentine produced a black and white print, a video-grab from the CCTV coverage.

'This is you, sir. Seven thirty on Sunday. At the Bluebell.'

'It wasn't anything to do with ... that boy.' Odd, thought Shaw, that after nearly two decades he still thought of Bryan Judd as Norma Jean's twin — but then Norma Jean would, perhaps, *never* get any older.

'I'd like a straight answer, Mr Orzsak, or we will go to St James's. I know you want to avoid that. Can you give me a straight answer?'

Orzsak struggled out of the chair, hauling himself upright with both hands on one arm rest. He retrieved a laptop computer from a pile of papers on a sideboard and switched it on, the pale light glowing warmly in the shadowy room. It was an odd clash of cultures – the latest iMac, beneath the patriarch's portrait. Orzsak found a wireless link and went online via Firefox to find a website: www.giveatoy.org.uk.

'I run this,' he said, standing back, and Shaw noticed that his left hand was shaking even though it hung loosely by his side.

'People come online and offer used toys for the children's wards at the hospital … I run round in the car and pick the toys up. Anything within twenty miles. On Mondays I ferry the items to the Bluebell and add anything decent to the trolley. It's always been at the Bluebell because that's where the original children's ward was – before they rebuilt the hospital site. One of the volunteers goes round the wards on Wednesday and Friday. Sundays the kids come to the toy store room – we call it the Toy Library. We set everything out. They can borrow for a week. I've always done it – I started with Mother. So I always go Sundays – it's the highlight of the week.'

From the sideboard drawer he brought a box full of newspaper cuttings. He gave one to Shaw – the *Lynn News* for September 1980. *Bluebell 'Toy Library' Silver Jubilee* – the picture was a crowd of children's faces, a younger

Jan Orzsak in the background holding a giant teddy bear, a woman beside him with the same face – like a moon, with a ring of fat at the neck.

Orzsak took the cutting back, went to put it in the box, then slowly tore it in half and went out of the room, returning with a set of keys attached to a ring in the shape of Mickey Mouse. He was crying, but he did it casually, as if it was of no note.

'CRB checked?' asked Valentine.

He shook his head. 'We began back in the eighties – no checks then. Then, when it was required, I was wary, because of Norma Jean. My arrest was on record – it may have been enough. And since my arrest there have always been those who gossip, build bricks from straw. So when the hospital asked I said I'd been cleared by the church – St Casimir.' He glanced up at the oil painting. 'I just never took them the paperwork and they didn't require it of me. I ...' he thought carefully about the right words. 'I support the unit – with my time, with some money.'

He went to the window and leant on the TV – a flat-screen, latest technology.

'So I lied. The last thing I wanted was the police here. Again.' He cast a murderous look at Valentine. 'An innocent lie,' he said. 'But it damns me. You will have to tell *them*. They will ask *me* the questions they must ask. And now I am condemned because I lied – and why did I lie, they will ask. They must not take risks. And I am a risk now. So – it's over, that part of my life. Thank you for that.' He was still looking at Valentine, but he handed the keys to Shaw. 'Take these back for me – the Toy Library's below Sunshine Ward, on Level One. This is all they need. Perhaps you could tell them I am unwell. But that is up to you. I was there on Sunday – as your picture shows – and there were several witnesses. I didn't leave the library.'

Valentine, frustrated by the neat confession, couldn't keep a note of disgust out of his voice. 'And you have no sexual interest in these children? How about Norma Jean?' He felt a sudden duty to ask the questions Jack Shaw would have asked if he was still alive – because if Jack had crushed this man's fingers to get to the truth then Valentine knew he'd had good cause. He'd looked in his eyes and seen something that night in 1992; something hooded, something cruel.

Shaw felt sick, as if he was watching a blood sport. They should leave; Orzsak's alibi was likely to be rock solid. They could charge him with obstruction for the lie, but they didn't have the time to waste. And it wasn't likely that Orzsak would change his story about Norma Jean after eighteen years of silence.

'I didn't hurt that child. I've never hurt a child.' Orzsak stood back, rounding his slumped shoulders as if facing a bully in the street. 'Your suggestion disgusts me.'

'Why did you stay here, in this street?' asked Valentine.

'Leaving would be a confession.' Orzsak's eyes widened, and his chin came up, determined, despite Valentine's aggression, to have his say. 'I have nothing to confess. Have you asked *him* why he's still here? Andy Judd? Asked *him* why he lives on this street? Asked *him* where he put his daughter's body? I think he guards it.' He dropped the torn picture into the cold grate. 'He'll rot in the hell I know God has made ready for him.'

29

On the doorstep they stood in the sun. Shaw thought the smell of heated pavements was the best thing about the city. Opposite, the Bentinck Launderette was open for business. He could see a woman working inside, on her knees, pulling sheets from a drier – but it wasn't Ally Judd. He checked the tide watch: it was one o'clock. They had two hours before meeting Peploe at Theatre Seven. Time for a working lunch.

'Let's get a sandwich,' he said, heading for the Crane.

The pub was full, every table taken, mostly workmen off the dockside. One had his feet up on a stool, the soles of his boots showing. As Shaw ordered, Valentine touched his shoulder. 'Check the boots,' he said. 'Must be pretty common on the quay.'

Each boot sole was encrusted with blakeys, the steel plates used to protect the shoe from wear and tear. One of the dockers saw Shaw's glance, and put one boot down, the sole cracking on the wooden floor.

The landlord left the one-armed bandit in order to serve them: a pint for Valentine, a half of Guinness for Shaw. They left two cheese sandwiches under a glass dome and bought crisps and nuts instead.

There was enough noise in the room to talk unheard.

'Andy Judd not in?' asked Shaw, not even bothering to flash the warrant card. The landlord was hairless, scrubbed, with a sovereign ring on the hand he used to pull the beer, a clean blue shirt with a white collar, open at the neck. An old-fashioned publican, keeping up appearances.

'No. Maybe he saw you coming, which is bad news. He's a bloody good customer. Best I've got.'

'Dodgy liver,' said Valentine.

'Yeah. It'll kill him. They won't give him a new one either – not till he stops drinking. Day he does that he'll be as stiff as this counter.' He tapped it once, letting the ring crack against the wood.

'You here when the kid went missing?' asked Valentine, leaning familiarly on the bar, playing with a packet of Silk Cut. 'In '92? Mr . . . ?'

'Shannon. Patrick – it's over the door.' He poured himself a drink in a small glass which might have held a half-pint, but probably less. 'I was here when she was born, mate. We had a party in the street. Twins. That was a bash. I'm Bry's godfather – bugger all that means.' He laughed, shaking his head.

'And Sean – the eldest. What about him?' asked Shaw.

'You think it did for Andy, losing the kid, you should of seen what it did to Sean. He was at sea – but they got a message to him, flew him back from somewhere . . . Rosyth, maybe. Kept wandering the streets trying to find her. On the rough lots, looking in fridges, or down on the Fleet, poking around in the mud. It didn't make sense, but he never forgave himself – he'd always looked out for her. Bryan – he was just close, like they were one person. But Sean, he'd been the big brother, the guardian. Then one day, six months after she'd gone, maybe a bit more, he just went. He couldn't take it, all the reminders – and he couldn't look at Bry.' He served someone else, then came back, rearranging a bar towel. 'Paper says he went in the furnace – that right?'

Valentine nodded, pushing some coins over the counter for some pork scratchings.

The landlord cleaned glasses manically, twisting a clean cloth.

'Happy couple, right – Bryan and Ally?' asked Shaw, leaning on the bar, timing the question to match a gush of silver coughed up by the one-armed bandit.

The landlord leant over the bar, the cloth twisted between his fists like a ligature. 'Fuck knows. You listen to the gossip round 'ere you'd think everyone's got a secret. Life's tough, they got through, so that's pretty much a victory.'

'Just asking,' said Shaw.

'Bry come in?' asked Valentine.

'Not really. Christmas. He and the old man were chalk and cheese. It happens. He drank down at the Retreat, by the dock.'

'Neil?'

'Oh yeah. Comes and gets his dad for meals. He's like a sheepdog, that kid. Mummy's boy.' He shook his head. 'It's always one family that cops the shite in life – you'd think it'd be spread about a bit. Neil tries hard for his dad, all the time, but Andy's not interested. He's a bit bitter, is Andy. Toxic, more like. But Neil just keeps plodding away. Bit pathetic, really. I'd have left Andy to rot years ago.'

'And the Organ Grinder,' asked Shaw. 'Ever heard of him?'

The landlord worked a bar cloth over the woodwork. 'You can try the jukebox if you like – might be one of those kids' bands.' He smiled, enjoying his own joke.

They took their drinks outside. Valentine sat on the kerb, a place he'd loved since childhood. After a minute Shaw went back for more crisps and to refill his DS's glass.

'There's a kid,' said Shaw to the landlord. 'In the street. Wears a cat mask sometimes. Bit of a snub nose,' he added, pushing his own up, stretching the nostrils.

'Yeah. That's Joey, my grandson. They live upstairs, his mum and him. Father pissed off sharpish. Good riddance to the tosser.' He pulled himself another drink and let it fall down his throat in one fluid movement.

'He seems to know Andy Judd – that right?'

'Sure. Like I said, I'm Bry's godfather, and Andy did for Joey. He's a good one, too – treats and that.' He stopped polishing the counter, stopped playing the part while no one but Shaw was looking. 'He's a good man, Andy is. Like I said, he's poison to touch, if you get near. And the booze's got him – but in here ...' He hit a fist against his heart. 'Loyal. No problem.'

Shaw went back outside, told Valentine what he'd heard, and then they were silent, standing together. 'It's this street, George,' said Shaw eventually. 'It all comes back to this street. It's not just Bryan Judd. Or Blanket. Or what's been going on at the hospital. There's something else. Something we're missing.'

Standing in the middle of the road, on the old railway

lines, he did a 360-degree turn. A minibus swung into Erebus Street and pulled up by the launderette. On the side was a branded motif: *LYNN PRIMARY CARE TRUST – A COMMUNITY COMING TOGETHER.*

Andy Judd got out, running a hand through the shock of white hair. He didn't pay the driver, who pulled a U-turn and left. He took a few steps towards the Crane, saw them, and turned instead into the launderette. Shaw didn't have to ask Valentine to make the call. He got through to Twine, told him to get Andy Judd's medical history and a contact number for his GP. One priority question: did he have a regular appointment at the Queen Vic? As the DS made the call Shaw saw Ally Judd come out of the church, closing the little lancet door behind her, then walking down the side of the nave towards the bench by the Victorian semi-circular apse, the seat Blanket had sought out on that first afternoon he'd come to Erebus Street. She walked quickly to it, head down, as if hurrying from a painful encounter. They saw her find the bench, sink down, and then cover her face in her hands.

'Martin'll be in the church,' said Shaw. 'Keep him busy for ten minutes, George. I'm going to see if I can get a private word with Ally Judd.'

Shaw cut through the graveyard, where the noon sun had left the stones without shadows. If she'd come here to get out of the heat it was a poor choice; the church walls shimmered with it, and a cypress sapling beside the bench seemed to wilt with the effort of staying green. Shaw paused by a memorial; an angel on a plinth, giving her a few more moments of peace. He thought he could hear her crying, but he couldn't be sure.

He looked up at the grey-silver leaves of the cypress. There was a reason, he thought, that they always planted such trees in graveyards. It was evergreen, of course – a symbol of life uninterrupted by death – but there was a specific reason, he was sure. The detail eluded him, and so it was with just a little shock of recognition that he did recall something else, consciously, for the first time, something retrieved from some distant half-baked lesson on Greek mythology: that hell's waiting room, the entrance to Hades, was Erebus – the personification of darkness and shadow.

A breeze stirred and he forced himself to take a step forward, his boot crunching on a broken beer bottle, so that she looked up, and he saw her eyes were red rimmed, her flesh puffy and without shape, as if it had been hastily fashioned out of Plasticine. He sat easily on the hot grass, leaving her the space on the bench alone, his legs crossed like a Buddha.

'Father Martin is in the vestry,' she said. 'There's a meeting, about rebuilding the hostel. It's going to be thousands, but the insurance will pay.' She tried a smile that went horribly wrong.

'If you're not telling us the truth it will unravel – lies always do,' said Shaw. A blackbird flew into the dust which had collected in the ditch at the root of the wall, flapping, shrieking as it took a bath.

She looked straight ahead, focused on the mid-distance.

'Neil doesn't know, I'm sure of that,' said Shaw. 'That's because he's an outsider. And an innocent, in an odd way, despite the tattoos and the martial arts. And he's all about holding the family together, so he'd be angry, really angry, wouldn't he? If he thought you'd cheated on Bryan.'

They heard a klaxon sound on the distant docks, marking a change of shift. The noise made her jump, so that she had to rearrange her hands on her knees, then curl one of her feet up and under herself. Shaw noticed that on her lap was an apple, green, with a single ice-white bite mark.

'But Bryan? That's the real question,' said Shaw. 'Did Bryan know you were having an affair with Thiago Martin?'

She stood then, and looked around, trying to see if there was a way out, not just out of the sun but away from the question. She turned and walked to the grave-yard wall, within which were set some headstones. With her back to Shaw she picked up a cypress leaf, examined it, then turned.

She looked into Shaw's eyes and he was sure she was concentrating on the moon-like one, knowing it was blind. 'Not until a few days before he died,' she said. Her voice had become oddly formal, as if she was giving evidence from a witness box. 'The water main burst up on the main road and we lost our supply. A woman comes in to help, she was there and didn't know what to do. She rang me, but I'd left the mobile in the launderette. So she rang Bry. He got someone to take half a shift and he cycled back. He found me, us, together, upstairs at number 14. It was the end of everything.'

'An end to the affair?'

'Yes. Bry was in pieces. He was trying to put his life back together. Trying to stop the drugs.' Shaw wondered if she really thought that was true – or was she forced to think well of the dead? 'I had no right to wreck that. Thiago left. I said it was over, told Bry it was over – if he wanted it to be over. It was all I could do, and it's what Thiago wanted too. Bry said, that night, if it was over he could forgive.' She sat back on the bench and held one hand on top of another. 'Promises were made.'

'Which you broke on Sunday night?' asked Shaw.

'That was a mistake.'

'What time was this "mistake"?'

She bent her head back, and Shaw wondered if she was calculating.

'At six. We always met at six. But not at the house – I came here. I left Martha in the launderette. She's a friend,' she added. 'She's there now.'

'Thank you,' said Shaw, standing. 'Six until . . . ?'

'Until you saw me in the street.' She sat back on the bench and pulled her legs up, embracing them for comfort. But Shaw thought the movement was oddly relaxed, and he wondered if she was better at concealing the truth than he'd thought. This woman was the still heart of the Judd family, around which the turbulent men seemed to revolve. Shaw could see that she was someone used to keeping secrets, and he wondered how many others she kept.

'Do you have to speak to Thiago?' she asked.

'Yes. I have to speak to Father Martin. Of course. And I have to ask you this: are you lying to me, to us, again? Did Father Martin really stay with you on Sunday night or did he go up to the hospital? Did he want to confront Bryan, perhaps? Because if Bryan had let you go . . .'

'No,' she said. 'He'd never do that. He respected Bry's decision – the commitment I'd made.'

'No he didn't,' said Shaw, angry that he'd let his sympathy for this woman cloud his judgement of her. 'You were – if we believe you both – in bed together when he died. What kind of respect is that?'

She shrunk back at that, the eyes focusing again on the mid-distance. Valentine's footsteps echoed down the tarmac path, and as Shaw turned to him the DS's mobile rang. Valentine listened, mouthed the word 'Twine', then rang off, walking away so that Shaw had to follow, out of earshot of Ally Judd.

'Hospital says Andy Judd's a regular outpatient at the liver unit; he's on a programme of steroids and was diagnosed in the initial stages of cirrhosis last May. He's on a dietary regime. He is *not* on the transplant waiting list because of his continuing alcohol abuse. He attends Mondays and Thursdays – 10.30 to noon. Twine had a word with the consultant. Between us and the gods, the prognosis is poor. He'll be dead in a year – less, if he's lucky.'

Shaw thought about the gods, and the trip into the underworld of Erebus – a land of shadow on the banks of the river of the dead. To cross into Hell you had to pay the ferryman. But this was a dusty street on a summer's day in Lynn, not a legend. Perhaps, in this world, you could pay to avoid the trip. 'Unless,' he said, looking up and down the street, at the paint peeling from the window frames, an ugly stain of damp on the side wall of the Crane. 'Unless he can find a hundred and fifty thousand pounds. That was the price, right? If he had that kind of money he could buy himself a second life.'

30

The latticework of the old gasometer stood against the evening sky like the bones of a dinosaur, the neat criss-cross of the steel ribs framing the drifting moon. A star shone through as well, low over the rooftops of the town's North End. Valentine left the Mazda in Adelaide Street behind a skip but under a street light, checked the car locks, then led the way through a gap in the fence, out onto the wasteland beyond, a few acres of shadowless abandoned concrete, stained with rust.

Shaw followed. He didn't like following, but this was Valentine's big moment, the break that just might blow open the case. They'd put out a description of the man they'd found on the sands through TV and radio that afternoon. But George Valentine hadn't just waited for someone to call in; he'd hit the phones, working his way through his old contact book, then gone out on the street, tracking low life down to the old haunts. On a street corner outside a pawn shop that had closed fifteen years ago he was approached by a tramp, offering a name. But not there, not then. He had to turn up in person to collect. And there'd be a payment. Not just cash.

'Wait,' said Valentine, pushing forward through some thorns, out of sight.

Shaw watched Venus creeping across a steel-framed square of evening sky, on the coat-tails of the moon. For him, in contrast to his DS, it had not been a productive afternoon. He'd met Dr Gavin Peploe in Theatre Seven – half-lit, mothballed for the afternoon. An oddly threatening room, full of the dull glints of surgical trays, unlit lights, and the dead eyes of electronic monitors.

Peploe had repented of his earlier fit of bad temper. Charm itself, he showed Shaw the pre-op facilities, the scrub room, the electronic screen which rolled back to create a double op theatre. Shaw had news too – the HTA audit team had completed the examination of the first three organ banks: the NHS facility. No signs of any illegal activity. That left Theatre Seven's bank D.

'But it is inconceivable,' said Peploe, both hands laid flat and down on the operating table itself. He was smart enough to avoid patronizing the DI. So he tried to explain just how inconceivable it was that a black-market organ transplant had been performed here, at the heart of an NHS hospital.

'It's the scale of the necessary conspiracy which makes it unthinkable,' he said. 'For an operation – all right, maybe a surgeon, anaesthetist, a nurse. Three people. But that's not the point; you need the recipient. They could walk in, but they aren't going to walk out. Where are they cared for? If it's an op with the donor present they need to be prepared – and then they need to recover. So, they go back to a ward. Which ward? Where's their records? The GP referrals? And don't forget, the key piece of evidence here is the human kidney found on the incinerator belt. It was placed in a waste bag from the children's ward. That means – that *demands* – that everything else is clandestine too, without records or documentation. Believe me,

Shaw, this is a backstreet black-market operation. It didn't happen here.'

Venus slipped behind a girder. So Shaw was left with a question: if not in Theatre Seven – or any of the NHS theatres – where? His mobile vibrated on silent mode. He looked at the number: Lena, ringing from the cottage. He was going to take the call but something made him stop – she'd want to know where he was because he'd forgotten to send her a text at five – a daily ritual. But he'd planned to go back to St James's before going home, for one last run-through of the CCTV of the Castle Rising crash. He was still tussling with the decision whether to take the call when Valentine came back, summoning him with a cursory beckoning movement of a hand, pale now in the gathering dusk. Shaw pocketed the phone, promising himself he'd ring when they were done.

'Why's this character called Pie?' asked Shaw, picking his way over a decade's worth of fly-tipping – a fridge, a pram, the innards of a mattress. It was all Shaw knew about Valentine's informant, that and the fact he'd been channelling information to St James's for the best part of fifteen years.

'You'll see,' said Valentine.

Shaw didn't like the idea that Valentine was in control, and wondered if *that* was what was strangely unsettling about this sudden twist in the inquiry. He thought about demanding an answer, then let the moment pass.

'Did Dad know this guy?' asked Shaw instead, wishing instantly he'd kept the question to himself. And he should have used his name and rank. 'Dad' was too personal, an invitation to be intimate.

'Sure. We ran him together.' Valentine stopped, breathing heavily. 'But the deal tonight is as always – we've never met – OK? He's a stranger. Last thing he wants is us reminiscing about his days as a copper's nark.'

Shaw thought just how impossible it would be to take orders from George Valentine on a daily basis. And, for the first time, he wondered if Valentine felt the same way about him, and that if he did, then what a nightmare his life must be from the inside.

Soon a path appeared in the rubbish, trodden through the weeds and teasel heads, crushed glass catching the moonlight. It led to a break in the steel retaining wall at the foot of the old gas holder. They climbed through to find themselves looking down twenty feet into the circular base. A perfect O, eighty yards across, a rubble floor dotted with fires. Shaw thought of a Bronze Age encampment, the flames the only human light within a thousand miles. There was something about the homeless that always made him feel like the ultimate outsider. It wasn't just a world he couldn't enter, it was a world that frightened him, because it was the antithesis of home.

Cardboard-box sleeping shacks dotted the perimeter. There was a smell on the air: cider and warm dog. The nearest group – four tramps sitting on beer crates – stood, and one whistled a single, vibrating note. A terrier barked wildly until one of the men cuffed it with a rope. They listened while Valentine explained that they'd had a message from someone called Pie saying that they should come tonight, when the sun was down. They were alone. Valentine lifted his arms out, his raincoat over one.

'I don't know which one he is,' Valentine lied, looking round.

They were ushered on, across the circle, to the ruins of a single-storey brick building. The roof and one wall had gone, but within the sheltered room which remained a large fire had burnt down to glowing embers. Shaw tried not to peer at the faces, a chiaroscuro world of watching eyes. And like the Mona Lisa's, all of them following him.

The man Shaw took for Pie sat in what looked like the front seat cut out of a wrecked car, his legs out straight. His name was in his face. Black skin, Afro-Caribbean features, but marred by splodges of white, mottled flesh. One of the pale patches extended into his hairline, and there the black hair was streaked white too. The piebald man. A human magpie.

Shaw shook his hand, aware of the odd symmetry of their asymmetrical faces. His with one blue eye, one moon-blind; Pie's with one eye surrounded by black skin, the other by white.

Valentine pulled up a crate and Shaw sensed that the exaggerated sense of ease was only partly manufactured – the DS was genuinely at home here, amongst the rootless. From his raincoat pocket he pulled out a full bottle of Johnnie Walker, twisted off the top, and put it on the warm ground by the fire.

Five tin mugs were filled – one each, and another for a man who sat back on the edge of the shadows, long hair covering his face. Only his legs were in the light, in pinstripe trousers, frayed, and stained.

Pie hadn't said a word. He held a hand up against the

light still lingering in the sky, and Shaw saw his fingers were cluttered with rings. 'The finger gone here,' he said, pointing at the index on the right, just below the knuckle. His voice was subterranean, a rumble like a tube train.

Shaw nodded.

'The paper didn't say much,' said Pie.

Shaw thought about what more he *could* say. They'd kept the details of the corpse they'd found on Warham's Hole guarded for good reasons, principally to make sure they weren't led astray in the inquiry by the usual telephone calls claiming responsibility or giving false information. 'The body had been in the water some time – maybe forty-eight hours.' Shaw took a breath, calculating that a risk should be taken. 'He'd lost both his eyes.' There was an intake of air around the little camp fire, a drawing back of feet from the heat. 'We'll have to wait for the pathologist's report, but there's every chance his corneas were surgically removed.'

Pie looked behind him into the shadows and the hidden man drew in his legs.

'Pearmain,' said Pie, then spelt it out. 'That was his name. P-E-A-R-M-A-I-N. We called him John 'cos he was London, not 'cos it was his name.'

'When was this?' asked Shaw.

'Six months ago. He disappeared overnight. He just wasn't there any more.'

Shaw looked around. 'Isn't that what's good about this life – that you can just disappear?'

'He left stuff – a dog, a bag with boots. People don't do that, even people like us,' said Pie.

But that didn't work, thought Shaw. The body was fresh. Where had he been for six months? 'Got any theories?' he asked.

'We don't need *the-o-ries*,' said Pie, stretching the word out. 'We *know* what happens.' Shaw watched as a line of whisky trickled from his lower lip. Valentine leant forward and put a £50 note under the bottle.

'Every six, eight months,' said Pie. 'He goes out and finds them – two, maybe three. With Pearmain there were two more: one they called Foster, the other ...' He looked back into the shadows for help. The voice of the man in the tattered pinstriped suit said, 'Tyler.'

'Right. Three of them that time. The same night. We don't know how they ...' He searched for the word. 'Select. They're offered cash. Fifty pounds there and then. A promise of the rest after the thing's done.'

Shaw felt a desperate need to spell this out, to stop trading in euphemisms. 'They're being propositioned – to sell body parts. Organs? For cash?'

'It's a buyer's market,' said Pie. The man in the shadows laughed. 'The promise is a thousand. A kidney. Bits of liver ...' He licked his lips. 'Slices. That's fifteen hundred. Skin grafts. Tendons. Veins. There's a list. It's big money – for us, a fortune.'

'And these other two – we know they really did disappear, like Pearmain. They didn't just move on?'

'They hung out, the three of them. And they left stuff as well, in their shack. A Thermos, a wallet. Stuff you never leave, anywhere, unless you're asleep, right there.'

'Did they come back?'

Pie used a boot to rearrange the ashes in the fire. 'No

one does. That's part of the deal.' Pie thought about that. 'Part of what they *said* was the deal. But if Pearmain can turn up on the sands … But the story they were given was straight-up: they get the money – cash; they get to recover, then a free trip to a new town. And they don't come back – ever.'

'Not ever?' asked Valentine, offering Pie a Silk Cut which he turned down. 'So how do you know what happens?'

Pie ignored him. 'I've given you info. It's good info. There were no strings, but I want a favour. I'd like a favour. For him …' he nodded into the shadows. 'Because he said we should tell you.'

The man in the shadows stood, shuffled into the light, then sat comfortably on his haunches, like a cowboy on the Great Plains. His hair was drawn back in a ponytail. Shaw recognized the man he'd rescued from the upstairs bedroom at number 6 Erebus Street, the man he'd seen curled in a bundle of fear on the floorboards as the house burnt beneath him, the man who'd walked out of the Queen Vic two days ago.

'Mr Hendre,' Shaw said. 'We've been looking for you.'

'I can discharge myself, I just didn't fill in the forms. I understand that you'd like to interview me – well, this is it.' The voice was modulated middle class, and Shaw recalled Hendre's original profession – accountancy. 'You saved my life. This is the payback. Then that's it.' Hendre held the lapels of the pinstripe jacket together despite the heat of the fire. 'I don't go on the stand, and I don't ID anyone. I'll tell you what happened – you do what you like with that. By noon tomorrow I can leave. I'll tell you where I'm going, but I'm leaving.'

Hendre felt inside the jacket for a quarter-bottle of Scotch, then drank, keeping that for himself. He took two inches off the level in the bottle. Shaw recalled Liam Kennedy's character sketch of Peter Hendre, and the observation that he was clean on drugs and alcohol.

'I can't promise,' said Shaw. 'But there's a good chance. Your best chance.' He looked around. 'Your only chance.'

Hendre put a knee down, folded himself forward, and took a piece of wood out of the fire to light a roll-up. At first Shaw thought he was nodding, but now he saw it was a tremor, the whole skull vibrating at a high frequency.

'I was at the Sacred Heart of Mary a year ago. Out in the day, in the nave at night. They didn't like anyone drinking so I kept it secret, drinking in the day, then I'd sober up in time for the free food. I give it a bash sometimes, but I don't need it every waking hour. If they caught you boozing they'd put you on those drugs that make you throw up with it. I didn't want that. So I played the game.' He swigged at the bottle again. 'It worked. It still works. That's the problem with good people – they want to believe the best of you.'

A laugh ran round the circle. Hendre looked at his feet. 'Maybe I fooled them, maybe they didn't give a fuck. Anyway, I was out on the rough lots by the abattoir sleeping one off last summer when I woke up. There's a grass bank, and I'd curled up on it. I'd got a book off the travelling library – *Anna Karenina* – and I'd opened it up and put it over my face. The first thing I knew there was this pain, searing, in my thigh.' He touched the bunched muscle just below his groin. 'There was someone there, I just remember a shadow leaning over. And a car ticking over – on the track there. Then I blacked out.' Hendre shook his head, the ponytail jiggling at the nape of his neck.

Pie threw a broken crate on the flames, which reared up, the air shimmering in the sudden blast of heat.

Hendre stood, opened the jacket, and pulled a T-shirt free of the belt so that they could see his skin, the edge of the pubic hair, the navel, and to one side a scar.

'I woke up with this.' An incision. From Peploe's description Shaw was confident it was the result of a kidney removal – keyhole surgery, two small scars, six inches apart, one for each surgical tool, like the mechanical hands in a seaside arcade machine, fishing for a cuddly toy.

'Where did you wake up?'

'A room. Blank concrete walls, pipes in the ceiling. There was a kind of hum, like a machine. A metal door with rivets. Just the bed, linen, a neon light. I was shitting myself, and I could feel the pain in my side. We'd talked at the hostel about the Organ Grinder. Rumours, gossip. Some stories had trickled back on the grapevine.' They all laughed at a private joke. 'But nobody really knew shit – though they knew someone was out there, and what they wanted. So I had to just lie there, knowing what they'd done to me.'

'Did you see anyone?'

'I waited. It was really quiet, except for that hum. Nothing outside. Then I heard someone coming. First off, I heard voices – through the wall. Really low, almost just a murmur.' Hendre closed his eyes, conjuring up the scene. 'There were two locks, then he came in. He looked foreign – a tanned face, but not like a summer holiday tan, a natural one. Good looking, smooth, black hair.' He searched for other details. 'A gold ring on one finger. When he spoke there was a strong accent, with a sibilance. Spanish, I guess, or something like it.'

'Portuguese?' asked Valentine, unable to keep the insistence out of his voice.

Hendre shrugged. 'He said I'd agreed to donate a kidney, that they'd offered a thousand pounds.' He laughed. 'That's crap. But I guess it made him feel better. Anyway, it's academic, because there wasn't going to be any money 'cos they couldn't use my kidney. He didn't say why, even when I asked. But, you know, it's kind of obvious.' He took another two inches off the whisky level in the bottle. 'I stayed a few days, then they gave me two hundred – two hundred fucking quid; drugged me up again and dumped me back at the Sacred Heart of Mary. I had a week to get out. Find somewhere new. If they ever saw my face again in Lynn they'd pick me up. If I talked about what had happened I'd pay a price. He had a knife, this bloke, and he got it out, pressed it right up here . . .'

Hendre pressed an index finger into the soft flesh under his right eye.

'Eyes. He said they could get a fortune for those. But no donors – unless they're dead. Pissed himself laughing at that. He said I'd have trouble reading Tolstoy after that.'

'Tell me more about the room,' said Shaw.

He shrugged. 'What's to tell? It was hot. Always, like a constant heat, but there was nothing in the room, no radiator, and the pipes were in the ceiling. The lights never went off – no, they did once, like a quick power cut, but there was emergency lighting outside 'cos even in the dark I could see a light through the keyhole. When they opened the door to bring in food and drugs – it was always the dago – I could see out into a corridor. Narrow, lit – but, like, not a lot. Darker than the room. Bare concrete walls. And pipes again – services, I guess – taped up on the ceiling.'

Shaw caught Valentine's eye, knowing they were both thinking the same thing: the hospital basement, Level One, with its maze-like corridors. 'And the hum?'

'Yeah. Always, like you were inside something.'

Pie retrieved a large plastic bottle of white cider from under his crate and drank. Over by the edge of the gas holder they heard shouts, two figures fighting, locked in a dance. Dogs barked, and shadows ran to break them apart.

'Why'd you come back to Lynn?' asked Shaw.

'Bit of luck. Unfinished business. Before this life.' He looked around the fire at the faces. 'I had another life. I fleeced a couple of old dears of their money. I thought they'd die. They didn't. It was just bad luck. I got barred, started living on the streets. It's not much of a qualification, right – dishonest accountant. Well ...' He laughed, swigging at the bottle. 'Actually, you can make a good living at it, but you're not supposed to advertise the fact.' He stood. 'After they dumped me back at the church, after the op, I got the warden – that kid Liam – to try and find me a place to go. I needed a fresh start. I'd done some work for the church – legal advice, nothing fancy, you'd get better off the CAB, but this way it was discreet. So they knew me. They got me a billet up the coast at Hunstanton – there's a church and some sheltered housing. It's OK. I've done a bit more work. Then I got a letter, the warden again. Guess what? Another old biddy I'd been working on really did peg out, and she's left me something to remember her by. Legit. Sweet. I don't have a bank account. I have to face up tomorrow at ten at White & Angel, in Queens Street. Then I'm out of this dump. I could be a rich man. Or maybe not – she had cats, so perhaps I get to feed the fuckers.'

All the faces round the fire smiled.

'And the Organ Grinder?' asked Shaw. 'That night of the fire – how come you *knew* he was in Erebus Street?'

'Because he knew I was back.' He slugged the whisky again, leaving his lips wet. 'The monkey told me.'

His hand was trembling now, in perfect rhythm with his skull. 'It had been a year. Christ, I hadn't said a word, nothing, even when some of the old guys at the hostel asked where I'd been. I thought, fuck it, I'm not saying a thing. I thought it'd be OK for a night, two, back in Lynn. I asked the kid to put me in the hostel and he said he could – they had spaces, as long as I was clean. I said I was.'

'And I'd be inside, out of sight. But the first evening – the night before the fire – I walked, I have to walk, get under the sky. So I went down by the docks, out along the Cut, then back. There was someone behind me. I heard the footsteps when I cut through the alley into the street – I was running then. He wasn't hiding the steps, smashing his feet down, like a beat, behind me. I got back to the front door, I was fumbling with the keys, and this kid came up. Arse hanging out of his trousers, some kind of mask on his face, like a cat. Cheeky sod – he asked for a ten-pence piece. I gave him one, just for asking. When he took it he grabbed my hand.'

Hendre held up his fist, clutched. 'Then he said it – just flat, like a line he'd been made to learn. "He knows you're back." Just that. Then he pointed at his eye – just like the wop did. Then he ran.'

31

'It's Level One,' said Shaw, wiping condensation from the windscreen of the Mazda. They were parked in Erebus Street, facing back up towards the T-junction, the dock gates behind them. There were lights on within the Sacred Heart of Mary, the tracery of the windows and the Victorian stained glass glowing in the dusk. White light that spilt from the frosted windows of the Crane. A late summer storm had cooled the air, so that the tables outside were empty, although the pub windows were open, allowing a thin trace of jukebox sound to leak out under the orange street lights.

'Got to be,' said Shaw. 'The sound, the heat, the pipes. We're out of time today but set it up for the morning, George. I want Level One ripped apart. We should have looked before, because if they were regularly getting rid of human waste down there then having the whole deal there – on the doorstep – it's perfect.'

Shaw covered his eyes, trying to dredge something from his memory. Something Liam Kennedy had said. *I hear voices ... We all hear ...* 'Down on Level One there's a room allocated for a group called the Hearing Voices Network,' he said. 'Kennedy mentioned it. I saw the door, down near one of the exits to the main car park. Get that checked specifically – I want to know what's behind that door.'

Valentine didn't move a muscle, because he wasn't convinced Level One was the answer. 'And you think they'd take that kind of risk? If anyone had stumbled on anything – a recovery room, the theatre itself – they'd be dead in the water. At least upstairs they could blend into the background.' He pushed in the Mazda's cigarette lighter. Shaw got out before he could light up, then leant back in.

'Get to Phillips, or Peploe, and tell them we want Level One sealed off tonight. The areas they have to use, round the lifts, the offices, the rest, we'll do those first thing and they can have them back. It won't be there, anyway – my guess is it's out on the edges somewhere. But let's do the best we can. Tell Twine what's up; give him the background. I want everyone up to speed by dawn. All right?'

The doors of the Crane opened and DC Campbell came out. She'd insisted the landlord wake up his grandson Joey – the child Pete Hendre thought was the Organ Grinder's monkey.

'Nothing, sir,' she said. 'But he was pretty scared. Said he'd never run an errand like that, and he didn't know anything about any organ grinder. I'll get family liaison to have another go in the morning. But there are limits. He's seven years old.'

'Thanks,' said Shaw. 'It was a long shot, anyway. See you tomorrow.' They watched her walk to a parked Citroën, then make a call on her mobile, before driving off.

Valentine looked at his Rolex. 'We done?' he asked.

'Almost. The statement you got off Father Martin is a perfect match for Ally Judd's – to the minute. So what's going on? They're having sex upstairs while Bryan Judd's meeting his killer up at the hospital? Maybe. Or are they covering something else up? Then there's that medical degree. Given what we're uncovering here, that's a detail I can't just leave. Clearly Martin isn't the man Hendre met when he woke up after the op – he knows the priest. But the accent's a coincidence. I'm going to give the priest another run round the block – then go home and sleep. Can you get uniform to run the Land Rover out here for me? Leave it by the Crane.'

'Sure.' The Mazda coughed into life.

'And, George. Tonight – finding Pie, then Hendre, that was good work. Well done.' He thought about smiling but knew it wouldn't look right. The Mazda was doing 50 m.p.h. by the time it reached the T-junction, then backfired as it turned out of view.

Shaw entered the Sacred Heart by the side door and was surprised to find that, despite the hour, a service was in progress. He found Liam Kennedy just inside the entrance, perched on a pew end, probably to discourage late visitors from the Crane, Shaw guessed.

Shaw knelt beside him.

'Midnight Mass?' he said.

'Tomorrow is the feast – the birth of Our Lady. We've always held a service on the eve. A vigil. It's popular, with those of a certain age. It's just ending.'

Shaw thought he wouldn't like to see what unpopular looked like. There were a dozen in the congregation itself, the hostel men gathered separately to one side, in front of the devotional candles, seven or eight of them, like human bundles, motionless, huddled together.

Father Martin was at the altar, his back to the nave,

cleaning the chalice with muscular movements which made his arms work beneath his vestments. A spotlight picked out the polished silver of the tabernacle, its doors open to reveal the gold leaf of the interior. The congregation knelt, or worked rosaries between their fingers, except for one man who had fallen asleep at the pew end, his head back.

Father Martin blessed the congregation and asked it to go in peace. Parishioners began to melt away, while the men of the hostel moved as a group down the nave towards the makeshift kitchen. Martin spoke to a few people at the door and then turned to Shaw, already unfurling the stole at his throat.

'Can I help?'

'Dinner's late,' he said, watching the men cluster around a tea urn which Kennedy had wheeled into the light. A biscuit tin attracted them like birds around grain.

'Just a treat, actually – they all ate earlier. It's our feast day tomorrow, so …' He laughed. 'A celebration.' He opened his arms as if to emphasize the contrast between that concept and the gloomy interior of the church.

'Can we talk alone?' asked Shaw.

Martin led the way into the small room behind the altar and began swiftly to pull off his vestments.

'You lied in your original statement – Ally told me the truth this afternoon. I'm sure you know that by now. You were upstairs, in bed, together.'

He was pulling the cassock up over his head and so Shaw couldn't see his face at that moment, but when he straightened up he was smiling. 'And why does that matter?' He pulled the bow on the white surplice.

'The truth matters.'

'Ally has to live in this street, Inspector. I can leave. I will leave, maybe soon. But she'll have to live with the truth we leave her, or whatever version of the truth is left.'

'You think people don't know?'

The smile again, revealing expensive teeth. 'You English – sometimes you don't see yourselves for what you are. People know many things. What they say to your face can be very different. She can live with gossip and innuendo – she does. She despises them anyway. We don't owe them any kind of truth. But we don't have to ...' He searched for the colloquialism. 'Rub their noses in it.'

It was the closest Shaw thought he'd get to a confession, so he moved on. 'Ally came to see you at six. Bryan Judd died at between seven forty-five and eight thirty. Did you go up to the hospital to see him?'

'No. I had no reason to.'

'Not true, Father. Surely, not true. Ally would not have broken off your relationship but for the fact that Bryan had found out about it and wanted her to stay with him. She felt she should. She felt she had a duty. She'd already broken her promise. But perhaps that was a final gift to you?'

Martin looked away and Shaw knew he was right.

'Did you go up to the hospital to confront Bryan with her betrayal? To force him to release her – openly – from the promise she'd made?'

Martin folded gold-threaded cloth into a wooden chest and locked it.

'I didn't go to see him. I was here.' He took a black leather jacket from a hook and shrugged it on.

Shaw believed him, persuaded not by his words, or the logic of his arguments, but by the fact he couldn't imagine the priest using violence. The hands were too studied in their movements: academic, considered. But he still had that image in his head of the medical certificate hanging in the priest's study. 'Do you have access to the medical records of the men here, and at the hostel?'

'In theory. We keep files, and I think there's a summary of the relevant medical details. That's really Liam's domain. Why?'

'You have a medical degree.'

Martin set his jaw. 'I'm at a loss to discover why I should feel guilty about *that*.'

'Someone has been selecting homeless men off the streets of Lynn – some of them from your hostel. These men are being offered money to donate organs as part of an illegal traffic. Two of them, at least two of them, have not survived their operations. I'm asking you whether you fulfilled the role of broker. I expect whoever it was would be well paid. You have ambitions to bring about change in your country – that must cost money? For publications. For travel. *Politicization* – that's the term? And I understand your reticence – we know you've been struck off. The Brazilian authorities are sending us the relevant documentation.'

He laughed in Shaw's face. 'There – that phrase. You've never lived in a police state, have you, Inspector? They say things like that all the time – euphemisms for control. Be careful. You're a good man, I think. In my country many good men are ashamed of what they do at work – and then go home to their families.'

Shaw glared at him, aware he had no evidence at all to support his accusations. But he didn't back down. 'I want to see inside the presbytery. I could get a search warrant – do I have to?'

Martin's eyes went dead. 'In my country the police rarely observe such niceties.' He patted his pocket and they heard the keys jangle. The priest led him through the graveyard to the door of the presbytery. Shaw stepped over the threshold first, still unsure what he was looking for, unsettled by the priest's sudden submission.

'Bedroom?' he asked.

He knew it was an invasion of privacy, but he felt he had to provoke Martin, to break down the emotional distance that separated them.

The stairs were dark wood, with a band of carpet that ran only down the middle of each step, held in place with brass stays. A long landing on the first floor ran the length of the house, the doors off it impersonal, like a hotel corridor. Martin's room was at the back, the last door.

The duvet was turned down on the single bed, but as Martin went to sit on it he flicked it back into place, covering the sheet.

There was a wardrobe with a mirror attached between two doors, and a bedside table, bare except for a reading light, some loose change, and a bible. It was as impersonal as a monk's cell, except for the small, wooden chest set under the window.

The sash was up, and Shaw walked to it, looking down

into an alleyway which separated the church from the house, leading out into the graveyard through a wooden door the shape of a bishop's mitre set in the brick, a Gothic flourish.

'I'd like to look in the chest,' said Shaw.

'You've come this far,' said Martin. Shaw could feel the anger the priest was holding in, the micro-muscles in his face tensing and untensing as he tried to keep control.

Shaw put a hand on the lid, lifted it, and looked down at a damask cloth covering the contents. The outside had been plain, but the underside of the lid was decorated with carved images of birds, flowers, and fish. He traced a finger around the image of a fern leaf. 'This is new, surely?'

'My father had it made. The wood is very old, actually – eighteenth century. But the carving and construction are contemporary. It was a twenty-first birthday present. A leaving present.'

Shaw breathed in the slightly musty scent of the chest. 'The wood?'

'Muirapiranga,' said the priest. 'The bloodwood tree.'

Shaw didn't react; just let his fingertips play over the carving. He pulled the velvet cloth away to reveal some books, leather-bound, a bible, two framed pictures of figures from the nineteenth century, both on high-backed chairs taken in full sunlight outside a stone building; a brass telescope, a wooden chessboard and what looked like a box for the pieces, a sextant, and a doctor's stethoscope. He laid each out on the bed.

'Heirlooms,' said Martin. 'My inheritance. I'm the youngest son – so nothing else. But you'll know all that,

283

from the files.' He spat out the last word as if it was a curse.

Martin nearly had him then, because Shaw was going to ask him about his family; but instead he remembered to turn back to the chest and the ruffled green baize cloth at the base. Beneath it was a velvet purse, about a foot long. He lifted it out, undid the gold-thread knot, and, using an edge of the material to cover his own prints, drew out a knife, the sheath silver, blackened with age, the handle the same, overworked in tracery.

'My grandfather's,' said Martin, but the tension in his voice made the word stick in his throat.

Shaw drew the blade and found to his surprise that it was not a blade at all, really, more like a short rapier, as clean as a surgeon's scalpel. What had Dr Kazimierz said of the wound in Bryan Judd's chest? That it had been delivered by a knife, narrow as a fencing épée.

Shaw held the blade up to the light.

They both heard the sound of footsteps from the alleyway below, two sharp metallic taps on stone. Shaw stepped to the window and leant out; the path, lit from above, was empty except for a hedgehog, ambling arthritically towards the rear yard. But the little doorway was open, and as Shaw leant further out he saw the shadow of a running man, flitting against gravestones, the sound of his footfalls deadened by the grass.

32

George Valentine felt good, dangerously exalted. He'd caught Mrs Phillips in her office on the mobile and told her to close Level One. He'd listened for five minutes to twenty reasons why it couldn't be done, then he left her to do it. And he had the power to do that, he knew, because of what this case had become. The death of Bryan Judd had looked like a low-life killing on day one; but now it looked like the kind of case that could make a career. Interpol, the national press, TV, radio – the feeding frenzy would start as soon as they released the gory details. It was just the kind of case Valentine needed to back up his next application for promotion. After the call to Phillips he'd gone up to the Queen Vic and spent an hour with Paul Twine, planning the search of Level One. After a brief word with St James's he'd secured a team of twenty uniformed officers for the legwork. If there was any trace left of the room Pete Hendre had woken up in, or the operating theatre he'd been through, they'd find it by noon.

They kicked him out of the Artichoke at midnight, but not before he'd refilled his hip flask while buying his last pint. He should have gone home then, back to the tall dark house in Greenland Street, but he already knew exactly what he was going to do, and knowing he was drunk didn't stop him doing it. So he turned up the London Road to the city gate, and took his usual seat under the spreading tree opposite Gotobed's Funeral Directors and Monumental Masons. That always made him laugh: 'monumental masons', as if they were giants.

As he laughed the cold beer bubbled up in his throat and he coughed into his hand, doubling up. He had a sudden image of what he'd look like from the outside looking in, and he knew it was a blessing Julie wasn't alive to see it. It was an odd comfort, knowing someone was beyond being hurt, because they were dead.

When he unfolded himself he heard a key turning in a lock and watched as Alex Cosyns opened the front door, watched the terrier jump down the steps, and then turn to walk towards the park. Valentine's heart was racing, not a fluid acceleration but a lurching and painful surge. He'd been wilful as a child, impetuous, but middle age and disappointment had allowed sloth to dim his unpredictable nature. But this was like the old days – he knew he couldn't stop himself, just knew he'd go to bed tonight having had a thorough look at the inside of this man's house, the inside of his life.

He watched the walking shadow fade away. Within a minute he was on the step, sliding his St James's security card down the door jamb, the lock springing. He stepped in, closed the door, and flipped on his torch. A bachelor's house: no carpet in the hallway, letters in a pile on a table holding a cordless phone. In the front room a media centre, an armchair, an exercise bike. The kitchen was MFI – new – with the cupboards full of tins and nothing in the fridge except milk. He ran up the stairs and felt his heart give an irregular beat. At the top he stopped, feeling sweat break out on his face. One bedroom had a duvet on a single futon, and a wall of photos – all stock-car racing. Winner's podium shots, pit crew, but none of the sponsor – Robert Mosse. The other bedroom was an office, as neat as any room in a doll's house, with the desktop clear except for a paperweight holding down a single cheque made out for £1,000 to Cosyns signed by R. M. Mosse. And a scrap of notepaper held in a little wire clasp which read TK 1956.

There was a footstep, outside the room, on the uncarpeted steps, and a dog's claws skittering. The Yale on the front door was so well oiled he hadn't heard it open. He felt the euphoria drain away. He looked at his watch: 12.28 a.m. He'd been a fool, and now – unless he could construct a plausible story – he'd just chucked away that promotion. Shaw had laid out Superintendent Warren's instructions in a formal letter: he was not to approach Cosyns, or any other witness or suspect connected to the Tessier case, either in person, by letter, or by phone. And here he was, standing by his bed. He walked quickly to the top of the stairs and threw the torchlight squarely into Cosyns's face. 'Don't move – police. Back down the steps, please – hands to the wall.'

Cosyns didn't move; the man had the ability to maintain an almost eerie calm. 'I live here,' he said. 'Who the fuck are you?'

Valentine pulled out his radio and let it crackle. It was on an open channel and they could hear a squad car calling in from a pub fight in the town centre.

Cosyns backed down the stairs, flipping the light

switch, leaving his hand there, as if he was considering plunging them back into darkness.

There was a picture on the wall Valentine had missed because it was behind the door – Cosyns, with a girl aged six or seven, both sitting on the bonnet of the souped-up Citroën. Cosyns took it off the wall and held it out. 'I live here – look.'

Valentine got to the foot of the stairs. 'We got a call – someone forcing the door. I live round the corner. It was open.'

'Right,' said Cosyns, smiling easily, and reaching down to unleash the dog. 'But it wasn't when I left.' He examined the door jamb. 'Nice job – clean as a whistle.' He looked past Valentine and up the stairs. 'Nothing up there, then?'

Valentine shook his head, helpless now, knowing he was losing credibility with every passing second. He took a step towards the door and the dog growled, its lips peeling back to show black gums.

'I didn't see the warrant card,' said Cosyns.

Valentine took it out, wishing the light wasn't on. Cosyns stepped forward quickly and held the wallet lightly, looking at the name and the picture. 'Right. DS Valentine.'

Cosyns stood to one side, back against the wall, a smile on his face. 'Reggie,' he said, and the dog cowered at his feet.

Valentine walked past, pulled the door open, and looked out. 'I'll get a patrol car to keep an eye out – you need to check the contents.'

'Right,' said Cosyns, readjusting the position of a

mobile phone which he'd left on the hall table. 'Can't be too careful.'

Valentine made himself walk away without looking back. If he had, he'd have seen Cosyns at the front room window, the mobile in his hand, listening to the ring tone.

The line picked up. 'Bobby,' he said, the tone familiar, but strangely threatening.

33

Wednesday, 8 September

Shaw stood on the sixteenth-floor balcony of Vancouver House looking down on the Westmead Estate. The rising sun was on the far side, so he was in the dawn's shadow; cool, almost chilly. Cars on the tarmac below looked like Dinky toys. In the flats opposite – a ten-storey block – lights were on in bathrooms and kitchens. Steam leaked from pipes, as if the insides of the flats were boiling. Shift work on the docks, or in the canning factories, meant that places like the Westmead didn't do night and day like the suburbs did, just an infinite grey siesta. He could smell a breakfast cooking somewhere, fried bacon on the breeze, and something else, something spicier.

He looked at his watch. He shouldn't be doing this; he had to be at the Ark at eight, and he needed to know what Valentine had organized for Level One. Tom Hadden had already sent him a text about the knife he'd taken into the lab the night before from Father Martin's bedroom: no traces of blood, but the inside of the sheath held microscopic traces of bloodwood – a broad match for the traces found on the MVR torch. It wasn't a fingerprint, but it was a powerful piece of physical evidence linking Father Martin to the scene of the crime. He'd ordered a cast made of the knife-tip. Father Martin had given a statement and been released. He stuck to his original statement, and Ally Judd continued to provide him with an alibi for the time of the murder. Which suggested another way forward: a formal interview with Ally Judd, under caution at St James's.

So, he really didn't have time for this. He looked at the door he was standing outside: Flat 163. His wallet held a small see-through pocket in which he usually carried a picture of Fran, but behind it was another passport-sized picture. He slipped it out now. Jonathan Tessier, just nine, an uncanny resemblance to Shaw himself at the same age: the wide high cheekbones, the tap-water eyes. He went to knock, hesitated, knowing that once the door was open he'd have lost control of events. But he had to do it; he'd promised Lena he'd do it – for them.

He'd arrived home the night before elated at the progress they'd made. He'd spent twenty hours a day on the murder inquiry from Day One; but when he got home all he wanted to talk about was the Tessier case, because he'd gone back to St James's and watched the CCTV again. It was like a living memory now, those black and white images, shuffling around the floodlit junction.

He'd sent a text ahead and she was there to meet him on the beach. She'd brought a bottle of white wine from the fridge and two chilled glasses. The stoop was pine, the wood cool and worn, so they'd sat on the steps. Low tide, so the beach seemed to stretch to the horizon, where a necklace of lights marked the anchorage for freighters, waiting to slip into Lynn when the tide turned.

'You look tired,' she said, pouring his drink.

'I watched the tape,' he said, as the almost colourless

Chablis filled his glass. 'The CCTV of the car crash a few days before the Tessier boy was murdered?' He felt inside his RNLI jacket and produced a black and white print of the scene – the wrecked Ford, the Mini pulled up in the shadows, the three blurred figures of the young men in baseball caps.

'There's something I'm missing. Something that's not right.' He readjusted the picture so that she could see, but she was staring out to sea. 'Lena?' he asked. But she still didn't turn to him, and he knew by this gesture that tonight they wouldn't make love. On the drive home, and the walk along the beach, he'd realized how much he wanted her, and the transformation that it always brought – the energy it released, the sudden alteration of everything, like a thunderstorm.

She was dressed in a loose sweater, with her arms out of the sleeves but tucked inside for warmth. She pulled up a leg and curled it under herself so that he didn't see her hand slip out until it had put something on the wooden stoop.

It was a small tub of yoghurt: Madagascar vanilla.

'What's that?' he said, but already he could feel the blood rushing to his heart. She held herself away from him, as if he was a fire and she didn't want to get burnt. And he didn't recognize her face, the focus on the middle distance, the ugly broken line of the mouth; and it made him realize that for a long time – he couldn't guess how long – she'd arranged her face for him, like a screen around a hospital bed. But he was too desperate to know the answer to his question to ask himself what she thought she was hiding, what it was she didn't want him to see.

'It's what nearly killed Fran.'

'What do you mean?' His voice was loaded with anger; and guilt, because he knew he'd done nothing since he'd got back to the beach but talk about his work, not the daily work of the CID but his own private case, the one he'd inherited from his father, the one he'd promised to end.

She turned to him then, her face slumping, her mouth open in a silent scream. 'It's what nearly killed Fran,' she said again deliberately, knowing that despite the word 'nearly', this was still a form of punishment.

'Lena – tell me. Tell me now.' He'd have given anything to keep the threat out of his voice.

Her eyes blazed in response. 'Now.' It was close to a shout. 'Now – it's convenient *now*? What about five hours ago when I phoned – I never phone, Peter. You know I never phone.'

He'd been waiting in the dark on the edge of the gas holder for Valentine. He'd clocked the number; why hadn't he rung back? He'd been in two minds because he'd promised himself that second viewing of the CCTV from Castle Rising.

'I'm sorry,' he said, knowing instantly that he'd done the right thing – got the word out before it was too late. 'Jesus. Lena – what happened?'

'She ate the yogurt,' she said, hitting out, knocking her glass over, sending the carton out into the sand.

'Get it back,' she said. 'The nurse said we should keep it. Make a note.' Her voice was cold and hard, the anger washing out of it like the tide over the sand.

Shaw fetched it, then sat down on the wine-damp wood, not quite touching her.

'I gave it her for tea. I didn't think – I haven't bothered since she was tiny.' At birth Fran had been allergic to milk – all milk. The first reaction had been the worst – not quite fatal, but her throat had swollen, blocking the air supply, the eyes and face bloated. After that they'd kept her clear of milk products for five years – then, gradually, they'd edged them back into her diet. There'd been no reaction of any kind for three years.

'How bad?' asked Shaw, quickly throwing an arm round Lena's shoulders, tight enough so that she couldn't pull away.

'Bad. It's my fault. This crowd was in from Burnham Thorpe – a family of six. They all wanted suits, they all wanted boards – the final bill was nearly four thousand pounds – so I did her a pizza and put it out in the kitchen and just called her in off the sands. So when I found her . . .'

She covered her mouth, rocking slightly with the memory, and Shaw understood that part of this was *her* guilt, not just his. 'I didn't know if it had been too long. If she was . . . So I felt for her pulse. I couldn't find it. And she was puffed up – the way she used to – her eyes closed. And there's no Piriton in the cupboard.' She kicked out, sending a sheet of fine sand forward like a shell burst.

'I rang you. Then I rang Scott on the mobile – he ran down with some from the lifeguard post at Hunstanton. And then, just for no reason, she was conscious – right then, when he got here. So we gave her the Piriton.' She laughed, and Shaw felt her shoulders relax an inch, the blades moving beneath the skin. 'Five minutes later she was running about like a rabbit.' She laughed again, looking around as if to recapture the image of the moving child.

'I'll check,' he said, lifting a knee.

But she held on to him. 'I have – every ten minutes. She's sleeping. Leave her.'

She let out a long breath, like a death rattle, and buried her eyes in the crook of his neck.

'I want you to end this obsession with the child,' she said. 'One way or another. Either drop it or end it quickly, one way or another. Solve it, Peter, or walk away.' She lifted her head and looked into his good eye. 'Jack destroyed his life for this, Peter. And we know why – because the boy looked like you, because it could have been you. Have you ever thought why that was – why he was . . .' she searched for the word. 'Unbalanced by that?' She held his head. 'It was guilt – because he'd let you grow up without being there. He couldn't be there for you, so in a rush he thought he'd make up for it by being there for Jonathan Tessier. Which was selfish, because it only made him feel better, not you. Don't let this happen to us.'

Later, as he lay in bed, listening to the sea creep back up the beach, Shaw realized how much of a relief that word had been: 'Us.'

34

He'd woken at dawn, listening to the seagulls scratching on the roof. He didn't need to recall specifically what had been said between them – it was there, already part of the memory bank he'd carry with him for the rest of his life. And it wasn't his life that was the point. It was Fran's. She could have died, and that would have destroyed them, because he wouldn't have been there. He always answered if Lena phoned. But he'd been blinded – she was right – blinded by the conflicting pressures in his life, between his home and his job, and between his case and his father's case. And the Tessier killing *was* an obsession; dangerous and disfiguring in so many ways. His problem was that he could no more walk away from it than walk away from himself. But in the darkness before dawn he had made a fresh appraisal of his failure to solve the case so far. Was it really such a baffling crime? Or was his inability to make progress really a reflection of his own inner conflict: the fear that if he found the truth, it would be an uncomfortable one?

He'd swum then, at dawn, seeing now that Lena was right, he'd overlooked so many more direct avenues of inquiry. It was a case he'd worried at, like a sore. Watching his hands rise above his head as his backstroke took him out to sea, he decided he must return to first principles, and talk to those with a direct recall of the night Jonathan

Tessier died. He'd made a pact with himself. Six weeks. For six weeks, he'd rake over the ashes of the case once more, and if, at the end, there was no prospect of fire, he *would* walk away. For Lena's sake he'd walk away – even if he did leave part of himself behind.

He'd decided to start here, on the Westmead, because he wanted an answer to Lena's original, and perceptive, question: why would a gang caught on CCTV at the fatal crash at Castle Rising go on to murder a nine-year-old boy just because he stumbled on them respraying the car? There had been reports of the accident in the local paper, and on the radio and TV – but why would a boy take any notice of that? It was nothing to do with him, or the small world in which he was living out his summer holidays. Even if he had sensed something sinister, and children were certainly gifted at that, he could have been bought off with a crisp £10 note. There had to be another motive.

In the block of flats opposite an alarm rang, the sound travelling across the concrete canyon to Shaw as he stood on the balcony outside Flat 43. A seagull glided between the high-rise blocks, below him, so that he could see the feathers on its back ruffled by the breeze. The digital numbers on his watch flashed seven o'clock, so he knocked on the plywood door, knowing she'd be up, because he'd checked out her shift pattern with a quick call to the Queen Vic.

Angela Tessier, the dead boy's mother, answered the door with a toothbrush sticking out of her mouth. 'What?'

'I'm sorry – I wondered if you had a few moments.

DI Shaw – Lynn CID. It's about Jonathan's death.'

She turned on her heel without a word and walked into the shadows of the flat. Shaw followed, down the corridor into the front room, which faced east and caught the full sun. There was a flat-screen TV, sound-deck DVD/CD player, a poster of Amy Winehouse.

'You've got a minute,' said a voice, echoing slightly in a bathroom. She came in, bustling, picking up a mobile, an iPod. Shaw knew from the file she was forty-three, a nurse at the Queen Victoria. But she looked thirty-five, the face animated by a sense of purpose. Her waist was narrow, circumnavigated by a thick leather belt. She'd looked after her figure and her eyes were a stunning green, like snooker-table baize. They looked at each other, and she didn't seem fazed by Shaw's lunar eye. She went out, then came back with a small cup of pitch-black coffee.

'Fifty seconds,' she said, but her voice wasn't un-friendly.

In the file on the Tessier killing there'd been a husband mentioned, Mike, a salesman with a carpet warehouse. But this was her world now, and Shaw sensed there was no one else in it, not even the ghost of Jonathan.

She read his mind. 'Mike left. We didn't handle what happened very well. But we still talk – we're friends. So – if your question's for him, I've got a number.'

'No.' Shaw hesitated, suddenly aware that he was unprepared. He didn't know where to start, so he had to tell the truth.

'My father was DCI Jack Shaw.'

'I know – I figured that out. Shit happens. I think he got the right man, so does Mike. But he fucked up.' She looked around, and Shaw thought she was trying very hard not to relive the past. 'And now life goes on.' She straightened out the smart blue uniform, adjusting a fob watch. 'And on.'

'I think Jonathan – on that evening – I think he went after the ball but got distracted, and he ended up on the far side of the estate by the lock-up garages. I think he saw a car there – and some men, working on the car. I'm pretty sure that's why he died.'

'Mosse was one of those?'

'Yes. I think he was.'

She put the cup down. 'It's a bit late.'

'I know. It's the car that's important. Was he interested in cars? Would he have been able to recall the make, for example? You know how some kids are fixated on machines.'

'No. Jon wasn't like that. Some boys, they just don't like boys' stuff. Football, maybe – but even that was just something to do. Books were the thing. That kit he was wearing was from his grandad – Celtic. But he didn't really care.'

Shaw didn't understand. 'But he'd played all that day ...' He stopped himself saying it was the day he died.

For the first time Shaw saw that she was distressed by trying to recreate the memory. Holding the fragile Italian coffee cup with both hands she stared into the bottom. 'He wasn't in the flat because we had my father with us – Mum had just died. It was very difficult here. He sort of broke up on us – so we got Jon out. If we'd known better, we'd have let him stay, share the emotion. But that's

299

hindsight. At the time it was too raw for us, let alone a kid. It was just one of those things.'

Shaw admired her for that, for not taking the easy way out and blaming herself.

'It was sudden – your mother's death?'

She laughed. 'You could say that. Some pissed-up kids killed her on a joyride. And her best friend. Out near Castle Rising. They never found them, the joyriders. That was the week before – the Tuesday.'

For the first time Shaw could hear a tap dripping in the kitchen.

'What was her name? Your mother?' He didn't want to know – he'd go back to the files for all the detail – but it bought him some time to think, because a single fact had just transformed the crime, like stepping into the hall of mirrors.

'Watts. Agnes.'

Shaw nodded.

'Does that help?'

'Maybe.'

Shaw walked to the window, looking down on the Westmead, cars scattered over the acres of tarmac between the blocks. He hadn't been honest with himself about the Tessier case, because he'd always thought on a secret level that he'd never find out the truth. And now, for the first time, looking out over the squalid estate where it had all happened thirteen years ago, he thought he might be wrong.

'At the time did anyone think there might be a link between Agnes's death and Jon's?'

'No – why should there be? It's a cliché, Inspector –

but shit happens. Especially on the Westmead. Just because we're one family doesn't mean it can't happen twice in ten days. Anyway – your dad had Mosse. We all know he did it. No one ever suggested that a gang of them had done it. Why should they? And they had a motive – they said he thought Jon had scratched his car. It all happened so quickly, didn't it? Chief Inspector Shaw knew about Mum's death – but no, I don't think they thought there was any link at all. They tried to find the car that caused the crash – that was another policeman, I can't recall the name, I'm sorry. But there was no registration number, so it was useless.'

Something in the way she said it made Shaw realize how stupid he'd been not to go back, not to talk to the witnesses, the people who were there that night – not just George Valentine. But the real victims, the ones without a police pension.

'Look,' he said, turning, stopping himself from saying that they should all have been asking themselves another question that first day of the original inquiry: not *who* did it – but *why*. Because the idea the boy had died in a tussle over a vandalized car didn't stand up in the light of day. It was possible, but hardly probable. They'd left motive to look after itself – a fatal omission.

'There may be a link. It's possible that this car – the one I said was in the lock-ups – is the one that killed your mother. There's a link, you see, between that car crash and Jon's death. There was a fleck of paint on his football shirt, it's a match for the car involved in the crash your mother died in.'

She sat down, fumbled in a heavy-duty handbag, and

produced a packet of cigarettes. When she'd lit one she stubbed it out.

'Fuck,' she said, and rubbed her hands into her eyes. 'I'm sorry.' Her mouth broke into a zigzag line. 'It's OK. It's a shock, bringing it all back.'

He sat on the sofa, trying not to push her too far with questions. And he was thinking fast himself, trying to straighten out the line that linked the shadowy CCTV footage at Castle Rising and Tessier's broken body. He opened his wallet and took out a folded print of the still from the CCTV – the Mini in the rain, under the floodlights at Castle Rising. He placed it on the table so they could both see it, and again, with even more force, he knew he was missing something vital in that black and white image. 'That's the car,' he said, touching the shadowy image of the Mini under the pine trees on the verge.

She stood, blowing her nose. 'I need to think about this.' She jotted down a mobile number on a corner of the local paper then ripped it off. 'Ring me, after work. The shift's over at two. I can't think now.'

Shaw walked to her car; a Ford Fiesta, the tyres slightly flat, a dent in the off side deep enough to show the metal beneath the paintwork. They hadn't talked as they'd tip-tapped down the stairs – the lift was out of order – which meant he'd had time to try and work it out. The problem was, even now that he'd established a link it didn't explain why the child had been murdered.

'Was Jon upset about his grandmother? Were they close?' he asked as she looked for her car key.

She checked her watch. 'Sure. Well, not really, to be

honest. We didn't see a lot of her – or Dad. Mike rubbed them up the wrong way – not good enough for their only daughter. For Jon the only upside was the dog. They'd got this puppy – a terrier. Cute thing. He loved it, so when she died he just asked Mike outright. Could we have the dog? But that was the really weird thing. The police said they'd watched the CCTV of the crash and they were pretty sure these kids took it.' She covered her mouth quickly. 'They left Mum there to die – but they took the dog. Can you believe that?'

35

The Ark was already bathed in early morning sunshine, the brickwork sickly orange, shimmering in a mirage created by the morning rush-hour on the ring road. Shaw had a large sheet of paper spread out on the Land Rover's bonnet: a plan of the Queen Victoria hospital, Level One. The spreading, almost organic chains of rooms and corridors reminded him of a map he'd once seen of the Valley of the Kings. Ancient designs, superimposed on shapes, on patterns long lost. Valentine leant on the side of the Land Rover, a mobile to his ear, getting the latest from Twine.

Shaw drank from a takeaway cappuccino, bouncing on his toes. Valentine cut the line to the murder suite. 'We've got two hundred rooms – well, they call them rooms, some are nothing more than cupboards,' he said. He didn't have a hangover, despite the late-night binge. But the confrontation with Cosyns meant he hadn't slept. So he was struggling to keep it clear, keep it simple. 'But they'll check them all. They've checked one already – the Hearing Voices Network. Nothing – just a PC, a few chairs, and a kettle. Most of the rest are going to storage – loo rolls to splints, scalpels to intubation bags, whatever the fuck they are. And the services, gas, electric, oil tanks. Foodstuffs for catering – tins, oils, dried food. Stairwells, lift shafts, piping. You're right, it's a maze.'

'All it needs is a Minotaur,' said Shaw, realizing that, in an odd way, perhaps it had one.

'My guess,' said Valentine, 'is that as soon as Judd turned up as crispy duck they packed up shop.' He snapped his fingers, then drank from a plastic cup, picking tea leaves from the end of his tongue.

Shaw studied the map, unmoved by Valentine's pessimism. Hendre's description of the room in which he'd woken up was a match for Level One – down to the incessant hum and the metal riveted doors. But was the operating theatre down there too? Could a patient have been taken up for the operation, then back down? That was more likely. What about one of those convenient gaps in the schedule at Theatre Seven? Then the patient recovered in secret – but never far from the hospital's vital services.

Valentine rummaged in his coat pocket and produced a faxed statement. 'This is the best Middlesbrough can do – it's a note of the interview with Ben Ruddle, Norma Jean's boyfriend, taken six weeks ago.'

The conversation had been chaotic, and Shaw noticed that whoever had conducted the interview had scribbled a note in the margin:

Alcohol/uppers/disco biscuits!!!

Ruddle had told the social worker he was living rough because he liked to see the sky. He'd given up the job at the market garden because they'd made him help out on deliveries and he didn't like the van. And he had to leave anyway – because he had something he had to do. Valentine had highlighted the paragraph:

R says he has score to settle. Advised to avoid violence. R says too late for that. Advised to seek counselling – offered further appointment. R request for funds to travel – refused. Offered shelter place for ten days – refused. R terminates interview.

'And there's this,' said Valentine, producing a black and white passport-style picture stamped with a prison number. The image bore little resemblance to the file picture from 1992 – the face had filled out, hardened.

It might have been Blanket: dark, Celtic, the wide gap at the bridge of the nose.

'Question is,' said Valentine, 'why'd he come back?' Shaw thought his way through an answer – because he'd loved Norma Jean, because he'd never stopped grieving for the child he'd lost, and now he had a chance to make the pay-off, buoyed up by drugs and booze. Maybe. But did Ruddle know who had killed Norma Jean? Or had he come back to Erebus Street, on the anniversary of her death, to make up his mind?

They heard the bells of St Margaret's on the Tuesday Market chime the hour. Inside the Ark they found Justina Kazimierz ready to begin the internal autopsy on the body they now suspected to be that of the man known as John Pearmain, itinerant tramp, whose corpse they'd found on Warham's Hole, minus the tell-tale upper joint of the second finger on his right hand, and minus his corneas, as well as the rest of the contents of the orbital cavities.

Shaw got into a surgical gown, then pushed his way through the heavy clear-plastic swing doors into the morgue, followed by Valentine. The stone carved angel looked down on the aluminium tables. Four were empty. A fifth held Pearmain's body, naked and white, like alabaster. The sixth was covered with a plastic shroud over an unseen corpse. Shaw had been dreading this moment since opening his eyes that morning, but as soon as he saw the flesh that John Pearmain had become he knew he'd be all right. This wasn't the remains of a human being any more, but lifeless meat, pressing down on the mortuary table with all the finality of stone.

Kazimierz didn't bother with any pleasantries. 'ID is confirmed, by the way – although the missing finger didn't leave a lot of doubt. His medical records are extensive and held at the GP centre which runs a clinic for the men at the Sacred Heart, so we've got matches on teeth, and a skull fracture.'

She began dictating notes into a headphone, making a brief external examination. 'Three points of interest, externally,' she said. 'The eyes, obviously. Both have been removed. One can only surmise that was in order to cut out the corneas – it's not necessary to remove the whole eye to do so but a lot easier if the body is not going to be subsequently viewed by relatives. Gunshot wound. The bullet went through the heart. Luck or skill? Who knows, but my money's on skill. And this . . .' She used a gloved hand to indicate a scar on the lower abdomen, left side, which meant she had to lift the corpse slightly. Valentine winced at the sound of creaking joints.

'This will, I suspect, turn out to indicate a kidney removal. I'll know once we open him up. There are other operative scars – all long healed. We'll take a look inside in a minute. But first . . .'

She turned to the other occupied mortuary table and pulled the shroud clear as if she was launching a new

307

model at the Motor Show. Beneath was the body from the storm grid, the skin pockmarked by the crabs so that it looked like the surface of a table tennis bat.

'This will be Dr Rigby's last post mortem examination for the West Norfolk Constabulary,' she said. 'I suspect an early retirement is about to be announced.'

Shaw stepped in. 'What did he miss?'

She laughed into her face mask. 'What did he catch is an easier question. The subject's overweight, so there are folds in the skin, and there's the pitting. But there's no excuse . . .'

Valentine noted the stitched autopsy incision down the chest bone and relaxed slightly, letting his eyes follow the pathologist's fingers as she held apart two folds of skin on the lower abdomen.

'Keyhole again; two incisions – just like Pearmain. I've ordered up the records on the other two names you gave me – Foster and Tyler, we may be lucky and get an ID. There are other scars.' She indicated a ten-inch incision on one leg, running into the groin. 'Vein removal . . . the key point, however, is that only the keyhole kidney surgery is recent. Very recent – perhaps less than forty-eight hours. All the other scars have healed, and healed well. That's why Rigby missed them. But that's not all. There's something wrong with the kidney keyhole surgery – the stitches are poorly executed, and the wound itself, the interior trauma, shows signs of post-operative pyrexia . . .'

Valentine failed to deliver a polite cough.

She touched a finger to her forehead. 'Sorry. Jargon, I know. Well, it's an infected wound. That could have been caused by a whole list of things. We know the patient wasn't elderly, and he looks reasonably fit, even though overweight, so that tends to suggest he became infected because the conditions in which the operation itself took place were less than pristine.'

'And the botched stitching?' asked Shaw. 'Could he have died on the table?'

'No. Absolutely not. There is some healing of the wound – very little, but some. No, death is post-operative. But, as I say, the work looks very – well, amateurish. Which hardly matches the evidence of the keyholes – an advanced procedure – or the other scars, which all appear perfectly professional.'

The pathologist straightened her back. 'We may know more once we've looked inside Pearmain's body. Which is why we're here.'

She smiled broadly at Valentine, pinging the surgical gloves on both hands, turning back to the eyeless corpse.

She made the initial surgical incision, holding the blade of the scalpel up to the green-tinged sunlight coming in through the old chapel windows, before pressing down into the bloodless flesh, running a wound from shoulder tip to shoulder tip, then down the line of the sternum to the pubic bone. Shaw stepped in to watch but he could hear Valentine's laboured breathing behind him. The DS had gone for the full face mask. He was ten feet away, and he wasn't getting any closer.

The Stryker saw created a thin film of bone dust as the pathologist cut through the ribs, then lifted clear the chest plate.

She made a quick examination of the principal organs. 'Oh dear,' she said. 'Now that is *not* what I expected.' She flipped the microphone away from her mouth, thinking, working the autopsy glove down between the fingers of her left hand with her right index.

'Tell me,' said Shaw, as the pathologist re-examined the outer flesh on the abdomen wall.

She flipped the microphone back into place and told the tape. 'The left kidney, the one beneath the surgical incision, is missing – as we would expect. The right kidney is in place – here.' Shaw stepped an inch to one side to let the floodlight illuminate the plump organ, the colour of a bean in a plate of chilli con carne.

Her hands dropped inside the torso cavity. 'And here, the liver – which is in situ – but you can see the scars? Someone has performed a hepatectomy, a partial removal of the healthy organ. A graft, if you like – common now, but sophisticated. *This* isn't some backstreet surgeon-barber at work. There's nothing amateurish about *that*.'

'Why would you need a bit of healthy liver?' asked Shaw.

'Transplant. Essentially it's grafted onto the failing liver in the recipient and takes over some of the workload. Very popular, of course, because you can have a live donor, not a cadaver. LDLT – live donor liver transplant.'

'So three different procedures?' asked Shaw. 'The corneas, the kidney, and the liver graft. At least three. Timings?'

She smiled, looking at Shaw as she might have looked at a favourite son. '*The* question. The corneas post-mortem, the kidney before that – maybe two weeks, but the liver … I'd say that happened between six to eight months ago. The liver has partially regenerated itself at the point of the internal scar – the external scar is almost entirely healed.'

Shaw thought about the timescale. They thought Pearmain had been taken off the streets about six months earlier. That's when the liver op would have taken place. Then he returns to the operating table for a kidney transplant. Then he dies and the corneas are removed before the body is dumped. Where had he been between the operations?

Meanwhile the other victim – possibly Foster or Tyler – has had several procedures as well, and then dies after a botched kidney removal. An operation which had taken place in the last few days. That didn't make sense either.

'Can we match either of these two to the organ we found on the incinerator with Bryan Judd – the kidney?'

'We can try,' said Kazimierz. 'It's not Pearmain's – the blood group is wrong. The other one – Rigby's floater – is a match for blood, but the rest of the tests will take time. At this stage all I can say is that we can't rule him out.'

Finished, Kazimierz made notes, walking back out into the CSI office on the far side of the partition. On a desktop was a bagged plaster cast of the knife Shaw had taken from Father Martin's bloodwood chest.

'As for this, it's possible the wound in Bryan Judd's chest was produced with this weapon. Possible. Nothing more.'

They broke for coffee. Valentine took his mug outside with a cigarette.

Kazimierz took Shaw to her desk. There was a pile of thin manila files.

'These are the parish records your team collected from

the Sacred Heart of Mary,' she said. 'They're effectively, in part, a précis of the medical records held on the men by the team of GPs who visited the church as part of the community health programme. The parish files are actually very good – they made copies of medical cards, other records, any repeat prescriptions they collected for the men, plus a written note from the doctor. Then they've added in their own observations: records of weight, for example, diet, etc.'

Shaw butted in, aware that he should have asked this question at the start of the inquiry. 'Is that usual, that a church would have copies of medical records, other documents?'

'No. I asked. It all goes back to the priest ...' She consulted her notes. 'Dr Martin? The GP admin people said he'd made a request to copy over the files and other information to aid his research work on the impact of poverty on health – particularly bone structure. That was his specialist area – rickets. He'd written academic papers on the work he'd done in Brazil – the São Paulo shanty towns. I've checked the references: reputable journals, important work.'

'Right,' thought Shaw. 'Unfortunately he was struck off in '94, which might explain why he failed to flag up his interest in the files to me. Even if it was a lie by omission. He said Kennedy, the hostel manager, looked after the files. He didn't mention his own interests. That's the innocent explanation – that he was trying to carry on his work, but knew we might check back on his record.'

Kazimierz thought about that, and then picked up three files, weighing them in her hand. Valentine came back in and edged himself onto a table top. 'I've studied the files for the three missing men: Pearmain, Tyler and Foster,' she told them. 'We know which one is Pearmain – he's from Warham's Hole. The floater may well be one of the other two. I've also got Hendre's file, and we know he underwent an operation and lost a kidney, but it was no good to them – almost certainly because once they got it out it was clearly diseased from alcohol abuse.'

The pathologist dropped the files and used both hands to massage her neck.

'Hendre *is* the odd man out,' she said. 'It's bizarre – he's the only one of these men with a history of alcohol abuse. Long term, from early teenage years. The reported mental problems – paranoia, anxiety – may well be related to that. In contrast, look at Tyler, for example. Council care, reform school, recidivist. Nicotine was his addiction; two hundred a day at one point.'

'Bloody hell,' said Valentine. 'Human kipper.'

'Indeed. But not a drop of alcohol, according to the records. Which means his kidneys were in perfect condition.'

She pushed the coffee mug aside.

'Which was all in the files . . .' said Valentine.

'All in the *parish* files.'

Her grey eyes pulsed with light. 'I cross-checked. The GP files are held at the hospital because the funding comes from the primary care trust. They are a decent match with the parish files *except* in the case of Hendre. The file on him up at the Queen Vic is completely wrong – he's listed as forty-six years of age, for example. He's thirty-three. So I checked through and found the obvious mistake. Hendre's file had been accidentally mixed up with those of a Pete Hendry – with a "y". And his kidneys were fine. So, if you were asking, which you aren't, I'd say whoever selected these men did so using the hospital files. That's why they made the mistake. If they'd used the parish ones they'd never have gone near Pete Hendre.'

Shaw and Valentine looked at each other, then back at the pathologist. 'Where are both sets kept and who has access?' asked Shaw.

'The parish ones were, I understand, under lock and key in the presbytery. The hospital records are held in the usual way and accessible to doctors on a case-by-case basis.'

'Which doctors?'

'Good question. GPs at the community health centre – and those with sufficient seniority on the hospital staff.'

Hadden thudded through the Ark's main doors. Shaw knew that in major inquiries the CSI man hardly slept, setting up a makeshift bed in the organ loft above the lab. He looked ill, his eyes puffy, with the ghost of a sunburn across his freckled forehead.

'Sodding sands,' he said. 'No shade.' He caught Shaw's eye. 'Wait – I've got something for you.'

He booted up the PC, then tapped his way into his e-mail basket, then leant back so that Shaw could read the note from the Forensic Science Service at Birmingham. The milk bottle used for the firebomb attack on the electricity sub-station had been drunk from by the neck, so they'd matched the DNA extracted from saliva against all those whose samples had been taken in the inquiry so far and they'd got a direct match, high-probability, with

Andy Judd. Plus they'd found his prints in Jan Orzsak's front room, on a shard of broken glass from one of the fish tanks.

'So Andy Judd set out that Sunday to inflict a little more exquisite pain on Jan Orzsak,' said Shaw. 'Either because he believed he'd murdered his daughter, or because the vendetta deflected attention from the fact that he himself had been the killer.'

But was that his *only* motive for cutting the power, thought Shaw. They knew a bit more about Andy Judd now and it made him increasingly wary about brushing him aside as some kind of disturbed vigilante. First, there was the eighteen-year-long feud with Bryan Judd about the death of his twin sister, Norma Jean. That, surely, was the definition of bad blood. Second, while Andy Judd had an alibi for the time of his son's death, it was underpinned by his network of friends in the street – hardly witnesses beyond reproach. And now they knew he was a regular outpatient at the hospital. A man in desperate need of a liver transplant, an operation he couldn't get because of his addiction to alcohol, and his inability to overcome that addiction. Was there another reason that Andy Judd – or someone who had power over him – wanted darkness in Erebus Street the day Bryan Judd died? A darkness which had also shrouded the abduction of the homeless Blanket from the Sacred Heart?

36

Andy Judd was in the lairage, the covered area at the
back of Bramalls' abattoir, where the cattle were held
before being sent down the metal-screened race into the
slaughterhouse, the corridor in which the cattle got their
first scent of death. But Valentine couldn't smell it, just
the sour aroma of singed bone from the saws. Shaw
raised a hand to Judd, who was edging a cow towards the
sinuous metal entrance to the race using a metal prod.
He was dressed in a white overall, one quarter of which
was stained a vivid red. Shaw thought what a dead
metaphor 'blood-soaked' really was.

The cow kicked, suddenly jittery, and the noise began,
the idyllic lowing of the field taking on an edgy urban
panic. Judd whacked the animal with a metal prong, and
sent it careering into the metal barriers, which flexed with
the weight. Somewhere a circular saw cut through flesh
and bone.

'Go there! Go there!' shouted Judd, making the cow
skitter and run behind the curtain wall, followed by the
next, and the next.

Judd stood still, waiting for Shaw and Valentine to
cross the yard, the white overalls and cap he wore making
his skin look butter-yellow. Again, Shaw was struck by
how diminished he looked, like a man wasting away, to
leave just the bones of what he'd once been. Judd worked

a rag between his hands, cleaning away the sweat and saliva from the cow.

Shaw was about to speak when they heard the first percussion, the bolt gun fired into the brain, the slaughtered animal collapsing against the stun cradle. The impact made something inside Shaw recoil in sympathy.

'I'm working,' said Judd.

'Well, actually, you're being interviewed by the police,' said Shaw. 'That can continue here, or at St James's, but frankly, what you do next is up to me, not you.'

Judd looked around. 'I can't just stop.' By their feet was a metal gutter, and as Valentine watched a trickle of arterial blood began to flow down it, bubbling oddly, as if it was boiling. He began to breathe through his mouth.

'All right,' said Shaw. 'If we can talk. But I'm telling you now, Mr Judd, that if I don't get some straightforward answers to my questions we will end this conversation under caution at St James's. Do you understand?'

All the cattle had gone now, the open concrete yard dappled with dung. Judd nodded. 'Down here,' he said, following the path the cattle had taken. They heard another stun bolt fired home, only just audible now above the rising panic of the cattle crowded in the race.

Judd's job was to keep the line of cattle organized so that at regular thirty-second intervals the next cow could be sent forward through a pair of metal swing doors, beyond which the bolt-gun operator dispatched the animals. After that they could just see the main butchery unit, steaming fresh carcasses moving in a production line from hell, dripping blood into the gutters which radiated a sickly metallic heat.

The noise – half animal, half machine – meant Shaw had to shout. 'The day Bryan died, Mr Judd . . .'

But Judd turned away, and at a signal Shaw must have missed walked the cow to the barrier, setting his shoulder against its side and inveigling it through. Shaw watched him as they heard the bolt gun, the blood gushing at their feet, and he saw Judd's face shiver with the distaste that even he couldn't hide. They could see the dying animal kicking beneath the swing doors as its carcass was dragged away. Then the sound of a saw cut through the air, making Valentine step backwards, his black slip-on slipping into the gutter. Judd tried to smile. 'That's the sticking, that noise. They take the heads off, then bleed them.'

He was looking at Valentine, which was a mistake, because the DS's foot now felt warm and sticky, and that made him feel sick as well as angry. As he stepped in close, feeling the power that only controlled aggression can supply, he told himself that anger was good, as long as it was directed – channelled – like the blood. He could smell the stale whisky on Judd's breath, and he wondered if he'd had a drink that morning already. *That* was something he'd never done, although there'd been days when he'd thought he'd die if he didn't. He felt a sudden contempt for this man.

'We've got your prints in Orzsak's house – and DNA off the bottle you used to bomb the sub-station. You're fucked, mate.'

What was left of Judd's self-esteem drained out of him like blood from a carcass.

'Mr Judd,' said Shaw, aware that Valentine's aggression

had rocked Judd, 'I don't believe you did this to torture Jan Orzsak – well, not just for that, anyway. Something else happened that night on Erebus Street, at the Sacred Heart. A tramp was abducted. He had to be bundled out – I think there was a car waiting nearby, if not on the street, to take him away. And that was much easier in the dark and with the diversion you'd set up outside the Crane – the party, around the fire. So I think you made those firebombs to cut out the power as well as to get into Jan Orzsak's house. The question is, who told you to cut the power?'

Judd took one of the cows by the halter, taking off his hat, and Shaw noticed that he couldn't stop himself trying to soothe the animal, working his fingers into the hide, around one ear, and clicking his tongue.

'No one told me to do it.'

Shaw thought he'd aged suddenly, almost while they were talking, as if he'd allowed something to catch up with him which had taken a sudden, terrible toll.

'I got pissed, it was Norma Jean's day – the day we lost her.' He looked defiantly at Valentine. 'I loved her very much. We all got talking outside the pub about how he'd got away with it, Orzsak, how he was still there, taunting us. So I got a coupla bottles and some old rags and filled 'em up with paraffin from the heater in the flat. Once we'd knocked out the power we just walked into his house. He deserves everything life's saving for him. I had two bottles left over. I don't know who chucked 'em in the hostel. That wasn't me. I don't know anything about the tramp down at the church.'

He forced himself to gather in the next cow, running a hand down the face, between the eyes, which were wide with terror.

'And I suppose you still don't know who the Organ Grinder is, or where I could find him?'

'You're right,' said Judd.

The cow went through, and they all looked away as the bolt gun fired.

Shaw took out the artist's impression he'd drawn of Blanket. It was due to go out on the networks that night – they'd done a deal, holding it back from the papers so the TV would headline with it.

'There's been some very ugly business done on this street, Mr Judd – a lot of innocent people have been hurt. Worse,' said Shaw. 'Weak people, defenceless people, desperate people. People like this ...' He held up the drawing. 'This man is the latest, he's the one taken from the church the night Bryan died. I think you know where he is, and what's been done with him, and why.'

He held the picture up to Judd's face as he tried to look away. 'I want you to think about this man, and what might have happened to him, and whether you're responsible in some way, in any way.' Judd took the piece of paper in his hand. There were a lot of emotions struggling not to surface. Then he looked at Valentine and Shaw, and shuffled one foot, trying to keep his balance.

Judd went to hand the picture back.

'Keep it,' said Shaw.

He looked at it again. 'What's happened to him?'

'Men like this are offered money, Mr Judd, for organs,' said Shaw, sceptical that Judd didn't know already. 'A few hundred pounds. Some of them end up dead. Rich people walk away with a new life. And you're telling me you don't know anything about that? Are you telling me you wouldn't like to be one of those rich people?'

Judd went along the line, smacking the animals, keeping them in single file. When he came back Shaw could see that, at last, some emotion was in his eyes. He wondered what life was like watching animals die.

He dropped his eyes to Shaw's boots. 'I don't know anything about that.' He seemed utterly defeated, as drained of blood as the carcasses hanging on the hooks.

'There's a car outside,' said Shaw. 'You're going downtown. I'm arresting you for the arson attack on the substation and the criminal damage to Jan Orzsak's house.' Shaw read him his rights.

The bolt-gun operator came out, smoking, looking curiously and openly at Judd. They all followed the race into the yard.

'One fag?' said Judd, out in the sunlight. 'Please.'

Shaw nodded, and watched as the old man's hands shook as he tried to light up. Then, deftly, with one hand he snapped the match and let it fall on the sand. That family habit again, the broken V-shaped match.

'There's one thing in particular I don't understand,' said Shaw, placing his feet apart. 'Why precisely did Bryan think you were responsible for Norma Jean's death? I know he felt in his heart she'd died. And he knew that you'd both fought over the baby. But why did he think you'd killed her?'

Judd looked down at the gore on his once-white overalls. 'Blood – he'd seen blood.'

'That's not in the statements,' said Valentine. 'There's no mention of blood – where did he see it?'

Judd's head was lost in a cloud of cigarette smoke. 'In the bathroom. He went up to check she was OK – I'd cut myself shaving, put a hand out, I s'pose, and left a mark. Later, when we knew she was gone, he wanted to know if it was her blood. Fuck. It was mine. And he'd felt her drowning, gasping for air. That's what he said. So he just strung it all together: that we'd fought, that I'd hit her, drawn blood, then held her under. He didn't tell you lot – sometimes I wish he had. But he wouldn't. Instead he tormented me all those years, and I've tormented Jan Orzsak.'

They let him finish his cigarette alone.

Then they walked him out into the street, and when he saw the squad car he looked at it as if it was an obscenity. Valentine opened the rear door and covered Judd's head with his hand, protecting it as he pushed him down into the seat. A uniformed officer sat beside him, another in the driver's seat. Shaw looked in the window and saw that he'd unfolded the ID sketch of Blanket on his lap. When Judd saw him he jerked his head away, but Shaw had seen that he was crying, the tears clearing a channel in the dust and blood on his face.

37

They watched Judd being driven off, his white hair visible through the rear window beside the PC, and then walked to the Land Rover. Shaw got on the mobile to Twine for an update, while Valentine fetched drinks from the Crane: a pint and a Coke. While he waited at the counter he thought of telling Shaw about his late-night visit to Alex Cosyns. If Cosyns complained he'd be on better ground – although not that much better – if he'd owned up first. Plus, he had found something material to the case. Robert Mosse was making payments to Cosyns. Why? What was more, traceable payments. Valentine was certain that if they could get access to Cosyns's bank account they'd find a regular income from Mosse – that must be how he'd paid for his lifestyle, how he'd kept the Citroën on the stock-car circuit, and how he'd managed to afford a messy divorce without any apparent pain.

'Blackmail,' Valentine said to himself as he took the drinks back to the car. But as soon as he was in the passenger seat he felt less confident. Perhaps Cosyns wouldn't complain, which would be suspicious in itself. So why risk being hauled up in front of DCS Warren when he could keep his head down until he had something copper-bottomed, something that would get Mosse into custody.

Shaw had been thinking too. He had an almost over-whelming desire to tell Valentine everything he'd found out about Jonathan Tessier's last day alive. Because it all made sense now. He could lay the pieces out, one by one, leading from the crash at Castle Rising to the moment the Tessier boy followed a bouncing ball off that football field. Perhaps he'd wandered down to the lock-ups by chance – or, more likely, he'd seen the dog, broken free perhaps, or out on a walk on the lead. The terrier he'd been in love with, the one he wanted for his own. So he'd followed the dog back to the lock-up – and inside, what had he seen inside? The car, buckled, still scarred from the crash. He'd have started talking, asking questions, wanting to know if he could keep the dog after all – but that's the last thing they could let him do. And buying him off wouldn't help: £10, £20 – how much to stop an excitable child blurting it all out once he'd got home? There wasn't enough money in his little world for that. Perhaps they'd got him inside the garage, closed the doors. Someone had strangled Tessier. A cold-blooded killing? Shaw doubted it, but they couldn't have kept the kid for ever. He'd have wanted to go, they'd have tried to stop him, tried to keep him quiet. In the end they didn't have a choice: he had to die. And then they had to get rid of the body. A job that had fallen to Robert Mosse, if the forensic evidence of the glove found at the scene was to be believed. He had a car nearby, parked up above ground to avoid the vandals. Had he run it round, backed it in, loaded up the child's body? But why was it Mosse who'd taken that risk? Shaw thought about the CCTV of the crash at Castle Rising. Had Mosse been there – the unseen figure in the front passenger seat? Because if he'd ever ended up in court his career would have been over. The Law Society could live with a misdemeanour, but being party to the killing of two innocent elderly women, and abandoning them when he could have called for help, was a crime no one could, or would, overlook.

But when Valentine returned from the bar Shaw hesitated, unable to take him into his confidence. After all it had been Shaw himself who'd read the Riot Act to his DS about continuing with the Tessier investigation; now he was proposing to tell him he'd done just that. What if, instead, Shaw tracked down the lock-up itself? Then he'd need help, on the ground, securing any hard evidence they could, evidence they could both take to DCS Warren. That's when he'd need DS Valentine – not now, with the Judd inquiry in full swing.

Shaw drank his Coke. 'So – what do we think? We can do Judd for arson and the break-in, but anything else? Is he tied up with the organ trade?'

Valentine shook his head. 'Not in my book. It's a coincidence. They could have got Blanket out of the church without the power down. And the sub-station was attacked at noon, hours before the kidnapping. There's no guarantee it wouldn't have been restored by then. I don't think Judd's in on it – no way. The only thing on his mind was getting into Orzsak's house.'

Shaw was going to argue the point but stopped when he saw DC Lau's Mégane turning into Erebus Street, tyres screeching. She pulled up, window-to-window with the Land Rover.

'Sir. Audit team's just finished running through the organ banks. Nothing in A, B, and C. They're the NHS banks. But D's full of surprises.' She handed him a computer printout: a list of unmarked tissue samples; six organs with no documentation: five kidneys and a section of liver. 'The doc in charge says there's also a few yards of tendon, vein tissue, and skin. All commercial, apparently,' she added. 'All missing.'

Shaw thought about it, flexing his arm. 'Hadden?'

'He's down there now. They're happy to hand it over as a crime scene. Doors are sealed and crime tape's up.'

'Peploe?'

'Secretary says he phoned in ill this morning – left a message. Home address is one of the flats in the old Baltic Flour Mill on the quayside. I've got uniform checking it out.'

'The yacht?' asked Shaw.

'*Monkey Business*,' said DC Lau. 'Secretary says Peploe uses it for clients – whatever that means. Regular berth at Wells-next-the Sea – just off the harbour.'

Shaw rang the harbourmaster at Wells, an ex-navy man called Roger Driscoll who commanded the RNLI's hovercraft at Hunstanton. Shaw apologized for the call, but did he have any information on the location of the yacht *Monkey Business*?

'Sure – but it isn't a yacht, Peter. Think Jackie Onassis, but without any sense of taste. It's got a flying bridge.'

Shaw knew the type. Sleek gin-palace lines, smoked-glass cabin, then a second deck on top below the bristling sonar and satellite navigation gear. It was what any self-respecting yachtsman would call a 'white boat'. He'd had

Peploe down as a wooden-boat, chart-table, under-canvas man. But perhaps the yacht was just for the girls, or rich private patients. Or something else? He conjured up Pete Hendre's description of the room he'd woken up in: the constant hum, the metal door, the flickering lights. Might he have been on board? But there'd been no movement, so if it was the yacht it would have had to have been in dock. Or beached?

'Personally, I don't go near any boat that's got patio doors,' Driscoll was saying. 'But then I haven't got half a million quid to waste.' He said the log book showed *Monkey Business* had motored out of harbour on the late-evening tide the night before. She hadn't any crew, but given the gear on the bridge she didn't need any. The boat had been registered at the harbour for five years in the name of a company – Curiosent; there was a telephone number and an address. She left for the Med each summer for three months. He knew the owner only as Gavin.

'Charming, tanned – there's usually a girl too, and usually a different one for each tide,' said Driscoll.

Shaw heard a burst of static, a metallic conversation, then Driscoll was back. 'Want me to find him? He's got a transmitter on board and we've got his ID. Give me five?'

Lau gave Shaw her iPhone, on which she'd tracked down the website for Curiosent. It was a company offering minor surgical procedures ranging from laser ops to cure snoring to vasectomies. Eight surgeons were listed; Shaw recognized three names from the list they'd been given at the Queen Vic – including Peploe's.

Shaw's mobile rang. It was Driscoll. 'Peter. Some-thing's wrong here. I've got a fix on Peploe's boat. She's about half a mile off Norton Hills.'

Shaw pictured the coastline in his head. Norton Hills was a line of sand dunes off Scolt Head Island. It was a stretch of coast made up of a maze of marshy channels and miles of shallow water.

'She afloat?'

'According to my charts she can't be. Tide's nearly at the bottom so there's four feet of water, less. She needs ten feet to get off the mud.'

'Will she sit?' It was one of the Norfolk coast's lethal dangers. A traditional keeled boat caught on the sands will eventually tip over as the tide falls.

'Don't know. Some of those big boats have a split hull – but not all. We have to presume the worst. I've tried the radio. She's receiving, but no answer. And there's a haar building about a mile off, with an onshore wind. It'll be over the sands by low tide. I've got radio contact with a couple of the local boats out there – visibility's down to thirty feet already, and falling fast.'

'A shout, then?' asked Shaw. It was Driscoll's decision, as commander, to call out the hovercraft. But he'd have heard the enthusiasm in Shaw's voice. As pilot Shaw had been forced to resit a test after losing his eye. He'd passed with flying colours. As the examiner had pointed out, beyond twenty-five feet everyone effectively has one eye, the benefits of two just a few inches apart being confined to close quarters.

'Right. I'll get us crew,' said Driscoll.

'I've got a passenger,' said Shaw. 'See you at the landing.'

He put the phone down. 'George. Get your raincoat. You're going to sea.'

They took the Land Rover and Shaw slapped an emergency light on the roof. As he drove, Shaw felt his mobile vibrating as Driscoll set in motion the automatic call-out. Valentine watched the sea go by on the left as they followed the coast. He didn't like the look of it – the sky was picture-book blue, the white waves gently folding on the sands, but further out there was a haze, and the horizon was gone, the sea and sky welded together without a joint.

The Lifeboat House at Old Hunstanton stood on a track leading to the sands, a café opposite, with tables outside. Shaw had a picture of the landing taken in 1920 – a Model-T Ford parked outside, ladies in small hats and knee-length skirts running barefoot in the sand.

The maroon had brought the usual crowd, holidaymakers keen to see some drama on an otherwise dull, hot afternoon. The RNLI shore crew was already marking out a path for the *Flyer* down to the sea, a distant smudge of blue over miles of dry sand. Shaw got his suit on, his helmet and a lightweight windcheater, and checked the radio link with the HM Coast Guard at Hunstanton. They ran up the doors on the new boathouse, and the hovercraft lay within, the skirt deflated, so that it sat like a cat in a basket. Shaw got in the pilot's seat, fired up the two diesel engines, and felt the craft rise, swaying slightly, the sound a distant roar through the helmet buffers.

He checked the controls, then swung round in the seat to see that the crew were in place: navigator, two crew, and Valentine, in a blue passenger's weatherproof, crushed into a seat with a double belt. Driscoll, a late arrival, climbed aboard and took the seat next to Shaw's in the cockpit. He flicked a switch, turning silent warning lights, then reported the launch to the RNLI tracking station. A sonar blade turned above them and the navigator reported that he had their position on monitor. A moving map lit up in front of Shaw, showing the hovercraft as a red circle on a see-through OS map.

Edging *Flyer* out through the doors, Shaw flipped down the visor on the helmet as the sand began to fly, a cloud drifting, so that when he got clear of the old beach huts he couldn't see his house along the beach. They crossed the tidal sands in a cloud of sand and noise, Shaw juggling the joystick to balance the ailerons behind the two spinning propellers which drove the *Flyer* forward. The sea, when they reached it, was like liquid mercury, an unruffled expanse which looked oily, almost syrupy. Shaw swung her east, accelerated to top speed at 30 knots, and hugged the coast. Onshore he saw a pair of horses skittering near Thornham as the engine noise hit them. Off Brancaster they cut through a sailing race, scattering twelve-footers, as Shaw took a short cut across the sands off Scolt Head.

Ahead he saw the incoming haar, a wall of phlegm-white mist, as unbroken as the white cliffs of Dover. They'd ride into it, settle her on dry sand, and try to find the yacht on foot.

Shaw slowed to 10 knots as *Flyer* slipped out of the

sunlight. The mist smelt of ammonia and sea-salt, oyster-fresh. The density of it cut the heat so that it felt like they'd slid into winter, the sudden depressing grey ahead of them, the partly lit edge of the haar retreating behind them as if they'd stopped still and the mist was sliding over them. Shaw swung *Flyer* in a loop, tracing the edge of a bar of sand dried golden before the mist had swept landward. Then he cut the engines, the skirt sank, and they landed with a kiss.

One crewman took the navigator's seat and monitored the radio while the rest climbed over the skirt. A turning halogen beacon was activated on the cabin roof, the beam cutting into the mist, sweeping around them like a lighthouse beam.

Driscoll was out on the sand last. 'Right. Let's do north, south, east, west. Don't lose sight of the light. Take a hailer – ping it if you see her. You OK?'

Valentine was watching the water form a moat round his black slip-ons. 'Sure.'

'That way,' said Driscoll, pointing north. 'There's a compass on the cuff of the jacket.'

Valentine looked at the little needle, then set out. Shaw went east, encountering only the skeleton of a conger eel in the first fifty yards. He stopped, looking down at the plastic cartilage, then back at the distant light. He walked another fifty, his eyes beginning to lose any sense of proportion or relative distance. It was like being lost in a giant sauna.

The single electronic ping, when it came, was eerie, echoing round him. He ran back to the hovercraft and then saw the others heading north, along Valentine's trail.

With a measured stride he followed, hitting every other footprint. When he reached them he could see it too, a bizarre apparition, the million-pound gin palace high and dry. The hull had cut down into a small creek so that there was enough support to keep her upright. In a grey world *Monkey Business* was blindingly white. A light shone from one of the cabin windows on the first deck. Somewhere they could hear the crackle of a radio on an open frequency.

Driscoll threw a weighted rope ladder up and over the deck rail so that it hung down uninvitingly. Shaw climbed first, then held it still for Valentine, who fought to hold on as it corkscrewed under him. The deck was clean, sluiced, spotless; the brass fittings managing a dull gleam despite the gloom.

'Dr Peploe?' Shaw felt an idiot shouting, and was unnerved by the echo bouncing back off the impenetrable fret. The first deck was largely enclosed in smoked brown glass. He walked to a glass door, tried to slide it across, but it was locked. He pressed his eye to the glass but could see nothing within except a fly on the inside: a bluebottle, then another.

They climbed to the second deck up a teak staircase with brass runners. Half of this deck was open at the sides and housed the cockpit. It looked like the flight deck of a 747: a sonar pattern in vivid green on black, the radio signal mapped out in decibel bars.

Red warning lights flashed on the engine monitor display.

There was a hatch down into the deck below which opened with an expensive click. Four carpeted steps led down into a saloon the size of a volleyball pitch. The heat within was stifling despite the filtered glass. Two sofas in a crescent shape took up the main space, along with an exercise bike, a flat-screen TV and a wall of books. The room smelt of polish and not being lived in. Outside the tinted windows the mist pressed up against the glass.

A central corridor led aft from the saloon, teak doors on either side, one into a dining room, another into a Jacuzzi. Another at the far end led to the master bedroom, the bed itself filling most of the cabin, the ceiling a single mirror. In the corner was a spiral staircase leading up to a perspex hatch marked SOLARIUM. A small electric illuminated sign read IN USE.

Shaw climbed until he could get his shoulder up against the hatch. Then he paused. There was a sound, and he looked up through the perspex. Bluebottles, hundreds, wheeling in a demented reel, the iridescent colours making them look like creeping jewels.

Shaw took a breath, pushed the hatch, and the hinges creaked. He climbed another step, bending at the waist, using his body as a lever. Another step, then all his strength applied to unfurl his body. He felt the air-pressure pop in his ears. Then he felt the flies, pouring past him, thudding off his skin in tiny percussions, probing his eyes, his nose, his lips. Forcing his legs to climb, he stumbled into the solarium. The roof was a tinted green-glass bubble, dotted with flies, the hum of the insects amplified in the bowl of the room.

Suspended in a semi-circle were four sun lamps, like operating-theatre lights, the panels emitting a soft cherry-red glow.

Gavin Peploe lay on a sunbed in a pair of yellow beach shorts. His skin was tanned, taut, and his chest and legs showed the well-toned muscles, but even on a million-pound yacht death was ugly.

The flies, spooked by the open hatch, were beginning to return to their meal, massing in the eye sockets and around the nose. Sweat sprang from Shaw's skin. He walked to the wall where a thermometer hung: 49°C, 110°F. The surgeon's skin had burnt on the upper surfaces of the knees and chest – a red burn, black at the edges.

He heard Valentine gagging below. Shaw pulled up the windcheater so that it covered his mouth and nose, zipping it closed.

When had he last seen Peploe? Twenty-four hours ago. If he'd come across the corpse at a crime scene in the open air he'd have guessed it had lain there a week, maybe more. In the oven-like solarium, under the tanning lamps, Gavin Peploe's body was already in an advanced stage of decomposition.

He heard Valentine's footsteps on the short staircase. He appeared, holding a grey handkerchief to his mouth.

They stood either side of the corpse. A glass, empty, was on the bedside table beside an iPod and a mobile phone, the concentric rings edged down the side of the beaker showing that the water had evaporated by degrees.

Peploe lay flat, his head supported by a velour inflatable pillow. There was a thin patina of vomit on his lips and chest. The eyes were open, crowded with flies. Shaw tried to close the eyelids, brushing the insects aside.

'I've radioed,' said Valentine, coughing as something crawled into his mouth.

Shaw felt dizzy in the heat, sick at the sight of such a vibrant, churning death. But he made himself take an inventory of the scene, so that he saw what was in Peploe's right hand. The fingers had come open so that the object they held had almost dropped free onto the sunbed. It was a plastic sweet dispenser in the shape of a dragon – a cylinder in which candy could be stored, then flipped up into the dragon's mouth, then knocked out like Tic-Tac mints. It was Play-Doh yellow, with red and blue stripes. The dragon's mouth was open where the next sweet should be, but they could see that instead of a sweet there was a pill – blue, oval, resting on the plastic pink tongue, like an offering.

38

Who really knew Gavin Peploe? Within six hours they'd built a picture of the man, a picture not entirely consistent with that of the carefree high-living bachelor. Peploe's ex-wife collapsed when informed of his death by a WPC on her doorstep in Virginia Water, Surrey. She'd remarried but had maintained regular contact with her former husband. She told a DI from Windsor CID that they'd simply married too young. Peploe was an epileptic, she said, who had taken AEDs – anticonvulsants – since adolescence. He also had a mild marijuana habit – a well-known recreational means of controlling seizures. His harelip had been corrected by surgery at the age of thirteen. Up until then he had had a severe facial de-formity the removal of which, his wife said, enhanced a tendency to personal vanity and a need to prove himself as a man who could attract women. It was a vice she'd grown to understand, but could never forgive.

Initial forensics from the yacht were inconclusive. Justina Kazimierz's examination of the victim in situ found no wounds. The burning of the skin under the lights and the sun had been post-mortem. She suggested either an accidental or deliberate overdose as a possible cause of death. Some of the pills from the dragon dis-penser had been sent for analysis at the Forensic Science Service. Hadden's CSI team had found no evidence in the solarium, or anywhere else on the yacht, of its use as either a floating operating theatre or a recovery ward. The ship's galley stores were empty except for a few cans of beans, vegetables, and cooked meats, as well as a small supply of bottled water. The engines were in working order, the warning lights on the bridge indicating simply that the screws were out of the sea.

'If Peploe was running a black-market trade in illegal transplants, where are his customers?' Shaw asked Valentine. They were at the Costa Coffee stall in the entrance to A&E at the Queen Vic, in the queue, taking a break from the murder incident room which was running at full tilt. Shaw had just briefed the team on the discovery of Gavin Peploe's body. Outside night had fallen and a revolving emergency light on an ambulance lit the forecourt. 'The rest I can see, George. But how do you get your clients? You can't advertise – or perhaps you can. Online? We should check that out.'

Through a side door was a small concrete patio with picnic tables, each surrounded by a few hundred cigarette butts. They took a seat, enjoying the cool air.

'Find your waiting list first,' said Valentine.

Shaw sipped the coffee, listening now.

'You're rich, you're dying, you need a kidney. Local hospital says maybe a year. But you're rich, you don't *do* waiting. You go private, they say six months because there's a list there too. And even if you've got the money, they're regulated, so you need to meet requirements: weight, diet, lifestyle. Then someone suggests there's another way. You can jump the queue – all the queues.'

Shaw crushed his paper cup and laid both his hands,

palms down, on the wooden table top. 'So we've got our surgeon – Peploe; we've got our operating theatre – here, Theatre Seven. Recovery rooms? On Level One's my bet – the search didn't find it but you're right, soon as Bryan Judd turns up dead they wipe it out – not a trace. Clients – there's a system, like you say, because we know there's a demand. Which leaves the supply – the donors. Homeless men, desperate for cash, willing to take the ultimate risk, to leave themselves defenceless for a thousand pounds – fifty pounds down and the rest if they survive. What don't we know?'

Valentine sighed; he hated this kind of rationalization, treating a crime like a textbook example. 'We don't know whether Peploe killed himself because he knew what we were about to find in the organ bank, or whether his death was an accident, or even murder. We don't know who the Organ Grinder is – the man on the street, finding and collecting the donors. We don't know who Peploe's accomplices were. And we don't know who killed Bryan Judd or why – which is where we came in. That do you?'

Shaw licked the chocolate off the lid of his coffee.

'Doesn't mean we can't try and think it through.'

Valentine spat in the dust.

'Bryan Judd fits in to the organ trade,' said Shaw. 'He makes sure the waste from the ops gets nicely disposed of. That's vital. They could burn it domestically, but they'd have to get it off the site, which is dangerous – stupid – if you can do it right here.'

Above them a thin line of smoke from the incinerator chimney caught the moon.

'Let's think about Judd's life,' said Shaw. 'He earns pretty much the minimum wage in here. He's caught up in this scam with Holme for which he gets a supply of Green Dragon. That's been going on a year, or more, so he's hooked. Plus, he gets whatever he's paid for dumping the human waste. My guess is that's not much, either, otherwise he wouldn't need Holme. So – summary is, our man is on the bottom of the feeding chain, and he's just alive. He gets his basic wage and some top-ups for turning a blind eye on the incinerator belt and giving Holme a heads up when drugs are going to be destroyed.

'But then, on the day he dies, things get worse. Holme goes up to the hospital to spell it out for the last time. He's going down; there won't be any more Green Dragon.' Shaw pinged the corner of the paper cup. 'Holme was going to be out of the picture – pretty much permanently as far as Judd was concerned. So Judd had to face up to the fact he'd have to get his gear somewhere else – and he needed the cash to get it. What are we talking about, George? A hundred pounds a week, one-fifty?'

Valentine nodded. 'Depends on how much he got through, but the cases I've seen – they're heavy users. So at least that.'

'So Judd's facing a crisis. He needs extra cash. What if he asked Peploe or the Organ Grinder for it? Perhaps he even added in a threat – that he'd blow the lid on the organ trade if he didn't get it. Because this isn't some little two-bit money earner, is it? We're talking organized crime, even if it isn't exactly the Mafia.'

Valentine, drawn into the analysis, took Shaw's crunched cup and turned it over, tapping the top. 'One thing – the candle mark on Blanket's back. Maybe that's the sign. But why'd you need to do that if you're the one who's collecting him?'

Shaw smiled. 'So there's two of them right there – one selects, one collects.' A bat, attracted by the insects circling in the light spilling from the glass door, swung round their heads.

DC Twine had tracked them down to the café. He took a seat, unscrewing the top on a bottle of still water. 'Bit of luck. Peploe's secretary at the hospital seems to know her boss pretty well – she's up to speed on his pills, anyway. She says he was on a course of anticonvulsants, like the wife said. The dragon's head dispenses lamotrigine. He told the kids they were sweets if he had to take one in public. He always carried a bag of boiled sweets too, so they got one as well.' He looked at a note he'd taken in a neat pocket book. 'He also took carbamazepine as a syrup – probably each morning – and gabapentin as an emergency measure. They were in a plastic bottle in his pocket.

'Problem is, Tom says the pills in the dispenser aren't lamotrigine. We'll have to wait for the official analysis from the FSS. The colour and shape are very close, but he thinks it's definitely something else. He showed the pharmacist at the hospital and she spotted them straight away. He thinks they're sodium nitroprusside. The A&E department holds them for use in emergencies to produce a sharp drop in blood pressure. One pill – never more. Even one, given to a patient with normal blood pressure, could be fatal. Two – and Peploe always took two as a dose – would be fatal.'

Shaw closed his eyes and pictured again the image of Peploe taking the pills. The quick, habitual double shake, the medicine dispensed onto his hand and then straight into his mouth. He hadn't looked. Why would he? Anyone who knew him would know that about Gavin Peploe: he never looked.

'It could have been suicide,' said Twine. 'He'd know the effect.'

Shaw shook his head. 'Think it through. It doesn't make sense. Why were the pills in the dispenser? You don't decide to commit suicide and then dream up ways to make it look like an accident. Unless it's an insurance scam – and I think we can rule that out. If he wanted to top himself he'd have just taken them. No – I think someone swapped them. Then left him to administer his own poison. Someone who didn't want Gavin Peploe to talk.'

39

Lena was asleep in the cottage, so Shaw let himself into the small office behind the Beach Café and switched on the iMac. He wouldn't sleep yet, so he might as well do something. The likelihood that Gavin Peploe had been murdered meant the inquiry had to be reappraised. The whole squad had been paged and told to attend a briefing at 6.30 the following morning on Level One. Outside he could hear the tide washing in, and a night breeze in the tall grass in the dunes.

As the iMac screen blossomed he tried to push Peploe's face from his mind: the saliva in a colourless line across the tanned skin, the crowded eyes. He tapped into Google, then to the local council website, following the links to the Burney Housing Association which now ran the Westmead Estate. Garage rental was outsourced to a private company called OffStreet. It had an online register listing the sixty-three lock-up garages on the Westmead. Eight were empty and available for rental at an annual fee of £40. Management of the service on the ground was provided by a warden – Mr D. Holden. An address in the nearby Shinwell Flats was listed, together with a telephone number.

Shaw checked his watch: low tide, and 10.36 p.m. It was late, but patience wasn't his strong suit. He rang and a woman answered, who said Don wouldn't mind the call, because he was so bored he was watching *Newsnight.* Shaw assured her it was a routine inquiry.

Don Holden's voice was a surprise; high and reedy, happy to help. Shaw had four names and wanted to know if any of them matched the tenants on the current roll. Four names: the three Askit apprentices he suspected were on the CCTV of the crash at Castle Rising, and Robert Mosse. Don said he'd be a minute and came back with the register. It was all on paper, always had been, because he'd been on a course for the computer but his fingers were too big for the keys. Shaw waited.

No match.

Did he have the register for past years? Yes – back to 1995. Before that he'd burnt the lot because it was a small flat and they had a cat to swing. Could he check back? Shaw sat, breathing in the sea air through the open window, as Holden went over the old registers.

No match.

Shaw laughed, thanked him, and rang off. He walked out on the sand and watched the distant white line of surf breaking out towards the horizon. He took a small rubber ball from his pocket and began to bounce it up against the wooden side of the café, catching it despite his one-eyed vision by gently moving his head a few inches from side to side – a technique which effectively gave his brain two images of the moving ball from which he could build a 3D image. He caught the ball three times perfectly, but missed the fourth by a good foot. It was a skill he'd have to hone.

He pocketed the ball and glanced up at the small sign set over the entrance to the café. It had been a big step

343

forward this summer, getting the drinks licence. Next year they might open in the early evenings, see if they could build up a trade. The sign's white lettering shone in the moonlight: *Lena Margaret Hunte; licensed to sell beers, wines and spirits to be consumed on the premises.*

Everything to do with the business was in her name – and she'd never taken his. He went back to his desk and found the file he wanted in the top drawer. The records on a juvenile court case from 1996, a case he'd been drawn to because of its links to the death of Jonathan Tessier. Three young men – Bobby Mosse's gang – had admitted terrorizing a small boy called Giddy Poynter. The boy's mother had tried to set up a Neighbourhood Watch scheme on the Westmead to try and curb vandalism on her floor of Vancouver House. The gang locked Giddy in a rubbish bin overnight, having tossed in half a dozen rats to keep him company, just to teach his mum a lesson.

Shaw read through the note on the proceedings until he got to a section in which each of the three gang members had been given the chance to produce an adult to speak on their behalf. They'd admitted the charges, but this was in mitigation. Two had produced fathers but the third – Alex Cosyns – had called his mother, a woman who described herself as the common-law wife of his father. She'd kept her maiden name. And there it was – Roundhay.

Shaw rang Holden back and asked him to check Roundhay in the list of tenants – but he didn't have to.

'Yes. Of course – that's a big family on the Westmead, Inspector. They've always owned a lock-up – that's number 51. They might even have 50 as well, but I'd have to look that up.'

Shaw told him not to bother; one number was enough.

The picture in Shaw's head was like a snapshot from a family album – in 1990s colour, brash and glaring. A hot Sunday afternoon, the lock-up garages baking, a small boy standing at an open roll-up door, a puppy yelping. At the side of the door two numbers screwed into the woodwork: 51. Then the snapshot moved, coming to life, so that the child was free to move. Someone said something and he took a step inside, out of the sunlight, then another, and then he was gone. For ever.

40

Valentine walked home along the quayside. The incoming tide brought with it the remnants of the cool mist which had acted as a shroud for Gavin Peploe's yacht. Out in mid-channel a freighter had slid in along the Cut from the sea, deck lights ablaze. The sound of a radio playing music to a Latin beat bounced over the water. The ship swung in the tide, the stern coming round towards the quayside so that she could enter the Alexandra Dock. The steel starboard side came to within fifty feet of the quay, towering over Valentine.

He stopped, lit a Silk Cut, and watched the ship glide towards him, skewed, the great mass edging sideways. The engines churned up chocolate-coloured water. On the side was painted a huge flag. Something exotic, thought Valentine; the Philippines, perhaps? Some banana republic? A blue flag, a yellow rhombus, within which was set a blue sphere of the night sky with studded stars, and a curving green band containing letters.

'Tin-pot,' he said to himself. You could always tell a country that had its arse hanging out by the fact that it had a flag cluttered with rubbish: coats of arms, emblems, flowers, you name it – they'd stuff it on the flag in the hope that no one would notice that the country was on its uppers.

The flag flying from the mast was different, something

corporate – black with white letters that he couldn't read because despite the drifting mist there was hardly any wind.

Smoking, he read out the words on the coloured flag. 'Ordem e Progresso.' He thought it didn't take his education to work that one out. Order and progress. Trite, he thought, flicking his cigarette end in the water, then turning away.

Fifty yards down the quay he stopped, in no hurry to get home. The house, despite the summer's day, would be cold – especially the bathroom, which always offered up the worst moment of his life, the last look in the mirror each night. He lit another Silk Cut, and thought about Alex Cosyns – about the cheque from Robert Mosse, and who he knew on the regional fraud squad who could wriggle him access to Cosyns's bank account. There'd been no complaint from Cosyns. Which was good news, but also unsettling. He shivered slightly, rolling his shoulders.

He looked back along the quay when he heard the odd, taut complaint of the buffers on the ship meeting the wooden piling which protected the concrete wharf; just a glance, a random moment which, he would later have to admit, probably saved his career, maybe even his life.

The name on the stern of the ship was written in blue letters ten feet high:

MV ROSA.

41

Shaw woke a millisecond before the phone rang. Or was it the second ring? He could never quite catch the echo, but sensed it was there, bouncing round the dark room. He could smell Lena; her skin was so close, a subtle mix of sweat and salt. He fumbled with the receiver trying not to think it must be bad news. It was George Valentine.

'Peter. I need to show you something – outside the Crane, on Erebus Street.' For once Valentine's voice was free of the corrosive edge of antagonism.

Lena turned away in her sleep.

Shaw propped himself up on an elbow and looked at the harsh red numbers on the alarm clock: 12.55 a.m.

Then he made a mistake. 'Is this really necessary, George?'

He heard Valentine draw on an unseen cigarette. Shaw knew he shouldn't have asked, shouldn't have questioned his DS's judgement. George Valentine was his partner, and he'd got the best part of thirty years' service under his belt. If he rang his DI in the middle of the night he had a reason – a compelling one. Shaw knew what Lena would say, and the word 'trust' would be at its heart. So he made himself cut in. 'Sorry. Course it is. I'll be there in twenty. Don't move.'

There was no sign of the moon when he pulled the

Land Rover into Erebus Street – just the orange splodges of the street lights, and the green, throbbing neon sign announcing 24-HOUR WASH, although the launderette was closed.

Valentine sat in the gutter, a pewter flask in his hand, his lips wet, so that they caught the light. In the sudden flood of headlamps he stood arthritically, like a deckchair unfolding. When Shaw got out of the Land Rover his DS didn't say anything, just led the way to the dock gates, following the sunken iron rails in the tarmac. The gate to the wired compound for the electricity sub-station stood open.

'The lock here was broken – that's how Andy Judd got in with his bottle of paraffin,' said Valentine.

From the small yard within they could see up into Jan Orzsak's house, where a single light shone through the frosted glass of a bathroom window. A shadow moved inside, and Shaw imagined Orzsak standing at a mirror, trying to forget whatever nightmare had woken him up, shifting his weight off the crushed slipper.

'We missed this,' said Valentine. He brushed his way through the hawthorn bushes to the far wire, the perimeter of the dockyard, and there they found another metal gate.

'This is neat,' said Valentine, holding out a padlock on his hand. The heavy-duty shackle had been filed through. The hinge screamed as the gate swung in. They walked out onto the barren acre of concrete, on which had been painted the giant number 4. A rat dashed left and right, left and right, seemingly following a path only it could see, as if it were negotiating an invisible maze.

Valentine pointed down the quayside towards the moored ship.

Shaw read the letters painted on the stern, and felt his blood run deliciously cool.

'*MV Rosa*,' he said. 'MVR.'

His second thought, after he'd stopped the elation flooding his brain, was that it could be a coincidence. 'Was she here on Sunday night?'

Valentine nodded, looking at his black slip-ons. 'I rang the shipping agent – she sailed Monday morning at dawn. But she was here, Berth 4.'

'*Well done*,' said Shaw, thinking fast, putting together pieces of a jigsaw which suddenly seemed to fit – like Pete Hendre's description of the room he'd woken up in, with the steady mechanical hum, and the iron door. Like the bodies on Warham's Hole and on the storm-drain grid. Like the torch and the wristband: MVR.

'You haven't been aboard?' He bit his lip, recognizing that he'd done it again, shown his lack of trust, because only an idiot rookie would be stupid enough to blunder aboard.

The cold edge returned to Valentine's voice. 'Agent's meeting us at the dock office – I've told him if he contacts anyone on the *Rosa* he'll be a shipping agent in Murmansk by the weekend. He's OK. Old school.'

The *Rosa* was silent except for the dribble of a bilge pump into the black oily water. They strolled away from the ship, keeping to the shadows of the hawthorns that grew through the wire fencing, round the edge of the Alexandra Dock, to the gates into the Bentinck – the inner dock – aware that by now they'd be on the CCTV.

On the far side of the dividing swing-bridge between the docks was a 1950s office block, two-storey, the upper one having a plate-glass window providing a view of the quays. A light shone, but half-heartedly, the blue glow of computer screens fluttering. A fascia board read CONSTABLE SHIPPING AGENTS.

Valentine spoke into a crackling entryphone grille.

'DS Valentine, sir. We spoke twenty minutes ago.'

They heard the automatic bolts shoot back. Inside was a windowless room in which sat two women, both wearing thigh-length skirts – one leather, one red silk – stockings, and loose blouses – one in gold lamé, the other silver, spangled with red dots. One had a cut lip, the other a puffy eye; tears stained the make-up on both.

Shaw thought they looked like hookers from central casting.

'Girls,' said Valentine. He knew them both, regulars from the small red-light district on the outskirts of the North End. Neither was older than twenty-five, but he knew they'd already been on the streets a decade.

'Fuck off,' said one, winking at Shaw. The other one hit her, but it was only a make-believe blow, and it made them both laugh bitterly. They clutched each other's arms and glared at Valentine, united in their antagonism.

'Come up,' crackled a voice from the entryphone outside. They climbed to the office. The ship's agent was called Galloway, a thick-set Scot with a permanent five o'clock shadow and short arms that hung like weapons from his shoulders. A Cairn terrier cross was at his feet, chewing the cardboard packet which had once held a beef sandwich. Galloway waved a mobile phone at them. 'Just getting one of your mob out to take the girls in – bit of a bundle over a client.'

Shaw shook his head. 'Do us a favour – cancel. Tell them we're here. Do it now.'

Galloway did so and killed the call. He didn't look that happy about being given orders in his own office. 'Next?' he said.

'What would the security guard at the gate do if he spotted two men like us wandering the dockside and then turning up here?'

'If he was awake, he'd ring me,' he said.

They stood in the silence. 'He isn't awake very often,' said Galloway. 'That's how the girls get on here. We're trying to keep the hookers off the dock. Mind you, these two were in the boot of a cab,' he added, shaking his head. 'Ship owners don't like it. They like the vice onshore.'

'That's the girl *we're* interested in,' said Valentine, pointing at the *Rosa*. 'What can you tell us?'

Galloway punched some computer keys. 'I've drilled down for the stuff you need ... She's a regular. Dutch owners. Basic run is from here to Vaasa – that's Finland; godforsaken hole, too. You wouldn't even get a shag there, let alone a drink. She takes grain, scrap metal, brings back timber. Three and a half thousand tonnes – which means she's a neat fit for the Kiel Canal, so we're talking five, six days, each way. Nearer six now the EU's kicking up about energy efficiency – they have to trim their speed, burns less fuel. Then there's a regular two-way contract to Rotterdam. She's just come in from that, carrying ...' He checked on screen. 'White goods – fridges, mainly.'

'And she was definitely here Sunday night?' asked Valentine.

Galloway nodded, scooping up the dog.

'Crew?' asked Shaw.

'Er ... standard seven. Captain is Juan de Mesquita – John to us. First Officer's Dutch, engineer is a Pole, couple of Russian ABs, then two Filipino deck crew – one of 'em's the cook. Good, too – I've had the grub.'

'All aboard?'

'Yeah. Probably. They don't need permission not to be – except from the captain. EU nationals don't need a passport. They'll go into town in the morning, shop while she's being unloaded. Then it's grain to load, and she should make the tide tomorrow night.'

Shaw shook his head. 'She's not going anywhere.'

'Technically, she's Dutch sovereign territory,' said Galloway, folding the short arms across a barrel chest.

'The dock gates are British,' said Shaw. 'And they're staying shut.'

Galloway shrugged. 'OK, but you'll have to deal with the owners. Every moment she's in the dock she's losing money. I'd need authorization – I don't know – the chief constable's office, something like that. In writing. I'm not trying to be difficult, but this is what I do. I protect the owners' interests.'

Deck lights died on the *Rosa*, leaving just the bridge lit. Shaw called the dog, which nuzzled his hands. 'We need your help,' he added to Galloway. 'I can't tell you everything, but I'll tell you as much as I can.'

It took Shaw a minute to give him the bare burnt bones. The case in a nutshell: Judd's death at the hospital, the other two bodies they'd found – both with evidence of transplant scars. The search for the operating theatre, the recovery rooms – somewhere that hums, that's hot, with the service cables in the roof, and steel doors. And the nagging clue: MVR. The torch, and the wrist-bands.

'You mean like this?' asked Galloway, extending his wrist out from a shirt cuff. On it was a white band, and he turned it to reveal the tell-tale letters MVR. 'Crew's been flogging these for about six months. They're raising cash for Mercy Ships – you know? Charity ships. They sail into some godforsaken port in Africa and start offering cataract ops for free, vaccination, that kind of thing.' He jiggled the band. 'It's a good cause.'

'It's guilt,' said Shaw. 'Crooks can surprise you just like honest people do.'

Galloway opened a drawer on his desk and retrieved a bottle of whisky. The label was Dutch. He poured it into three tea mugs and divvied them up.

'So,' concluded Shaw, sipping. 'What I want to do is watch, see what happens. They may just keep their heads down – I would. They don't know we've got the torch or the wristbands – although they may well know we've picked up the two floaters, so perhaps they've guessed. But they won't know we've made the link. And I guess they have to come back, right? They haven't got a lot of choice.'

'None. She's run by the owners. Contracts are in place. They want her in Lynn, she's in Lynn.'

Unless, of course, the owners were in on the game, thought Shaw. He made a mental note to check back on the ownership, on the ship's history, and the captain's track record.

'They'll know we're up at the hospital turning the place over,' said Shaw. 'And the death of one of the surgeons – Peploe – has given us a conveniently silent prime suspect. If they're greedy, or desperate, they might just think they're in the clear. I don't want anyone on the ship alerted. Let them think they're sailing Saturday morning. Can we put someone in here . . .'

Galloway looked round at the dishevelled office. 'Sure. The glass is tinted so they can't see in. I usually go aboard for the paperwork, so they don't come here. You'd be safe. There's a secretary, telephonist, but they're good girls. Leave it to me.' He walked to the glass and looked at the ship. 'There's dockside CCTV – a camera on the gate, one on the quay. There are screens at security. Mind you, the picture quality's crap so don't get your hopes up.'

'I'll get you that letter from the chief constable – and the Port Authority. You'll be covered,' said Shaw. He asked to borrow a pair of night-vision binoculars.

The light was eerie, a kind of low-voltage purple. He focused on the security booth at the gate, two hundred yards away – a blaze of neon, the cap of the security guard just visible through the plastic counter glass.

'He's asleep all right.'

Then he looked at the *Rosa*, tied to the quayside, the only link between the two worlds a thin gangplank. No, not the only link, because there was the thick power cable as well, like a snake.

Something clicked into place in Shaw's mind, like a virtual plug into an imaginary socket.

He sat down, composed the question. 'How come the ship takes power off the quayside?'

Galloway put his hands behind his head, revealing two large patches of sweat-stained shirt. 'We're a green port. That means once the ships tie up they have to switch to UK power, which is generated inland from biomass. Costs a fucking fortune – nobody likes it, but that's the way it is. If the UK's gonna meet its emissions targets this is the kind of nonsense we have to live with.'

'So Sunday lunchtime, when the power went, they'd have to switch to the generator?' Shaw tried to recall the dark shape of the ship beyond the dock gates, but he couldn't see any lights in his memory.

Galloway thought, then frowned. 'Well, the others did – the *Ostgard*, the *Waverley*, the *Rufinia*. They all switched to generators 'cos I had to go aboard to do the paperwork during the afternoon and they all had power. But I did the *Rosa* when she came in about ten that morning. Then I went home. I do that – just to frighten the wife. But Monday morning the bloke on security said there'd been a cock-up on the *Rosa* – soon as they'd docked and hooked up to the shore-side power they'd taken the chance to strip down the generator 'cos it was way past its maintenance date. So when the power went pop they were buggered. Took them till after midnight to get it up and running again.'

Shaw and Valentine exchanged glances. At last, the link between the seemingly chaotic events on Erebus Street and the illegal traffic in human organs. Shaw tried to imagine the scene on board as the power failed at mid-day on Sunday: the frantic activity, the generator useless.

He pressed his forehead against the tinted glass and looked at the *Rosa*. Then he scrolled down his mobile call list until he found the number for Andersen, the electricity company engineer they'd talked to in Erebus Street on the Sunday night. He answered on the third ring. Shaw guessed he had the kind of career where a call in the middle of the night wasn't unusual. Shaw had a simple question: the power on the quayside, did it run through the Erebus Street sub-station, and if it did, where was it coming from now? Simple answers: yes, to one. Now it came from a divert they'd set up from the power supply on the Bentinck Dock.

'Can you monitor the supply to a specific ship?'

'Sure,' said Andersen. 'I'd have to get into the other sub-station – it's over by the grain stores.'

'Can you do that? This is confidential, so low key. Then let me know as soon as there's a peak in the supply – anything substantial. The ship we're interested in is the *Rosa*.'

'Why?'

It was a fair question and he needed the engineer onside. 'It's possible the *Rosa* has been used as a kind of floating hospital – an illegal floating hospital. If they tried an operation on board the arc lamps alone would chew up the power supply. I want you to tell me if there's a peak like that.'

Andersen said he'd be in position in an hour.

Then Shaw swung the glasses round to the old gates at the bottom of Erebus Street. The light still shone from Orzsak's bathroom, but it wasn't the only light now. Above the Bentinck Launderette the lights were on, glimpsed through curtains, and only visible in the dark interlude when the 24-HOUR WASH sign wasn't lit green – a livid light, echoed by the stark illuminated cross on the apex of the roof of the Sacred Heart.

'OK,' said Shaw. 'For now, we wait.'

42

Shaw took the first watch. He set up a desk by the observation window, put his mobile on it, a coffee cup alongside. From inside his jacket he produced the CCTV print he'd taken from the footage of the fatal road accident at Castle Rising which had killed Jonathan Tessier's grandmother – and apparently set in motion a chain of events which had led to the nine-year-old's murder.

The print showed the Mini after the impact, parked in the shadows under the trees. The offside wing crumpled, but otherwise intact. The two-tone paint job, a radio aerial, and a roof rack. Raindrops speckled the windows, except where the wipers had kept the view clear for the driver.

He sat back, letting his mind slip into neutral. Out on the quayside nothing moved. On a moonless night the shadows didn't move. He tried to conjure up a memory of Erebus Street on that Sunday night: the fire burning, Blanket's abduction from the church, the attack on the hostel, Ally Judd slipping home from the presbytery, and the ship, in darkness, just beyond the dock gates at the end of the street.

Tiredness overwhelmed him, so that he slept for a nano-second, waking up with a heart-thumping start. He stood, both hands on the glass, looking out on the bleak dock. There was one vehicle parked in a bay by the grain store, an HGV, towing a container trailer which was empty. One of the Eddie Stobart fleet. Shaw guessed the driver had reached the legal limit on his hours and had been forced to leave his lorry and find a room for the night in Lynn. Or he was fast asleep in his cab. One of the floodlights bounced off the curved windscreen, which was filthy with dust from the docks, except where the glass had been swished clean by the wipers.

Shaw's heart missed a beat. He looked at his CCTV print, at the window within a window cleared by the windscreen wipers. He'd seen it so many times – and yet hadn't seen it. He looked out of the window at the HGV, back at the Mini, back at the HGV.

'Jesus,' he said, burying his head in his hands. He'd known all the time – or he should have realized he'd known. The paint he'd tracked down through forensics was for a batch of Minis for *export*.

'Anything wrong?' asked Galloway, who was playing computer games silently on his desktop PC.

'No, just the opposite. Here, have a look.'

Galloway came over, his knees slightly arthritic, the mug of whisky still in his hand.

'What's the difference between this windscreen,' said Shaw, touching the print, 'and that ...' He pointed at the HGV.

'This windscreen's covered in water – that one's covered in shite.'

Shaw shook his head. 'Nope. This one ...' he said, letting his finger vibrate on the print of the Mini. 'This one is left-hand drive. See – the shape of the cleaned area

360

is reversed. It's about the only external difference you'd see in a British car converted to left-hand drive. If you didn't switch the wipers the driver would have the diminished vision, not the passenger.'

'Well done. So what?'

'This picture was taken a few moments after a fatal crash. One man got out the driver's side, two out the back. At least, I thought it was the driver's side. But it isn't. *The driver is still in the car.* There were four of them. But the driver's smart enough to stay out of sight.'

He gave Galloway the surfer's smile. He felt a flash of joy in his life, like a distant view of the sea. 'Got any more of that whisky?'

43

Jan Orzsak stood on a chair in the hallway of his house, a picture of his mother, cut from the family album, held to his chest with one hand. He'd been standing still for nearly two hours and the pain in his legs was making them shake. Around his neck was a noose he'd made from a bed sheet, the end attached to the newel post of the banisters above.

The dawn sun shone through the 1930s stained glass over the front door. The light – blue and yellow – caught dust motes in parallelograms of colour. A heavenly beauty, he thought. And the fittingness of this thought made him smile.

He'd heard the six o'clock siren on the docks. He wondered if he could die by inaction, if he just stood and let the world grow old around him. He'd almost taken that decision when there was a sharp knock on the door.

The intrusion broke the spell. Whoever it was tried to flip up the letterbox, but he'd had it nailed shut after the latest dogshit package. 'Mr Orzsak?' said a muffled voice. 'We saw the light. I'm sorry, can we talk? It's the power engineers – from next door.'

The last twelve hours had been the worst of Jan Orzsak's life, and he was determined – as a determined man – to make sure the agony did not persist. He'd lived a private life, and it was a kind of death to have people crawling all over it. He'd take what was left of his privacy to his God. He'd been a just man, and he'd kept God's law, so he didn't fear meeting him. There was only one great sin, and he knew God would forgive him for that.

He'd set the DVD player in his room to Chopin, a nocturne, playing in a continuous loop. It had reached the closing bars. There'd be silence in a minute and then all he had to do was step off the chair, and it would be over. But how many times had he listened already to those same closing bars? Twenty? Each time the beautiful music demanded another performance. A final curtain-call.

The knock at the door was more insistent. 'Mr Orzsak. We need to cut the power. I can't go ahead unless you agree. Ten minutes, sir, then we'll be done and out of your hair. Sir?'

Beyond the front door he could hear the foreman muttering – stringing together profanities.

The music died.

Orzsak felt very cold, the blood rushing to his heart, the sudden certainty of what was to happen next making his vision clear. He gripped the picture to his heart and he thought what a child-like impulse that was, and that made him even more determined to go back there – before all this happened – back to a time of innocence.

He stepped off the chair into the spangled air.

Weightless, for a second, he felt sublimely happy.

44

Shaw rang the head of security for the docks, an ex-DI from Peterborough called Frank Denver, at 7.01 a.m. Shaw thought the timing was acceptable – but wasn't surprised to discover otherwise. When Denver had stopped shouting about being woken up Shaw told him the good news: that there was every chance a series of major crimes had taken place within the docks, unnoticed by either his security staff or the Lynn CID. His cooperation was now urgently required. He didn't have a choice.

Denver arranged for a taxi to call at the dock security booth and pick up the written record of vehicles entering and leaving the quayside, then drop it at the agent's office. The CCTV footage from dock security was available at the booth – there was a back room for viewing and DC Birley was on his way down to start running it through. The Port Authority manager was told that on no account was he to meet any request from the *Rosa* to leave Lynn; if asked, he was to say that the Home Office had an immigration issue and was sending up an officer to interview the captain.

Shaw arranged for a former colleague in the Met to liaise with Whitehall to make sure they had a credible set of case notes to begin an inquiry. Meanwhile, Shaw got Twine to search for the *Rosa* online; he wanted details on ownership, crew, and cargoes.

At ten DC Jackie Lau arrived by courier motorbike. She took over surveillance while Shaw settled down with the security log. The record for Sunday, 5 September, the day Bryan Judd died, showed thirty-five vehicles in, thirty-seven out. Shaw dispensed with all commercial vehicles: HGVs, container lorries, and Port Authority personnel. That left a BMW series six which had come onto the docks at 7 a.m. The Monday record showed another early-morning visit. He rang Birley, who'd just slipped into the dock security booth office, and told him to run the tapes covering the quayside for those periods. It took him twenty minutes to locate the BMW parked by the *Rosa*'s gangplank at 7.06 a.m. It was booked out at 8.13 a.m. At 4.30 a.m. the next morning it returned, leaving at 5.13 a.m. Each time there was a chauffeur. The man who was the passenger – dropped on the first morning, picked up the next – was grossly overweight and walked badly. The *Rosa* sailed at six on Tuesday morning.

The BMW's registration plate led them to a car-hire firm in Lynn. The vehicle was still on hire, at a private address in Burnham Overy Staithe, a village deep in the heart of 'Chelsea-on-Sea', booked out in the name of a Ravid Lotnar.

Shaw left by taxi, meeting Valentine in the Mazda on the Tuesday Market in a lay-by on the east side. First, news from St James's. Andy Judd had been charged with arson and criminal damage and then released on police bail. Three conditions: he had to report daily at St James's, had to stay within a mile of Erebus Street, and he had to keep away from Jan Orzsak.

Valentine also had a brief run-down on Ravid Lotnar gathered online. He was an Israeli, and a man of some substance; rich, but not in the super-rich league. Aged seventy-six, married, with six children. Born in Slaný, Bohemia, the son of a Jewish printer. Fled to the USA with his mother in 1938. Emigrated to Israel in 1947; now the MD of a publishing company which produced one of Israel's national newspapers, and a string of magazines. The registered head office was in Tel Aviv. His home address was also in the city.

'Jewish,' said Shaw, as they picked up the coast road running east. 'Peploe gave me some files, background material on the organ traffic trade. Israelis are major customers – know why?'

Valentine drummed his fingers on the steering wheel; the Mazda was trapped behind a caravan. 'Money?'

'Nope. It's one of the few developed countries which do not recognize the concept of brain death. That seriously reduces the supply of organs for transplant, which forces thousands onto the black market. Which means we are almost certainly about to meet our first organ transplant customer.'

The radio crackled. It was Birley. He'd cut into the CCTV footage at hourly intervals for Sunday. The power had gone at 12.15 precisely. Luckily, the CCTV cameras were on a circuit which fed the new dock, so had remained live. He was able to see that at dusk most of the ships had switched to their onboard generators and had begun to show lights. The *Rosa*, however, had remained in darkness until 12.13 a.m. Shaw worked with that time frame: if an operation had been under way on the *Rosa* it had been cruelly interrupted by nearly twelve hours of darkness. He tried to imagine the chaos on board, the botched operation, and the freezers, slowly warming.

They got to the village and turned off towards the beach, the lane snaking through an ocean of reeds where the spring tides flooded the marsh.

'One other thing,' said Valentine. 'Bad news. Twine's picked up a note sent out by Lincoln CID. They're looking for background info on a Benjamin David Ruddle – the father of Norma Jean's baby. He's alive and well in one of their cells and has given Erebus Street as his home address. Little fucker; killed a prison officer with a Stanley knife as he walked home through the park after dark. Then he just stood there with the knife until he got picked up. Claims the bloke abused him at Deerbolt. Other than that, he ain't talking.' Valentine shifted his weight, trying to reduce the pressure on his bladder. 'Look's like he's settled that score.'

'So he isn't Blanket.'

'Nope. Less he's a quick mover. Plus Twine says he looked at personal details – he's thirteen stone. Kennedy says Blanket's eight, nine tops.'

They'd reached the house. A new wall in Norfolk stone, an iron set of security gates with a security keypad. Staithe House itself was minimalist modern in blinding Greek white, but hidden beneath a grove of pines which had been forced to bend with the wind until they caressed the building, softening its lines, making it part of the sinuous wave of dunes. A pair of Dobermann pinschers ran down to the gates to greet them, mouths open and wet, like flesh-eating plants.

Shaw got out and stood pressing the call button, then identified himself when a voice crackled. There'd been a series of burglaries in the Burnham area, he explained, all on properties owned by the letting agency Mr Lotnar had used. It was a routine check, with some timely advice. A voice said to wait. Somewhere he could hear splashing in a swimming pool, and the screams of women. The dogs disappeared to the sound, presumably, of an inaudible whistle, and the gates opened.

A silent servant, a young man dressed in black shorts and a black T-shirt, said his name was Charlie and led them into the house, guarding them for twenty minutes while Mr Lotnar readied himself to meet them. Shaw noticed that Charlie was all muscle, with the kind of biceps that need daily care. They sat in an open-plan living room, spotless, in dark polished wood, watercolours of the north Norfolk coast spotlit on the white walls. Shaw asked for the toilet and started climbing the stairs, waiting for directions.

'First left,' Charlie said, trying to work out if he should stay with Valentine or follow Shaw.

Shaw found the toilet, washed his hands, left a tap running, then slipped along the corridor to a bedroom door. He pushed it open and stood on the threshold. A set of leather cases stood open, packed neatly with clothes. Then he heard a sound that didn't fit, a kind of rhythmic mechanical breathing. He followed the sound back to the top of stairs and into the opposite wing. But he'd only taken a few steps when a door opened and a woman stepped out onto the expensive carpet pile: a nurse, immaculate private-healthcare white, the sound of the machine louder, swelling in the hall.

'I needed the loo,' said Shaw.

She pointed behind him. 'First left at the top of the stairs.' The voice had a syrupy sibilance, and Shaw guessed she was an Israeli too.

He went to the toilet, turned off the tap, flushed the loo, and padded down the stairs, rubbing damp hands together. They all sat amongst the dark polished wood, feigning patience. A buzzer sounded, the noise coming from an antique desk set in the bay window. Charlie took them through into the back garden, which featured an emerald green lawn in alternate stripes, and a pool that sparkled. Lotnar was in a recliner, and Shaw wondered what he'd been doing while they'd been decanted through the house. Had he been upstairs with the machine that mimicked breathing? A woman in a bikini stood drying herself with a fluffy towel in front of him. Shaw couldn't help thinking that her business was her body: tanned, toned, and as curved as the sand dunes. She took a lot of time making sure the skin on her thighs was dry.

Lotnar didn't introduce her, or the other two girls in the pool, floating topless on lilos, their breasts pale against deep tans.

'Inspector.' Lotnar didn't get up. In fact he didn't look like he did a lot of getting up. He weighed, Shaw guessed, at least twenty stone. His torso sagged in a pair of Bermuda shorts, like a Walnut Whip, the overhang of fat covered by an expensive silk shirt, the top six buttons open.

'I'd like to talk privately, if that's OK,' said Shaw. 'We have some information concerning these break-ins which is confidential.'

Lotnar shrugged and dismissed the girl. She went to frolic with the others in a half-hearted way, but they made enough noise to cover any conversation. That was the way Shaw wanted it; only Lotnar was going to hear what he had to say.

He gave Lotnar a version of the real reason they were in his house, a version Shaw thought would worry him just enough: that there had been a murder, evidence of an illegal trade in human organs, and links with a ship in Lynn docks.

Lotnar's face froze, and with a hand he began to pat the Bermuda shorts.

'Why did you visit the *Rosa* on Sunday morning, and why did you stay aboard until the following morning?'

Lotnar's smile contained two gold teeth. 'Inspector, Inspector . . . I visited an old friend. Beckman – the engineer. A wandering Jew. A Pole. He rang – he knew I was here. We had some food, then too much vodka, much too much vodka. So I slept it off. This isn't a crime, is it?'

Shaw coughed, the chlorine from the pool making his throat hurt. 'The scar's in your groin. I hope it was a neat job. It's in the groin because the new kidney is attached to the urethra – but you'll know that by now. The man who donated that kidney is missing, by the way. But when the lights went out they had someone else on the operating table – a man called Tyler – he's dead. Not such a neat job. But then he wasn't paying.'

Lotnar's smile slid off his face like an iceberg calving.

'I can't let you – or anyone – contact the *Rosa* for the next forty-eight hours,' said Shaw. 'That will mean taking everyone into custody. But there is another way.'

Lotnar was thinking fast, and Shaw could see that he hadn't yet given up all hope that his money could buy a way out of this – a way out that didn't involve a prison cell.

'I'm an ill man, Inspector. Yes, I have a new kidney. There is a perfectly legal record of the operation, I assure you. A private hospital near my home in Tel Aviv. That is why I am here. To relax, to recover. I have telephone numbers if you wish to check . . .' He took the mobile out of his shorts, began scrolling.

Valentine had it off him before Shaw had even thought what he might be doing.

Lotnar held his hands up, showing them clean palms.

'DS Valentine will stay with you while you change, Mr Lotnar,' said Shaw. But Lotnar didn't move. 'You'll need an overnight bag.'

'A better way,' said Lotnar, licking fat lips. 'You said, there might be a better way.'

Shaw took a seat. The girls were out on towels now, rubbing suntan lotion onto slim backs.

'You have an Israeli passport?' asked Shaw.

Lotnar nodded, eager now, seeing that there was a way out.

'We'd need a statement. I can't promise you won't be called to give your evidence in person – but it's unlikely. You are one, I suspect, of hundreds. Perhaps you are a victim too . . .' Shaw watched the girls mixing drinks from a trolley the T-shirted muscle had just wheeled out. 'Just tell the truth.'

'A lawyer,' said Lotnar.

'You can have a lawyer before you make a formal statement. But I don't have much time. The *Rosa* is back in port. Tell us the truth.'

Lotnar's throat was dry so he asked for a drink. Shaw said he could have one but he had to talk to Charlie first – in front of them. There was a deal, and Charlie was in the deal too. Lotnar took Charlie's mobile and gave it to Valentine. He told him to fetch drinks, to ring nobody, to cut the landline.

Lotnar's account was chillingly businesslike. His health had deteriorated badly eight months earlier. One kidney had failed, the other was just 20 per cent efficient. He'd been confined to his home in Tel Aviv, undergoing twice-daily dialysis. He had expensive medical insurance and was on a private clinic's waiting list for a kidney transplant. But donor organs were rare in Israel, and while his money could buy him a place on the scheme, it couldn't get him to the front of the queue and it couldn't buy him a kidney. There were other problems. Even his own doctor told him he needed to lose five stones before the operation and radically alter his diet and reduce his alcohol consumption. A medical agency in Haifa made inquiries on his behalf at European and US clinics. All had waiting lists and insisted on a pre-op examination. The US offered the best opportunities, but he'd have to fly out and effectively live in a clinic on dialysis while the queue shortened. And the US surgeons would also demand that he met strict criteria before the procedure was undertaken – including a complete ban on alcohol. It might take months to get on the operating table.

Meanwhile, he *was* dying. One of the senior consultants at the Tel Aviv clinic told him there was another way. That phrase again, and Lotnar rolled it round with his fat lips: 'another way'. Lotnar paid the consultant $10,000 to find out what that other way was. He was given a number in Cyprus to call. A man answered the phone, took his details, and told him to wait. Nothing happened for a week. Then, suddenly, at his bedside a young man appeared. His name was Rudi and he said a new kidney would cost Lotnar $150,000. This, Lotnar could afford, although he resented every cent. Rudi was given a duplicate set of his medical records and in return Lotnar received his instructions. He needed to rent a house within an hour's drive of the Norfolk port of King's Lynn. On the morning of Sunday, 5 September he should arrive by car at the docks and ask for the MV *Rosa* and its captain, Juan de Mesquita. He should have had no alcohol for a week beforehand, no food for twenty-four hours, no water for six.

He did as he was told. He was taken to the captain's room. He lay down for four hours. Somewhere, the captain said, his new kidney was being removed from its healthy – and willing – donor. He didn't ask any more questions. It was hot, he remembered, and the first sign that something was wrong was when the fan stopped revolving over his head. He heard footsteps on the metal stairways, people running. Voices: angry, impatient, in many languages.

Then de Mesquita had come with a bottle and two glasses. There would be a delay. The main power supply had failed and the engineer – a drunken Pole called

373

Beckman – was ashore in some whorehouse and they couldn't get the generators to cut back in. But they'd find him, it just meant they had some time to kill. Six hours, perhaps. So – a drink. Just one – because the doctors said that was OK. But he never saw these doctors.

Lotnar slept. When he woke, the cabin was dark. A few minutes later the lights flickered on and the fan's blades began once more to turn lazily overhead. De Mesquita gave him the anaesthetic. He'd held his hand as they watched the fan turn. It was the first time he'd regretted his decision, lying there, with this man who'd just pumped liquid sleep into his vein.

And that was all he recalled until he woke the next morning. He was in the captain's cabin. They had a wheelchair at the foot of the gangplank. Charlie had returned in the BMW. The pain had been distant, his body soaked in barbiturates. He'd passed out on the journey. But that night, in the bath, he'd examined the small scars: neat and bloodless. And that was the word Lotnar used. 'Bloodless,' as if there were no victims.

'Did you pay in cash?' asked Valentine.

Lotnar seemed to shake himself out of the memory. 'No, by cheque – an offshore trust. I've got a note . . .'

'We need the name,' said Shaw. He stood. 'And no after-care? Nothing?'

'No, that was part of the deal. I had to set that up. I'm fine. Thriving,' he added, patting his thigh. The girls were at the far end of the pool, lying together, their heads touching.

'The *Rosa* is trapped,' said Shaw. 'It's not sailing anywhere. You make any contact at all, or allow anyone else to make contact, and our deal's off.' He looked around at the flowering borders, the bent pines, the distant marram grass on the dunes. 'And you stay here – until it's over. Break your word and you'll have the best functioning kidney in the British penal system.'

As the gates closed on Staithe House the dogs rushed from around the garage block, baying, throwing themselves against the railings.

Shaw let Valentine drive. He felt an almost overwhelming urge to spell it out, tell someone outside his own head what had really happened that night on the dockside beyond the gates at the bottom of Erebus Street. The car was steamy, the windscreen smeared with dead wildlife. So Shaw wound the window down and spoke out of it, letting the wind cool his skin.

'So the *Rosa* comes into port. They've already got Tyler somewhere – on board? Maybe. There's something there we don't understand – not yet. Then Lotnar arrives. By mid-morning on the Sunday the donor's on the operating table and the recipient's eager to get under the knife next. Then the power goes. So – here's a hypothesis. Tyler's healthy kidney has been removed, but there's no power. He's still opened up, on the table, and they can't keep the kidney, because the temperature's rocketing. What do they do? My guess is the theatre's below the waterline so there's no natural light. Candlelight, torchlight? Whatever, it's panic. They botch sewing him up, and the wound gets infected. Within twenty-four hours he's dead. Just in time to get dropped off at sea as the MV *Rosa* heads for Rotterdam.'

Valentine swung the car round the roundabout at

Hunstanton, clogged with tourists heading down to the beach. 'The other corpse – on the storm-drain grid – what about him?'

'Don't know. What we do know is that back on the ship that night they've got a paying customer who's still a decent kidney short of a full set. So they wait – for two things. The power, yes. But they also need a new donor.'

Valentine let his own window down. Out at sea a flotilla of sailboats was off the sandbanks, catching a brisk wind.

'We know the deal on the street. The Organ Grinder picks up the donor, who's already been selected by someone with access to the medical records at the hospital. But this time the timescale is a few hours, not days. So they can't follow routine. But there's one thing on their side: because the power's down on Erebus Street thanks to Andy Judd's toxic hatred for Jan Orzsak, the power company tells everyone the line's down till, what, midnight or later. So at least with the lights out, getting the donor is easier.

'They know Blanket's a match and he's in town, so whoever does the selection finds him and marks his coat. The Organ Grinder calls. But Blanket turns him down. So the Organ Grinder does what he's good at – he drags his donor out into the street, in the dark. Maybe a car's waiting, or maybe he bundles him down the back alley to the dock gates. By midnight Blanket's on an operating table. Is Peploe the surgeon? Maybe. The playboy lifestyle doesn't come cheap. The lion's share of that hundred and fifty thousand is all his. The rest get the crumbs.'

Valentine slammed on the brakes, cursing a cyclist weighed down with camping gear.

'Who killed Bryan Judd, and why?' he asked.

'If we're right, someone had to get rid of the waste from both ops – including Tyler's kidney. So they go to the hospital. Either it's the first time, or it's what they do every time. Maybe that's Peploe.' Shaw clicked his fingers. 'Tell Mark to keep an eye out on the CCTV for a cyclist. But Judd won't play ball – or catches him slipping the stuff on the belt – or demands a bigger cut if it's a regular system. My money's on the last. They argue, Peploe kills Judd and puts the body on the belt. They spot the body in the furnace and shut it down, just in time to hear Peploe's shoes running for the exit – cycling shoes.'

Valentine shook his head. 'That's crazy – it's one kidney. They could just weight it and put it overboard. They don't need Judd.'

'But the fact is the kidney was there,' said Shaw. 'Know what I think? I think this is a system. This isn't just one op – over months, over years, it could be hundreds. Sure they could dump stuff, but why take the risk if there's a better way? The furnace is foolproof – so I think they used it. Like clockwork. A system, like I said.'

Over the rooftops of the North End they could see the superstructure of the *Rosa* as they approached Erebus Street. Valentine parked by the dock gates. As soon as he cut the engine Shaw's mobile rang. It was Paul Twine. 'It's Orzsak,' said Twine. 'Tried to top himself in the house but one of the builders went up to tell him they were taking down the power for half an hour – didn't get an answer. Then he heard a sound, legs kicking out, hitting the banisters and the wall. So they broke the door down. He was swinging on a rope. He's down at A&E. Looks like he'll live.'

45

Shaw stood at the dock gates at the foot of Erebus Street, and despite the windblown rubbish and weeds he could see the *Rosa* along the quayside, a single crane hauling crates from the open hold. Across the deserted concrete quay was the agent's offices – Galloway had been right, you couldn't see anything behind the tinted, tilted glass of the first-floor offices. DC Campbell was still on shift, and Birley was still in the security booth at the gates checking back over the old CCTV cassettes. On board the ship the two Filipino crew were working, but the ABs had gone ashore, a plainclothes unit tailing them through the Vancouver Shopping Centre. Captain de Mesquita had invited Galloway aboard for coffee – a regular courtesy. Shaw had advised him to take up the offer, keep his eyes open, but play it straight. Don't even think about a few clever questions.

Shaw turned his back on the docks and looked up the street. A sign hung in the window of the Bentinck Launderette: BACK IN 20 MINS.

The sun pounded down, and Shaw stood in an ink-blot of shadow. He saw Father Martin locking the door of the Sacred Heart of Mary, with Ally Judd beside him. They walked through the gravestones to the presbytery, close enough to share a shadow, while she held the back of her wrist to her lips and the priest held her by an elbow, his neck bent down to listen to something she was trying to say. Shaw recalled the last time he'd talked to Ally Judd – in the shadows by the cypress tree behind the church. He'd sensed then that she still harboured secrets about the Judd family. Did she share those secrets with her lover?

Shaw and Valentine traced the line of the hot rails up the street and then crossed into the graveyard. Shaw touched the stones as they threaded a path to the door, and he thought how odd it was that even on the hottest day tombstones were always cold. Father Martin's door was open, the interior cool and dark, a single Virgin Mary in blue and white lit by an unshaded bulb. At the end of the hall corridor there was another door – green baize, a servants' entrance into the old kitchen. Father Martin came out, businesslike, head down, and only saw them when he was almost upon them.

His face was almost unrecognizable; both eyes were black, a bruise disfigured the left cheekbone and the upper lip was split and stitched. He held up his mobile. 'I was just calling. If you have a second. I've been hearing confessions. Ally came to me – but I think it's for you, as much as me.'

His eyes looked everywhere except at Shaw.

In the small plain kitchen Ally Judd sat on a chair beside the washing machine, upon which she laid a hand, as if it was a touchstone. On the floor was a large laundry bag. She had a glass of water before her and she held a wad of tissue to her mouth. When she saw them she tried to stand, knocking the chair backwards, but she didn't seem to hear the crash. Martin put the seat back in place, and with a hand on her shoulder pushed her down, as though she were lighter than air.

'Who did this?' asked Valentine, gesturing at the priest's mangled face.

'It's all right,' said Martin.

Shaw thought about that; in what circumstances could that kind of beating be all right?

'Was it Neil, Mrs Judd? Was it Neil who did this? He found out, didn't he – about both of you?' Or did Neil know something else, wondered Shaw. Was this really just about a secret love affair?

Martin shook his head for both of them. 'That's not what Ally has to say. Just show them,' he said.

It was a letter, in a plain envelope, marked simply with her name. The handwriting in the note was neat, purposeful, and in aquamarine.

Ally.

I got your letter, finally – I was at Colchester, in the glasshouse. I'm sorry, you know I am, to hear that he's dying. I didn't want that, and I don't want it now. He's my father – still my father – despite what Bry says he did. What I think we all know he did.

So I've come back as you asked. I'm here now, with you, but you won't see me. Don't try to find me. I have to keep in the shadows – the Red Caps will come here – or they'll get the police to watch out. I just don't want you to feel alone. And don't tell anyone. When the time is right I'll talk to him. You want me to make my peace? I don't think I can do that. But I can tell him I love him.

Again – don't look for me. But we can meet. On Thursday,

at noon, I'll be in The Walks, on one of the benches by the Red Tower.

    Sean

'You should have shown me this,' said Shaw. 'This is from Bryan's brother, isn't it? Sean? When did you get it?'

'A week ago. It was left at the launderette.'

'What did Sean say when you met?'

'He didn't turn up,' she said. 'I waited, right by the Red Tower, but nothing. And there's been nothing since – like he's gone again, and the only thing to prove he was here is this.' She touched the letter, making the paper crackle, then pressed her hands against her cheeks. 'And then we saw the newspaper – the artist's impression of the tramp who went missing from the Sacred Heart.'

She pulled the piece of paper from her pocket, a scrunched-up copy of Shaw's forensic reconstruction of the face of Blanket.

'It was him, you see – looking out of the page at us. Right here, amongst us, watching. And now he's gone.'

'You're sure this is Sean?' asked Shaw.

She nodded. 'That's Sean.'

'What did you tell him that brought him back?'

'That Andy's dying. I promised Sean when he left that I'd always make sure he knew if there was bad news. About Bry, or Neil, or his father. He couldn't stay, not after what had happened to Norma Jean. Every time he saw Bry he said the pain was as sharp as it had always been – and the guilt. He was the one who inherited Andy's strength, he'd have been the rock – our rock. But he couldn't stay, and he couldn't let go, not for ever. So I was his link.'

Father Martin moved his hands to the nape of her neck, and Valentine watched the movement. The priest knelt beside her and took her face in his hands. 'Everything, Ally. You must.' Shaw noticed the contrast between their fingers, his tanned with the gold ring, hers bleached and powder dry.

She turned her face to them. 'I should have told you about the blood. On that Sunday – the night Bry died. Late, after midnight, I went down to the shop because when the power came back on all the machines began a new cycle. One of them had jammed – a piece of clothing caught in the seal. So the water was leaking. Bloody water. When I got the stuff out it was covered in blood.'

'Clothing? What kind of clothing?' asked Valentine.

'A pair of overalls.'

'Did you recognize them?' asked Shaw.

'They could have been a stranger's,' she said. 'The shop was open – I'd left the latch up. So – anyone, I guess. Anyone in Erebus Street.'

'But they weren't a stranger's, were they?' asked Shaw.

She pressed her knees together and Shaw thought she was considering a lie, but Father Martin watched her, waiting.

'No, they weren't. There was a name tag – they were Andy's.'

46

DC Mark Birley stretched out his legs under the table which held the CCTV screens in the security booth at the dock gates; his left leg was bandaged from the game on Saturday, when the opposition fly-half had raked his boot down Birley's shin bone, lifting the skin away, damaging the muscle. He looked at his left fist where the knuckles were still swollen. If he'd hit him any harder he'd have had to arrest himself. He grinned, drank some cold coffee, rubbed the heel of his palm into his right eye, and focused again on the screen.

He was good at this, he knew enough about Peter Shaw's methods to know that. The DI didn't do Buggins' turn – he worked out what you had a skill for and made sure it wasn't wasted. Since the inquiry had begun Birley had spent eighty hours in front of CCTV screens, because he had an eye for detail and the strength of mind to concentrate when every nerve in his body wanted sleep. Beside the table was a pile of video cassettes running back a month. His job was to locate the *Rosa*'s dockings, then see if he could pick up the registration numbers of any cars making double visits. And any signs of a bicycle, too – high-tech, a racing model, with a pannier.

He watched the film at treble speed; cars swishing across the quayside, HGVs, the stevedores swarming like ants when a ship came in. The date/time display on the screen buzzed forward. His finger hung ready over the pause button, waiting for the *Rosa* to appear off the dockside. There! It docked, in Keystone-cop time, and the captain's Volvo was winched off the fo'c's'le onto the quayside. He ran the film speed down to real time and began to make a note.

Despite his level of concentration he was still half listening to the real world. A car engine idled as someone pulled up at the barrier. In the outer office he heard the security guard separating the glass screens so that he could take the driver's ID and paperwork.

'The *Rosa*,' said a woman's voice. 'Captain should have left a note.'

Birley stood quickly, moving to one side so that he could see through the hatch to the security window. He watched the guard flicking through a pile of documents.

'Here it is …' He made a note and passed a book across for the woman to sign. Birley clocked the car: a Vauxhall Zafira, new, spotless, with a parking permit in the window marked QUEEN VICTORIA HOSPITAL — SENIOR STAFF.

Then she was gone. Birley stepped into the guard's booth. Turned the book round to see the scrawled name.

Mrs Jofranka Phillips.

47

By the time Shaw was in Galloway's office on the dock-side Jofranka Phillips's car was parked at the foot of the gangplank and she'd gone aboard, carrying – according to DC Campbell – nothing more than a paper bag from Thorntons.

'So she likes chocolates. Anything else?'

'Nothing,' she said. She looked at her notes. 'Dark glasses, black summer dress. One of the crew met her at the top of the gangplank – they kissed, cheek-to-cheek, like friends would.'

'Right – George, ring Ravid Lotnar. He told us he could get a set of documents to prove his operation had been legally conducted in Israel. Get me the name of the hospital.'

He asked Galloway if he could use his broadband link. The Scot said he'd need a minute to finish an e-mail. Shaw bounced on his toes, reviewing in his mind the interview they'd just completed with Andy Judd under caution at St James's, with the duty solicitor present. They'd hauled him in quickly before he'd any time to discover that his eldest son had been living secretly in Erebus Street. Or did he know? That was the problem with the Judd family: trying to see its internal workings, its alliances and feuds, was impossible – the more you looked, the less you saw.

'What's going on?' Andy Judd had asked, running his fingers through the wallpaper-brush hair. 'This is fucking harassment,' he said, turning to the solicitor, a woman in a cheap suit. 'You got that down? I'm spending my life in this place.'

It was well after opening time and Judd was sober, which didn't suit him. He held a pea-green cup of tea on a saucer, but every time he tried to lift it to his lips he'd given up. They'd been talking for an hour: question, answer, question, answer ... routine, aimless, designed to confuse the suspect. Every time Valentine got up to take a cigarette break – which was every ten minutes – he'd ostentatiously taken his packet of Silk Cut with him. Judd didn't just have a craving for nicotine, he had a dependency; they could see it was beginning to make his yellow-stained fingers shake.

Then Shaw showed him the artist's impression that Ally Judd said was an accurate depiction of his oldest son.

'This was in all the local papers, TV. I gave you your own copy too.'

'Yeah – so?'

'Your daughter-in-law says it is unmistakably your son, Sean.'

'Looks like him, all right. You'd think I'd come and tell you that? I can look after my own ...' He regretted that, they could both see it in his eyes. Because he couldn't look after his own.

'He came back because you're dying. But he couldn't – didn't – feel he could talk to you. Why was that? He thought Bryan was right, didn't he? That you'd killed Norma Jean?'

Judd had leant in over the narrow interview table. 'He was keeping his head down. We knew – everyone knew – he'd broken out of the glasshouse. Like he's gonna knock on his own front door. Give me a fucking break.'

'So you knew he was back in Lynn?'

Judd whispered to the solicitor. 'I don't have to answer that question,' he said, smiling through wrecked teeth.

'Can you explain how a pair of your overalls came to be found in the launderette, Mr Judd – soaked in blood – on the night your son died?'

The solicitor stiffened, as though she'd got a shock off a cattle fence. But Judd pushed her hand aside when she tried to place it on the table in front of him. 'I've got a bag of special tokens – Ally gives 'em to me. I work in an abattoir. You've seen it – seen what I do. You got me in here to ask a fucking question like that? That *is* harassment. You've got me on the arson charge – there's a date, for the court. I'm sticking my hand up for that – OK – so well done, boys. Isn't that enough?'

He hadn't missed a beat and the explanation had been fluid and calm.

'But that's not how it works, is it?' said Shaw. 'The abattoir collects the overalls and gets them washed in town, on contract. But not this set of overalls. And not on the night your son died.'

Judd's eyes widened. 'It's Bry, isn't it? You still think I killed him? You think I don't love my kids? You think I don't ever wake up and not think of them first? I'd die for them.' He fingered a gold cross which had fallen out of his open-necked shirt, and Shaw noticed the contrast between the fragile filigree of the icon and Judd's swollen working hands.

'There's twenty – more – who'll tell you I was out on the street that day – by the fire, drinking. I didn't kill Bry – I didn't go anywhere near him. It was cow's blood on the overalls. Your lot in the white coats too stupid to work that out? It's not *Silent Witness*, is it?'

Shaw didn't have an answer to that, because there was one irritating flaw in Ally Judd's statement: why had she put the blood-soaked overalls *back* in the wash? Andy Judd had been released, still constrained by the conditions of bail previously set.

In the shipping agent's office overlooking the Alexandra Dock Galloway finished his e-mail exchange and Shaw took his place at the computer, punching two words into Google: Kalo Kircher.

He'd been a fool. Phillips's tangential link with Israel had been a coincidence he should have checked out. DC Twine's summary of her background had included the fact that Kalo Kircher's children supported a charitable medical programme in Israel. Ravid Lotnar – the *Rosa*'s last patient – was an Israeli citizen who had tried to claim that there was documentary proof he'd had his organ transplant in his own country.

Shaw watched the spinning wheel on the screen as Google searched the worldwide web. The first page returned was headed 'The Kircher Institute'.

Shaw clicked the link. The Kircher Institute was a hospital in Jerusalem offering basic medical services to both the Jewish and Palestinian populations. He worked his way through the site for twenty minutes, then called Valentine over to look at the screen. There was a picture showing a street in a suburb of the city, a whitewashed building behind a set of railings.

He gave his DS a single A4 sheet he'd printed out – a history of the clinic from the website.

The Kircher Institute was founded in 1968 by three brothers – Gyorgy, Hanzi, and Pitivo Kircher, all doctors, based in the United States. The hospital is dedicated to the poor, and named for their father, Kalo Kircher, a pioneering surgeon of the 1930s. In 1970 it offered outpatient services. The first surgical ward opened in 1973 – it now holds nearly 200 patients. No charges are made for the services given. Funding is largely undertaken in the US amongst the Jewish community – although significant donations have been made (see list) from organizations such as the United Nations, and World Jewish Relief (WJR). The Kircher accepts patients on a needs-first basis, irrespective of religion, ethnicity, or sex. The clinic has led a campaign within Israel to amend legislation to allow the removal of organs for transplant from patients certified as brain dead.

Valentine's mobile rang. He took the call, listened, then cut the line. 'Campbell's with Lotnar now. He says he was given the documentation as part of the deal. Operation is listed as taking place at the Kircher Institute ten days ago.'

Shaw called up a newspaper archive story to show Valentine. The headline was 'Funding Crisis Threatens Kircher'.

He tapped the screen. 'Two of the founding brothers are dead, the third – Hanzi – is struggling to raise enough cash in the US to keep the Institute open. Its director on the ground in Tel Aviv says here that the hospital needs annual funding of 3.5 million dollars – he's appealing for ordinary Jews and Palestinians around the world to make contributions. The Israeli government won't help. The Institute's campaign on organ retrieval is seen as too controversial. Without some cash, it's going to close.'

The report was over a year old. But the website was live – the clinic still open.

'How's that for a noble motive?' said Shaw. 'Keeping that clinic open demands a regular, substantial flow of income.'

They both looked out through the tinted windows as the sun began to stretch the shadows of the cranes on the dockside to breaking point. The lights on the *Rosa* stood out in the dusk, the hold pontoons now slid firmly over the cargo of grain.

A taxi arrived with pizzas and coffee.

Twine sent them an e-mail via the office network – everything he'd managed to track down on the history of MV *Rosa* and her crew. The ship was eight years old and had been built in Valparaiso, Chile, though she was Brazilian registered. Originally called the *Estanca*, she'd sailed regularly from São Paulo to Tilbury carrying what was termed general cargo – that was foodstuffs, timber and scrap metal. She'd been bought by her present owners, a shipping company based in Basle, three years earlier. The owners were Swiss, anonymous, and appeared on no known criminal record according to Interpol HQ at

Lyon. The same could not be said of her captain. Juan de Mesquita, a Brazilian national, had been jailed by a court in Haifa in 1991 under a newly ratified law for 'aiding and abetting human traffic for the harvest of organs'. He and his co-defendant, a Filipino male nurse called Rey Abucajo, had been jailed for four years and ordered to pay nearly £40,000 compensation to three men they had inveigled into donating kidneys for transplant. De Mesquita and Abucajo were merchant seamen who had bought a flat in the suburbs of Tel Aviv, where the operations had taken place. Previously, de Mesquita's record had been unblemished, and he'd had his master's ticket for a decade. The operation to arrest the pair had been partly organized by the International Maritime Organization.

'Tel Aviv,' said Shaw, training night glasses on the bridge of the MV *Rosa*.

'How'd a character like that get another ship?' asked Valentine.

'Let's get Interpol to try the Swiss owners again,' said Shaw. 'Get Twine to organize it – get the paperwork started. It'll take for ever, so the sooner we start the better.'

They watched another small coaster coming through the Alexandra Dock, out of the Hook, carrying TV sets, according to Galloway. It slid into Berth 2 on the far side, dwarfed by an artificial mountain of scrap metal. Fork-lift trucks swarmed like rats, and a necklace of HGVs queued to unload. At the bottom of Erebus Street a bright light burnt in the hawthorn bushes where the power company team had left it on for security. The old sub-station was still not yet ready to be switched back into the grid. A light shone from Jan Orzsak's house, overlooking the work. Shaw presumed that he'd been released from hospital after his failed suicide attempt.

The air-conditioning in the office was making Shaw's throat dry so he glugged two pints of cold milk he'd ordered delivered with the pizzas.

'And she can't sail?' said Valentine, nodding at the *Rosa*.

'Not unless I say so,' said Shaw. 'So we wait.'

'For?'

Shaw didn't answer, but swung the field glasses over the scene one last time. Berth 4 was still deserted, a flash of last-minute rays from the sun gilding it gold. He focused on the electricity sub-station. His heart stopped, missed a beat, as he watched the gate in the perimeter wire swing open. Two figures emerged, one supporting the other.

Campbell had picked up the movement too and scrabbled for a pair of binoculars. 'It's a blind spot,' she said. 'Just there, by the gates. I talked it through with Mark – the CCTV's too far round behind the container park. They won't be on film.'

And they knew it. The two figures didn't take a step onto the quayside, but skirted the container park, disappearing into the maze, then re-emerging opposite the gangplank to the *Rosa*. They both sat, their backs to the metal container side, in the shadow. But Shaw could see them well enough with the night-vision glasses.

It was Andy Judd, and his son Neil.

48

'And you think she'd risk it – right here, under our noses?' Valentine lit a Silk Cut and flicked the match into the dock. He didn't look convinced. They were outside on the quay, in the dark, getting air, although the heat was bad – the whole dock a giant storage heater re-radiating the day's sunshine right back into a muggy night sky. The *Rosa* was 200 yards away, the three crew decks lit. They'd watched Andy Judd and his son for an hour, waiting in the shadows until darkness had fallen. At ten precisely the *Rosa*'s gangplank lights had gone off for just thirty seconds. When they'd flickered back on they were gone.

'Phillips thinks we've shut up shop, that we believe Peploe's our man,' said Shaw. 'And let's think about that, George. What evidence did we have on Peploe? Untraced human tissue in the Theatre Seven organ bank. And who had the keys to the organ bank in those vital few hours before we ordered the search? Phillips. What if she just swapped tissue and organs from A, B, or C into D? She could have set him up. She'd already done a fine job painting a character portrait for us: the playboy with the expensive lifestyle and the private patients. She left us to join up the dots. She knows we're looking for MVR, but she thinks we're looking up at the hospital.'

A rat swam across the dock, the V-shaped wake geometrically perfect.

'And she must have seen Peploe take the epilepsy pills often enough,' said Shaw. 'Who's got access to the hospital pharmacy? Senior staff. And how convenient is it for her that our principal suspect is dead. Maybe Peploe was in it with her, but it's possible he wasn't. Either way, to her, he's better dead.'

Valentine shook his head. 'If Andy Judd's the patient, where'd the money come from? You said a hundred and fifty thousand dollars a shot – he works at the abattoir, for Christ's sake.'

But Shaw was ahead of him now, fitting pieces together. 'Well – think it through. We can be pretty sure, can't we, that Bryan Judd was involved in the organ-trafficking. And if he was on the inside then there's every chance Andy and Neil were as well. But Bryan was there . . .' Shaw pointed at his own feet. 'In the middle. Even that far down the food chain he'd have picked up a pay cheque. Perhaps they promised him an op for Andy at cost price. Perhaps there's honour amongst thieves. Or . . .' And it was the first time the thought had struck. 'Or, he did something special for them. Something that would buy Andy Judd the op he desperately needs to stay alive.'

Valentine looked towards the *Rosa*. There was a light on the bridge, but no sign of anyone on watch.

A seagull came in through the floodlights on the far berth, and flapped over their heads. Shaw's mobile rang. It was the power engineer, Anderson. 'Hi. The power load on your boat just went up – about five minutes ago.'

'Significantly?'

'Well, if it's going to lights, you're talking enough to

play five-a-side football by. And the base level's high, too. I've tracked back to the last ship in, which was four thousand tonnes – a bit bigger, in fact. Power consumption on board her was half what it was on the *Rosa* an hour ago.'

It was warm, even out on the quayside, but Shaw still felt a cold sweat breaking out.

He swore, then cut the line. 'They've started,' he said. 'Doesn't make sense. Judd can't be a donor, so where's the healthy liver coming from? Neil?' He nodded to himself, because that made sense. What had Justina called it? LDLT: live donor liver transplant. Or did they have the organ they needed on ice? He'd been a fool, thinking that they had to wait for the donor to turn up. 'Ring Twine. Get me a unit down here – fast,' he said to Valentine, unable to keep the tension out of his voice. 'Faster.'

By the time Shaw reached the *Rosa* he was running, certain now that he'd waited too long.

The gangplank to the ship was metal, ribbed, and set askew. As Shaw climbed he glimpsed the oily water below in the three-foot gap between the hull and the wharf, a porthole's light reflected as a lazy, unmoving oval. Strapped to the side of the gangplank was the three-inch-thick power cable. The ship hummed with power, a note low enough for Shaw to feel it in his bones. A door stood open at the top. He looked over his shoulder and saw Valentine behind him. Back-up would be twenty minutes. The rule book said he should wait. But for once he didn't have time for the rule book.

He stepped over the metal threshold into a stairwell, immediately struck by the carpet – a corporate flecked blue – and the spotless stainless steel banisters. On the wall was a sign – POOP DECK – and a plan of the *Rosa*. The corridors and serried cabins reminded Shaw of the map of Level One. He stood for a second listening; somewhere laughter came in short, drunken bursts. Galloway had said the crew was seven strong. He looked Valentine in the face, about to ask if he was up for going on, but the look in his DS's eyes told him it was a question he didn't need to ask.

They climbed towards the noise. One flight, two, then three, before stepping through another door into a corridor. Again, the odd feeling that he was on a cross-Channel ferry – the antiseptic smell, the blue metal doors, the carpet, the helpful signs.

Footsteps were suddenly near, and round a corner came one of the crew – a Filipino in spotless white shorts, carrying a towel. He stopped in his tracks, then turned and ran. They followed for twenty yards, then a sharp left and a door ahead, a sign which read MESS.

The crew were ready for them, all standing, tensed, the smell of fear in the airless room as solid as the cool metal walls. There were two tables with banquette seating, a wall-fitted flat-screen TV, a shelf of videos and DVDs; two portholes, thrown open. There were six men in the room and none of them spoke.

Shaw flashed his warrant card. 'Captain?'

No one spoke again.

'Anyone speak English?' asked Valentine, walking in to see that they'd been watching a DVD – no sound. Porn: two men, one woman, the smiles and gasps as fake as the suntans.

'I speak English,' said a small man with his fists held at his side. He was a European, with grey hair and a neck as thick as his skull. 'The captain is sleeping.' The stillness in the room was uncanny, and for the first time Shaw heard the trickling of bilge pumps.

Shaw knew they'd be calculating too, trying to work out if these two policemen were really stupid enough to come aboard without support. He tried not to show that his heart beat had hit 120.

'George, stay here. No one leaves. I'll get the rest on the search.'

Valentine's mobile trilled and he flicked it open to see a text from Twine.

FIVE MINUTES AWAY

'Unit 3's at the gate as well,' said Valentine, leaning back against the metal wall. 'You lot can sit.'

They subsided slowly, like tower blocks on a demolition site.

'You,' said Shaw, pointing at the man who spoke English. 'Name?'

'Albert Samblant, First Officer.' The man looked Shaw in the face, unable to stop his focus falling on the moon eye.

'Right. Tell 'em to sit tight. No one's going anywhere. Then I want you to take me to the captain's cabin.'

Samblant spoke to the crew in English, Spanish and French. Then he led the way, his short legs working crab-like, so that he seemed to sidle down the corridor.

The captain's cabin was another ladder up. Samblant knocked, then stood back. Shaw noticed that he was sweating, the smell pungent, and that he kept covering his top lip with the bottom.

'Open it,' said Shaw.

Albert shrugged, rattling the lock, but the door wouldn't open.

Shaw knocked once, twice, then took two steps back, swivelled onto his left leg, and kicked out – making contact at a point precisely three inches above the lock. The door and jamb buckled, so that the second kick left it hanging from a single hinge.

The room stank of cigarette smoke and a plate of chorizo and beans which was on the small table, untouched. There was an ashtray containing a single match – broken to form a V. Shaw tried to understand what that meant – that Andy Judd had been in the cabin? Maybe.

The First Officer hadn't moved. He stood on the threshold as if barred by an invisible trip wire.

There was one other door and Shaw pushed it open to reveal a shower room. The air was still heavy with moisture, the mirrors misted. Sitting in the shower, the curtain wrapped round his neck, was a man with a face the colour of a rotten peach, a film of vomit dripping from his chin to his naked chest. No one, Shaw instantly knew, with a face like that, had ever taken another living breath. The rest of the body was blotchy but white, a thin stain of urine running away from the corpse in a spiral towards the plughole.

Shaw's heartbeat was painful now, and the almost physical shock of seeing a corpse sparked a massive release of adrenaline in his bloodstream. He went back to the door of the cabin, took hold of the T-shirt round the First Officer's neck, and dragged him to the threshold of the shower room.

'Is this the captain?'

'Jesus,' said Samblant, trying to cover his face. Then he threw up, missing the toilet bowl.

Shaw got hold of the corpse under the armpits. The flesh was still warm. Lifting the body away from the tiled shower wall, he tried to unwrap the plastic curtain which was clinging to it like a second skin. When he'd got the material away from the neck he felt for a pulse. He was appalled that a body could be at once so hot and so dead. The captain had been fifty, maybe more, just the hands and face browned by a lifetime afloat. In the base of the shower there was a tide mark, a thin line of dirt, red and gritty. Shaw ran a finger along it and looked at the smudge, smelt it, worked it between thumb and forefinger. It was red sawdust.

'Bloodwood,' he said.

'Where's Phillips?' he said to Samblant, who was sitting against the wall beside a washbasin. A dark saddle in his jeans around his groin showed that he'd wet himself. He still held shaking hands across his face. Shaw pulled the meshed fingers apart, grabbed his chin. 'Where's Phillips, the surgeon?'

But there was still enough fear in this man to summon up the nerve for what must have been one last lie. 'Gone. An hour, two.'

In the corridor they heard footsteps and Twine appeared at the door. He took in the scene. 'Unit's here – six officers. Another on the way. Search the ship?'

'Yeah. Get one of the crew to help, but don't believe a word anyone says. Tear it apart. Especially below the water line.'

49

Twine's team searched the *Rosa* in twenty minutes: six decks down to the engine room, eighteen cabins, the forward stores, the galley, the mess room. Nothing. Then they did it again, this time using the plans on each deck to block off each room shown, and with a dog team they'd called in from St James's. Nothing. The Port Authority got them a skeleton crew for the quayside so they could roll back the last pontoon to reveal the cargo – three separate holds brimful of grain, the surface of each as untouched as a beach at dawn. Then they edged down the side of the deck to the fo'c's'le and checked that. Again nothing, just cable, anchors, and rope.

Shaw was back in the mess room when Twine reported in. 'We're doing it again.' Shaw laid his hands out on the mess table, aware that stress was making his joints ache. If the operating room wasn't on board, where was it? They hadn't actually seen Andy and Neil Judd go aboard – perhaps they'd gone somewhere else, the surgeon too? The containers on the dock? That was possible. Metallic. Hot. But did they rumble and hum? The dockside cranes would make them vibrate. Or the HGVs edging past in first gear.

'OK, Paul. Rustle up the dock manager – I want all the containers opened on the quayside. Now.'

Twine went, and Shaw was pretty sure he saw Samblant

exchange a glance with one of the crew. Everyone shifted in their seats, fresh cigarettes were lit. Either they were relaxing, or they were pretending to relax.

He rang Birley at the dock gates. 'Mark? Run the CCTV back to when the *Rosa* was in port last time – see if you can ID any of the containers on the dockside that night. Then compare that with what we've got out there now. OK – do it.'

He looked at the crew. One of them smiled, a fatal error, because you couldn't fake a smile like that.

'Stand up,' said Shaw. They all stood, exchanging glances, and one or two now suppressing smiles. They thought they were safe, and that made Shaw certain they weren't. Valentine came in with DC Lau.

'Search them,' he said. They did a two-hander, shuffling each one forward and then pushing them through to the galley. Nothing.

'OK – strip off,' said Shaw. They piled their clothes on the mess table and stood, their faces showing something else now – anger, betrayal, shame perhaps, so that the tension in the room was electric.

Six naked bodies. Six clean naked bodies. 'Clean as whistles,' said Valentine. All except for the white charity bracelets on each wrist. But they *were* clean, and that's what Shaw had missed, until now.

'The ship's got two thousand tonnes of grain on it – the dust's everywhere down by the hold, but everyone's spotless,' said Shaw. 'The ship's spotless.' He ran a finger along the table top. 'Why?' he asked Samblant, stepping inside his personal space. 'Why's everything clean?'

'We don't touch the cargo,' said Samblant. 'It's loaded,

unloaded, by the shore crews. We've all got cabins, showers. Why shouldn't we be clean?' Then he bit his lip, hard, until Shaw saw a speck of blood appear.

Shaw thought about that, and the bloodwood dust in the captain's shower room. He tried to call up a mental picture of the single sheet of A4 Twine had put together on the history of the *Rosa* – a ship's CV. He couldn't recall its original name, but he remembered its trade – running timber between São Paulo and Tilbury for five years in the early 1990s.

'So why, and how, did the captain get covered in sawdust?' he asked. He held up a finger, still smudged red. 'Muirapiranga – bloodwood,' he said. Samblant's eyes faked confusion, but Shaw could see that the emotion he was trying to mask was fear. He didn't get an answer to his question – but that didn't matter. Because he knew now – not only why, and how, but where.

50

Shaw was in the dark – not the dark that is the absence of light, but a suffocating presence; on a vertical ladder, a hoop of steel at his back, both hands on a rung, his feet on two. The air was so hot it felt like a blanket, and he could imagine letting go and just sinking into it, hanging there in the velvet blackness. Then the hatch above opened and a light burnt down into the well like a laser beam. Dazzled, he closed his eyes, then looked down. Below him, perhaps thirty feet, was the deck of the hold. He was in a vertical tube, like an empty packet of Smarties. Number 3 hatch. He'd already been down number 1, number 2 and number 4. At the bottom of each he'd found a bulkhead door, which they couldn't force open because there was 4,000 tonnes of grain on the other side.

He looked down again. This one had to be different.

Above him he heard boots rasping on metal rungs. DC Twine stopped ten feet above his head and looked down.

'I got a certificate,' he said. 'Just in case.' Over his shoulder he had an automatic carbine. Twine was one of a dozen officers at St James's with firearms clearance, but he still required a magistrate to clear the issue of the gun.

'OK,' said Shaw. It didn't make him feel any better because now he was the filling in the sandwich – between the gun and whatever lay below. He looked at Twine's finger, curled round the trigger, which was in the locked position. The DC's hand was smudged with red dust from the ladder rungs.

They climbed down, in silence, trying not to let their boots grate on the rusted metal. At the bottom Shaw jumped down the last three feet into the well of the hatch. There *was* something different. In the other hatches the base of the shaft had been empty, but here there was a metal cradle, like a seat, enclosed in steel crash bars and connected to a cable which ran up the side of the well to the square of light above. Shaw imagined it rising slowly, pulled by the capstan on the deck, a vertical bosun's chair.

Twine stepped down beside him. They'd got a routine now, so Shaw radioed Valentine on the deck above, told him they were going in, then he put his shoulder to the metal door, spun the central lock, and Twine used his leg to try and force it open.

It opened, unlike the first three – the hinges oiled, an almost silent entry, the only sound a faint exhalation, like a breath.

They stepped out into a large space, a hold, but this one was empty, and had what must be a false deck above, so that it was only ten feet high. A single emergency light in a frosted box lit the whole scene, like a lamp under water seen from fathoms above. Above them, thought Shaw, would be grain. But beneath the grain was this hidden hold, empty except for a nest of HGV containers set against the port side. There was a door open, but the view was obscured by heavy plastic sheeting. Beyond it burnt lights, figures moving, casting kaleidoscopes of shadow.

Shaw took a breath and it caught in his throat. There

was dust in the air, and when he squatted down he could feel the sawdust on the floor – five years' worth from the thousands of tonnes of bloodwood the *Rosa* had once carried across the Atlantic.

Twine released the lock on the carbine. He'd seen that out here in the hold they were not alone. A man sat on the floor outside the first container, his back to the bulwark wall which separated the holds, his head in his hands. He looked up now, and they saw it was Neil Judd, his hair and clothes soaked with sweat, both hands gripping his knees, which he pressed together. The moment he saw them his body tensed and Shaw thought he was going to stand. But he seemed to assess the moment, and his fragile body relaxed, deflating; and Shaw noticed a burning dog-end in his hand. Around him on the decking were spent matches, each one neatly broken in a V-shape. And Shaw thought that, with hindsight, that made more sense: that it would be Neil who would mimic his father, not Bryan, who hated him. Judd stretched out his legs so that they could see the soles of his shoes and Shaw noted the double Blakeys on each – little sonic transmitters, designed to rap on the floor, the pavement, steps; sending vital sounds back to Judd's damaged ears, so that he could keep his balance.

The hold was a box of noise: a generator rumbled, and the electric cables which ran along both walls thrummed with power. The heat was counteracted by a set of air-conditioning units, the size of a pair of fridge-freezers, the outlet/inlet grilles vibrating. Shaw walked forward towards the hanging plastic door, which was marked with a diagonal red line.

'Don't,' said Neil Judd. 'Please. It's too late. Let her finish.'

'I can't do that,' said Shaw; but he stopped, trying to think it through. If Andy Judd was on the table, under anaesthetic, then the donor had already lost his – or her – liver, or at least, part of it. Perhaps Neil Judd was right, perhaps it was too late.

'Dad will die if they stop now.'

Shaw walked to the door and then turned to face Judd. The light was glaucous, as if they'd all been drowned, and were floating – suspended – while Jofranka Phillips finished her work.

'Then I need to know all that you know,' said Shaw. Twine stood with his back to the ship's hull, looking at Neil Judd, the carbine held level. Beyond the plastic doors, even against the background noise of the generators and coolers, Shaw could just hear the occasional top-of-the-spectrum clash of surgical instruments, like cutlery in a busy restaurant.

'I helped load the *Rosa* many times,' said Neil Judd. 'Once, we did it in record time, so they said to come aboard to the mess. We drank, ate their food, talked about our different lives. One of the Filipinos was into martial arts, and they had this gym set up on the pontoon deck. So I worked out – showed him what I could do. I knew they wanted something – something back. But I thought I'd wait and see what it was, 'cos I'm not stupid.'

He adjusted the hearing aid in his left ear. 'And they had girls too ...' The smile disfigured his face with the effort of trying to look weary of such vices. 'Then one night they said there was a man living in the church hostel that they wanted to get a message to. That I'd know which one he was by the mark on his coat – this was winter, last winter, when it never stopped raining. I found him over on the waste ground by the Baltic. The deal was good, so I didn't have a problem. Fifty pounds up front, then a thousand afterwards. He took it, so I just walked him back that night – to the ship. If anyone said no I was to say that I'd be back to ask again. But if that happened, I didn't get my money – so I didn't take no for an answer.'

Sweat seemed to suddenly spring from Judd's young face, like jewels, so with one fluid movement he took off his T-shirt, then used it to towel his narrow chest and tattooed arm.

'Two hundred quid a time, they paid me. Like I said, I didn't need it. I'm OK. But Dad was getting worse, and even if he didn't say as much, we knew he was dying. And that was crazy because they could help him if he'd just stop the booze. It was like Mum said it was going to be – that I was to watch out for – that he'd just self-destruct. It was what was on the inside that would get him. I promised her that wouldn't happen. She said I was the man now, that it was down to me.'

Inside the operating theatre they could hear a suction pipe sucking liquid from an incision.

'The mark,' said Shaw. 'The mark they left on the men – the candle?' Judd's eyes widened with the realization that this man knew more about his life than he thought was possible. Shaw saw an image then of Patigno's *Miracle at Cana* on the wall of the Sacred Heart. The memento mori on the velvet drape – but in this version, unlike the original, the candle had been omitted.

Shaw heard Twine shift his boots and the next second the plastic curtains opened. A man, Filipino, stood in the opening, a silhouette in a surgical gown.

'Tell her,' said Neil Judd. 'Tell her it's all over – but she can finish.' The man looked at the carbine, the open hatch door.

'Rey?' said a voice within.

He retreated without a word.

Three uniformed officers came through the door to the hatch, all armed. Twine briefed them. They all waited, awkward, like nightclub bouncers.

Shaw squatted down in the dust, trying to see into Neil Judd's unfocused eyes. 'So you were the Organ Grinder?'

'I didn't know I had a name,' he said. 'But I knew they were afraid of me; the story was out there, like a legend. It helped, the fear, because it meant hardly anyone dared to say no. Before I did the work for them they had others. Sometimes they bungled the job – so the news had got out, but only whispered. When the ship came in I could . . .' He rubbed his fingers together. '*Feel* the fear.' The excitement made the biceps in his tattooed arm twitch.

'But this time – the last time?'

'They didn't need me every time,' he said. 'I didn't ask why. I saw the captain and we had some food, booze, but they didn't want a donor. They had other sources – that's what he always said. Then, that Sunday, the power went.' He laughed bitterly, and again Shaw was struck that it wasn't a genuine emotion, but a mimicked version, like a child copying an adult. 'All because Dad wanted to keep his little vendetta going – because he thought it proved to us that he was innocent. I didn't know he was planning it. I'd have stopped him.

'They had a client on board the *Rosa* – everything ready to go. They'd got a kidney out, ready. But once the juice went the temperature soared – the fridges too. It was chaos. That's when Rey called. I had to find a donor. Really quickly. And that's when I saw my chance. So I said I wouldn't do it, that it was too dangerous, 'cos normally I had time to watch them, time to see if there was a routine that I could cut into. I said that, if they were really desperate I'd do it, provided they gave Dad the op. For free. We made the deal – right there on the mobile. Then they said they'd found me someone at the hostel, that he was called Blanket, and they'd marked up his coat.'

'And you didn't know who Blanket really was, did you?'

Judd ducked his head and threw up, a thin trickle of bile, his body convulsing in rhythmic waves like a cat being sick.

He started telling the truth before the rhythm had ceased, so that what he said came in broken phrases. 'I threw the money at him … got him …' He looked up suddenly and Shaw saw tears spilling out of his eyes. 'Got my brother, by the scruff of the neck.' He wiped a hand across his mouth. 'I think he knew it was me, but I didn't recognize him, or the voice. I was a toddler when he left home, so he's a stranger – was a stranger. I hardly had a memory of him. I just thought – I have to do this. So I hit him.'

They both looked to the perspex door, as if the lost brother might walk out, large as life.

'Then you dragged him aboard?'

'Down the alley, through the yard. Then there was a second problem. They got the engineer back on board but he was pissed-up, so they put the generator back arse about face and when the juice ran it blew the fridges – nearly all of them – so most of the stored stuff – tissue, tendons – it was all useless. They said they knew where Bry worked. That it was ideal, that I had to get him to do this, to put all the waste through the furnace, because they needed to clean out the fridges and it was too dangerous to drop that much at sea. So I said I'd go up and ask him, and I took the waste from the op they'd had to abandon – the kidney, the rest – I took that with me, to show him how easy it was, and because they wanted to clean up the theatre when the lights came back on. It was all in a Tesco bag, wrapped, sealed . . .'

He looked at Shaw for the first time, as if that one domestic detail had brought back the horror of what he'd done. 'I went home 'cos I'd got his . . .' He stopped, his throat filling with fluid. 'Sean's . . . blood, on my shirt. The lights were out so the street was chaos. One of Dad's overalls was left hanging on the stairs where Ally leaves them, so I took those. Then I ran – up to the hospital.

'I knew the layout up there from when I was a kid and I'd go up in the holidays – take Bry's lunch up. And I knew he went out on the ledge for a smoke. So that's where we talked. I was waiting for him. I told him how easy it was. Then we went inside 'cos I was going to show him. I picked another bag which was nearly empty, ripped the plastic, and stuffed my bag in.'

'But he didn't want to do it, did he?' said Shaw.

Judd shook his head. 'It was stupid,' he said, driving the heel of his palm into his eye socket. 'I said we had to do this for Dad. That just stopped him, like a statue. He said he was enjoying it, watching Dad die.' His eyes locked on Shaw's, desperate for someone to say he'd done the right thing. 'He said he knew what he'd seen the day Norma Jean went missing, knew what he felt. That Dad deserved to die. I told him that I'd promised Mum – that the past was Dad's burden, whatever the truth was. But he still said no. We fought when I put the bag on the belt. I'm stronger than they all think, 'cos of the workouts. It was an accident.' Even he didn't sound like he believed that.

'What did you stab him with?'

He used both hands to roll up one of the legs of his jeans. A screwdriver was taped to his calf muscle, the head sharpened to a murderous point, like a snapshot from *Taxi Driver*. 'The lights went out – a power cut – and he lunged for me in the dark. I threw him back, and I heard him crash into the metal instrument panel.' He touched the back of his skull. 'I knew he was dead – that he'd die – right then, because when the emergency lighting came on I could see him pinned to the metal, his arms jerking. He was gonna scream. I couldn't let that happen. So I walked forward and put the screwdriver in his chest, just once, so he'd be quiet.'

Shaw let him have the euphemism unchallenged.

'Why's the skipper dead?' he said.

'Ally showed me the note from Sean last night, asked me if I'd seen him. So I knew then what I'd done. I'd brought him here for this . . .'

413

He stood, wanting to get away, Shaw sensed, up to the light.

'So I went to de Mesquita when I brought Dad aboard. I wanted to know where they went – the donors – when the ops were done. I could put it right then – bring him back. I wanted to know where I'd find him. But of course part of me knew, knew instantly, when they found that corpse on the sands. And I thought – can that be true? *Can that be true?* And then I thought I'd been a fucking fool.'

He was sobbing now, pushing his palms into his face as if he could compress the tears. 'The captain said they always dropped them out at sea. He'd been drinking, which loosened his tongue. And I guess he thought I was one of them now, that there was no way out. It was just the words he chose. His English ain't good. So perhaps I should have forgiven him. But he said they dumped them when they'd *served their purpose.* He was standing in the shower, naked, shameless. I don't think I can live with the truth. I was fucking sure he wasn't going to live with it.'

He looked up quickly at a noise from the operating room. Jofranka Phillips parted the plastic curtains. She still wore a surgical gown, the chest bloodsoaked. Shaw thought how cool she looked, revealing her fingers as she pulled clear the gloves.

'Thank you for waiting,' she said. Just like that, as if she'd just come out of her office at the hospital.

She turned to Neil Judd and even managed a half-smile. 'He's going to be fine.'

51

Friday, 10 September

Jofranka Phillips joined Shaw in the mess room once she was satisfied with the condition of her patients. She didn't know the donor's name, she never asked such questions. Their only mark of individuality was the white wristband, to set them apart from the recipient. De Mesquita's job was to set up everything – all she did was the operations, assisted by Rey Abucajo, the nurse who had worked alongside Mesquita throughout his 'career' – the very word she used, as if there were a certificate awarded for such a crime. She saw the clients – rich, replete, and white. And sometimes the donors – the pallid, mottled bodies of the homeless, or, more often, just the prepared organ or bone or tendon, taken from storage.

Dawn was still an hour away. The night had taken its toll on Phillips, who covered her face with her long fingers.

'Tell me about your father,' said Shaw, knowing it was one question she'd feel compelled to answer.

'He died before I was born. By the time I arrived his life was over, but its shadow was on all of us. And has been ever since.'

Shaw hardened his voice, impatient with the self-pity in her answer. 'Your brothers?'

'They felt, and I feel, that he would have wanted us to make recompense.' She'd chosen the word beautifully. 'We are innocent of his guilt, of course – but families don't work like that, do they? It's the stigma, attached to the name, to the blood.'

'And the Kircher Institute needs money?'

She laughed, closing her eyes. 'Millions. My brothers coped, then old age has overtaken them, and then death – only Hanzi now, and he is bedridden. So they turned to me. And I felt helpless, impotent. I'd been to the Kircher, of course, and I'd become involved in the campaign to change the law, to allow the removal of organs from the brain-dead. I was interested in the subject, aware of the market. I thought I could do this, that if we were careful with collecting our donors, if we offered them this' – she searched the dictionary in her head – 'this opportunity, then there was nothing evil in this, and that great good would come from it. I posed as a client, and met Juan de Mesquita. The *Rosa* had already been converted by then, but he had no steady supply of donors, and the surgeon he used was on the edge of the law – in Germany, near Hamburg. It was too dangerous. I solved his problems.'

'And the money?'

'Went to the Kircher. All of it.'

'And you don't see the irony in that? That your father died of shame because he experimented on prisoners. Innocents.'

'We pay the donors. They are treated well. Very well.'

Shaw conjured up what he hoped was a cruel smile, seeing again John Pearmain's body on Warham's Hole.

'You don't know, do you? You think Rey is here just to assist in these operations? They needed you for this. For the transplants. But other things are simpler ... cornea grafts, tissue removal. You didn't think of that, did you? And you believed that all the donors walked away. Just like that. With a fat cheque?'

She drank more tea, ignoring the question, although he could see that it had troubled her deeply because the blood had drained from her face and her lips were hardening into a murderous line.

'And Gavin Peploe? Why did he have to die? Because you are his murderer, I'm sure of that. Where was the ultimate good in that? Because he *was* an innocent, wasn't he? A playboy, maybe; a man who sold his skills in the private market. But not a bad man.'

She couldn't keep the revulsion she genuinely felt from disfiguring her face. 'Neil Judd said he would go to you with everything if we did not do this operation for his father. I had to make time. We can't change the schedule for the *Rosa* without the owners' permission. I thought you might find her here on the quayside – that what was on board, hidden, might be found. A diversion was needed.' She dropped her eyes, ashamed, Shaw knew, that she'd resorted to such a euphemism. 'He administered his own poison,' she said, as if the difference between good and evil came down to a technicality.

'You switched the pills – knowing that he never looked.'

'I don't think you can prove that, and I doubt you ever will.'

Shaw's mobile, sitting on the table top, buzzed and

shook, like a bee pointing the way to honey. A text on his mobile from DC Lau:

EREBUS STREET – POWER SUB-STATION – 187

The code for a suspicious death.

Phillips wouldn't say another word. She wanted her lawyer.

'I wish you would talk to us now – because it might be important – it might save lives.' She watched him. 'Because, even now, there is so much I don't understand. Neil said that he didn't always fetch the donor – that the captain said there was another "source". And the man we found dead out on the sands – and the one in the docks – they'd given ...' He let that word hang between them. 'They'd given organs several times – and tissue. Which begs the question, where were they between the operations? Do you see? There's still something hidden.'

She remained silent, even as Shaw walked her to a squad car on the quay. There she stood with the door open, to take one last look at the ship. 'He'll do well,' she said. 'Neil's father. The liver will regenerate, but only if he stops the drinking. There's a drug, his GP should be told – now. Even if he goes to prison – because of the fire – he needs to take it. It'll make the alcohol repugnant to him ...' She looked about her. 'Like ashes.'

Shaw turned and walked away without giving her the comfort of an answer. He moved quickly through the night shadows which still stretched across Berth 4. The gate to the sub-station stood open, the yard crowded with building gear: a cement mixer, a pallet of new bricks, the glittering innards of the new electrics wrapped in industrial clingfilm.

The roof and walls of the original listed building still stood but the gear within had been removed and the floor broken up. Lumps of reinforced concrete stood in the yard. In the shadows within Shaw could see Tom Hadden, and then, suddenly, the interior was bathed in bright white light, an arc lamp blazing. Shaw stood on the edge of a trench, a slit so dark by comparison that it seemed to suck in the heat as well as the light so that he shivered, staring down, waiting for his eyes to find a line, a shade, a pinpoint – anything to make sense of the absence of shape and meaning.

Flints first, glistening, where they lay in strata amongst the clay. Then at the bottom, many shapes, in pale outlines. A human body. The shock made him fall forward slightly so that he had to suddenly drop to his knees, looking down at the familiar bones of the dead, but turned on one side, the knees up, and the shreds of something wrapping it – a dress as a shroud.

Hadden edged the light nearer so that the grave was lit. The corpse was slight, five feet tall, the skull complete, the teeth still in place, all in place, but ugly in the lipless mouth.

Hadden squatted down beside him. 'Andersen, the engineer, says they found some bones late yesterday. St James's rang me – you were on the ship. And she's not going anywhere. It's a girl – yes. Early teens.'

'I think I know her name,' said Shaw. 'There's something on the chest,' he said. Hadden stepped down beside the body.

'What is it, Tom?' said Shaw. 'Jewellery?'

Hadden slipped something into a plastic evidence envelope and reached up – laying it on the ground with a kind of reverence that Shaw didn't understand until he saw what it was.

'Fish skeleton,' said Hadden. 'There's twenty – twenty-five. I'm no expert but they're bony fish – tropical.' He held another in a second bag in his hand. This one was as delicate as a ship in a bottle.

Shaw told him what he knew of Jan Orzsak's obsession with his tropical fish; the favour he'd asked of Norma Jean that last summer of her life – that she feed them while he was away. How she'd promised she would and how, on the day she died, Orzsak had confronted her with the consequences of her failure to keep that promise: the dead, resplendent fish.

'I see,' said Hadden. 'There was one in her throat. I think he pushed her down, Peter, pushed her head down into the tank of water, amongst the dead fish she'd killed with her neglect. There's a crack in the jawbone too. That's typical if she was held under; she'd strain for air until the bone broke.'

Shaw took the envelope and held the tiny skeleton up to the light. 'It's a beautiful thing to be buried with,' he said.

Shaw understood now why Jan Orzsak hadn't left the street in all those years, why he'd taken the opportunity to move next door to the site. He was his victim's guardian, and the keeper of his own secret. But for this, the chance discovery of her bones, he'd have lived out the rest of his years knowing she was there, knowing Andy Judd was hated by his own children – condemned to a lifetime under suspicion – for what he, Jan Orzsak, had done. And he'd persisted with this lie knowing that Andy Judd's world had been reduced to a single wish: to bury his daughter, to know, finally, that her body was at peace.

But Orzsak wasn't at home now. He'd been brought back to Erebus Street by community ambulance at six the previous evening. He'd made himself a simple meal – two boiled eggs, with the stale sliced bread toasted. Then he'd selected the best bottle of wine he had left in the rack. He'd gone to bed, knowing sleep was a mercy he was denied. At just after six that morning DC Lau, in an unmarked car by the dock gates, had seen him leave his house, walk the street and weave his way through the tombstones towards the presbytery of the Sacred Heart of Mary. Ten minutes later she'd watched as Orzsak retraced his steps through the graveyard, followed by the priest, who'd opened up the church.

The small neo-Gothic side door was still open, the

interior cool, despite the low dawn sun which streamed through one of the Victorian stained-glass windows. The light revealed something Shaw had missed before – a figure of Christ, the wounds of the crucifixion still bleeding, the bland face looking askance, hung high over the altar. The men slept in the nave, rolled in their blankets, innocent of the crime that Shaw guessed was even now being confessed under this same roof for the first time.

Shaw stood in the silence, listening, managing to pick out a steady, insistent whisper. Three confessional boxes stood to one side, but there was light in none of them. Looking back up the aisle towards the great doors and the shadowy mural, he saw Orzsak, kneeling in a pew, Father Martin beside him, a hand on his shoulder. As Shaw walked towards them Orzsak stood, and Shaw felt that gravity had won whatever battle it had been fighting with this man for a lifetime. He stepped out into the aisle, moving as if he was under water, the folds of fat on his face looser, his jaw slack, his bottom lip down, wet and pink.

Shaw stood in his path. Orzsak almost fell, then steadied himself by holding on to the end of a pew.

'An honest confession?' he asked, and Orzsak couldn't stop himself nodding.

'Really?' He turned to Martin, who wore a confessional stole over a white T-shirt and jeans. 'So he's forgiven?'

'Absolution isn't mine to give,' he said. 'That will come later, possibly. In another life.'

'I know how you did it, Mr Orzsak. You hid her body in the basement that first night,' Shaw said. 'I checked the original report of the officers who searched the houses.

None of the rest had a basement. But yours had been dug out for the wine, hadn't it? When your mother bought it in the sixties. All you had to do was conceal the door.'

Orzsak moved his knee, a tiny stamp. 'A trapdoor,' he said.

'And you had time; she died at – what – six? We didn't get to the house before ten. And after that you had all the time you needed not to hurry, not to make a mistake. Her body was in the basement; they were rebuilding the electricity sub-station – that's right, isn't it? Sometime then – '92, '93?'

'The next spring,' said Orzsak, a slight sibilance on the 's'.

'So easy enough for you, because you were in the industry – power supply. In fact, were you on the job?'

Orzsak looked away, suddenly tired of the questions.

'So one night you ran a car to the dock gates and slipped her body into the waiting footings of the floor – an extra foot, beneath the clay. Then you just sat back and waited for them to pour the concrete. Your secret then, until Andy Judd's little spasm of vengeance led us all to this . . .'

Shaw looked up at the mural of the wedding feast around the doors.

'What I don't understand is why,' said Shaw. 'Why she had to die.'

Orzsak considered the implied question, as if it were an abstruse point of contention in a philosophical debate.

'She came to me crying,' he said. 'Not for what she'd done to me, but for what she wanted to do to her child. The unborn child. She'd taken all this life from me

423

without a thought. Just a regret. And she so misunderstood my grief that she would bring this to me – this plan to kill her child against the wishes of God. Not just my God – her God. Do you know what she asked me . . . ?' A trickle of saliva left the corner of the bow-like mouth. 'For money. She said she had the courage to do it – but not here, amongst her own people. Her doctor had suggested Norwich – a hostel. But she wanted to know if she could ask me for help – for "pocket-money", she said. It was the obscenity of that. The childlike obscenity. She wanted to take that life away. But she didn't deserve the one she had. I felt God's wrath within me.'

Shaw didn't believe most of that. 'So you killed her – drowned her – held her head under the water of the tank. But you killed the child as well – that doesn't make sense.'

'I was angry.'

'Just angry?' asked Shaw. He thought about the relationship between the lonely bachelor and the child who had become a woman. 'Or jealousy? You didn't know about Ben Ruddle, did you? You didn't know that Norma Jean wasn't a child any more. What did you really feel?'

'I won't speak, not again,' said Orzsak. 'Not about this.'

Father Martin sat, pulling the purple stole of confession from around his neck. He'd heard many confessions, Shaw guessed, but none that had taken him so far into the depths of human pain: Orzsak's pain, the pain of the teenager who had died that night at his hands, and the pain of the father, an outcast even to his children.

They heard footsteps and Ally Judd appeared from the vestry, holding a tray of coffee cups, a nightgown only partly concealed by a raincoat. Behind her came Liam Kennedy, rubbing sleep from his eyes, in only shorts and a sweatshirt. He tried to look floppy, at ease, but Shaw could see the tension that made him hold his arms at an awkward angle, as if in pain.

Ally handed out coffees. Orzsak shook his head so Shaw took his. The liquid was hot, gritty, and pungent. Shaw was always astonished at how such a simple thing could make him feel a splinter of joy, even here.

Kennedy stood watching the men sleep.

'And what do the voices say today?' asked Shaw of Kennedy.

He shook his head, as if clearing it of other thoughts. 'They've been silent.'

Shaw stood and looked back down the nave to Kennedy's painting, completed now to the halfway stage above the pointed arch of the main doors – Patigno's *Miracle at Cana*.

'I did wonder why you'd left it out – the candle, the ultimate symbol of memento mori, of the passing of time, of death. In the original there's a rather fine one, in a gold holder, at the centre of the table ... just there, to the right of the skull.' He walked to the wall, pointing up at the velvet-covered table, heavy with rotting fruit.

But Kennedy wouldn't look. Instead Father Martin walked towards the mural, as if seeing it for the first time. 'Yes, you're right,' he said, tapping a finger on the cold stone wall.

Valentine appeared at the small door with two

uniformed PCs. Shaw shook his head a fraction and they melted away.

'You couldn't bring yourself to paint the candle, could you, Liam – because that was the sign, the signal, that you used to mark each of the victims after Mrs Phillips gave you the names.'

Kennedy came alive then, realizing for the first time that he'd made mistakes, that good intentions didn't mean he hadn't committed a great sin. 'This is rubbish. Selected who – for what?'

Shaw ignored him.

'The second time we met you, Liam, here, in the church, you were wearing a T-shirt with a slogan. Do you remember?'

Kennedy licked his lips. He did, and he put a hand over his heart where his pulse was beginning to race.

'Voluntary Service Overseas,' said Shaw. 'I checked you out with their London office. They passed me on to Tel Aviv. You were at a kibbutz in 2008. A whole harvest – a good worker, even if you weren't Jewish. And political too – speaking up for the Palestinians, for their rights on the same land. But that wasn't so popular, was it? So you went to Jerusalem to work for an organization that didn't discriminate – the Kircher Institute. And you could use some of your IT skills, at last. You helped them build their website. And when you came home you kept in touch, which is how you met Jofranka Phillips. But you were ill by then, and the voices were part of that. So what could she give you in return for your help? There's a room up at the hospital – for the Hearing Voices Network. We had a look inside. PCs, an office.

I checked out the website – it's good, Liam, really good.'

Kennedy turned to Father Martin. 'This *is* rubbish.'

'And she'd have told you what she told me. That the donors each had a choice. And that once they'd taken that choice they'd be looked after. No evil could come from that. Is that what she said?'

Kennedy held a coffee cup but he put it down now because his hand was beginning to shake.

'I'm not here to listen to you deny this,' said Shaw. 'I'm here because there is still something I don't understand. It was one of your little kindnesses, I think, at first, to collect the men's pills from the chemist. At first I thought that was it – that was how you were able to select the ones that Mrs Phillips could use. And it might have helped – but it wasn't good enough. No, she had the files, up at the hospital, so she didn't need you for that. But I checked with Boots.'

He took a list out of his pocket.

'And that's what I don't understand, because only yesterday you picked up a prescription for Paul Tyler – and he disappeared six months ago. And there are others, men who haven't been listed here, on your records, for months, even a year. So my question – and it's an urgent one – is why. If these men have gone, why do you still collect their drugs?'

In the silence they could hear the uneven whirr of the electric clock over the vestry door.

The blood drained from Kennedy's face.

'I gave them to the captain,' he said in a whisper. 'He said they needed them – where they'd gone. That's how they got away – on the *Rosa*. To the south coast.' He

427

looked around. 'That's what he said.' His shoulders slumped.

'Was he lying to me?' Kennedy asked, though Shaw could see he already knew the answer. It was the moment, Shaw thought, when Liam Kennedy realized he was a holy fool.

He stood, adjusted his jeans, and noticed for the first time the uniformed officers who'd slipped into a pew by the door.

'I want to speak with Father Martin before I go,' he said. 'Can I?'

But Father Martin was already walking away, down the nave, with Ally Judd at his side. He knelt at the altar, crossed himself, then left his church without looking back.

53

On the *Rosa* Neil Judd was lying on a bunk in one of the crew cabins. It held a single bed, a fitted cupboard and a shower unit, slightly smaller than the one in which he'd squeezed the life out of Juan de Mesquita. He'd collapsed while being helped up the ladder in number 4 hatch. In the end they'd got him in the bosun's chair and winched him up to the deck. A doctor had given him a sedative and advised a period of rest before trying to transfer him to St James's. A uniformed woman constable sat at the foot of the bunk. When Neil Judd woke at eleven she brought him to the mess, where Shaw was having breakfast prepared from supplies in the galley: cereal, milk and toast. A pot of black coffee seeped a delicious aroma into the small room. He'd spent an hour running various versions of events through his head, and he was still disturbed by what he didn't know. He was reluctant to leave the *Rosa*, sensing that the ship still held more secrets than it had so far revealed.

Shaw put an evidence envelope on the table. He was struggling still to think of Neil Judd as a killer, rather than a victim himself, the baby brother left as a guardian angel for a father he probably didn't hate but almost certainly despised; haunted by the fact that he'd slept through the trauma which had ripped his own family apart and that he was too young to recall his missing siblings, Norma Jean

429

and Sean. He'd deserve whatever the court decided, but he deserved the truth as well.

Shaw unpopped the envelope seal and slid the delicate skeleton of the fish onto the table.

'We've found your sister's body. It was buried in the foundations of the electricity sub-station at the foot of Erebus Street. These were with her – and many more like them.'

Judd laid a finger on the delicate tracery of the bones – a dorsal fin, as fine as a scrimshaw comb.

'We think Jan Orzsak worked as a consultant for the power company in the 1990s. There is other forensic evidence, potential evidence – the body was partly wrapped in a blanket, a roll of carpet. We've recovered human hairs. We're confident we can bring the appropriate charges.'

'My father . . .' said Neil Judd, trying to understand all the implications of this gossamer-thin skeleton.

'Yes. An innocent man. Not a killer.'

The word made Judd jolt, as if he'd been stung. He drank some coffee Shaw offered him, and then asked a favour Shaw couldn't refuse. 'Can I see him? I want him to know that I know. I'm strong enough now – much stronger.' He cracked the joints of his fingers.

'He's in the hold,' said Shaw. 'They won't move him until they're ready.'

Judd stood. 'I can climb down. Please.'

The vertical shaft was lit now by a line of halogen lights. Shaw went first, then Judd, then DC Birley. The three of them descended like abseiling mountaineers. The operating theatre looked very different. The plastic screens had been removed, a team of three NHS nurses had been brought in from the hospital, the two patients – as yet still not sufficiently recovered to be winched vertically up the shaft – lay on operating tables at the end. The donor was still unconscious, but he fitted the description of Terry Foster, the man who'd gone missing with Pearmain and Tyler. Andy Judd was awake, his eyes fixed on the girder above. Phillips's instruments and much of the medical kit had been taken up the shaft. Shaw noticed that the donor's wrist was still encircled by one of the charity bands.

Neil Judd went to his father's bedside and took his hand, standing at a slight distance, then stepped closer, pushing back white hair from the old man's forehead. They put their heads together to talk.

Shaw could see now that the metal container which had held the operating theatre had two internal doors, not one. Three CSIs in SOC suits worked at the other door, one cutting through a padlock with a fine saw, overseen by Tom Hadden.

'No key?' asked Shaw, joining them.

'If anyone's got it they're not telling us,' said Hadden. 'Which makes me even more determined to get through. It leads into the other containers. My guess is they contain stores, the fridges.'

Shaw thought about that and took a step back, but then the padlock gave and Hadden spun a circular lock. When the door finally gave there was a sound of escaping air, like a Tupperware lid being popped.

It took three of them to swing it out and back and the light flooded in to reveal a corridor, unlit, the steel walls stained with rust, glistening with condensation. An image flashed into Shaw's head from *Run Silent, Run Deep*, a Second World War film set aboard a submarine, the crew sweating in the silence under an oily sea or dead in an airless tomb.

It was an eerie image, so that when he saw something move in the shadows it made him flinch, as if from a blow.

Out of the ash-grey shadows came a man, walking towards them, shuffling, a hand to his side where a bloody bandage encircled his flesh. The smell was fetid, the stench of humankind, and, thought Shaw, the sweet smell of rotting fruit. It was an image out of a nightmare, and the thought that broke into Shaw's mind was that he was relieved that Fran wasn't there to see it – because it would haunt a child's mind, as it would his.

'Sean?'

Neil Judd stood at Shaw's shoulder. The word seemed to stop the shuffling man in his tracks, and he swayed, then sank to his knees.

Neil Judd ran forward and helped him up, and when their heads were together it became obvious that they were brothers, even now, because Sean Judd had lost his mop of hair.

Shaw and Valentine pushed past, down the corridor, which at first seemed to end in a blank wall. As his vision adjusted to the gloom, however, Shaw could see that the end wall contained another door. Beyond it was a room which doubled back towards the operating theatre.

Inside were six beds, three of them occupied, each occupant held to the bedstead by a single handcuff. The first raised his head from a grimy pillow and held Shaw's gaze with jaundiced eyes – a look which was both rational and unhinged. 'Thank God,' he said simply, and let his lids fall, his body relaxing into unconsciousness.

Standing there, Shaw's mind locked, as if it was unable to complete a difficult computation. But he knew what he had in his mind – the image of Liam Kennedy, collecting prescriptions for men who should have been long gone. But they'd been here, waiting to fulfil their purpose, a living organ bank. And another image: the sudden darkness on that Sunday when the power had failed. The chaos here in this room, the fear and the anger. Had they been handcuffed then, he wondered, or free?

One of the other two men sat up, then rolled from his bed, tugging the bed frame with him, holding a hand up, trying to cover his face. In the third bed a man lay still, bandages around his head. The man on the floor began to scream, a thin wail, gathering strength. Shaw was still struggling to understand what he was seeing, and in his confusion he tried to find a parallel from his own experience, but all he could call to mind was a painting by Hieronymus Bosch, a nightmare vision of hell. The man in the corner stopped screaming and pointed at the man with the bandaged head.

The heat in the room lay like a second skin. The men were dressed only in shorts, so that Shaw and Valentine could see the scars. Several on each. And the long, stitched lines along calves and arms where tendon and tissue had been removed.

The man in the corner told them where to go next – not with his voice, but with his eyes, which kept flickering to the other door, into the third container.

Shaw opened it quickly because he knew if he stopped he might not be able to go on. There was no lock. His fingers searched inside for a switch while he stifled a childhood fear that some unseen hand would grab his wrist in the darkness. Neon tubes strobed into life, revealing a line of industrial fridges. He looked at Valentine, unwilling to believe, then flipped the lid of the nearest.

Two men lay in the ice, their many scars a vivid blue, the bodies naked. One had had a leg removed, the stump a dull terracotta. Valentine walked past Shaw and opened the next: a man, ice like a blanket around him through which only lips and hair could be seen, and the toes – breaking through. But the skin looked patched, black in places, and disfigured. Shaw remembered that the *Rosa*'s power supply, when switched on that night after the generator had been reassembled, had blown the circuits, so that the contents of the fridges had begun to rot and they couldn't have let the power engineers run a cable aboard – not that night, anyway, because of the chaos on the ship. Eventually these men had been refrozen, but now their flesh was useless.

Shaw wondered if he was in shock. Time seemed to have slowed down, and when Valentine spoke it was like listening to a voice underwater.

'They kept them alive – for this?' asked Valentine.

Shaw walked back into the next room. The man in the corner had begun to shake rhythmically, keening softly now. In the corridor he felt the first comforting hint of the cooler air from the operating theatre. And when he got there a sight which halted, for a moment at least, the slide towards trauma: the two Judd brothers, their hands held across their father's body, the old man's eyes open, dimmed with tears.

54

The stock cars circled the arena as if locked together, a screaming high-velocity scrap heap of painted metal wrapped in exhaust fumes. Above rose a cloud of summer dust, like a nuclear mushroom, climbing into a towering column in the hot, windless evening air. The sun was setting through this prism of dirt, so that everywhere the light was red and golden. Valentine watched the last race; or rather, he looked as if he was watching the last race. But his field glasses did not swing as the cars went past. They were fixed instead on a spot in the pits opposite. The man he was watching wore a spotless mechanic's jacket, reflective glasses, and a baseball cap with a logo Valentine couldn't read – although he knew what it said: TEAM MOSSE.

The air was soaked with petrol so that he could taste it on his lips – iron, and the astringent kick of gas – so he pulled the third can of beer out of his raincoat pocket. The first had been iced, this one was warm, and as he pulled the tab he let the froth explode in his mouth. He was pleased it was the last race because his back ached, and the noise was making a small bone in his inner ear buzz like a trapped fly.

A chequered flag the size of a picnic blanket waved

and he saw Alex Cosyns's car go past in the leading pack of three, and then a blazing replay screen showed the final yards in slow motion, with a flashing white-on-black tickertape line reading WINNER – TEAM MOSSE. As the chasing pack swept past a piece of chassis span off one of the cars, followed by a few strips of burnt tyre. The crowd, about 8,000 strong, screamed with delight as the disintegrating car failed to pull out of the bend, the offside front wheel crumpling so that the whole vehicle carried on, catching the crash barrier, tipping, then riding ahead on its roof.

But Valentine wasn't watching. He'd found his target again in the pits opposite: Robert Mosse, standing alone, hands on hips, watching Cosyns bring in the winning car. When the driver got out Mosse stopped clapping and lit a cigar, turning away, and it was a mechanic from the next pit who patted the winner on the back. Valentine wondered again why Robert Mosse was sending Cosyns £1,000 cheques and then cutting him dead in his moment of glory. Cosyns didn't register the slight, simply accepting a bottle of beer from the man in overalls and calmly sipping it as he watched the replay of the final lap.

Valentine dropped the can, half finished, in a bin and began to thread through the crowd towards the exit gates. There'd be a kind of circus finale, with all the cars circling, but he didn't need to see that because he was here to find out where they kept the Team Mosse trailer. Cosyns housed the car in the garage beside the undertakers, but there was no room for anything else, and Valentine had executed a drive-by surveillance of Mosse's tasteless suburban villa – there were three garages, but all standard length, so they couldn't keep it there. Besides, they already had three cars: Mosse's BMW, a 4×4, and another stock car, but this one was always up on bricks. That hadn't been a drive-by observation – he'd had a decent drink at the Artichoke and thought, fuck it. So he'd parked round the corner and had a sniff, put a torch beam through the little window in the garage side door. What harm was in that? He was building up a picture, that was all. Keeping his distance. And this was just one of the bits that didn't fit, finding the place where they kept the trailer.

Outside the arena it was chaos, like some nightmare version of the Monte Carlo Rally, with people running for their cars, trying to beat the inevitable traffic jam. The sun shone from a thousand windscreens. Valentine found the Mazda, zigzagged to the gates, and slipped into a lay-by next to a mobile tea van. He had the window down so the smell of fat and bacon filled the car.

He kicked open the door but left the engine running.

His mobile rang. He'd changed the ring tone to play the theme from *Ghostbusters*, and it still made him laugh.

GUILTY PLEA

The text was from Shaw, on his way back to Lynn from an informal meeting in Peterborough with the CPS, who were involved in an international effort to prepare the case against the organ traffickers – a case set to cause an international sensation.

Andy Judd was due before the magistrates the following morning to lodge a plea, and had waited until the last moment before agreeing to the deal on offer to both him and his son Neil. Andy Judd would plead guilty to arson at the electrical sub-station and criminal damage at Orzsak's house – astonishingly, his only crimes. The prosecution would agree to a non-custodial sentence. In return, Andy Judd would appear as a Crown witness in the trail of those involved in the illegal trafficking of human organs. His own complicity would be overlooked. Neil Judd would also appear for the Crown, and escape prosecution for his part in recruiting donors. However, he would separately stand charged with the murder of his brother once the main case was concluded. Liam Kennedy would not appear at all; the stress of discovering the true consequences of his 'selection' process had triggered a crisis in his mental condition. He was being held at a psychiatric unit in Coventry, and had been assessed as unfit to face trial.

The Crown's case would further be strengthened by testimony from the three men discovered still alive in the hold of the *Rosa* by Shaw and Valentine – and Terence Foster, the donor in the operating theatre: brave men who, it now seemed, had come close to saving themselves on that Sunday night the power had blown on Erebus Street. In the sudden darkness they'd planned a rebellion, and when Rey Abucajo had opened the door by torchlight to select a replacement for John Tyler they'd coshed him, pushed him out, and barricaded the door. And that was why Neil Judd had been forced to go out on the streets for a fresh donor. When Rey Abucajo eventually returned with the rest of the crew to force his way through the door he'd come armed. The man they'd known as John Pearmain had been shot dead as an example to the rest, then taken away to the operating table to make his final contribution to the market for human organs. His body had gone overboard with Tyler's as the *Rosa* sailed out of the Wash, weighted down in the waste bag which had come ashore on Warham's Hole. All four witnesses lived for the moment they'd take the stand.

Interpol was making progress in establishing when and where the *Rosa*'s hold had been adapted to conceal the operating theatre and makeshift ward and organ bank. The complexity of the wider investigation – which had been handed to a specialist cross-border unit at New Scotland Yard – meant that the trial was yet to be allocated a date in the legal calendar. Counsel's best guess was currently spring 2012. None of the accused had been granted bail. Lawyers for Abucajo had indicated that their client would testify that the dead captain had administered lethal injections to those donors who had outlived their usefulness in the living organ bank. It was a ploy unlikely to save his skin. Jofranka Phillips's case would be more subtle: a jury would have to decide the extent to which she'd known the secrets of the *Rosa*. Initial estimates of the number of men who may have died on board the vessel during its two-year career as a floating operating theatre varied between eight and thirteen. The final figure might be far higher.

Valentine sucked the life out of a Silk Cut. Then another. Was there another way out of the Norfolk Arena? He was about to walk back and check with the security guard by the entrance when Mosse's soft-top BMW came into view, taking the corner onto the main road at 60 m.p.h., purring past, the Limousin leather hood folded back behind the rear seat.

A minute later, less, Cosyns swung out in his own BMW – a second-hand model, the offside wing dented – with the trailer behind carrying the Citroën, a winner's laurel leaf wreath hung over the bonnet aerial. At the rear window he saw a small dog scrabbling, its nose to the glass.

Valentine slipped the Mazda in behind the trailer, up close, where he wouldn't be seen too often in the BMW's side mirror.

Following, he felt fleetingly happy, with the local radio giving out a forecast for the beaches, the heat making the plastic seats soft with that smell that brought back a memory of childhood holidays.

They hit the ring road, went east, then skirted the town, so that Valentine was beginning to think they'd pick up the coast road, but then one roundabout short they cut back into town, round the Magnox power station, and into the Westmead Estate. Valentine's breathing became painfully shallow, because in all the years since the Tessier case he'd never found a single line of evidence which linked Robert Mosse *back* to his childhood home and the scene of the crime – except for the disputed fur glove. In fact all the members of Mosse's little gang had put as much distance as they could between the estate and their adult lives. Cosyns had moved away, Voyce had gone to New Zealand, Robins to the Midlands, then prison and a string of psychiatric hospitals. But here Valentine was, following Cosyns right back to where it had all begun.

He dropped the Mazda back a hundred yards as they drove past the triangle of ground worn down to mud by kids' football, the pitch where Tessier had been playing that summer's day in 1997. A narrow slip road led beyond it, past low-level residential blocks built in the late eighties, then round the community centre into the dead ground between the estate and the old coastal railway – a deep cut full of dusty shrubs. Here were serried ranks of wooden lock-ups, access tracks of compacted dirt running between, and he saw the trailer turning into one, backing out to negotiate the corner, then disappearing. Valentine pulled a U-turn and went back to the football pitch, where he parked outside a Spar shop. He left his raincoat and jacket in the car, bought an evening paper and a fresh pack of Silk Cut, then strolled back towards the lock-ups. The battered BMW was parked in the third alleyway, the doors of one of the lock-ups just closing automatically on the trailer and Citroën. Blue doors once, now flecked in peeling paint.

He walked down the alley, clocking the numbers on most of the lock-ups: some just painted, others broken. The garages were built in pairs, each sharing a centre wall of breeze blocks and each pair separated by a narrow gap. Keeping the front of Cosyns's lock-up in sight he edged closer, then slipped into one of the gaps opposite. A goods train went past on the old railway line, but when the silence returned he could hear something in it: the low rumble of an engine, throaty and visceral, coming from the lock-up. He noted the number: 51. He backed further down the narrow gap, behind some rubbish – two old pushbikes and an ancient rusted pram. Behind him he had an exit if he got spotted. He'd wait for Cosyns to go, then check out the lock-up. The engine rumbled on. The noise was subterranean, but rhythmic, oiled, and flawless.

So he should have wondered why, twenty minutes later, he could still hear it.

Shaw watched the holiday traffic creeping west as he approached the outskirts of Lynn. His mobile buzzed in its holder on the dashboard. He pressed a key to open a picture message: Fran on the beach holding the string of a kite. Out to the north, over the sea, the sky was a vivid stretched blue. As he reached the ring road he fought and won against the temptation to return to St James's. He had a fortnight's holiday, and it started now. Lena had obtained planning permission for an extension to the cottage: a shower room and bathroom, utility room, and a boot room so they could come straight off the beach without leaving a ton of sand in the cottage. He'd been nominated site manager, which meant two weeks on the beach watching someone else work.

He accelerated to 70 m.p.h., testing out his latest toy – £17,000 worth of second-hand Porsche 911. The car was a fifteen-year-old oddity he'd tracked down on the internet through a specialist car dealer. He'd seen a recommendation for the model on a website run by the Partially Sighted Society. It was one of the few relatively modern cars with a narrow 'A' bar – the strut between the windscreen and the side window. In new cars these 'A' bars were inches thick because they disguised a roll-bar. And they'd been edged forward for strength. The result was that any monocular driver had a serious restriction on visibility. The Porsche had an elegant, thread-like 'A' bar, set back, giving Shaw excellent vision on both sides. This was his new code, to deal with his disability

443

rather than just muddling through and pretending it didn't exist.

He thought about driving straight home to the beach but decided there was one thing he needed to do first. On the dashboard there was a Post-It note with a number in black felt pen: 51. At the last roundabout on the ring road he pulled off to the left and ran into the North End, then round to the edge of town and onto the Westmead Estate. He drove past Valentine's Mazda without recognizing it because the DS had put it through the car-wash that morning. Down by the community centre there was a telephone box under a security CCTV camera, so Shaw parked there. As soon as he'd robbed himself of the forward motion of the car the heat crowded back in. There was something about the architecture of housing estates which made the sun unbearable – the scorched grass, the reflecting windows, the blank concrete. But it was more than that. It was the way the estate captured the idea of being trapped. The sound of a lone ice-cream van seemed to make it worse, the reedy call-sign horribly harsh: the whistled theme from *The Great Escape*. He thought about staying in the car and going home, running to the cottage, getting back in the sea – leaving this until he was back at work. But Lena had been right, he needed to exorcize the ghost of Jonathan Tessier. This was a loose end, and he could tie it up in ten minutes. It didn't cross his mind to ring Valentine for back-up, despite the fact he'd promised himself he would.

He'd been a young DS, just posted to Lynn from Brixton, when he'd first been sent out to the Westmead to take a statement from a man who'd been attacked getting his car out of one of the lock-ups. The victim had been backing out when the driver's door had been pulled open, he'd been dragged out, and hit with an iron bar. They'd taken the car – a Morris Minor in pristine condition. It had turned up at an auction in Retford eight months later, although that was its third sale since the theft thanks to a fake logbook and new plates. Shaw had asked to take the victim's statement at the scene as soon as he'd got out of hospital. They'd worked it out then – that the thieves had been in the gap at the side of the garage, waiting for their moment. So he knew the layout, the 'manor', as his dad would have called it; because there were lots of different landscapes in the city, but one of the most thrilling was the landscape of crime.

The lock-up at the top of the first row was numbered 160, the next 121, then 120, 81, 80, and then 41. He kept walking but glanced down the next alley and saw a battered BMW parked, but nothing else. He knew 51 was down there, but he felt exposed, approaching from the front, so he walked on past 40, to the last alley, looking to double back using one of the gaps. But there was a car in this alley and it didn't look right at all. It was another BMW, but this one had a soft top, and its black paintwork was waxed to a patina which made it look like there was an invisible inch-thick layer of glass covering the paint. This wasn't a third-hand BMW. This was new. It was a £40,000 motor car. He touched the bonnet, felt the warmth of the engine on his palm.

He looked inside the car and saw a pair of reflective sunglasses on the passenger seat. The roll-top reeked of leather. Maybe, thought Shaw, the driver was just stupid, because if this car stood in this alleyway for another hour one of the Westmead's locals would open it up like a can of baked beans.

He chose the nearest gap between lock-ups, clogged with stinging nettles but easy enough to edge down. Brushing a path through, he stopped to untangle a thread of blackberry thorns. He could hear an engine, low and visceral; a big sporting engine. Each of the lock-ups had a small rear door, wooden, with a single window, although most were boarded up now for security. The one at the side of number 51 was covered in a metal sheet of corrugated iron.

The throbbing engine made the iron door vibrate. Using the sound as cover, Shaw tried the handle and, despite the rust and the thick, flaking blue paint, it turned noiselessly, the door opening in on well-oiled hinges like the lid of a musical box. The interior was gloomy and unlit, and appeared to be empty. He went inside and closed the door behind him, letting his eyes assemble the greys and blacks in the half light which came in through a mossy skylight. The air was laden with lead. He went to breathe, coughed once, then doubled over.

Down on his knees the air was clearer. He wanted to call out but knew if he inhaled enough of the fumes to do so he'd pass out. Looking across the stained concrete floor he saw that the breeze-block wall between lock-ups 51 and 52 had been taken down and replaced by a steel joist. A trailer carrying a stock car stood sideways, beside it a Mini, up on blocks, the paintwork a rusted quilt – but Shaw could see the underlying colour, and it made his blood chill: mustard yellow, the colour of the microscopic globes of paint they'd found on Jonathan Tessier's football shirt. The bonnet of the Mini had been removed, the engine cannibalized, the seats ripped out. A Mini: left-hand drive.

Could that be true? Could this be the car that had crashed at that lonely crossroads thirteen years earlier? After the murder of the child they'd have been too scared to move the car, even if they had resprayed the vehicle. Perhaps they'd never finished, traumatized by what they'd had to do, and focused on the desperate need to get rid of the boy's body. Robert Mosse would have been in custody for the killing – but they must have hoped, even then, that the case against him was fatally flawed, but most of all that he wouldn't talk. If they kept their nerve, sat tight, they might get away with murder. After Mosse was freed the vehicle was too hot to put on the streets. A double fatal hit-and-run was one thing, but child murder was in a different league. They'd have been paralysed, so they'd just waited, hoping. And Jack Shaw's myopic investigation had let the moment slip, because he should have turned the Westmead over, looking for more evidence, but he was convinced he had his man, and that was all the evidence he'd need.

Shaw heard something else then, a whimper. Unexpectedly close, a dog barked. Still crouching, he made his way round the trailer until he saw a figure lying on the floor, spreadeagled, face obscured under the vehicle below the exhaust pipe, which was churning out blue gas. A small terrier dog snuffled at his trouser leg, pulling at a pair of racing overalls.

Shaw grabbed the man's feet and dragged the body

towards the door he'd entered by, where the air was clearer, the dog barking now in a rhythmic pattern of yelps. He felt for the pulse: none. The man's face was the colour of wallpaper paste, a thin line of saliva running from the corner of the mouth. Shaw knew Alex Cosyns from his mugshot. He recognized him now, even as he took the jawbone in one hand, putting his other over the man's nose, and opened the airway, bending down. He was looking down the pale throat when two hands clamped around his own throat from behind, closing on his windpipe, locking. Instantly he had no air, and the force of the grip made one of his vertebrae crack. He didn't panic. He worked his strong legs against the floor, trying to get the toe of his right boot to grip so he could get some upward leverage. At the same time he used his elbows to strike upwards. He heard a rib snap, and was pretty sure it wasn't his. He got his other foot into a corner of something – he'd seen an old bookcase against the wall, the shelves crowded with paint, bottles, jars. The dog, silent, gripped his trouser leg in its teeth and hung on despite the violent outward kicks, but he managed to make a decent contact with the wooden bookcase, because he heard it fall, a cacophony of broken glass. He struggled on, but now – shockingly – he knew that he was watching himself struggle, as if he'd floated clear of his own body. He was aware with a kind of pathetic insight that what his body was doing – the crab-like violent star-kicks – was not enough. He didn't black out, he faded away, as if the image of his own struggle was a film clip he didn't have the time to watch. He took one thought with him, left in his brain like the line a firework traces in the

448

sky on bonfire night. It was a laughable, trite thought. He should have gone straight home.

Shaw knew he was still alive when he heard the sound of a trolley wheel squeak. It was mundane enough to rule out the possibility he was in heaven, or, for that matter, hell. If he opened his eyes he knew there'd be pain, but he steeled himself and tried anyway. His eyelids parted stickily, and through his good eye he saw a hospital room. White sheets, white walls, a blanket exactly the colour of the one that used to cover his bed as a child – a sort of nursery blue. He wasn't lying down, not flat, but perched up, with something holding his neck almost vertical, so that he could see forward to the foot of the bed.

The second time he woke up he knew he was alive because of the pain: like cramp, but in the muscles at the base of his skull. He was aware of a surgical collar, lifting his chin, locking his head into position. There was a small wheeled trolley at the foot of the bed with some greetings cards on it, one a seascape in the precise shade of green his daughter always used. On a chair by the trolley sat George Valentine. He had his legs crossed and Shaw noticed he'd bought himself a pair of new shoes: black slip-ons.

'Cosyns?' asked Shaw, but he didn't hear anything, so he tried the word again. His voice sounded like a pencil sharpener.

'Dead on arrival,' said Valentine. 'Staged suicide is my bet. You got in the way. It's early days, but Tom says there's traces of morphine on Cosyns's lips, in the nostrils.'

449

'I should be dead,' said Shaw, irritated now by the collar, which made his head feel like a medicine ball, the weight crushing his spine.

'I heard the bookcase fall – I was opposite, staking the place out,' said Valentine. 'I tried to get the door up, heard something inside, and the dog yelping. By the time I ran round the side the back door was open. You were inside on top of Cosyns. He was dead. You're not.'

Shaw told Valentine what he'd done, up until the moment he felt the hands round his neck. A summary as compressed as a black hole; all that mattered rolled into a tight ball. How he'd tracked down the lock-up number, how he'd found the link with the fatal crash at Castle Rising, how he knew now that Mosse had been at the wheel, and that was why the other members of the gang had a hold over him. And the black BMW with the soft top.

'Was it Mosse who attacked me?' he asked, when he'd finished.

'Probably, though we can't prove it. You didn't get the number of the BMW?'

Shaw went to shake his head but the pain stopped him dead so that he closed his eyes, tears spilling out of one.

'We shook down Mosse's house last night,' said Valentine. 'And the car. Nothing. Wife says he was home at the time. Domestic bliss.'

Shaw thought about the hands round his neck. 'I thought I broke his rib.'

''Fraid not. Bruised – but he plays Sunday football for a side out at Wisbech. One of his mates says he took a knock last week.'

'Why were you there?' asked Shaw, but even as he heard the words he slipped out of consciousness. Then his eyes were open and it was getting dark outside, and the blanket was red not blue. But Valentine was still there – or he'd gone and come back.

Shaw closed his eyes, trying to remember the question he'd asked and had no answer to. When he opened them again George Valentine was still there, the bedside light on, and the DS had a new sticker on his lapel: Alcoholics Anonymous.

'You advertising now?' he asked, nodding at the badge.

'Your wife was here – she'll be back in an hour.'

'Why were you there?' asked Shaw, knowing he was picking up where he'd stopped.

'I followed Cosyns home from the Norfolk Arena. I've been tracking him, seeing what came up. I didn't know where they kept the trailer. It seemed like a loose thread. I haven't got a life, so I thought I'd tie it up. Mosse left the arena first – in a BMW soft-top.'

'What does Warren say?' asked Shaw. Detective Chief Superintendent Max Warren had made it clear to both of them that the Tessier case was a closed file. He'd clearly failed to make it clear enough.

'When he stopped shouting he was pretty good about it,' said Valentine. 'He said if we were going to work on the case it was probably about time we got some fucking results. Because if we're right, Mosse is clearly prepared to kill to make sure he never pays the price for what he did to that kid.' Blood flushed Valentine's face.

Shaw went to speak but Valentine held up a hand. 'Let me do the pitch – I've done it once with Warren. He went for it, so hear me out.' He heaved in a double lungful of air, and Shaw wondered, for the first time, if he'd live to see the end of the case.

He put a cigarette, unlit, between his teeth.

'It's a cold case – an ice box. We ain't gonna get any fresh forensics. No one's going to tell us anything we don't know. We've got to move on from Tessier. Find a new way in.

'There were four of them – Mosse, Cosyns, Robins and Voyce. Once the case against Mosse collapsed they went their own ways: Voyce to New Zealand, Robins into crime – he went to Ashworth in the end, a secure psychiatric unit, and then to Bellevue, here, on the edge of Lynn. That left Cosyns and Mosse in town. Mates – whether Mr Up-and-Coming wanted it or not. That's the crucial bit, 'cos Cosyns isn't in that league – divorced, a job keeping a hearse on the road. It doesn't take a lot to see what's happened. Cosyns leans on Mosse for help – just a bit perhaps, then more. Because he isn't gonna starve, is he – not while Mosse needs his silence. I've been asking a few questions about our Mr Mosse and it seems he's no ordinary solicitor. He's studying for the Bar. Should be called later this year. That'll treble his earning power – there's already a new house, the new BMW, kids at private school. Warms your heart – just a snotty-nosed kid from the Westmead. So he's got all that to lose.

'Then we turn up, fresh as daisies, trying to reopen the case.' Valentine ran a finger round the tight collar of his grey shirt. 'I had a look round Cosyns's house. He's been getting money from Mosse – cheques at a grand a pop. He came home while I was there. It's not blackmail exactly, but it's as good as. In thousand-pound instalments.'

Out in the corridor a metal tray hit the floor like a cymbal.

Shaw didn't say a word so Valentine ploughed on. 'My guess is that Cosyns pushed his luck. Upped the ante. If we were that close to him, he let Mosse feel the heat too. Mosse doesn't like the heat. He leaves the Norfolk Arena first, gets back, parks, and waits for Cosyns. I reckon it isn't the first time he's killed to stop us getting to the truth.'

'Go on,' said Shaw, aware now that his DS had been running his own private investigation. But he was hardly in any position to show his anger, or a sense of betrayal.

'I checked it out. Robins died in Bellevue in May this year – cut his wrists open with a brand-new Swiss Army knife. The local nick got involved because there was a suggestion he had help – a visitor, day before they found him. Name and address left at the front gate were false. I showed the orderly a picture of Mosse. He couldn't be sure – or wouldn't. But it's possible.'

Shaw closed his eyes. 'Why?'

'Don't know,' said Valentine. 'But I do know whose name pops up in the visitors' book those last few months – Alex Cosyns's. What'd they talk about? Did he tell Mosse about the visits – turning the screw?'

A nurse came and put a tea cup in front of Shaw which he couldn't pick up.

'So that leaves Jimmy Voyce,' said Valentine, holding up a piece of paper on which was written what looked like a short piece of code.

TK 1956

'I found this scrawled on a note on Cosyns's desk at his house. It's a flight number. Stansted, last week, incoming from Istanbul, a connection back to Auckland. Passenger list includes James Anthony Voyce. Why the return trip? My guess is they'd talked about money. And how easy it is to get, if you know the right people.'

'Where's Voyce now?'

Valentine smiled, and Shaw realized how unusual that was. He looked twenty years younger.

'Fuck knows. But Warren's lifted the ban – said it didn't seem to make much difference what he said anyway. The Cosyns case is open, so's Tessier's. We're on it – with one condition.'

'Which is?'

'We talk to each other.'

'About what?'

'About tracking down Voyce, and making sure we're there when he tries to put the frighteners on Robert Mosse – because if he does do that, and that's got to be why he's here, then there's a really good chance our man will kill again.'

'Try to kill again,' said Shaw, closing his eyes. He heard Valentine get up, open a window, and strike a match. A wave falling, exploding around him in white surf, was the first image in a dream. But he woke almost instantly, with a heart-stopping jerk, because he'd felt those hands again, locked round his throat, trying to take his life away.

The next time he opened his eyes Fran was standing there holding Cosyns's terrier dog – the one he'd taken from the car that night, leaving the passengers and driver for dead. The one Jonathan Tessier had loved. For the first time Shaw wondered why Cosyns had done it, and whether it was a tiny act of contrition, to save the only life in that car they hadn't shattered. And he'd have felt an empathy with the animal, because his father had bred them.

His wife was behind his daughter, trying to smile. 'George had it in the car when he came round to tell us what had happened. It's ancient.' Lena shook her head.

She came to the bed and laid a hand on his forehead. 'George said Fran could have it, if it was OK with you.'

Valentine had gone. Shaw was too horrified to speak.

'Is it, Dad?' asked Fran. 'Is it all right?'

Acknowledgements

I would like to thank three people for bringing *Death Watch* into the world. My new editor at Penguin, Kate Burke, has swiftly created an atmosphere of calm professionalism which is reflected in the final manuscript. My agent, Faith Evans, has tirelessly driven forward the quest for better writing and more substantial characters. Midge Gillies, my wife, is a sure sounding board on all aspects of story-telling.

Special thanks go to Trevor Horwood – my copy-editor – who allows us all to sleep more easily at nights. Jenny Burgoyne, again, made sure Trevor gets sleep too. Bridie Pritchard provided belt and braces.

I have returned to a growing team of specialists to check details and seek advice. They include Paul Horrell on motorcars, Alan Gilbert on forensics, Martin Peters on medical matters and James Woodman for advice on clinical matters. This time round we have added Nick Bonsor, of Read & Sutcliffe Ltd, King's Lynn, for advice on all things nautical and for a tour of the port. Without this help, *Death Watch* would never have been written.

As always the characters in *Death Watch* are fictional. I have played with place names to enliven the language and the plot. For the record, the Italian painter Patigno did not exist and neither, therefore, does his masterpiece *The Miracle at Cana*.